35444001184547
YA SKU
Skuse, C. J
Rockoholic

WITHDRAWN

BAR   NOV 1 5 2012

D1052778

ROCKOHOLIC

Thompson-Nicola Regional District
Library System
300 - 465 VICTORIA STREET
KAMLOOPS, B.C.   V2C 2A9

ROCKOHOLIC

C.J. SKUSE

Chicken House

SCHOLASTIC INC. · NEW YORK

FOR MY SISTER PENNY.
FOREVER IN DEBT TO YOUR PRICELESS ADVICE.

Text copyright © 2012 by C.J. Skuse

All rights reserved. Published by Chicken House, an imprint of Scholastic
Inc., *Publishers since 1920*. CHICKEN HOUSE, SCHOLASTIC, and associated logos
are trademarks and/or registered trademarks of Scholastic Inc.
www.scholastic.com

First published in the United Kingdom in 2011
by Chicken House, 2 Palmer Street, Frome, Somerset BA11 1DS.
www.doublecluck.com

No part of this publication may be reproduced, stored in a retrieval
system, or transmitted in any form or by any means, electronic, mechanical,
photocopying, recording, or otherwise, without written permission of the
publisher. For information regarding permission, write to Scholastic Inc.,
Attention: Permissions Department, 557 Broadway, New York, NY 10012.

Library of Congress Cataloging-in-Publication Data

Skuse, C. J.
Rockoholic / C. J. Skuse. – 1st American ed.
p. cm.
Summary: Sixteen-year-old Jody Flook is known for doing stupid things, but
when she accidentally kidnaps her idol, rock star Jackson Gatlin, at his
only concert in the entire United Kingdom, and he does not want to leave her
garage, she is in real trouble.

ISBN 978-0-545-42960-3
[1. Kidnapping – Fiction. 2. Fame – Fiction. 3. Musicians – Fiction. 4. Rock
music – Fiction. 5. Best friends – Fiction. 6. Friendship – Fiction. 7. Wales
– Fiction.] I. Title.
PZ7.S43748Roc 2012
[Fic] – dc23
2011046582

10 9 8 7 6 5 4 3 2 1   12 13 14 15 16

Printed in the U.S.A.   23
First American edition, November 2012

The text type was set in Lino Letter Roman.
The display type was set in Champion and Old Typewriter.
Interior book design by Whitney Lyle

3 5444 00118454 7

I know someday you'll have a beautiful life,
I know you'll be a star, in somebody else's sky,
But why, why, why can't it be,
Can't it be mine?

PEARL JAM, "BLACK"

ONE
F-UNREAL

To our local newspaper, my grandad's death was "a shocking accident that brought Bristol city centre to a standstill." To my mum, it was humiliation beyond words and a week's worth of whispers from her colleagues at the bank. To me, it was a sadness that could fill a dry sea.

And now it's the funeral and everything's wrong. My grandad didn't want people wearing black. He wanted his mourners to come in saris, or wet suits, or grass skirts and hula gear. He wanted a big lavish send-off, too, with female bodybuilders carrying his gold coffin and, to round off the day, cannons firing his ashes into the sky.

"And I don't want it called a funeral, either, Jody. Invite people to my Body Barbecue. That sounds much more fun."

My mum is all gray skirt-suits and polished shoes, and anything Grandad ever did embarrassed the hell out of her. The announcement in the paper just read, "Funeral of Charles Nathaniel McGee. Donations to Cancer Research UK, no flowers, please." Everything had to be funereal. F-unreal. That's how I've felt all day.

And now we're at the snooty Torrance Lodge for the wake, and Mum and my sister are mingling with Scottish relatives we haven't seen for decades and trying desperately to find reasons for not being in touch. Several soap-smelling old women have delighted in telling me how I've grown up since the last time they saw me, which was probably before I was conceived, and now I'm hiding on the staircase, clutching my sketch pad, out of the way. I'll let Halley take the brunt of it. She loves the attention. They all think she's the super-star in the family, anyway, with all her sports medals and Olympic hopes and Duke of Edinburgh awards for community service. I've had enough of it. And as my gran-dad used to tell me . . .

"If you can't find anything useful to say, get the hell out of the way."

He'd once played drums in a band and had nipple rings and smoked weed and camped out in the mud at the Glastonbury Festival. He used to moon-bathe naked on the roof of his house, and he'd gone bungee jump-ing and skinny-dipped at the Great Barrier Reef. He loved Queen's "Bohemian Rhapsody," and used to dance around the living room with the mannequin he'd nicked from a skip outside Debenhams department store. He'd wanted heavy metal music and sushi and chocolate foun-tains at his wake. Not Sarah Effin' McLachlan and cheap frozen quiche.

I huddle into the banister, iPod earbuds in, hood up, looking like a poster child for teen angst. I close my eyes and imagine Jackson is singing to me, like I do when I'm trying to get to sleep at night. I imagine he's lying next to me, his breath on my face as he sings, that he's stroking my hair. When I open my eyes, Mum's throwing me one of her disapproving "Why don't you join in?" glares from the private party room where everyone is chowing down on cheese and ice cream. In the bar next door, five kids, apparently my third cousins, roll balls up and down the snooker table.

I just go back to sketching Jackson.

Feet approach. Nike high-tops with blue swooshes. Black skinny jeans. Wallet chain. White graffiti T-shirt. And one of my grandad's bluest waistcoats. I pluck the earphones out, and shove the sketch pad into my bag.

"All right, Precious?" says Mac, settling a glass of Coke down next to me on the stairs. "Sorry, I got sidetracked by this old bloke telling me about his prostate. Here you go, Presh."

"S'OK, I had Jackson," I say. He rolls his eyes. Mac's more into show tunes and Lady Gaga than rock, but he knows The Regulators are the sound track to my life, so he keeps a few of their songs on his iPod, just for me. I don't have my own iPod, and any cheapo MP3 players I buy usually get knackered or dropped down drains, so I borrow Mac's. I wind the earbuds around it and hand it back to him.

"Hang on to it for a bit," he says. "There's barely room for my arse in these jeans."

"Why d'you wear them, then?"

"*Because, because, because, because, because . . .*" he sings. It really bugs me sometimes how he can't give straight answers. I wonder if that's a gay thing.

"I've sexed up your Coke," he says. "Thought you could do with a perk."

I shake my head. "I'm not drinking today."

"Why? Because of Jackson Gatlin?" he whines sarcastically. Mac doesn't appreciate my obsession with Jackson. He calls him my "fictional fix." Because he's my hero. Because I choose to support Jackson's newfound teetotalism. Because I spend nearly all my wages on Regulators T-shirts, CDs, and limited-edition DVD box sets of all their South American concerts. Because they're my band, my sanctuary. Because, because, because, because, because . . .

"You need something to get you through the day," he says. "Might freshen you up a bit."

"I don't want it. I want my grandad." I take the moon rock from my hoodie pocket. I rub it, as though the grandad genie is going to plume out of it. But all I see is him in my head on that last day, sitting in his wheelchair.

"Don't Dream It, Be It," he says. Then he's gone. Down and down and down. The tray of drinks falls to the pavement. Our foot soles thump down the street. My screams. My fault.

I feel the rush of tears coming, like water surging up a broken pipe, but Mac sees it, too, and kneels down before me, placing one black-fingernailed hand on my knee.

"OK, maybe alcohol's not the best idea," he says in his serious voice. "It's OK, come here." I don't like Mac's serious voice. He sounds like a doctor or something. A doctor with spiky black hair with a shock of magpie blue flashed through one side. It smells like lemons, and hugging him is like hugging a warm summer tree.

"He'd have really hated this, Mac," I sniff, pulling back from his shoulder. "Every second."

"You're right. You know what I can hear him saying? 'Where's my bloody sushi?' 'Why'd you let your mother pick Valium FM? You canny dance to that!'" he says in a near-perfect imitation of Grandad's Scottish accent.

I smile, wiping my eyes. Some opera woman mourns over the buffet-room speakers. "I'm not going back in there. I swear, if one more hairy-lipped granny kisses me on the cheek and asks me how school's going, they're going to be booking the next wake here."

Mac sits on the step beside me. "Well, it's nearly over now, isn't it?"

"Yeah. And I've done nothing toward it. I've done nothing to make it better for him."

"Well, at the end of the day, your mum gave him a respectable send-off. She probably can't afford to do more, Jode. It all went smoothly, didn't it?"

And then it comes to me, like it's been stapled to my forehead.

"That's the problem, Mac," I say, getting up off the stairs and taking up my vodka-kicked Coke. "It's all gone way too smoothly."

"Whoa there, what are you going to do?" he says as I glug the Coke down, wincing at the huge injection of vodka lurking at the bottom of the glass. "Where are you going?" he calls after me.

"I'm going to change that bloody music."

Picture this: huddled groups of old people chatting over paper plates; the reek of lily of the valley and the rank smell of prawns. The tortured warbling of Katherine Jenkins comes to an abrupt end as I fix Mac's iPod to the docking station behind the bar, find "Bedlam" by The Regulators, and lock the volume control. Speakers crackle in all four corners of the room. The chattering stops.

Sunlight breaks through the metal-gray clouds outside and floods the room like honey. A guitar noise kicks in on the sound system.

Crank, crank.

More guitars, louder than bombs.

Crank. The loudest voice in the world screams . . .

"This is a warning, motherfuckers! You gotta deal . . ."

A huge grin splits my face. It's Jackson's voice.

"Surrender your weapons. It's gonna get . . ."

Crank, crank, crank, crank, crank.

"Reeeeeeeeeeeeeeeeeeeeeal!"

Before I know what my own hand is doing, it's sinking straight into a crystal bowl of pink Jell-O, grabbing a handful, and hoying a large rubbery splodge straight at the reverend's face.

I see Mac heading toward me, all serious face. He's coming to hold me back, talk me down, but I'm too hyped, I'm too riled, and some random kids (possibly the third cousins) are joining in.

Jackson's screeching through the speakers that surround me. He's cheering me on. One of the cousins lunges for the cherry pie and shoves a handful in my mouth. He laughs and I laugh and shower him with a plateful of mini lemon tarts, rubbing the custard into his hair. Another cousin grabs a fistful of chocolate mousse and flings it at an old lady in a green hat. More second and third cousins run in from the game room, squealing in delight and grabbing handfuls of sandwiches and puff pastries and hurling them at us and each other.

I catch sight of Mac, just outside the private party room. He's given up trying to stop what's happening. He's standing beneath a pink-and-white floral umbrella.

The barman shouts and gets a face full of fish-paste sandwiches. Old women squawk and flap and wheel out of the way. The crabby old man from the post office gets a hunk of raspberry sponge cake smack in his mouth. A waitress skids on the mandarin jelly. Fondue splats against the walls. Quiche plasters the windows. Light fixtures drip with shredded lettuce. Multicolored squidgy lumps rain down as cheese balls pellet the air like machine-gun fire.

"Give me what you got, don't hold back."

The air is thick with egg mayonnaise, salmon sandwiches, mini kievs, and cupcakes; the floor is a battlefield of bodies felled by blueberry pie and ice cream, all crawling and ducking out of the firing line. It is not a funeral anymore. It is a buffet bloodbath.

"This is my war, this is my waaaaaaaaaaaaaaaaaaarrrrrrrrr!"

With Jackson's help, I destroy that room. It is five manic minutes of loud music, helpless laughing, screaming, shouting, mayhem, magic, and mess. By the time me and the cousins have come to our breathless truce, it is a no-man's-land of sweet gunk and mangled pastry. I'm going to pay, we all are. My mum is going to go into rage overdrive with no shock absorbers and a double exhaust. But for these brief minutes, all is as it should be.

And I just know that somewhere in the universe my grandad is laughing his head off.

TWO
SMELLS LIKE TEEN BULLSHIT

So my mum goes supernova insane over my funeral shenanigans. She's convinced I'm either an alcoholic or a pothead, anyway, so it doesn't exactly surprise her, it just appalls her. I know I've reached the summit of Mount Deep Shit with this one.

"Stupid, inconsiderate little cow!" she shouts at me. She's managed a nice skid mark of chocolate mousse all up one side of her suit, and half her head is covered in whipped cream. Others mill about aimlessly behind her, like extras from *Dawn of the Dead*. There are lots of angry sighs from my mother in between frightful gasps at the mess and cries of "God knows how much all this is going to cost me."

"I did it for Grandad," I try to explain, shrimp cocktail dripping off me. "You wouldn't give him the funeral he wanted, so . . ."

"He didn't want a bloody funeral, he wanted a circus," she snaps. "It was ridiculous what he was asking for. Do you know how hard today was for me, Jody?"

"Yes."

Mum sighs angrily. Mum sighs angrily a lot. "Sighs angrily" is usually followed by "rubs eyes wearily" and "frowns exasperatedly." She's had a lot to sigh angrily about lately, I suppose. Money worries a-go-go. My alleged drug addiction. Dad gambling away our mortgage. My fourteen-year-old sister Halley's Internet buddy Liam turning out to be *not* the boy from One Direction but a fifty-year-old truck driver named Sid.

"It was very hard." She's going to cry, I think. I can see the water pooling in her eyes. "First your father, then the accident, bloody local newspapers on our doorstep, and now this. How much more humiliation do you think I can take?"

"Probably not much more," I say, before realizing that she probably didn't expect an answer to that.

And then she starts crying. And I feel the deep twist of dread inside me.

"He'd have loved it, Mum. He would."

She goes to step away from me, then steps back, but doesn't look me in the eye.

"You go and apologize to Donna and Vic. Then you go home, you get the wet vac out of the utility room, you bring it here, and you clean this room from top to bottom. And don't even think you're going to that concert tomorrow. Don't even think about it." Every word looks like it hurts her to say it, and just as she turns away, a tear drops from her face and onto the carpet.

It's late when I finally get back home from cleaning the Torrance. Me and Mum have another bust-up of egg-frying proportions and she goes all giraffe angry (i.e., when her neck gets all long and her eyes get all big) about me always siding with Grandad, never with her.

And then I go and drop the f-bomb and tell her to f-off to her face. I don't mean to, it just leaps out of my mouth.

She rips up my Regulators concert ticket and my life officially ends right there.

I can't think straight. I can't see straight. There's a festival of frustration in my head and the unfairness of it all just blinds me. I decide to leave home. I pack my rucksack with essentials — clothes, some Stephen Kings, my current Jackson sketchbook, toothbrush, the eBay shirt released from its frame on the wall — and leave her a note on the hallway table. It just says "Gone to Mac's. Bye."

Mac's waiting tables when I step through the main door of the Pack Horse, but he yells over to his mum that he's "taking five" and helps me up to the back bedroom with my stuff. The room's rarely used as a bedroom since it's hidden away at the back of the pub's living quarters, so Mac's dad, Teddy, uses it to stash his massive collection of DVDs, and Mac's two-year-old sister, Cree, uses it as her playroom.

Cree's a proper cutie — blonde and blue-eyed, just like Mac before he went black-haired and blue-streaked on his seventeenth birthday. Some afternoons he brings her into the day-care center where I work and she's usually all over me, but not today. She can tell I've been crying. For a while she just sits on Mac's lap, eyeing me warily. Then Mac whispers in her ear and she crawls across the bed to where I'm sitting and gives me a hug. She even does a little *pat-pat* on my shoulder as if to say, "There, there."

She's ready for bed and has not long had her bath. Her hair smells like marzipan.

"Thanks, Cree," I say, hugging her in.

She pulls back and looks up at me with her big blues. "Why you crying?"

"I'm just sad, that's all."

"Are you going to get dead?"

"No."

"Why you crying?"

"I'm just sad, that's all."

"Dody be sad?"

"Yeah."

"I got a doctor case."

"Go and get it, then, and we'll play doctors."

She scooches straight off the bed and runs down the corridor.

"You don't have to play with her," says Mac. "I can say there's a ghost in the wardrobe or something."

"It's OK," I say, picking at a loose thread on the top sheet. "I like being in Cree's little world. Anything not to be in mine at the moment."

"You did what you thought Charlie would have wanted. OK, it was insane and stupid and you've probably caused hundreds of quids' worth of damage but that's just what you do, isn't it?"

Mac's talking from experience. He's been there more than once when I've done something stupid and caused hundreds of quids' worth of damage, and he's usually the one to either apologize on my behalf, mop up, or carry me home. He's more like my social worker than my best friend. If it weren't for him, I'd either be paraplegic, pregnant, or dead by now.

"Mum hates me even more now," I mumble.

"She doesn't hate you. She just . . . doesn't get you. She didn't really get Charlie, either, did she? She wasn't like you two peas in a pencil case."

I nod. "The day after he died, she boxed up all his stuff. His books, his bongs, his clothes. Boxed it all up for the thrift shop."

"You never told me that."

"I got up in the middle of the night, took most of it back out again, and hid it in the garage. That's still his stuff. She just wants to forget he was there. Bloody china ornaments on the windowsill where his bongs used to be. Bloody paint samples on the mantelpiece, *two* days after. *Peach.* Halley's going to help her paint the living room. Mummy and golden baby together. Won't that be peachy? I don't even get a vote."

Mac flops back on the bed so the hem of his white waiter's shirt rides up a little on his stomach. He reaches his hand out and gives mine a quick squeeze. This would have been weird if we were in a soap opera and would have probably led to a momentous kiss, but Mac's not into me, not like that. I think he's gay but we never talk about it. He's still in the closet.

We hear whining out in the corridor. Alfie the Alsatian saunters past the open door with a pink plastic stethoscope in his jaws. Cree's running after him with her pink plastic doctor case.

"Alfie tooked it! Alfie tooked it!" she shrieks at us.

"Alf! Drop it!" Mac shouts and the dog immediately drops the stethoscope. Cree grabs it and comes back in to set up her little hospital on my bed. "Let's talk about tomorrow. Big day. What time do you want to leave for Cardiff?"

"I can't go now, can I?"

"What? I thought death itself wasn't going to stop you from going to that concert. You're not going to let your mum stop you going, are you?"

"No choice. She tore up my ticket. I've been on a diet for that concert and everything. Now I just want to eat until I puke."

"I'm sick of saying it — you don't need to diet."

"I do. I'm way too big for —"

"For what? Do *not* say for Jackass Gatlin."

"Well, he went out with that model, didn't he, and she's tiny. I should have stopped eating about four hundred pounds ago." I can see Mac's mouth grow wider and his eyes bulge like he's just seen an apparition walk through the wall behind me. He can't believe what I'm saying. A few months ago, *I* wouldn't have believed it, either. But ever since I saw Jackson with that twinkly model, and read that article about his "type" of woman, I knew it would never be someone like me. I wasn't size two. I wasn't blonde. I wasn't twinkly. But I could be. For Jackson. I would do anything for Jackson.

"What are you talking about? You. Are. Not. Fat. I just don't get it. So what, you think if you stick your fingers down your throat, Jackson's gonna fall totally in luurve with you, is he?"

"Maybe. Nobody as good-looking as Jackson would date anyone above a size minus zero."

I help Cree into her little white doctor's coat. Mac hates

it when I'm down on myself, which is pretty much all the time. It doesn't matter how many times he tells me I'm not fat, or how many times he shoves me into a dressing room in Topshop and urges me into clothes that aren't black to "bring out my inner goddess," I still think he's kidding himself. When I see the same face and lank brown hair and freckles in the mirror, I just want to smash it. Since Grandad died, it's got worse. He used to say my freckles were "an extra sprinkle of sweetness." But they're not. They're just not.

Mac sighs and fiddles with his friendship bracelets. It's awkward between us all of a sudden.

Outside the sky is gray and smoky, and the orange security lights are on all over the parking lot. There's quite a few cars in tonight, and a bus. Footsteps approach from the corridor and Mac's mum, Tish, brings in two plates of saucy sausage sandwiches.

"There you go, guys." She hands me my plate and strokes my hair and Cree's hair at the same time. Her nails are long and shiny red.

"Thanks." I sniff at my sandwich and pull a burnt onion from within. I don't dare remind Tish that I'm vegetarian at the moment — not since she's letting me stay and everything. And then I lift up the top slice of bread to see the sausages inside are as pale as my fingers. Yuck, they're veggie sausages. Bless, she remembered.

"My have a sammidge, Mumma?" asks Cree, injecting Mac's stomach with her toy syringe.

"No, you've had yours. Bedtime now. Have you called your mum, Jody? She'll be worried."

"No, it's OK. I've left her a note. I'll pay you some-thing. . . ."

She flaps her hand as if to say "don't be silly" and adjusts her vinyl belt back down over her spare tire. Cree steals a little mouthful of my sandwich and squeals as I catch her in the act.

"Come on, Creedence, bedtime," says Tish, offering the little girl her hand.

"No, my stay with Dody and my Kenzie," she flaps at her mum and hides behind me.

Tish looks at me. "It's fine," I say, blushing. "She's all right with us for a bit." Cree peeks out, holding up both her hands right in front of her face.

"Ten more minutes, then. Make yourself at home, Jody. You know where everything is. Kenz, you got some tables to clear, love. We're ever so busy."

"Yeah, yeah, I'm coming," he mutters.

"Thanks, Tish," I say as she totters out on her stilettos, shutting the door quietly.

"You're always ever so busy," says Mac, glaring daggers at the door. "Hate this place."

"Your mum's nice. Wish mine was half as nice as yours," I moan to him. He's still lying back on the bed with his arms over his eyes, his sandwich balancing on his stom-ach. "Wish I was you."

Cree is still chomping on my sandwich. I crane my neck to chomp the bread from the other side of it, which makes her smile. She has ketchup all over her little doctor's coat and the bottom half of her face, like a surgeon who's been eating the organs.

"Mackenzie," I say to him, eyeing Cree cos I know what she'll do and I love it.

Cree points her finger at me. "No, *My* Kenzie."

"No, *Mac*kenzie."

"*My* Kenzie," she shouts and flings herself on her brother's chest. He oomphs and his plate bounces off onto the bed. She laughs. There's now ketchup all over his white apron and onions all over the sheet.

"OK, OK," I laugh, clearing away the sandwich mess to the bedside table. I love being with them. I love not being at home. But how long will they want me here? I wonder. I'm not part of their family. I'm a Flook, however much I want to be a Lawless. This thought plunges me down deeper into my dread and reminds me why I'm here in the first place.

"Grandad told me once that when he was younger he saw Jimi Hendrix play at this club in New York and met him afterward and that night changed his whole life. Like, *completely.* He said something inside him just clicked open and he knew he had to change."

Mac strokes Cree's hair as she lies on him. "What, he fancied Jimi Hendrix?"

"No. It was more the rock lifestyle. So he quit his crappy job and went traveling and got tattoos and stopped being . . . what was that word he used to use?"

"Normal?" Mac suggests.

"Mediocre. That's what he said. He knew from that night on he didn't want to be mediocre anymore. I just . . . wanted that to happen to me. I wanted to have that kind of night at the concert. And I wanted Jackson to notice me. He's not just some rock dude, Mac. I love him. I guess that doesn't matter much now though, does it? I'm never going to meet him now."

"They never do meet and greets, do they?"

"Sometimes they do. Something was going to happen at that concert, Mac. Something great. It was going to be so good!"

Mac levers himself upward and strikes a dramatic pose, bursting into song. *"Could it be? Yes, it could. Something's coming, something good, if I can waaaaaaait. . . ."* Cree giggles in his arms and squirms to return to her doctoring. She's heard it too many times.

"Shut up," I laugh, feeling my cheeks begin to warm up.

He stands up on the bed. *"The air is humming, and something greeaaaaaat is coming!"*

"It's all a bloody joke to you, isn't it?" I say, throwing a pillow up at his face. He always does this, bursts into song when I'm trying to be serious or banging on about Jackson. He doesn't understand. That's OK, nobody does. But after everything that's happened with Grandad and the general shitness of my life during the last few years, the thought of no Regulators concert, no possibility of seeing Jackson for real . . .

"Grandad, do you like The Regulators?"

"Yeah, they're good. I can see why you like them, darling."

"I'm going to marry Jackson Gatlin one day."

"He's the one, is he?"

"Yep."

"Then you go for it, darling. Reach up high enough, you can have any star you want."

Mac sighs and jumps down to the floor. "The Regulators aren't the be-all and end-all, Jode. Jackson's just one of many thousands of shock-headed rock dudes who get girls all crazy for a few years until the next big thing comes along. And let's face it, his music isn't going to change the world. Women in labor scream more in tune than him. You're so infatuated, you've just forgotten what's real."

"No I haven't. I just . . . love him. And The Regulators. Going to that concert was important to me, that's all."

Mac looks like he's struggling to find the words. Then he says, "I guess love really is blind, then. And deaf."

I shrug. I'm too embarrassed to talk about it anymore. Even Cree is looking at me strangely. She's set out her doctor instruments on the bed and scribbled on a little plastic doctor pad. She leans over and presses a Band-Aid on my forehead. It's an over-used Band-Aid that several dollies have previously worn so it falls straight off. She burps in my face and I can smell onions.

Mac makes for the door. "You can still go, you know. To the concert."

"Yeah? You got any loaves and fishes you want to multiply while you're at it? I don't have a ticket, do I? I can't afford to just show up on the night and get one off the scalpers. They charge the Earth. And it's not as if I can invest in a Wonka Bar, is it?"

He takes a step toward me. "You know you can have my ticket."

"What?"

"You can have mine. I've never been that fussed about seeing them. You're the one who plagued the life out of me to get tickets. You're the fan. Makes sense for you to have it."

"Are you serious?"

"Yeah. If you don't mind going in on your own, that is. . . ."

"Mac . . ."

"Doesn't make any difference to me. You're not going to start blubbing again, are you?"

I launch myself at him, pinning him onto the bed. "YOU ARE AMAZING!" I scream.

"Thanks, for the deafness," he says, smiling as I push him back on the bed and kiss him all over his hot face. Cree's giggling her head off.

"You . . . are . . . officially . . . my . . . favorite . . . person . . . ever!"

He stops and looks at me. "Apart from Jackson Gatlin, I suppose?"

"Of course," I say. "Where is it, where's the ticket?" He rolls over onto his side and pulls his wallet out of his back pocket by the chain. He sifts through some receipts in the main section and then he hands it to me. There it is again. That beautiful ticket. The hologram. The writing.

CUTTHROAT PRODUCTIONS PROUDLY PRESENTS
THE REGULATORS
PLUS SPECIAL GUESTS
BECKON GALLOW
MOTORPOINT ARENA CARDIFF 23 MARCH
DOORS OPEN AT 7:00 P.M.
ADMIT ONE

I can barely see it through my tears. I kiss it. I stare at it. I hold it against my face. I move my fingertip over the lettering and make the little silver hologram shimmer in the light.

I look up at Mac and wipe my eyes. "Why didn't you say something before?!"

Cree starts bandaging one of my Converse with a length of toilet roll. Mac sits up and shrugs. "Just wanted to see you squirm. Have it. It's fine. Truly."

"Serious voice truly?"

"Serious voice truly," he says.

THREE
GET THERE EARLY, CURLY WURLY

5:00 A.M. — Mac grabs two cans of orange Tango and a fistful of Curly Wurly chocolate bars from behind the counter and we're off up the motorway toward South Wales. The sky's dark. I'm wearing black cargoes, my long black fleece coat, and, for the first time ever, the eBay shirt. Jackson's signed-for-charity, one-of-five-in-the-world, jellyfish-design T-shirt. Everyone will notice it and know how massive a fan I am. Jackson will notice it. He'll pull me out of the crowd and we'll duet.

6:05 A.M. — Mac parks at his cousin Alastair's flat and we walk to the arena. Fifteen people already at the entrance. Fifteen! With sleeping bags. Can't believe I didn't think of sleeping here. *Damn.*

6:09 A.M. — Mac gets out the Curly Wurlys, chomps his way through two of them, and calls it breakfast. We're lining up alongside a short wall and he jump-sits straight onto it, almost falling backward into the flower bed behind. I can't do that so I stand beside his knee. I'm going to starve myself today so I'm as thin as possible when Jackson sees me. Mac shoves the rest of the Curly Wurlys in my thigh pocket and disappears to sniff out a Starbucks.

6:39 A.M. — Mac's not back. I've eaten one of the Curly Wurlys. Still three in my thigh pocket. I take out my moon rock and twiddle it around in my fingers. I haven't spoken to any other fans yet.

6:49 A.M. — Still haven't spoken to the others. Think I've worked out why I don't want to talk to them. Regulators is *my* band, not theirs. I know other fans exist, of course. I go on message boards and see the crowd photos from the gig reviews in *Lungs* magazine. But when it's just me, listening to Jackson singing through my earphones, or just me watching the DVD, I can pretend The Regulators exist just for me, like Jackson's lying next to me and stroking my hair as he sings. I don't want to think about him stroking their hair, too.

7:03 A.M. — The sky is getting lighter. Some girls in front have their hair like Jackson. One wears the same outfit he wears in the "Tortuous" video when he's on the beach — black T-shirt, skinny jeans, and black DMs. A boy in a tank top is showing off a burning-rose tattoo on his upper arm, just like Jackson's. One girl has a zebra-pattern T-shirt on. This is because Wikipedia said Jackson's favorite animals were zebras. I started collecting zebra stuff when I read that. A week later, it said llamas.

7:22 A.M. — A white taxi draws up. Two emo versions of the spooky twins from *The Shining* clamber out the back. They both have purple and pink extensions in their long black hair, and are wearing black leather skirts, striped tights, black DMs tagged with Wite-Out, and matching T-shirts, which they've obviously designed themselves. I realize they've come as the conjoined twins from the "Freaktasia" video, where Jackson plays a ringmaster and he's luring all these freaks into his circus tent like some mad Pied Piper. One of the twins carries a small rucksack with loads of buttons pinned to it. One of the buttons says "Mrs. Jackson Gatlin." I want it.

7:23 A.M. — Mac returns with grande hot chocolates, blueberry muffins, and cheesy paninis.

"Is it vegetarian cheese?" I ask him.

"Yeah," he says. I know it's not. I resist it all for about a second and then dive in. Dammit!

"You talked to anyone yet?" he asks, pulling at the blue-tinged lashes on his eyelid. I shake my head and slurp my hot choccy in between bites of the best panini ever. Mac does a little dance to get warm. He's got this tricky routine he has to learn for one of his numbers, so every standing-still opportunity, he's at it. He's in our town production of *The Rocky Horror Show*, this musical about a geek couple who stay at this castle full of transvestites when their car breaks down. Mac's playing the head transvestite, Frank-N-Furter, and has to seduce the couple. It's well sketchy but Mac's going to rip it up.

The hot chocolate tastes like liquid sunshine. Sometimes me and Grandad used to sneak downstairs and have hot choccies with cheese-and-Marmite sandwiches. We liked dipping our sandwiches in the chocolate. Mum didn't like that, said it was childish. That's why we had to do it on the sly. I put my free hand in my pocket and clutch the moon rock tightly.

"That rock fell from the moon, Jody. Neil Armstrong himself kicked it down and I caught it. It's magic. You look after that."

"I will, Grandad, I promise."

8:31 A.M. — I catch the eye of Zebra T-shirt Girl but pretend I'm looking at the poster behind her. Three more fans turn up in a red Vauxhall Nova — a small red-haired girl with a photograph-covered bag, a blond boy in orange coveralls eating Sugar Puffs out of the box, and a lanky boy who looks like he's cut his hair and stuck clumps of it to his cheeks. Way too much random there for me.

8:38 A.M. — Mac and I sit on the wall and play with the piano and dressing-up apps on his iPod. The wind is cold but sitting next to Mac in his bomber jacket, it's warm. The Hairy Boy from the Vauxhall Nova asks Mac for "some herb or bounce or summing" and Mac says no, sorry. Then he asks him for "a light" and again, Mac says no. Mac doesn't smoke, because of his singing.

9:00 A.M. — People in suits and skirts *clip-clop* by. I'm glad I'm not at work today. I work at Bumblebees, this three-story town house that's been converted into a children's day-care center. The only two staff members I get along with are Alice and Serena, since they have at least heard of The Regulators, and Regs are all I like to talk about. But Alice breeds pot-bellied pigs and Serena thinks Chris Brown is a genius. And this is all we usually talk about.

9:31 A.M. — We run through Mac's steps for one of his *Rocky Horror* songs, "The Time Warp."

10:12 A.M. — Hairy Boy gives Small Redhead a piggyback. Then they make out for ages, slurps and all. Ugh. More fans join the line — boys in shorts, skinny girls in tights and ribbed wife-beaters. It's, like, minus ten degrees? I can't help giving them the warm evils. I ask Mac what "herb or bounce" is. "Drugs," he says. "What did you think it was, laundry detergent?" He laughs. I laugh, but I kind of did, yeah.

10:46 A.M. — A bus pulls up, drops off some fans and other people in work clothes who head toward town. As the bus pulls away, some lads lean out the window, gob on the pavement, and shout, "Sad wankers!" at us. I get the moon rock out and rub the smooth side against my cheek.

10:58 A.M. — There's nothing to look at other than the cinema posters opposite, so it calls for drastics: *OK!* magazine. We take the piss out of the celebs and their "Look at my endless sofa" poses for a bit, and then Mac starts up a random convo with Number 13 in the line about how pregnant weather girls annoy him. Number 13 looks like Hermione out of *Harry Potter*, but with black hair and not posh.

11:44 A.M. — A group of girls and one curly-haired boy in a green school blazer join the line. "Is this the Regs queue?" Green Blazer Boy asks, acting all drunk. Then I realize he *is* drunk. He takes a bottle of Jack Daniel's from inside his blazer and swigs it, making a face like he's drinking acid. It's morning and he's, like, fourteen? He laughs like all lads like him do, *hur, hur, hur.*

11:45 A.M. — "That's it, I'm going to have to go into town," says Mac, clapping his hands. "Or else my Visa's going to run off without me. Do you need anything?"

I shake my head. "Can't you wait another hour?"

"No wayski. I've waited this long." I sigh, then quickly regret it cos I know what Mac's going to say. "You wanted to get here early. Get talking to people. Make the effort. I'll be back about one with some munchables." He pulls his iPod from his coat pocket and puts it in my hand.

"Don't take up all the battery, and guard it," he squeezes my freezing hands around it, "with your miserable, empty, dried-up husk of a life."

I brighten immediately. "OMG, you sure? You are a legend."

"What's a friend for?" he says, finger encircling the pinky-yellow friendship bracelet on his wrist, one I made for him. "Keep it quiet, though, eh, Presh? They'll all want a piece of me."

I shuffle through Mac's iPod. I come to a song I've heard him singing before, by some band called Van Morrison. He sings it to me cos I've got brown eyes like the girl in the song. It's not screamy like I'm used to, but it's OK.

12:02 P.M. — A blonde girl in a "Team Gatlin" T-shirt goes along the line with a box of donuts and offers them to people. I say no. They've probably been injected with something.

12:15 P.M. — Pigeons peck the cake crumbs. Can't stop listening to that Van Morrison song.

12:39 P.M. — I can't ignore the fact that I really need the loo. I think I might just have to pee myself and send Mac to town again to buy me some more cargo pants.

1:04 P.M. — Mac reappears with a bargain bucket of chicken, chips, beans, corn on the cob, and coleslaw. I nip across to the cinema for a wee and when I come back I sit on the pavement and tuck in to the vegetarian options in the bucket. My mouth is flooded with the thought of chicken. I pick at the most vegetarian part of a drumstick, the skin, as Mac shows me what else he's bought — black skinny jeans, Topman T-shirts, lace-ups, a leather jacket, and a silver belt. He hands me a small white bag. Inside it is a zipper clip of that zebra from *Madagascar*. Mac still thinks I'm into zebras and presents me with trinkets like this whenever he sees one. I haven't told him about the llama thing.

"Aw, thanks," I say, taking it. "Did you text Alastair?"

"Uh, yeah. I'm meeting him at the record store after lunch."

"Good," I say, attempting to attach the zebra clip to my fleece. "At least you're not on your own. And you'll go round his place for tea, yeah?"

"Yes, stop worrying. You could come into town for a bit, if you wanted?" I shake my head. "Didn't think so. Not *that* worried about me, then," he sniffs, taking over and attaching the zebra zip pull for me since my hands are so frozen they've lost all function. "Go on, can't you come in just for a bit? Someone'll hold your place, won't they? Do you want me to ask?"

"No, I'm not going anywhere. I'm staying put until those doors open."

"All right, keep your hair on," he snaps. "Pardon me for wanting to spend some time with you."

"Mac, this day is about the concert, OK? Nothing else matters."

He mumbles something as he looks away and it sounds like, "Don't I know it."

"You know I can't leave. Look at the queue now. I'm sixteenth of sixty."

Mac sighs. "You won't get any closer. The first fifteen will get the best spots at the barrier."

"Why d'you say that? Don't say that. I've got as good a chance as they have."

"Yeah, whatever," he says, with more than a hint of haughty. He looks away from me and sniffs the air. "I'm going to dump this lot in the car and go back in for round two."

"Are you in a mush now?" I ask him.

"No," he snips. "Just fed up. So you're going to stay here until seven o'clock tonight, just sitting on the pavement?"

"No. I might stand up for a bit." I smile, but he doesn't. "Anyway, think of all the shopping you'll get done without me getting in the way and moaning. Bet you're in your element."

"I miss the moaning. It's not as fun on my own."

"Well, you won't be on your own for much longer, will you?"

"How do you mean?"

"If you're meeting your cousin?"

"Yeah, I s'pose." He's all jittery and the longer I stare at him the pinker his cheeks get. "You are meeting him, aren't you?"

"I told you I was, didn't I? Do you want anything else in the meantime?" He's doing everything he can not to look at me.

I shake my head. I haven't lost the use of my voice, I'm just cold.

"Right, I'm off, then," he says. "River Island's got a sale on. I'll see you later."

I watch him wander off out of sight. He can be so weird at times. One of the *Shining* twins is suddenly very close to my side and smiling at me. Her hood is still up.

"Your boyfriend must really l-l-love you, to hang around all day and not even have a t-t-ticket," she says, juddering with cold, or it could be a stammer, I'm not sure.

"He's just my friend," I say and try to smile. Our two-line conversation comes to an end, seeing as I make no effort. I'm a bit anti-boyfriend. None of them live up to Jackson so what's the point? I've only done it once with Seth Chambers from school, and it was rubbish. His family was downstairs watching *Britain's Got Talent*. I'd spent years dreaming about losing my virginity and, when it happened, it was all over before Simon Cowell let that middle-aged unibrow woman know if she'd made it to the semifinals. Sex is a waste of time if it isn't with someone like Jackson. If it isn't with someone I love as much as Jackson. And that's impossible.

1:57 P.M. — I offer the bargain bucket to the Smiley *Shining* Twin, who's reading a battered copy of *Jane Eyre*. Scary *Shining* Twin just sits on the wall and stares at me, but Smiley *Shining* Twin seems pleased. Effort made. Check off that box, Jody.

2:03 P.M. — The platinum blonde girl next to me in the "Team Gatlin" T-shirt waves excitedly and knocks my cold chips out of my hand. I apologize (WTF?). She has that glossy hair that I want. The kind of hair that model had, the one Jackson went out with. I've tried everything but my hair just won't gloss. I'm just destined to be overweight and un-glossy.

2:06 P.M. — A seagull shits in the bargain bucket.

2:21 P.M. — Mac's back, talking to Team Gatlin about how Superdry is overrated. He used to wear it, until everyone else started wearing it, then he went off it. He's so fickle. They talk for ages, swapping makeup tips and shopping bargains and trying to remember lines from *Mamma Mia!* They're acting like lifelong friends. He's got his back to me. He's so annoying when he ignores me. Really winds me up. I can't help it if this is the most important day of my life so far. Why's he being so pissy? I don't like it when Mac talks to other girls. It just reminds me there are girls out there who'd be a better best friend for him. Chatty, pretty girls who like shopping.

2:37 P.M. — Mac takes over from me so I can go to the cinema loo again, and asks me to grab a leaflet of show-times while I'm over there, which I do. When I come back, he announces he's going to see this Jennifer Aniston rom-com. Our section of the line has bunched up where people are mingling, getting to know each other. Small Redhead offers me a swig of vodka. I shake my head and play with the moon rock.

Something above catches my eye. Mac's waving out of the window at the top of the cinema. Part of me wishes I was with him. We don't get to do much stuff on our own anymore, not since his mum went back to working full-time. We've usually got to bring Cree along, so we have to go to some playground or petting zoo. We always have a good time, though. A laugh. I'd be laughing now if I was with him, not freezing my tits off sitting on the pavement. I force myself to remember why I'm here. I try sketching to kill time, but my fingers are too cold. I put Mac's iPod on instead and find a Regs song, "Plug It Up." I close my eyes. Eyes on the prize, Jody, eyes on the prize.

3:25 P.M. — Commotion surrounds me. A warm sensation creeps down the sides of my head. Laughter. I must have nod-ded off. People are squealing and scattering away from me. I pluck the earphones out and slowly start piecing the awful puzzle together. Green Blazer Boy has puked on my head.

3:26 P.M. — I stand up, my head hanging over, hot frothy sick running down my scalp and neck. Green Blazer Boy is apologizing and laughing at the same time.

"It's OK, it's not that bad," says Smiley *Shining* Twin. "There's not that much of it." She's pouring her bottled water over my hanging head and tearing out pages of *OK!* magazine to scrape my hair with. Scrunched-up pictures of Pippa Middleton and one of the Kardashians flutter about my feet.

"I'm really sorry," the Green Blazer Boy keeps saying, but he's laughing with his friends.

I'm so angry, I swear I can feel my own stomach acids spitting inside me. What if Jackson pulls me out of the crowd for a duet now? I'm going to stink of some moron's digestive juices and put him right off. "You aimed for my head, you shitwit."

"I so didn't, oh my God, I so didn't, I didn't even see you 'til the last second."

Shining Twin finds my face under my hair. "Do you want to clean up? I'll hold your place."

"No, it's OK. Oh God." I remove Mac's iPod from my pocket to inspect it. "Stupid prick," I grumble in Green Blazer's direction. He slumps down against the wall, dribbling mouth, pale as a window.

"Is the iPod OK?" says *Shining* Twin.

"Yeah, just surface splashes. Don't tell him. This thing means more to him than I do."

3:41 P.M. — The iPod's still working, thank Cobain. I stick it on shuffle. The first song is that one from *Annie* that Mac sings all the time, "It's the Hard-Knock Life." There's a burning in my throat and I want to sink inside the hood of my fleece and cry my eyes out.

5:24 P.M. — The cinema's all lit up and streetlamps are coming on. Smiley *Shining* Twin now has a pair of pink leg warmers on over her wrists. She is also now blonde, and she's tossing her long black wig from hand to hand. Other *Shining* Twin is sitting on the wall, knees hugged in, shivering. She still has black hair and large black-painted eyes. She's glaring at me. I'm a bit scared.

5:48 P.M. — The sky's completely dark. A Mercedes rolls up and a group of girls spews out, all squealing like mosquitoes. I'm in *such* a bad mood and I can't shake myself out of it. I stink of whiskey puke, I need the loo again, and I can't see an end to this queuing lark. And then, to make matters worse, I notice a girl from the Mercedes is wearing the eBay shirt like mine. *I'm* supposed to be the only one here wearing one!

6:09 P.M. — I feel the last Curly Wurly in my thigh pocket. The discovery briefly lifts my mood. I take it out and rip open the top but the whiff of my sicky hair puts me off, so I stuff it back inside.

6:23 P.M. — A shudder of excitement, or maybe it's just cold, ripples through my body. It's getting close now. The scalpers have turned up. Short men in baseball caps and striped track pants, shouting up and down the line. "Regulators tickets. Come and get your Regulators tickets here." Everyone just ignores them. People in suits and skirts and high heels *clip-clop* back from town. I look behind at the queue. It is endless now. There are hundreds of people lining up far into the distance behind me.

Mac appears in the crowd and pushes his way toward me. I'm so happy to see a familiar face, I want to cry. Must be the emotion of knowing that I'm finally so close to getting inside.

He notices my smell straightaway. "God, who's vommed?"

I nod toward Green Blazer Wanker, who is lying along the wall a few places down, his arms over his eyes. Said Green Blazer is propped under his head as a pillow.

"It's coming from you," says Mac, laughing. "You stink. Has he thrown up on you or something?"

"Yes. And he just stood there and laughed. He's pretty out of it, though."

Mac stops laughing. A flash of realization appears on his face. "Were you wearing my iPod?"

I pull it from my pocket. "It's fine, it didn't get wet. It was in my pocket."

Without a word, Mac barges his way through the gathered knot of people until he gets to Green Blazer Boy and yanks the blazer from under his head so his skull falls back on the wall.

"Hey!"

Mac leaps up onto the wall and leans down and grabs the boy's T-shirt, pulling him to his feet, wincing at his breath. He gets right in his face. He's so tall and fit-looking compared to Green Blazer Boy, who's all pale and as limp as a rag doll.

"Keep your puke to yourself, all right? Else next time, you won't be drinking out of that bottle, you'll be having it removed. Got it?"

The boy nods and Mac pushes him back into the leafless bush behind the wall. Mac comes back over to me, still grimacing like he's just picked up something really dirty.

"Oh my God, why did you do that?" I ask when he comes back.

He shrugs, pulling his hand sanitizer from his coat pocket. "Because you didn't." His face is hard and he's looking back in the direction of Green Blazer Boy, shaking his head. He would have looked quite heroic, if he hadn't been hand-sanitizing. He offers me some.

I hold out my hands. "That was a bit manly."

"Well, I'm a man, aren't I?" he says, scratching his nose with a black-varnished fingernail.

"I meant to ask, how was the movie?" Some security guards are talking into CB radios through the windows of the building. It's nearly time!

Mac shoves his fingers into his pockets. "Like you care, anyway. You're practically fizzing."

"I can't help it. It's nearly seven o'clock. We'll be going in soon."

"Must feel like you're getting paroled. OK, well, have fun. I'll see you later."

"OK. Thanks," I call out as he melts back into the crowd. He says something and puts his hand up but before I can ask him to say it again, he's gone.

7:00 P.M. — We're all bunched around the doors. They're going to open any second now. Yellow-shirted security people have appeared and big fat bald men in black shiny jackets are barking out orders not to push and not to run once we're inside. My phone vibrates in my pocket. It's Mac.

"I'll text you when it finishes, about eleven, I reckon. See the lamppost opposite the pub, the one with the orange sign on it?" I twist my neck around and look across the road to the pub, then across to the lamppost. "I'll park by that. I'll put my hazards on."

"OK. See you —" But the phone goes dead.

It's taking ages for them to open the doors. It must be almost quarter past now. I feel for the ticket in my fleece pocket next to Grandad's moon rock, make sure it's still there. Mac's ticket.

7:15 P.M. — The crowd swell is incredible. I'm part of this vast wriggling worm of people all desperately trying to be the first through the tiny double doors. Some older girls from "The First Fifteen" try to tell the black-jacket security men that people are queue-jumping. They don't care — they're too busy chewing and being bald. And then, after twelve hours of waiting, everything happens. People push, girls yelp, doors open, bags are searched, people push, girls run, men shout, "Don't run." "No running." "Crowd surfers will be ejected." Doors open. People push.

And then my adrenaline kicks in and I race to the front of the huge indoor arena.

"No running!" someone shouts. But I don't stop running — I keep on, *pelt, pelt, pelt,* and pump my arms until I make the final lunge for the barrier, slamming into it and gripping on tightly. Never mind the dodgy looks I'm getting from the blonde on one side of me and the bob haircut on the other. Never mind that I'm winded. I don't care. I'm where I need to be and for the first time today, I'm happy. I'm so happy I'm here. This is where it's all going to happen. I'm going to sing the loudest. I'm going to stretch my hand out the farthest. He's going to notice me.

FOUR
TOO POSH TO MOSH

The opening act, Beckon Gallow, is rubbish. Like a load of little boys jumping around demanding sweets. But I guess we all expected that. No one is here to see them, anyway — they are just the last hurdle between us and the heaven that is The Regulators.

I'm crammed in like a cow in a pen. The other cows pinned in around me surge forward. I have to go with them — there's nothing else I can do, unless I signal to one of the Yellow T-shirt Guys at the front to pull me out, but only desperation calls for that and I'm not giving up yet. Not until I've seen Jackson. A crowd-surfer kicks my head as he passes over the top of us, but I can't complain. Water is thrown at us from the front like we're starving orphans. At one point, a jet of water squirts me hard in the face, I assume to cool me down, but it just makes me temporarily blind.

Smiley *Shining* Twin must have attached herself to me. Every time I turn around I see her.

"This is amazing!" she screams in my ear.

I blink the water out of my eyes and nod as she flings a plastic cup of ice-cold water over her head. I don't think it's amazing at all. I've queued all day in the freezing cold and now I'm penned in like I'm waiting to be slaughtered, mooing along with the rest of them. I'm not even watching the opening band anymore — I'm concentrating on not passing out. Somehow I've drifted away from the front barrier and that hallowed row in front of Jackson and the catchment area for his sweat or his spit and now I'm all at sea and there's nothing to hold on to.

Then it happens. The best part of the day so far. The opening act, can't even remember their name now, announces "This is our last song . . ." and everyone in the place goes mad and starts cheering, but the crush on my rib cage gets about ten degrees worse. Their last song is fast and frenetic and suddenly we're so excited to be seeing the back of them, we all start headbanging and jumping around like epileptics on pogo sticks. Sweat is pouring into my eyes because I still have my thick fleece on. The eBay shirt underneath has become another layer of my skin. There's a mist above the mosh pit — a mist of hot body odor and teen hormones run amok. The song comes to an abrupt halt and everyone cheers. They go off and the stage goes black.

"Wooooo-hoooooooo!" screams Smiley *Shining* Twin. I realize then that I'm pretty much deaf but for a dull audience murmur and a tiny mouse screaming somewhere inside my inner ear. The herd relaxes back and I can start wriggling out of my sweltering fleece.

Nothing happens for ages. A roadie appears every now and again to twiddle knobs on the amps. Then the curtain at the back is lifted and, in that instant, the stage triples in size. A huge, sparkling new drum kit appears at the back and everyone cheers again. Jael's drum kit.

More roadies appear, placing mic stands to the left and right of the stage for Lenny and Pash and one right in the center. The center where Jackson's going to be, any moment now. I'm going to see him. I'm craning my calves trying to stand on tiptoes the whole time, desperate to get the first glimpse of him when he comes on. I'm passed a plastic cup with an inch of ice-cold water in it.

Amps are hefted around, switches are checked, someone runs from the left side to the right, talking into a CB radio for no apparent reason, and a wiry woman comes on and sets up a six-pack of lagers on the edge of the drum platform and two large bottles of water on the amps. Another cheer goes up. Those are Pash's lagers. That's Jackson's water. OMFG. His lips are going to be on one of those bottles any second now.

My chest is thundering. Behind the drum platform, another curtain pulls back to reveal a high staircase which leads right up to a higher platform running all along the top. I'm guessing this is where Jackson makes his entrance: I read in a *Lungs* magazine review of the Prague gig that he came down some steps at the start. I don't think I'm ready for this. I don't think I'm ready for what is about to happen.

More waiting. I feel the mass around me expand a little every so often, so I have managed to wriggle my arms out of my fleece and it is now down as far as my waist. I'm apologizing all the time to the bodies next to me for touching them as I try to knot it around myself. I finally do it. I'm soaked through but at least I might now begin to cool down.

As I finish tying the sleeves, the buzz around me grows louder. A roar comes up over us like a wave, and I start screaming, too, though I don't know why. It just takes me over. Something's happening but I've no idea what it is. I'm up on tiptoes, looking frantically around the stage for signs of something other than black curtains and mic stands and amps. And eventually I see a figure in the wings with a guitar.

It's Lenny Mortiro. Lead guitarist. He is the first on. The screams grow louder, like a million tiny bells, and the swelling mass tightens around me like a blood-pressure band. Lenny salutes us and strides over to his mic stand on the left-hand side. He's wearing the trademark kilt and white shirt with the sleeves torn off to reveal arms full of tattoos. He has a pink Mohawk. In Berlin it was green — I saw it on YouTube. A spotlight beams down as he sips some water, fiddles with an amp, and starts cranking up a guitar riff so clean and perfect you could scratch your back with it.

He is the Punk.

At that moment, there's another roar. I'm on tiptoes again, I can't see anything. Then Pash Fredericks appears in a long black vicar dress with a white collar thing and grabs his bass guitar from the same side of the stage, raises a hand to us, and struts across to his microphone. He's so tall, just as tall as I imagined. His hair is flattened and shiny and there's a cigarette dangling from his mouth. He goes to the drum kit to snap the ring off a can of lager. He swigs it, flicks the ring pull toward us, then goes to his spotlit mic and starts plucking his strings.

He is the Priest.

The crowd roar covers me like a boiling hot blanket.

I've never heard anything so loud. But when Pash's guitar joins in with Lenny's, they take it up a couple more levels. Lenny's wheedling away on one side and Pash is plucking for all he's worth. They're plucking on guitar strings, but those guitar strings could be running through the center of my body. I can feel each one, feel the vibrations inside me. I can feel it all! A steady surge forward of the crammed-in mass takes me out of my heaven and it's suddenly harder to breathe. I'm sweating buckets and I can feel beads of perspiration popping up all over my face. I raise a hand up to wipe my forehead and it gets pinned where it is. I can't get it down at all. I look like I'm answering a question.

Another roar from somewhere. Another figure appears, this time from the back of the stage. Where? Who? What?! It's Jael Dennehy. Oh my sweet Lord Cobain on High, it's Jael Dennehy and not only is he here, he is not wearing a shirt. He's just as V-shaped and tanned as he is in all my pictures but just as shy as he seems in interviews. His upper body ripples and bumps in all the right places but his head is dipped and covered with a straggly mass of hair. The screams around me are unspeakable. He has white board shorts on, high-top Nikes, and a mask on the top of his head. He lifts up one extremely toned arm to acknowledge us, gets himself comfortable on his stool, and pulls his mask down onto his face. He then starts banging away to a constant marching rhythm.

He is the Clown.

Everyone's going ballistic. Jael's drumming is so loud I swear the fillings are jumping out of my teeth. Strobe lights flash white-hot then orange, red, green, purple, pink, blue on the stage. All my internal organs quiver to the wheedling of Lenny's guitar. My legs shake to the timbre of the bass line. The air is sweaty and sexy, and grown men around me are shouting and screaming, and the stink of stale beer and eggy sweat is thick in my nose and my mouth.

And all at once it goes completely black. Lenny, Pash, and Jael stop thrumming and drumming. There's near silence onstage. Near glass-breaking noise in the crowd. OMG.

A single white spotlight beams down at the top of the staircase. OMFG.

And he's there.

He's standing there, his arms folded across his chest. His arms bound by his sleeves. He's wearing a white strait-jacket. Skinny white jeans. White DMs. He is Jackson.

He is the Madman.

They're all here now. The Punk. The Priest. The Clown. And the Madman.

The crowd noise goes up ten decibels even though Jackson's just standing there, completely still. I don't move either. For at least a minute he doesn't move and I don't move. Every pore on my skin is a goose bump. The crowd chants.

"REGS! REGS! REGS! REGS! REGS! REGS! REGS! REGS! REGS! REGS! REGS! REGS!"

I start crying uncontrollably. He's here. They're all here. Pasha John Fredericks, bass player, birthday 17 February, strawberry blond, chain-smoking, E-string genius. Leonardo Joseph Mortiro, lead guitar, birthday 6 July, quarter Italian, Mohawked, kilt-wearing, maestro wheedler extraordinaire. Jael Matthew Dennehy, drummer, birthday 10 March, mute, birthmarked, board shorts–wearing, sushi-loving, tub-thumper.

And Jackson James Gatlin, singer, birthday 3 September, beautiful, big blue eyes, messy brown hair, teetotaler, vegetarian, Stephen King–fanatic, broken-homed, bookish, bliss on legs.

Jackson has a head mic. He screams and it's like the twisting of a thousand knives. It's really Jackson. It's really him. Oh my God, he's there. He's here. I'm so close. Not close enough but still closer than I've ever been before. He starts to sing but the crowd noise is a wall. I can barely hear him. I'm crying so much I can barely see him. Then the amps are turned up and his voice runs up and down my body like fingernails.

I push and shove to get an inch closer, try and hang on to my place near the front, but you give a Regs fan an inch she'll take two and the second I move to make the break to get closer, bodies close in and I lose it, and suddenly I'm an inch farther back than I was.

"Jaaaaaaaaaacksssssssonnnnnnn!!!!!!!!!!!!!" I yell, but it's like nothing has come out of my mouth. He's not going to hear me, anyway. He's in the moment. There's about ten thousand people all screaming the same thing. Why would he hear *me*?

I'm up on tiptoes, trying to see as much as I can. He stamps down the stairs, his hair gelled up in a forest of spikes, and sings the whole first song with his arms bound across his chest. It's their slow love song, "Tortuous," from the new album *The Punk, The Priest* . . . That means they're going to do it in CD order. Jackson disappears from the stage for a couple of minutes as Lenny shreds through a solo. Nobody around me seems to know what's happened to him. And as "Tortuous" comes to its slow, melodic end, he reappears at the side. His arms unbound. His eyes wild. And I know what's coming next. And it's not going to be pretty.

It's gonna be "Bedlam."

And suddenly I'm tossed and pushed and pummeled around like a ball in a bounce house. Jackson flings his arms wide. He is feral. Possessed. Jumping off speakers. Snarling and screeching and kicking and spitting out at the crowd and they love it. Lights pulse green, red, white, flashing blue. The drumbeats smack us about the face and we just want more. We feed off him like vampires in a bloodbath. Vampire cows.

At the front, yellow-shirted security blokes stand as still as marble pillars, facing away from the stage. They're watching us and chewing, occasionally doling out cups of water from large blue bins and handing them to us. Every now and then I get an inch in the bottom of a cup and drink it down like it's the last water on Earth. Girls everywhere scream and cry, practically tearing their faces off. I recognize a couple from the queue. Team Gatlin and Small Redhead. I see Team Gatlin signal to a Yellow Shirt and he and another guy step up and reach over the front row to pull her out. Two songs in and she's had it. She's queued all day and they're pulling her out already. One body closer to the front row I get.

Then the worst thing happens, aside from me dying on the spot: Suddenly I don't know where the moon rock is.

I don't know why it occurs to me to notice at that moment, but I know it's not in my cargoes — just the last Curly Wurly and some candy wrappers in there. It's in my fleece pocket, tied around my waist, where it can easily fall out while I'm dancing. I stand still while everyone else is going nuts around me, and force my hand down to my waist to try and get it, apologizing again, even though they can't hear me, to all those bodies juddering and shoving up against me. It takes me a little while to reach it and I'm still desperately trying to keep my eyes on the stage to see what Jackson is doing, but then I get to my pocket and reach inside. And it's there. And I clasp it between my fingers and pull it out. I need to get it into my cargoes where I can zip it up safely. I can't lose it. I made a promise to Grandad.

"Bedlam" ends and a cheer goes up again. The cow mass relaxes slightly to cheer and I raise my hands out to clap, but suddenly song three starts and it's "Freaktasia," the circus song, another fast one, and everyone starts jumping about again. Fireworks go off behind speakers to the left, to the right. Something explodes behind the drums. The stage goes dark and some midgets run on with sparklers. Jackson's wearing a top hat and cracking a whip across the stage. A Goth girl beside me whoops and hollers and flings her arm in front of me, screaming "Yeeaaaaaah!" and as she does, her frantic arm knocks the moon rock clean out of my hand. It flies, I'm not kidding, *flies* toward the front of the stage and disappears down where the Yellow Shirts are standing.

It's gone. Shit, it's gone. Where the hell is it?

"Freaktasia" is in full swing and everyone's loving it.

But I can't enjoy it anymore. I have to get the moon rock, I just have to. Aside from my grandad showing up at the front of the stage, it's the only thing that will get me out of that pen. I have to get it, don't I? I imagine it getting kicked about, or some security guard chucking it into the crowd farther away.

I catch the eye of one of the Yellow Shirts and make the universal sign of "Get me the hell out of here." Everyone then guides me toward him and I'm like a baby being pulled out of a tight sucking hole. My body's being dragged across people's heads and I'm yanked out of there by my belt and arms. I'm plonked onto my feet and ushered to the left-hand side toward the St. John Ambulance people and a bin full of iced water. I'm handed a cup, but I don't take it. I'm scanning the floor. There's no sign of the moon rock, but I won't leave the front of the stage until I see it. I feel a hand try to move me along to a Yellow Shirt, who then shows me the way to the side barrier. The drink is shoved under my nose again. I don't want it — I just want to see the rock.

"Move it!" shouts the Yellow Shirt, right in my ear. "Go behind the barrier."

"No, I have to find my rock!" I shout back at him, scanning the floor. "Oh God, where is it?"

I look back along the line of Yellow Shirts at the front of the stage. They're all watching the cow pen. But then I see it, glinting on the floor in front of one of them. I'm sure that's it. I make like I'm doing as I'm told and head toward the side barrier, then at the last second, I do a U-turn and peg it back toward the front of the stage. It's like slow motion, every step is measured and I know each step could be my last before I'm taken down, but I make sure they're big steps. I nearly get there. I reach out, I reach for the moon rock, and arms grab me around my waist. I'm thrown down *oomph* style to the floor, the rock just out of reach. I kick and shout, trying to wrench myself out of the Yellow Shirt's grip, but it's like being inside a tire. Another one jumps on top of him and the squeeze on my ribs is even worse than being in the mosh pit. I'm going to pass out.

I want to shout but I can't. I can't get enough air in my lungs. I'm just mouthing, "Let me go, I have to get it, just let me get it." I'm crying now, though there isn't enough air to even fuel each sob. I keep seeing my grandad's face, hearing his voice in my head.

"It's magic, Jody. You look after that."
"I promise."

"Let me get my rock. Just let me get it!" I scream. Two of them are on me now. Another stands on my hand. And at that moment, I feel all of them leave me. No one's on my back. No one's on my hand. My sweaty hair is clinging to my face like wet worms. I'm lifted to my feet. Jackson is there. He's standing in front of me. All in white. And he's handing me my moon rock.

"Here you go. That what you needed?" he shouts breathlessly. I take the rock quickly and look at his eyes. They are soft and his face is sweaty and pale. Then he turns to the three burly Yellow Shirts and points his finger — his eyes all wild and watery and his face furious. "You manhandle one of them again like that I'll have you all fuckin' fired, got it? Bunch of pricks."

Some other security people, big burly men but in suits, dash in and maneuver Jackson back onto the stage, where the song, I don't even know which one, comes to its instrumental end.

Robotically, I shove the rock deep inside my cargoes and zip it up. Then I'm ushered back behind the barrier at the side of the stage. I. Cannot. Believe. What. Just. Happened. My mouth hangs open like a trapdoor. "I didn't thank him," I mumble as I'm pushed along.

Someone is beside me and hands me a cup of water. It's Scary *Shining* Twin, all sweaty, her T-shirt stuck to her skin like plastic wrap. I take the cup and pour the water over my head. I don't even feel how cold it is but there are little lumps of ice in it.

She looks like she's going to sink her teeth into my neck, but instead shouts something into my ear. I only hear her the second time. "What did he give you?"

I just look at her.

"Are you all right?"

And then she's getting farther away. And farther away. And I'm at her knees, her feet. And I feel my head fall back with a snap. And it hurts. Then all the lights go out.

FIVE

STEALING THE LIMELIGHT

Bright white room. Heaven? Am I dead? Is this the "something good" I wanted? Shit. I don't want to be dead! I'm not ready. I want to go to Italy. I want to swim with dolphins. . . .

Black uniforms mill around me. I'm soaked and freezing cold. Music thumps through the white walls. After a couple of blinks, I realize. I'm not dead. I'm still at the concert. I must be backstage. Hospital beds are dotted about the room. I'm lying on my side on one of them. Three songs. I waited all day in the freezing cold to hear a shit opening band and three songs. Now I'm proper bawling it. People in black uniforms look at me. It's so bloody unfair! My phone judders in my pants pocket.

I roll onto my back and take it out. Message from Mac. I squint through my tears to read it.

PRKD OPPO PUB OUT FRONT. UNDER STREET LITE WIV ORANGE SIGN. WEN EVA UR READY. M.

It must be eleven o'clock. That's when he said he'd text. I remember him saying it. The concert must be nearly over. I've slept through it!

I shove the phone back in my pocket. I'm still crying,

even more hopelessly now, like a toddler who's lost sight of her mum. I pat my zipped pocket. A lump. The moon rock's there. I daren't get it out in case it leaps out of my hand again. What am I thinking? Rocks can't jump, can they? A tear rolls down my cheek, into one of my almost deaf ears. I see Jackson's face as he gave the rock back to me. His shining, smiling face. I get the rock out and rub it against my upper lip. Pretty soon it's wet with my tears. My head throbs all over. Two girls are carried in by some more Black Uniforms, one of them is the Smiley *Shining* Twin, who looks like she's dying — not so smiley now. The other is the girl in the eBay shirt. She looks dead. Her head-band has fallen over her forehead and her hair is stuck to her face. One of the sleeves has been ripped right off the T-shirt. That could have been me!

"Are you going to be sick?" A girl about my age with a massive mop of fuzzy brown hair appears by my bed. She's in a black uniform like the others. She stares at me, eyes like buttons. Her badge says "Farrah."

"What's your name?" she shouts in my ear, like I'm an old woman.

"I . . . want . . . to . . . go . . . back . . . out . . . there," I squeak between breaths.

She shakes her head. "You're not in your right mind. You've been going in and out of consciousness for the last hour. Can you tell me what your name is? Did you come with someone?"

I start sobbing again. She thrusts a small white bucket under my nose. I shove it back at her and it tumbles to the floor with a clatter. A fat woman with short legs and a face like a plate waddles over and offers me a cup of ice cubes. I'm guessing she's the head Black Uniform. The Fat Controller.

"Did you find out her name?" says the Fat Controller to Farrah the Fuzz Monster.

Farrah shakes her head and goes to open the door a bit wider for three more Black Uniforms carrying in a blond boy who is wheezing like a pig stuck in a fence. They're just saying, "Breathe, breathe, that's it, just breathe," and I feel like shouting, *If he could bloody breathe he wouldn't be in here!* Farrah and the Fat Controller go over to see if they can help, leaving me with the cup of ice. I look inside. There's a small black hair in it that looks like a pube.

I want to see Jackson. I need to thank him. I can't remember if he touched my hand when he gave me back the moon rock. I moan as I cry, as somber as a ghoul. I drop the cup to the floor and make to get up off the bed, but my head spins and I can't focus. Maybe the Jackson-giving-back-my-rock thing was a dream, I don't know anymore. I close my eyes to stop the room from spinning and try to focus on the door. I make toward it quickly, hoping no one will see, but just as I think I reach the door, my head bangs against something. I've walked straight into the wall.

"Come on now, back to your bed, that's right," a voice says. An arm guides me back to my bed. It's the Fat Controller. "You're not well at all, are you? You've had a bump to the back of your head. You need to keep that compress on it."

"What compress? I haven't bumped my head. I just fainted or something. . . ."

"Yes, and when you fainted, you bumped your head. You need to keep pressure on it." She leans me back on the bed and picks up a cold white washcloth from a cart, folds it over, and presses it against the back of my head. "Now, can you hold it there for me?" She guides my hand to it to hold it in place. For a second my face is in her armpit.

"Now you stay put while we wait for the ambulance. We don't want you keeling over again."

Something in my chest collapses about six stories. "No, I don't want an ambulance."

"We do it for anyone with a head injury. You just missed the first one so we'll just wait in here for them to send the next, OK? Can you tell me your name now?" I shake my head.

Wheezy Boy's being sick and she rushes over to see if she can interfere. I look at the compress. There's a red patch on it, about the size of a fava bean. I put it back on my head and lie back onto it. I can't go to the hospital. Today cannot end like this! I can't stop crying. The room is still helter-skeltering around and I close my eyes briefly to make it stop.

The Fat Controller is arguing with another Black Uniform about how late the ambulance is and he's all shruggy and end-of-his-tethery because all the ambulances are busy at some antiwar demo in the city center. Music thuds through the walls — they must be nearing the end of the set by now. They'll be back on the tour bus and heading to the airport and far away across the Atlantic before I even know it.

After a little while the room slows down a bit and I

can see who else is there with me. Wheezy Boy is being sick again. A blonde in a Paramore T-shirt is sitting on a bed nibbling a cereal bar. I overhear her tell Farrah the Fuzz Monster that she hasn't eaten for two days. And when Farrah asks why, she shrugs and says, "For Jackson." Then they start talking about something that happened onstage, something I missed.

"God it was great," says Cereal Bar Girl. "The other guys stopped playing, and it was just Jackson and the crowd singing. *'I'm just a poor boy, I need no sympathy, because I'm easy come, easy go. . . .'* And we did the Scaramouche bits. God it was sooooo amazing! I didn't want it to ever end. I'm so getting a tattoo done tomorrow. I wasn't sure but I've made up my mind now."

"Bohemian Rhapsody"? Jackson sang "Bohemian Rhapsody," my grandad's favorite song? And I MISSED IT? I feel the tears come fast into my head and there's nothing I can do to stop them. I pull my knees up to my chest. There's a scrunching sound in my thigh pocket — the last Curly Wurly, untouched and sagging where it's melted in its wrapper. I pull it out and look at it but get one whiff of the chocolate and suddenly I want to cry again. Last time I had one of these, it was before. Before the puke, before Jackson and the rock . . .

I have to get out of here. I have to get back to Jackson.

I hear more applause through the walls. I lean up again and sit on the side of the bed; my head's going a little spinny but it's not as bad as it was. There are little dark specks in my eyes.

It is then that I see a tall black blob in the doorway. I try and blink away the blur in my eyes and when it comes into focus I can see who the blob is. It's Pash Fredericks, the bass player from The Regulators. I'm not even surprised to see him. I've read on the net that Pash does this sometimes, insists on being brought to the medical room to meet those fans who were stupid enough to faint after three songs. Lenny does it as well, sometimes. But never Jael and never *ever* Jackson. This could make up for it, I think, make up for my car crash of a day. If Pash comes over to me, hugs me, asks how I am, this might just save the day. I lie back, holding the compress to the back of my head with one hand, trying to will more blood to that part of my body, possibly even a bit of brain to come out, to get some sympathy. I'm clutching the Curly Wurly in my other hand and cooking up a plan to get Pash's attention, to make him remember me. He's always going on about chocolate and candy in his interviews — I'll give him a bite of the Curly Wurly. Yes, that's what I'll do. And then I'll keep it, take it home, and frame it, and then I'll have my memento of the night. A half-eaten chocolate bar from the least popular member of the band. Better than nothing.

"Hey, kid, how ya doing?" says Pash as he wanders over to Wheezy Boy and gives him his last rights. Wheezy Boy laughs. Cereal Bar Girl is bawling her eyes out, at which point he goes over and gives her a really tight hug. As he breaks away he goes to light up a cigarette and the Fat Controller stops him just as he flicks up the flame.

"Uh, not in here, please. It's against the law in this

country, in case you hadn't heard. And this boy's had an asthma attack," she says. He gives her a look, but tucks the cigarette behind his ear.

And it is then that another blob appears in the doorway. A white blob. Jael, possibly Jael. God, is it Jael? I can't quite see. I blink. No . . . it's not Jackson. It can't be Jackson. Jackson never goes backstage to visit the fans.

But it *is* Jackson.

Oh fuuuuuuuuuuuuuuuuuuuuuuuuuuuuuuuuuuuuuuuuuuuck.

Oh my God, oh my God, oh my God, Jesus, please no. Oh no. Oh no, I'm not ready. Oh I look a mess. Do I still smell of puke? This is too much. I'm going to faint. What will I do, what am I going to do?! This man is *the* most perfect man in the world and I look like crap! My mind is blank. I should be squeeing. I should be about ready to bungee jump off Cloud Nine, but I feel sick. I do want to meet him, ask him if it was a dream that he gave the moon rock back to me, tell him how much he means to me, how I'm an outcast like him, how my parents got divorced, too, tell him about the Stephen King books I've read, about the thirty-seven times I've watched their DVD, how his birthday is twenty-six days before mine. Tell him I'm his Number One Fan.

"Hey, how are you doing?" I overhear him ask Cereal Bar Girl. He looks gorgeous, still wearing his straitjacket, though this time he has hands poking out through the sleeves and the front is wide open. I can see his hands. His three silver rings on his right hand. I can see his mood ring, his actual mood ring that he always wears. OMG. He has a black string necklace on with a key pendant.

I can see his chest. It's sweaty. He has hairs!

Pash comes over to me. "Hey, how you doing?" Pash asks. I look right past him to Jackson.

"OK, thanks, Pash."

"What happened, you faint or something?"

"Yeah. I'll be OK." *Where's Jackson, where's Jackson, where's Jackson . . .* .

"Well, thanks for coming, great to see y'all, man, great gig." He holds his hand up to grab mine in a buddy way, then sees I'm holding the compress behind my head. I'm just about to offer Pash the Curly Wurly, but I've forgotten what it's called. All I can think is, *Wow, he's really cross-eyed. They don't show that on the posters.* He smells, too — *really* strongly of cigarettes. It's better than the hot meat smell of the mosh pit — armpit, more like — but it's still rank.

I'm just thinking about going into spasms to attract Jackson's attention when Pash moves on and Jackson makes the break from Cereal Bar Girl and heads my way.

But Cereal Bar Girl waylays him by trying to give him a hug (Jackson doesn't give hugs, I know that) and she's talking about this fan fiction she writes on her blog, but he's not interested. He's got strands of sweaty hair worming over his face and he looks like he's about to be sick.

"That's Claire with an 'i,' and I'm on Facebook," Cereal Bar Girl's going, but he's so not listening. I can't stop staring at him. He's kind of smiling but he looks so tired. There are wet black shadows underneath his eyes where his makeup has run. He actually looks quite ill.

Another blob enters in a gray suit, his blond hair stuck solid with hairspray. He has a really nasty little face, piercing green eyes, and skin that shines like plastic. He's flanked by two bulky security men in suits with curly earpieces.

He walks up to Jackson. He's angry with him, but he's angry in tones only I can hear, cos they're right by my bed. They don't seem to notice me, though.

"What was that about, Gat?" the man says to Jackson. "Why did you do that cover? I told you —"

"Yeah, well, you know me, Frank. Nothing really matters to me."

"Fucking song, why you gotta test me like this, huh? Do I not pay you enough or something?"

"I told you I was gonna do 'Rhapsody' tonight and you weren't gonna stop me," says Jackson, wearily, like he's about to climb up onto one of the beds and go to sleep for the night.

Blond Nasty Face glares at Jackson and digs him in the chest with his finger. He says something I can't quite hear because the security men's radios are crackling, Pash is laughing with a kid on a bed, and some first aiders in the corner are pulling back chairs to lie someone down on the floor.

"Don't give me all that 'You Don't Own Me' crap," says Nasty Face. "One phone call and I could convert you to a carpet stain and don't forget it." He goes right up to Jackson's face. "Don't fuck with me, Gatlin. And why the hell are you back here visiting these morons?"

"To piss you off," Jackson replies, all cool, but looking really sick at the same time. And not in a good way.

"You've had your take five to piss and pill up. Get back out there."

"I'm out," Jackson mumbles, rubbing his eyebrow. "I got nothing left tonight, Frank."

"Get back out there. They're screaming for an encore and you're gonna give them one."

Jackson removes a card of pills from his jean pocket and pops one out. "You said one night we could leave it as is. . . ."

"Not tonight. Did you know the guys from Glastonbury are here tonight? Oh yeah. Top row. They're checkin' you chuckleheads out."

Jackson drops the pill and swallows it down dry, placing the card back in his pocket. "Well then they've seen us. We played for two damn hours." Jackson rubs his eye. Frank cuffs him around the head. His hand is covered in big gold rings.

I recognize the blond guy then. I know his voice. He's interviewed on The Regulators' *Behind the Scenes* DVD. It's Frank Grohman, their manager. If snakes could talk, I imagine they would talk like Frank Grohman. All fast and raspy and chewy, cos Frank is always chewing when he talks. Pash jokes on the DVD that he's chewing on the flesh of his last intern — that's Frank's reputation for being a badass. Frank took over from their last manager just under a year ago before they started recording their new album. He's responsible for their faster, more frenetic sound, the longer touring schedules, big budget videos. He comes across as an arsehole on the DVD, too.

"You got five minutes," he says to Jackson. "We're

playing videos to keep them happy. Wipe that shit off your face, get out there, and give it everything you got, you hear me? Keep thinking Glastonbury."

"What if I don't got nothing left, Frank, huh? What about that? Can't we just go?"

"What's the matter with you? It's not the last train outta friggin' Auschwitz. You do another fifteen and then you can sleep on the bus 'til next Tuesday for all I care." Frank slaps him on the back. "Four minutes, Gat."

Frank's cell phone starts ringing and he takes the call, jabbing one chubby, gold-encrusted finger to his ear and disappearing out of the room, followed by the two bodyguards. Jackson is still for a minute. He wanders over to my bed, forcing a smile. Without thinking, I hold my arms out for a hug. He stays where he is and his lips have disappeared into his face like they're stapled together.

"Sorry, I forgot," I say. I thrust my hand forward instead. He holds his hand out and I drop the compress to take it. He has a very limp handshake, like a dead squid. But it's his hand. It's Jackson's hand! I smile, he doesn't. Doesn't even look at me.

I have no idea what to say so I say the first thing that comes to mind.

"You look tired." Which he really does.

He laughs and looks embarrassed. He starts fiddling with the key pendant around his neck. "Yeah. I am," he laughs again and rubs his eye.

His mood ring is glowing bright blue, like his eyes. His pupils are like pinpricks and make the blue bits of his eyes look even bigger. I'm not poetic enough to think of some fantastically beautiful description of Jackson's eyes. All I ever come up with are wanky things like that crushed blue ice you suck through a straw. But they're that blue. As blue as that ice. Chemical blue. He takes the card out of his back pocket again and drops another couple of pills. "Aspirin," he explains.

I laugh, but I don't know why. I can't stop staring at his eyes. I have to say something about his eyes. "Your eyes are like Slush Puppies."

"What?"

"Oh, uh, nothing. I'm . . . uh, eBay. I'm wearing the eBay shirt. Your shirt for charity."

"Oh. Yeah. I, uh, I hope you feel better soon," he says with some finality, but he's not looking at me. He's looking at the floor, swaying a tiny bit, like he's about to fall over. Then he takes a packet of cigarettes from his jacket pocket. He moves away, stands at the end of my bed, and cups the hand with the mood ring over a cigarette as he lights it. Fat Controller marches over.

"I'm sorry but we do have a smoking ban in this country," she says, just like she did before with Pash, and her nostrils go all cave-dweller big. He pulls the cigarette out of his mouth and just stands there looking down at her, head bowed. He scratches his fingertips through his scalp and laughs.

And in that moment, it's almost as though the scenery peels back and me and Jackson step out of it. Everything happens on the other side of the room. In the corner by Cereal Bar Girl, Pash slips over, probably on one of the many ice cubes scattered about the floor, and knocks his head on a plastic chair. There is immediate panic from everyone nearby and they all gather around him. Security guys are on their CB radios. Black Uniforms buzz around. The Fat Controller orders them about like she's queen bee. Everyone's preoccupied. Everyone is concerned about Pash. Everyone except Jackson. He stays right where he is at the end of my bed. He doesn't even seem to care. He puts his hands in the tops of his pockets. He stumbles a bit, and pulls them out again and steadies himself on the bed.

And that's when rational thought hops aboard the night train out of there. I *have* to talk to him again, I *have* to touch him again, to feel the tingle of him when he shook my hand. I have to tell him about my grandad and the moon rock and everything he means to me. *"Don't Dream It, Be It."* He has to know what he means to me.

Be it!

He turns around. And I just react.

"Jackson?" I say.

"Huh?" he slowly, painfully turns to face me.

"Do you want my Curly Wurly?" I blurt out, lurching to the end of the bed and thrusting the thing right up in his face.

O-M-F-G.

He looks at it all big-eyes, like it's diseased. He thinks I'm a whale. This sad, pathetic loser who has to have chocolate on her at all times in case of emergencies. Some real fat-ass.

"All right," he says, staring at it wide-eyed. He's still swaying about. "Take it easy."

It's still there, the Curly Wurly, thrust out before him.

I can't move my arm. It's locked like it's turned to stone or something. "It's OK, you can have it, take it," I insist, jabbing him in the cheek with it. The end I'm holding is limp in my iron fist, I'm squeezing it so tightly.

"I'll do what you want just . . . p-please, no drama," he says, like I've got a knife against his cheek, not a Curly Wurly.

He's just staring at it. There's a blur in my eye again. I blink it away, and as I open my eyes from the blink, he's there with his hands up in front of him. Not one person is looking our way, they're all too worried about Pash or having breathing problems of their own to notice. Oh. My. God. He thinks it's a weapon. Jackson thinks my Curly Wurly is a *knife*!

"Oh, no. No it's not . . ."

He turns toward the door and, without another single sensible thought, I place my palm on his back and we start walking. I look behind me. No one is watching us. *No one is watching us!*

"Where are we going?" he says, stumbling through the door.

"Uh . . . don't speak," I say. And all the time we're walking out of there into the cold night air, I try not to concentrate on the Mac side of my brain which is saying, *What the hell are you doing? He thinks it's a knife, he thinks your Curly Wurly is a* knife*! Tell him it's just a silver wrapper, tell him it's just a misunderstanding. Let him go, just let him go!*

But I can't let him go, I just can't.

Keep going, keep going, keep going. Don't look back. No one notice, please no one notice!

And anyway we're out the door now. "Put your hands down," I tell him, and he does.

The door shuts quietly behind us, and we're walking, across the silent bus parking lot, heading toward some tall metal gates. I look behind again. No one calls out. No one stops us. Two security guards are watching football on a small television screen inside a booth by the gates. We approach them and I slow my pace. *Please don't see us.* We walk past them. My hearing is so messed up I can't even hear what they're talking about. *Please don't see us.* It's like they're speaking through a cardboard tube. But they don't notice us and as we make it through the gates to the pavement on the main road, I rip my fleece from my waist and put it over Jackson's head. He's shaking. His walk is slow and his feet scuff on the ground like a kid coming down from a tantrum. I steer him around trash bins and speed bumps and burger boxes until we arrive around the front of the arena and cross the road. He mumbles something.

"What?"

"Where are you taking me?" he mumbles again, somewhere under my fleece.

I don't know what else to say to him. I rack my brain, trying to think of movies where people are being taken hostage. What do the bad guys say? I don't want to tell him to shut the eff up. He is, after all, still my hero. I just want him with me, that's all I know. That's all I want at that moment. "Just keep moving," I say and he does, slowly.

There are fans milling around outside the arena, and scalpers still trying to sell tickets for a gig that's pretty much over. Some guys stand on the street selling tour posters and cheap-looking T-shirts with band logos on them, and for a second I want to stop and buy one, but then I think I couldn't possibly buy anything now that will compare with what I already have.

Reality check: OMFG!

But I choose to ignore it. Don't think just do, don't think just do. We walk past them all, through a sea of cans, bottles, flyers, and cigarette butts, across the road toward Mac's car. Right where he said he'd be — hazards on, under the lamppost.

A police car whizzes past, followed shortly by an ambulance. A stab of fear slices through me. It's OK, they're not for me. I just pray no one works out what's going on. But I don't know what's happening, so I doubt anyone else will.

"Just walk, I'll guide you," I say as we cross the road. Mac is dozing in the driver's seat, wrapped up in his coat. I knock on the window and he jumps and fumbles with the door before pulling the seat forward.

"That was quick. Thought you'd be ages. Didn't you get a T-shirt or something?"

"No."

"Didn't they do an encore even? Stingy gits. Oh, are we giving someone a lift?"

I push Jackson inside first so he is sitting behind Mac's seat and then get in next to him and shut the door.

"Why aren't you sitting in the front —"

"Go, Mac, before we get caught in the traffic."

"Hang on, where does your mate live?"

"I'll tell you on the way, please just drive."

And he does. He puts his foot down and we are out

of there like a speed skater. We bolt through the town, straight through every traffic light, increasing speed until the orange streetlamps become blurs outside the windows. It starts raining hard. The wipers are on full pelt and they're squeaking loudly. We get to a traffic circle. Mac is looking at me in the rearview mirror with his serious face on. He adjusts the mirror to see the face of "my mate" but Jackson still has my fleece over his head so he adjusts it back.

"Are you going to tell me what's going on?" Mac says as we make it to a big traffic circle.

"Are we on the motorway yet?"

"Jody, tell me now. What have you done? Why's she under your coat?"

"Are we on the motorway yet?" I say again, more forcefully. He pauses, puts his foot down. We head along the edge of the circle. He flips up the blinker. We take the second exit and hit the rumble strips.

"Yes, we're on the motorway, all right?"

"So you can't turn back?" I say.

"No, Jody, for Christ's sake . . ."

I pull the coat off Jackson's head and he shakes his hair out. Mac adjusts the mirror and flicks on the reading light. "What the . . ." He flicks the light off and on again. Then he flicks it off and doesn't say another word.

SIX

JACKSON, TOO: FULLY LOADED

I tend to do stupid things when left to my own devices. Mac will testify to this, if it ever needs testifying to, as he's usually a witness. So I thought if anyone would understand why I took Jackson when the opportunity came up, it would be Mac. He knows how I feel about Jackson, so he should understand why I did it. But as we speed along the near-deserted M4 motorway out of Cardiff, it becomes clear that Mac is definitely *not* on the same page as me. I don't even think we're in the same library.

Jackson falls asleep as the car bombs along. In fact, he goes practically unconscious. And then, without warning, Mac pulls off the motorway at the next exit and hits the turn signal for the rest stop. Red-and-white lit-up signs for a KFC and a drive-through Burger King glow in the misty dark and the parking lot is empty except for two hatchbacks and a tourist bus. He pulls into a space near the entrance and switches off the engine.

"You need . . . to tell me . . . what the hell you've done," he says, very slowly, like he's had a stroke and is learning to talk again.

"Um," I begin, and then I try to remember being back in the first-aid room, hearing the music pumping and the Fat Controller and the St. John Ambulance people and Cereal

Bar Girl and Pash coming in and Pash falling over. "Well, Jackson came backstage, to see the fans in the recovery area. He shook my hand. And then his manager came in and he was really rude to him, kept swearing and stuff, and Jackson looked really fed up and he said he had a headache. I offered him my Curly Wurly —"

Mac holds up his hand to shush me. "Is that sex slang for something?"

I frown. "No, my chocolate bar." Mac is silent for another age and I gabble away to fill the void. "Anyway he came over and I didn't know what to do, my brain just went into overdrive cos I'd fainted and hit my head and I couldn't believe he was there and I didn't know what to say so I thought I'd offer him my chocolate bar and see if he would have a bite so I could take it home and frame it or something and when I reached out to give it to him, I think he thinked —"

"Thought."

"— thought it might have kind of been a bit of a . . . like . . . sort of . . . knife."

A looooooong sigh. More silence. He turns in his seat to look back at me. "He thinks you've kidnapped him? By force?" I nod. "Hmm?" he reiterates in that harsh way teachers do.

"Yes," I say quietly, so as not to wake Jackson up. "But he sort of relaxed, once I'd got him in the car. He didn't seem to mind. He hasn't freaked out or anything. Look at him, he's asleep."

"Why do you think that is, Jody?" Mac shouts.

"Keep your voice down."

"No, this is my car and I can shout as much as I want!" I look across at Jackson but he doesn't even flinch. Mouth agape, he is completely out of it. I raise a hand to feel for breath. "You didn't even see it, did you?"

"See what?" I frown.

Mac sighs again. "He's a tweak-head."

"No he isn't. He's just got a headache. I saw him take an aspirin earlier. He's been clean for, like, two years. . . ."

"Oh, wake up and smell the bullshit, Jody, please. Wild Man Rocker Jackson Gatlin? Angst-Ridden Jackson Gatlin? Drugged-Up Wastoid Jackson Gatlin? You bought the magazines."

"Stop it. Not all those stories are true."

"No, they are, you just don't want to believe them." Mac sighs for a third time, scraping a hand through his spiky black hair, and when he gets right to the back, he rubs it harder and harder through his hair again, like he's trying to sandpaper his head. The spikes don't move, though; there's that much gel on it. "Oh my nightmare day," he says. "Please, someone, *someone* tell me I'm dreaming. I mean, are you clinically depressed or something? Is there something here I'm missing? You've done stupid things, I know. I was the one who broke your fall when you tried to climb that telephone pole. . . ." Silence. Then he shouts. "*WHAT* the *HELL* have you *DONE*?"

Jackson stirs, but turns over and falls back to sleep, his face right up against the cold window. "I just saw an opportunity," I say, my voice shaking. "It's your fault."

"What do you mean this is *my* fault, how the hell is this *my* fault?"

"It was your Curly Wurly."

"Oh my God," he says, scrunching his eyes. "I can almost hear the soap dropping in the shower. Do you realize people will be out looking for him? Police? His manager? The press? They'll hunt us down. They'll search the Saxo. They'll find fibers!"

"No they won't. It's OK. I'll clean the car. I'll eat the evidence. Ow, my head hurts."

He laughs sarcastically. I feel I should speak, or at least make some noise. I hate that laugh. That's the "Jody, you are something else" laugh and it makes me feel stupid. Fat and ugly and freckled and embarrassed and stupid.

"I just wanted more," I tell him. "I wanted to meet him properly. To spend more than just thirty seconds with him. More than just a handshake. He came with me quite willingly. . . ."

"Because he thought you were going to stab him, you stupid cow!"

I flinch like he's pricked me with a pin. He calls me a cow all the time and I never get offended. But when he says it now, I don't like it. "I only got to see three songs, Mac. . . ."

"That does *not* entitle you to take home the lead singer, Jody."

"I know."

"Most people settle for a T-shirt or a poster. Not Jody. Jody wants actual *band* members."

There's an odd shuffling and clanking noise behind the car and all of a sudden there's a light knock on the back window next to Jackson's head. I scream and Mac jumps about two feet in the air. This is it, I think, it's the police. I'm beyond busted. A figure shuffles along to Mac's window and knocks again. But it's not the police, it's a sketchy old woman pushing a supermarket cart stuffed with trash bags. Mac catches his breath and goes to roll the window down.

"Don't!" I cry out. "She could have an ax or hairy hands or something," I urge him, instinctively clinging on to Jackson, like she might try and take him away.

He ignores me and rolls the window down an inch. She must be about eighty, and she's wearing a wool hat, long brown coat, and a Hello Kitty nightgown. Her face looks like a mashed-up envelope and she obviously has no teeth because her jaw seems to be chewing itself.

"Spare change?" she sniffs, holding her hand up to the crack in the driver's window.

"Uh no, not tonight," says Mac.

She peers into the car. "Who else you got in there with you, then?"

"No one," he says, and rolls his window back up.

"Have they got any change?" she asks again, more muffled through the window. We both watch her as she shuffles back around to Jackson's window, tries to clear the glass and have a good beak in at him. He has his face completely against the window so she must see him. She disappears around the back of the car and out of sight.

My heart is going like fist blows to a punching bag. "Do you think she saw him?" I whisper.

"I don't give a shit. In fact, I hope she did see him and

I hope she *does* recognize his face when it's plastered all over the tabloids tomorrow."

"Don't be so dramatic."

"You've kidnapped a celebrity, Jody. All right, he's not Princess Kate or the president or anything, but he's still famous. He's still in all the gossip mags. Once it gets out he's gone missing, presumed *kidnapped* from a concert, you're a ghost on toast."

"I don't care what you say, he was miserable in that room. When his manager was saying those things to him, all he wanted to do was to get out —"

"— and don't think you're bringing him back to the pub, either, no way," Mac interrupts.

I forgot. I no longer have a home, do I? I'm a house-guest at the pub. I can hardly bring home some other waif and stray to stay, can I? "Please, Mac, can he just stay at yours —?"

"No way."

"Well, what am I going to do, then?"

"I don't know. This is your problem, not mine."

"Where are we going, dudes?" a voice next to me pipes up. Oh, it's the rock star I kidnapped. He's pulling my pukey black fleece around him and he's shivering.

Mac snorts. "Oh nice, Ozzy Osbourne's back with us."

"Uh . . . to a pub," I tell Jackson.

"I need a burger," he mumbles, and falls back to sleep.

"OK," I say and I point to the Burger King across the parking lot. "They sell veggie burgers or cheesy some-things over there, don't they?" Mac throws me a filthy look. "I'll pay."

"Oh, I know you will." He starts the engine again, heading toward the drive-through ramp.

"Mozarella bites or something?" I say, turning toward Jackson.

"Burger," he mumbles, drool oozing from his mouth. He slurps it back up to speak. "I want meat. Bacon. Meat."

He eats *MEAT*?! And I went through months of eating rabbit food just for him!

"Ha!" Mac flicks on the mirror light and reaches over the back of his seat to lift up one of Jackson's eyelids. "Clean-living vegetarian, is he? Don't make me wet myself, Jody."

"He's just hungry. They did a long set tonight." That must be it.

"I know. I waited outside for most of it. Look at him. Any normal lead singer would be amped having ten thousand people calling his name. He should be bouncing off the walls. Look at him!"

So I do. I look at him.

"He's a rock star, Jody. It comes with the job."

The guy appears at the first window and Mac places the order for a Whopper with fries, mozzarella balls for me, and two Diet Cokes. Mac says he's not hungry. Big surprise. I hate his poor martyr act at times like this, not that we've ever had a time like this before, but he always does this. Goes without so I'll feel sorry for him. I don't feel sorry for him, not anymore. He can nail up his own cross. I'm not helping.

"He's not like all the others. Jackson's different," I tell him, getting my emergency £20 from my sock and handing it over.

Mac gets the change and flings it back at me, moving the Saxo along to the second window to pick up our food. "The only thing different about *him*," he says, "is that he hasn't choked to death on his own vomit yet. He's just as screwed up, just as miserable, just as fake."

And this is the point where I have had enough of his barbed little comments. "OK, fine, whatever, he lied. He lied on the *Behind the Scenes* DVD, he lied in that interview, Wikipedia lies, everyone lies, he's a drug user, he's not really a vegetarian, he's not really into zebras. I don't care, OK? I want him with me. And you are going to take us back to the pub, right now, me *and* Jackson, or I'm going to do something really, really, really . . ." And then I lose my nerve a bit and I stumble over my words and I can't think of a single thing that I would do if Mac didn't drive us back to our shitty little town. Back to Nuffing. Nuffing-on-the-sodding-Wold. So I just end the sentence on the third really.

And Mac says, "Really what?"

I've had a little more time, so I've thought of something. "I hope you never find out."

Mac twists back in his seat, does a few more sighs. Then he mumbles about the windshield being too steamed up and whacks the heat up full blast.

"Well, if you stopped sighing it might clear a bit quicker," I snap. He throws the straws and paper napkins back at me, followed by Jackson's burger and my mozzarella balls in turn. We hit the road again. For a second, I think that he's going to go back around the traffic circle and head back to Cardiff and that, if he does, I will never

ever *EVER* speak to him again. But he heads for the South West. He heads back toward the Severn Bridge. Back to Nuffing-on-the-Wold.

"Thank you," I say and he holds his hand up to shush me, then puts it back on the steering wheel where it grips hard. I slurp half of my Diet Coke — I hadn't realized how thirsty I was until now — and place Jackson's burger box on his chest with his fries. I eat my mozzarella balls in total silence, watching him. There's no stereo on. It's just the car bobbing along the deserted motorway toward the bridge, jolting over the odd speed bump and whipping past the tall orange streetlamps as the rain lashes down upon the metal roof. I'm usually ravenous for anything fried but this time I can taste every globule of fat, feel every artery snap shut, and pretty soon I have indigestion.

"Stop it," says Mac in the silence.

"What?"

"Looking at him, all cow eyes. You're not keeping him."

I haven't even realized I'm doing it. I'm just staring at Jackson. The car is so quiet and this is well odd, because when me and Mac usually go out in his car, he has the radio blaring and we're singing our lungs out to classic rock or doing Gaga impressions to make Cree laugh. But not tonight.

Every so often Mac sighs, or Jackson gargles or coughs, but apart from that, it's just road noise and the occasional other car overtaking us. I can't look at Jackson so I watch the pine tree air freshner and the jelly dolphin charm swinging together under the rearview mirror. It isn't until we're on the bridge, right in the middle of the bridge, that the silence is cracked by a sharp intake of breath and a deafening yell.

"Jeeeeeesus aaaarrgghh, oh my gaaaaaaaad, help me! Get it off me, get it off meee!!!!"

Jackson's burger flies off his chest and it's raining French fries as I'm pinned to the side of the car while Jackson flails and flips about in his seat, climbing across me to try and open the front passenger door. Luckily I've locked it. If I hadn't, he would have leapt out of the speeding car.

"Wh-what, oh my God, what is it?" I keep saying, utterly at a loss for what to do.

"What's he doing?" cries Mac, struggling to keep control of the car.

"Get it off me, get it off meeeeee!" he screams. Mac swerves and the car screeches onto the hard shoulder of the road and stops. Jackson crawls right across me, fumbles with the door locks and the handle until it almost snaps in his hand, and jumps through the seats and out of the car. Outside in the freezing night, he rips off his straitjacket and flings it upward. It lands. He grabs it again and flings it harder, high up and over the side of the bridge.

"Get off meeeeee! No, no get off, get off get off!"

He takes his boots off and flings them in the air, too, so he's just standing there, screaming in his white jeans. He rips his jeans off, with some difficulty because they're too tight and now wet from the rain that's lashing down on him, and he stumbles and falls over himself. I can't bear to watch. Cars zoom past and beep every so often. When everything has landed at his feet, he grabs each item in turn and hurls it over the side of the bridge and just stands there.

"Mac?" I say quietly. "What's he doing?"

"I think he's hallucinating," he whispers. "I've seen it before."

"Where have you seen it before?" I ask, my imagination running rampant.

"In the bar," he says defensively. "Duncan Buzzey used to be off his face most of the time. Used to tell my dad they were epilepsy tablets so he wouldn't kick him out, but I knew. He burned down the school science lab trying to make cotton candy. He was high on something then. And once he had a spaz attack in our parking lot cos he thought his clothes were infested with cockroaches."

"Is he going to be OK?"

Mac says nothing, not taking his eyes off Jackson, who's crouching in a ball. "Dunno, never comes in the pub anymore."

"I mean Jackson," I urge him.

"Oh no," he suddenly says, and grabs my fleece, pegging it out of the car and over to Jackson, who's now trying to climb over the side of the bridge. Mac covers him over with my coat and pulls him back, pinning him to the ground. Jackson doesn't seem to be struggling much and Mac's talking in his ear. They get up. Mac puts his arm around his shoulders and guides him back to the car.

"Get in the front," Mac tells me. "We need to lie him down. He's been sick."

"Is he going to be OK?"

"Just let's get him in the back, all right?" Mac's

helping me. Everything is going to be OK if he's helping me. Working together, we get Jackson onto the backseat and Mac has a spare blanket in the trunk that he finds and tucks Jackson in. Jackson's shivering and wet and I can see the puke chunks around his mouth. "You're going to be fine," Mac whispers. He plucks out a pack of Sticky Fingers wet wipes from the pocket behind the driver's seat and tugs out two of them, handing them to me. "Wipe his mouth."

"Don't leave me on my own," says Jackson shakily, tear tracks down both his cheeks.

"We won't. We'll look after you," Mac says. I wipe over his face, and Mac gets back in the front seat.

I ride shotgun. Mac's hair is soaking from the rain. The windshield wipers squeak manically as he starts up the engine again. "Is he going to be OK?"

"I don't know, do I?"

"You said 'we'll' look after you," I point out.

"It's just an expression, Jody," he says, all serious voice.

SEVEN
URINE FOR A TREAT

As journeys go, it's pretty awful. I have squeaky Diet Coke mouth and Jackson keeps shaking and slipping in and out of consciousness. He looks so pale and small. Kind of like Grandad when we saw him in the Chapel of Rest. White as marble and completely peaceful. At one point I reach back and stroke the side of his face. I can't believe he's here. With me. Then he starts snoring like an ogre, which cuts a nice jagged edge through the silence, tearing into Mac's already fragile mood.

We eventually roll into the parking lot at the back of Mac's pub around 1:45 A.M. Mac turns off the engine and gets out, pulling his seat forward and crouching down to talk to Jackson.

"We need to get you inside, OK?" he says to him, shaking his shoulder with the very tips of his fingers.

"Mmurgh?" Jackson garbles.

"You're going to stay here tonight and then we'll see about getting you home tomorrow, OK?" He snatches a look at me, then looks back at Jackson.

Jackson levers himself up, and then slips back down, trembling uncontrollably. "No. I'm not going back, I'm not going back there," he mumbles.

"He doesn't want to, Mac," I say, but Mac's just

concentrating on Jackson. He grabs him under his arms and heaves him out and there is an awkward moment when his coat (my pukey black fleece) flies open and I can't help but look at his underpants. I glance away, but I've seen all I need to. They're really wet. And the wetness is still coming, trickling down his leg. He's peeing himself. His head's lolling around like a balloon and he's peeing himself. He doesn't even *know*. O-M-F-G.

Mac doesn't notice the pee stream, which is good because if he sees that he'll have even more of a fit, especially if there's piss in his car. I look down onto the backseat. It's too dark to see a stain, just bits of shredded lettuce and squished mozzarella ball. I reach through the seats and gently press my hand against it. Feels a bit damp. I click my seat belt and get out. I go around and take Jackson's weight by putting his left arm around me as Mac locks up the car.

Chink, chink, chink, chink.

This sound is coming from the pavement alongside the parking lot. I look up to see old George Milne, one of the regulars, walking his sheepdog past the pub. We're in the full glare of the security light above the pub sign, and I smile nervously over at him. He doesn't respond. *Chink, chink.* I hope to God he's deep in thought and hasn't even seen us but that's probably too much to ask.

Together we help Jackson down the steps, through the back entrance of the pub.

There are three internal doors at the back of the Pack Horse, and Mac has keys for all three of them, but it just means that every five seconds as we're through one door, he has to stop, lean his side of Jackson up against the wall, unlock a door, prop it open, and come back and help me carry him. I feel like Chunk in *The Goonies* when he's locked in the freezer with the corpse. Jackson's heavy weight is against me, his head dangling over my shoulder. Mumbling to himself.

"Ssh," I whisper as I wait for Mac to open another internal door. His mumbling gets louder. "Please ssh!"

He starts crying then.

"What's the matter? What's wrong?"

"Everything. Everything's wrong! I don't want it, I'm not doing it. I'm not doing it anymore."

"Doing what? What are you talking about?"

Someday when I'm not so tired or confused or worried about being quiet or worried about what Mac's going to say when he opens his car tomorrow morning and smells the festering piss and chips, I'll look back on all this and laugh my head off.

Up the back stairs we go, and I'm taking Jackson's full weight as he has completely lost the use of his legs. We manage to get him as far as the landing outside the back bedrooms when —

"Kenz? 'S that you?" His mum's voice.

Mac claps a hand over Jackson's crying mouth to quiet him. "Yeah," he calls back.

"D'you lock it all up properly?"

"Yeah."

"Nighty night."

"Night, Mum."

Once through the back bedroom door, all three of us

collapse onto my nice clean double bed, except now it has a rock star, covered in piss and vomit, sprawled out in the middle of it.

"I'll get the sleeping bag out of the attic," says Mac, panting. "He can sleep on that and I'll take the bed. You can sleep in my room."

"No, I want to stay with him."

"Jody, we don't know this guy, all right? He's a complete stranger."

"He's not to me."

"Yes, he is! What we've seen in the past hour or so should have told you that."

"He's not a stranger. You've seen him in all my magazines, in my DVDs."

"Yeah, and so have you. And that's all you've seen him in. You've also seen what he's like in the flesh. Tonight, remember?"

"He's just taken something he shouldn't have tonight. He might have had a bad aspirin, my grandad couldn't get on with aspirin. Once he —"

"Your grandad got a rash when he took aspirin. He didn't try and throw himself off a bridge."

I actually harrumphed. And I didn't even know I *could* harrumph. "He'll be OK tomorrow. I want to stay with him. What if he's sick again? Are you going to come and wake me up?"

"You're not staying in here with him alone. End of."

"Well, you stay with us, then."

Mac sighs, hands on hips, then hand through hair. He

looks like he might fall asleep standing up. "I'll get the sleeping bag."

"Mac?" He turns around. "He needs some clothes. Underpants. He's kind of . . ."

Mac holds his hand up to stop me. "That's where I draw the line."

I'm not exactly relishing the thought of changing my idol's pissy undercrackers, but I have to, so it's OK. Jackson's my responsibility, my hero, no one else's. "I'll do it, it's fine," I tell him. "I change the kids in day care all the time when they've had accidents."

"Yeah, but he's one big adult accident, Jody," says Mac as he leaves the room.

I look at Jackson, lying legs akimbo on the bed, covered in everything. Thrillsville.

"OK, Jackson, I'm going to turn you over," I whisper in his ear, not that he can hear me at all. His face is smushed into the bed — he might as well be in a coma. I heave him over onto his back. I go around to the other side of the bed and delicately begin removing my black fleece from around him, just like I would a sleeping baby if I thought it was too hot in his cot. I see his burning-rose tattoo on his upper arm. I've only ever seen that in a poster. Wow. I run my fingers over it. It's even more beautiful in real life. I'm going to draw it again. I tried a few months ago but it went wrong. It didn't look like a rose. Looked more like a blossom.

Anyway, so I'm there, undressing him, and I begin to peel off his soaking underpants. I'm trying very hard not to look at his thing. I've never seen *that* before, not even in a poster. I try doing it with one hand so I can put my other hand over my eyes as a guard, and this seems to work. I turn to grab an empty plastic bag stuffed between the back of the wardrobe and the wall and I shove the underpants in there, trying not to let the smell register. I tie the bag, dropping it in the trash bin in the corner of the room. And then I can't help myself. I look.

"Whoa."

Jackson Gatlin, lead singer of The Regulators, lies totally naked on my bed. Everything on display. I can't stop seeing him at the MTV Video Music Awards a couple of months ago when they won Best Rock Video. If I knew then what I can see now when I was rewinding his acceptance speech, watching every single movement in his walk, the cute little scratch of his temple, the little smile to the camera as he picked up the award. Wow. Look at that. God. I can't stop looking at his thing! My eyes keep flicking to it. A little voice in my head keeps saying, *Go on, look again, just quickly, just a quick squizz.* It's not the most beautiful sight in the world, but these things never are, I guess. Even so, it's Jackson Gatlin's you-know-what. I can't even say the word. Every time I think the word I start going red as roses. I realize I need to cover his middle section up if I'm going to clean him up cos I'm just not getting anything done so I root through Cree's toy boxes along the wall and eventually pull out a *Three Little Pigs* pop-up book and open it up in the center, placing that over his thing.

I must be insane.

I have several recurring fantasies about Jackson and

this current image of him spread-eagled on a bed occurs in one of them. Except he's not in a coma and there isn't a Big Bad Wolf springing out from his crotch. Other more innocent ones include me and him on the *Ellen* show, me and him on a gondola in Venice, me and him shopping for baby furniture in IKEA, and me and him sitting on the sofa watching TV while I stroke his face. And now here he is. I have in front of me the living fantasy of millions of girls worldwide, including myself. Before tonight, he only ever existed on my TV. On a poster on my wall. In my sketchbook. On my MP3. And now he's here. But it's not at all like I imagined. I don't feel like I thought I would — contented, in love, fulfilled. I feel like that Greek-myth bloke who caught the wild bull. I can't stop shaking, and the smell of him is making me wretch. I make for the bathroom but as soon as I get in there, I see the packet of Cree's wet wipes on the back of the toilet. I rip out a handful and quickly return to Jackson to swab him down over his legs where the pee ran and then, carefully, underneath the book.

His eyes snap open and he levers up his head and it drops back down again heavily. Then again. "Mwagh . . . wh . . . what are you whez my . . . ooh that's nice . . . my backbez . . . I need my blackbez. . . ."

"Stay still," I tell him. He's still jibbering on and I can't help smiling at his helplessness. He sounds like Cree does when she's coloring and she's having a babbling little conversation to herself, evidently making perfect sense in her own head, but to others sounding like she's talking in fast-forward.

I imagine I'm just at work and swabbing down a baby who's wet the bed. Jackson passes out again. I'm just about finished washing him all over with the baby wipes, including the now crusty sick tidemark around his chin, when Mac returns and chucks a rolled-up sleeping bag onto the carpet below the window and a pile of his clothes on the bed. He frowns when he sees the book covering Jackson's knob.

"Oh God, I'm going to wake up in a minute," says Mac, rubbing his eyes with one hand and passing me a white T-shirt and some black underpants with the other. I set about dressing Jackson. Mac's found some old checkered pajama pants, too, and I put them on him as well. Then, me at one end, Mac at the other, we 1-2-3-lift him off the bed and down onto the sleeping bag. I look at Jackson's sleeping face. Apart from his straggly, greasy black hair and the stink of his breath when he exhales, he looks like an angel. I can't wait to see his beautiful blue eyes in the light of day.

"Oh int he gaw-juss," Mac sneers, slicing straight through my thoughts like an ax. He throws a blanket down on Jackson and starts stripping off the top layer of my bed, chucking it all in the corner. He flicks off the light. Apart from taking our shoes off, neither of us gets undressed, despite the fact my clothes, particularly my eBay shirt, are ten types of stinky. He lies down on the bare bed and I lie down next to him, like we've done a thousand times laughing, and a couple of times drunk. Except this time, we're not laughing and we're not drunk and we're joined by a comatose rock star. We're both listening to Jackson's rasping snores and lying side by side like two bedridden vampires.

"What are you going to do with him in the morning?" he says into the darkness.

"He says he doesn't want to go back."

"He'll feel differently in the morning."

"It *is* the morning."

"You know what I mean. You've got to take him back." I say nothing. "Jody, he's not some stray animal. He's not that rabbit you found in the park last Easter. He's a human being. You can't keep him in the garage like Skellig. I don't know what's going on in your head at the moment, if you've taken something or . . ."

"I haven't taken anything," I say. "I really haven't, Mac, you know I wouldn't."

"All right, but you can see how I might be thinking that, can't you? This is beyond . . . It's just beyond, Jode. It's because you do things like this that your mum thinks you're a pothead. This is . . . it's . . . like . . . you have to take him back."

"I know, I know. I just want to get to know him first, that's all. Just for one day. That's all I want. Please don't tell anyone he's here yet, Mac. You know he's my kindred . . . thingy."

"Grow up," says Mac. "You need to get real, fast. We are in the middle of a nightmare and I don't know how the hell we got here." I can feel myself beginning to cry. Mac hears my sniff. "Jody, don't."

"I can't help it," I huff. "I don't want to let go of him, Mac. You don't understand it, I know you don't, but I need him."

The only sound in the room is me crying for a little

while, until I feel something on my hand in the darkness. Mac's hand. "We'll sort it out."

We lie like that for a while. I need to feel him closer so I wriggle over to him and snuggle into his armpit. He doesn't move away so we stay like that. He must be coming around to my way of thinking, he must. The alarm clock on the dressing table flicks over to 2:35 A.M.

"Are you tired?" I say.

"Knackered," he yawns. "But I doubt I'll sleep."

But both of us must nod off, because within seconds, it seems, the lamp flicks on. Someone is waking us up. It's Tish, Mac's mum.

"Mum? What is it?"

"Ssh," she says. She's got a black baseball bat in the crook of one arm and a fast-asleep Cree in the other. "We've been burgled, loves. Your dad's downstairs talking to Brian and Steve."

I fling myself upright to look beneath the window. Jackson is gone. "Oh shit." Mac sits up, his hair all sticky-uppy and his eyes still sewn shut with sleep.

Tish comes around to my side of the bed. She strokes my head and kisses Cree's head at the same time. "The police are here, don't worry, all right?" She frowns. "What's that smell?"

She can smell the bag of pissy underpants. Oh God, what'll I say? I'm going to have to say I peed myself. But just as I open my mouth, Teddy's voice calls up the back stairs. "Tish?"

Without another thought, she takes Cree and scurries out in the direction of Teddy's voice.

Mac turns to me. I get up off the bed and go to the window, which looks out over the parking lot at the back of the pub. Mac's car's still there and the sky looks a bit lighter than it did when we went to bed. It's quarter past six on the alarm clock. We've slept about three hours.

"Shit," I say, scrabbling around for my gray hoodie in my rucksack and pulling it on. Then I crawl about on the floor, looking for my white DMs. They've gone. Mac gets up really slowly, like Frankenstein's monster just after reanimation.

"My Docs are gone," I tell him. He sits on the bed and starts putting on his Nikes. "Mac?"

"What?" he croaks.

"He's taken my boots. Where do you think he's gone?" I rub a grain of sleep from the corner of my eye, amazed it had enough time to form there in the first place.

"Bloody knew this would happen," he says eventually. "I'll get Alfie."

"Why? What's Alfie going to do?"

"He's an ex-police dog. He'll track him. We'll need something for him to get the scent." He sneers as I pick the pissy underpants bag out of the bin and offer him that. "Stunning," he says.

Tish and Teddy are in the bar talking to a couple of policemen when we appear downstairs. Mac's had to loan me a pair of his high-top Nikes, which I've secretly had my eye on for a while, anyway. I'm expecting carnage when we arrive in the main bar, like smashed glasses and an open register and stuff, but I can't see anything different. Teddy sums up exactly what's different.

"Well, the bastard had the munchies," he says, picking up two empty potato chip bags and a Curly Wurly wrapper from the counter. "These weren't here when I locked up. There's half a bottle of Smirnoff gone 'n' all."

"You're sure that's all?" says one of the policemen, who has a thick black mustache. He looks familiar. I think I recognize him from last Christmas. I'd just had a row with Mum and I tried to strip the holiday lights off the town tree to protest commercialization.

"Yeah, definitely," says Teddy.

With Cree still snuggled asleep in her arms, Tish pipes up in his defense. "Ted always leaves the bar spotless last thing at night," she says. "I can vouch for that."

"You told our operator they'd left a trail of destruction?" says the other policeman, who has a big nose and ginger hair. "Apart from two empty potato chip bags and a chocolate wrapper . . ."

"And what about me vodka, Steve? Eh? And all this?" Teddy points to an upturned ashtray on the floor and some pork rinds on the counter. The window looking out onto the street is wide open.

"Was there a lock on that window?"

"Yeah."

The policeman raises an eyebrow like it's on a wire.

"No. Not on that one, no. When they tried to get in once before, it was through the gents', cos that window overlooks the parking lot, see? So we had locks put on them."

"But not the ones in the main bar?"

"No."

"Alarm system?"

"No, we had it taken out. Kept going off whenever Alfie walked across the sensor. We haven't got around to having it put back in."

"And the dog didn't bark or anything . . . ?"

"No," says Tish. "We'd have heard."

The mustachioed policeman's eyebrows rise. "Well, your cigarette machine and your cash register haven't been touched and there's no sign of forced entry."

"There must be. The bugger got out."

"But he didn't get in," says Mustachio. He has a long white face, like a strip of stretched dough. "They may have been inside when you locked up."

"No, I checked," Teddy says, rubbing his chin. "I checked all around the place, there wasn't a soul here except me and me wife and the littl'un and they were asleep upstairs."

Ginger looks at me, then at Mac. I can feel my heart galloping up my windpipe. "And what about you two?"

"They came in about twelve-ish, didn't you?" says Tish.

"All right?" says Mustachio, looking right at me.

"Yeah," I say, looking so sheepish you could knit a sweater from me.

"They'd been to a concert. Mackenzie and his friend Jody," Tish explains. "Jody's staying here for a while." *Don't say where the concert was, please don't say where the concert was, Tish.* If the cops know about the concert and that Jackson is missing, they might put two and two together. They might do an upstairs search. They might smell the underpants bag Mac's holding behind his back. We might be arrested! But she doesn't.

Mustachio seems more preoccupied then with asking Mac about *Rocky Horror* and how rehearsals are going. I gauge from the conversation that his son and Mac used to take ballet together when they were kids and I can tell Teddy is awkward. He coughs, bringing Mustachio back to the matter at hand. "You didn't see or hear anything suspicious when you came in during the early hours of this morning?" the policeman says, turning to me. I shake my head.

"No," Mac says as Alfie wanders over and sits beside him, looking up at the policemen with utter contempt. "I'm surprised the dog didn't bark or something and let us know if someone was down here." He pats Alfie's head. Alfie yawns.

"I'm not," scoffs Teddy, his flabby jowls shaking in anger. "Bloody dog's useless. The inmates of Alcatraz could skip through here singing 'Jailhouse Rock' and he wouldn't hear it. You sure you locked everything up, Kenz?"

"Yes," Mac snaps. "God, you've talked me through it enough times, Dad."

"Yeah, well, your head's been all over the place with this bloody play, one minute you're here, next you're not. . . ."

"It's not a play, it's a musical, and I have to rehearse, don't I?"

"Prance about, more like."

"How would you know, anyway? It's not like you ever come and watch."

"I'm busy, aren't I? Trying to run this place. Trying to keep a roof over our heads. That's when someone isn't leaving the bloody door unlocked at three in the morn—"

"I didn't leave it unlocked, Dad!"

Cree yawns on Tish's shoulder. "Mumma?"

"It's all right, baby," says Tish, "go back to sleepies."

"Want my daddy," she says croakily and Tish goes to hand her over to Teddy, who's far too worried about the Curly Wurly thief to take her.

"Stay with Mum, there's a good girl," he tells her, and Cree turns her face over on Tish's shoulder and tries to go back to sleepies.

Mustachio turns to me and thins his eyes. "Didn't stop for a little drink down here when you came in late or anything, kids?" I shake my head.

"No," says Mac. Mustachio nods, then so does Ginger, like he's set him off. They both look us right up, then right down. Mac grabs Alfie's collar and beckons him to come along as we turn back toward the beaded curtain at exactly the same time.

"Where you two going?" asks Teddy.

"What do you care?" he snaps back at him.

"Kenz, don't be like that," says Tish.

"Taking the dog out," he says, and leaves the bar without turning back.

EIGHT

SOFTLY, SOFTLY, CATCH A JUNKIE

There's this weird *Exorcist* mist in the road as we step outside. Going for a walk through Nuffing town center on an evilly cold March morning is not normally my idea of fun. Going for a walk through Nuffing town center on an evilly cold *Thursday* morning is even less fun, knowing that I'm supposed to go to work today. And going for a walk through Nuffing town center on an evilly cold March morning, on a Thursday, with a plastic bag of pissy underpants and an even pissier best friend, looking for "a famous junkie wearing my old pajamas and your shoes" as Mac puts it, is just about the worst thing I can imagine.

Mac is ignoring me again as Alfie leads the way, and it's not just because he's tired. Even when Mac's tired he'll manage a song or at the very least a hum as we walk along. But not now. I wish he would smile, just for a second, for any reason at all. I hate seeing him cross or sad or serious in any way. It just isn't his nature. And he has the best smile. Even when I'm at my most horrible, he can cheer me up with his smile.

"I'll take Alfie for a bit," I offer, gesturing for Mac to hand me the dog leash as we lope down the hill.

"No, 'sfine," he says, marching on. "You won't be able to hold him." He does look as though he is straining to hold on, which is good because it means Alfie has Jackson's scent, but up until now he has only led us up one blind alley after another. First he takes us up the hill past the Torrance Lodge and down toward the railway station. Perhaps Jackson got on a train back to Cardiff? I put this to Mac.

"How the bloody hell would he have done that?" he laughs, but it's not a happy laugh. It's one of his "Jody, you're thick" laughs.

The cold wind claws my face like a winter wolf. "It's possible, though."

"No it's not, Jody."

"Oh. You think he wouldn't understand the train time-tables? I don't understand train timetables, either. Maybe you're right."

Mac sighs. "Not because he wouldn't understand the . . . because he's got no money, he's wearing pajamas, and he probably has no idea where he is, let alone where he needs to go."

"That's what I mean. Timetables."

Back up the hill again we go, past the Torrance, down toward the flank of shut-up shops waiting for nine o'clock — Nuffing is a market town, but between the seventeenth-century yarn market and houses signed THE OLD FORGE and THE DOVECOTE, they've still managed to crowbar in the odd New Look clothing boutique and Boots drugstore. Nuffing's just somewhere nice to drive through on the way to the Glastonbury Festival, really, there's no real reason to stop unless you live here. Alfie lingers in a doorway to smell a furry hood that's fallen off someone's coat, but it comes to nothing. We've been walking for an hour. I'm fed up, groggy, filthy, tired, and terrified all in one sullen lump. We give Alfie another whiff of underpants and *schoom*! Off he goes again, back up the street a little ways and through the alleyway leading to the back of the Playhouse Theater and some dumpsters. Mac still ignores me, and apart from checking the spelling on all the *Rocky Horror* posters in the theater window, he just carries on walking the dog and huffing. I check the dumpsters. No sign of Jackson at all.

"So what are you going to do with him, *if* we find him?" says Mac as we round the corner and head down into the center of town. Alfie sniffs right around the base of a post box outside Fancy That, the costume shop.

"I don't know," I say, which I know is the wrong answer as soon as it leaves my cold steamy mouth. Mac rolls his eyes as if to say, "Should have known," and lingers with Alfie by the doorway of the British Heart Foundation. "I should have stayed awake with him. I should have looked after him better. He needs looking after. He must have been scared to wake up in a strange place."

"No, I mean you have to call someone, Jody. This is going to be all over the news in a couple of hours, if it isn't already, you do know that?"

"Not the national news," I say.

"Yeah, the national news. And not just those nice-suited and booted BBC-type news bulletins, either. Paparazzi sites. Those nasty, money-grabbing, Princess Di–chasing wankers in dirty raincoats with a blood lust for down-on-their-luck celebs. And he's a major celebrity, Jody. 'Rock

Star Kidnapped' is going to make headlines, *world* headlines, no matter how many people know who he is."

"Nobody knows he was kidnapped," I say, watching as Alfie loops around the wire catalog basket outside the Argos store.

"They *will* know. That tramp woman from the rest stop saw him."

"She wouldn't have known it was him."

"Those cars that beeped at us on the motorway coming home? George Milne walking his bloody sheepdog past the pub last night? They all saw him."

I shake my head. "They didn't. The cars beeped for the sake of it. They didn't see him."

"George Milne definitely saw us. He definitely saw Jackson."

My voice is getting higher and higher with all my protesting. "He saw you, he saw me, and some drunk guy being helped out of a car. That's not suspicious. And George is about eighty and half-blind. He's not going to look at some breaking news flash on TV and immediately think, *'Ooh, I wonder if that was the bloke I saw outside the pub last night.'*"

"Think what you like but this is a small town, Jody, with even smaller-minded people living in it. Someone's bound to make the connection between a dark-haired girl leaving Cardiff Arena last night with a figure shrouded in a black coat and a missing rock star from said venue."

I sigh, my breath a great spreading cloud before me, and I pull the sleeves of my hoodie down over my freezing white fists. Alfie is still buzzing around every little nook and cranny in the town, his nose on the brink of discovery at every turn by the look of it, but every stop he makes is just another false hope. More faded dog piss. Another dropped potato chip.

Alfie lingers outside the post office. Then he stops altogether and sits down, panting and looking up at Mac. I look at Mac.

"What is it? What is it, Alf? What did you find?"

The dog dips his nose and then looks up again at Mac, panting, his tongue hanging out of his smiling mouth as if to say, "I told you I was onto something."

But there's nothing there. No sign of anyone or anything. Just some scraps of litter. Balled-up receipts. A couple of plastic bottle tops. A ring pull from a can.

No, not a ring pull. A key. A silver key attached to a long black string.

I bend down and pick it up. "This is his. It's Jackson's key pendant."

"Are you sure?" says Mac, looking awake for the first time this morning.

"Yeah, definitely. I remember seeing it on him, Mac. Backstage. This is his, I know it is."

Mac plucks a tennis ball out of his pocket and bounces it on the ground in front of Alfie, who jumps up and eagerly snatches it out of the air. And then Mac's all over him like a rash. "Good boy, good boy, Alf," he says, ruffling his back.

I hold the key between my finger and thumb. "God he's good," I say, looking at Alfie.

"Told you. He's ex-police. Didn't make it through his

training, but he's good enough for us. He's probably taken us to the exact same places where Jackson's been since he left the pub."

"He must be scared. If he's been to all those places, imagine how jittery he must be."

"I know," says Mac. "We're onto something now; we've got to keep looking."

We come to the walkway across the River Nuff, which leads to the library and the parking lot at the back of the Playhouse. Alfie leads Mac over it and to the right, along the bridleway toward the old stone bridge, which crosses the river a little farther down. That's when the grip of dread clenches me like King Kong's fist. Alfie is taking us along the river. What if he takes us down the bank? What if he takes us to a body? What if Jackson's dead? Oh God, oh God, oh God.

And I can't breathe and my chest is tight and I'm walking behind the dog and I know it, I know we're going to find Jackson with his face all puffy and bloated. And it's going to be my fault. It's going to be like finding Grandad all over again, only a million times worse, because when Grandad died, there was only me and Mac who really cared. This time, there's going to be photographers and journalists, not to mention hundreds of thousands of fans giving a whole big shit about this. It'll be the end of everything. My hot breath hits the cold air faster and faster. For the first time in ages I don't reach for the moon rock. I grip Jackson's key instead and I pray.

But then I see a man, wearing a white T-shirt, sitting on top of the stone bridge directly opposite the walkway.

Sitting on the bridge, like he's going to jump into the greeny-brown water below any second now. Mac and Alfie have carried on down the walkway.

"Wait!" I call after them, still watching the figure on the bridge. He's spinning an empty glass bottle in his palm. "That's him," I say to Mac. "That's Jackson. And the vodka bottle."

"Oh God," says Mac, coming back toward me on the walkway, dragging Alfie behind him while Alfie's pulling the other way. "The empty vodka bottle. What is it with him and bridges?"

"I think he's going to jump."

"You can't kill yourself, jumping in there," says Mac, almost laughing. "The bridge isn't high enough. And the water's only two feet deep."

"I'll handle this, OK?" I tell him, and begin walking down the rest of the path toward the bridleway that runs along the river at the side of the library.

"What are you going to say to him?" says Mac. I turn around and shrug, but keep walking.

"It's OK, Mac. I know what I'm doing."

I don't know what I'm doing, as usual. I don't have a single clue what I'm going to say. I've seen it in movies. People on building ledges. People on bridges. People with guns against their heads. What does the negotiator say to stop them from jumping or pulling the trigger? I can't think straight. I'm not in a movie and I'm not an actor. I'm on a tiny stone bridge across the River Nuff in a tiny market town in Somerset and I'm sixteen years old. What the hell do I know?

I stand on the bridge, watching him for the longest time, like he's a figure in a glass case at a museum. A glass case teetering on the edge about to shatter into more pieces than I can imagine. Something quacks on the bank.

"Jackson?" I say. "I'm Jody."

He looks at me, then snaps his head to look back down at the water. "Where. Am. I?"

"Nuffing-on-the-Wold."

"Where the hell is that?" He rolls the empty vodka bottle along the wall next to him.

"Somerset. In England. Y-y-you did a gig last night, at the Cardiff Arena. You were amazing . . . from what I saw."

"Where'd Cardiff Arena go?"

"It's . . . in Cardiff."

"Where'd Cardiff go?!"

"Um, why don't you come back off the bridge and we can talk."

"No." He bangs his fist down on the stone wall with every syllable. "I don't know where I am, I don't know what I'm doing here, why I'm not on the bus, I should be on the bus. . . ."

"The tour bus?"

He sniffs. He's crying! Then he stops crying and shouts. "Where's the goddamn bus?!"

I step forward. "Please, just come back off there and —"

"No, get away from me."

"I'll take you back to Cardiff, or you could give me Frank's number. . . ."

"No, Jesus, Grohman'll kill me!" He's laughing now.

"I can't go back. We should be in Venice . . . no, Vienna, Verona. Some 'V' place."

"But you just said you wanted to go back. . . ."

"No, no, no, no, no, no, I can't go back, I can't go back."

"OK, OK, so . . . what can I do, then?"

"I don't know. I can't go back. Grohman'll kill me."

"He's not going to kill you. I think the media or your fans would have something to say about that. Or the press. He can't go around killing his —"

"You don't know Grohman."

I take another step toward him. I hold the key out by its string. "You dropped this."

He snaps his head around. His eyes widen. "Gimme that!" I move toward him until the key is within his reach and he snatches it back. "Jesus," he mutters as he puts the black string back over his neck and looks down at the key. He kisses it.

"I'm sorry I've put you through all this," I tell him. He's still kissing the key. "It's just . . . last night, after the show, you came backstage, and I met you. I didn't mean to kidnap you. I saw your manager talking to you. You looked really sad. You must have thought I had a knife but . . ."

"I don't remember anything!" Jackson shouts. He draws his knees up to his chest so he is in an even more wobbly rocking position on the edge of the bridge. I can't catch my breath. He chants through chattering teeth, "I don't know where I am, I don't know how I got here, I don't know where my blackberries are. . . ."

"You have more than one BlackBerry? They must have been in your jacket or jeans."

"And where are they?"

"You threw them off the Severn Bridge."

"What? When?"

"Last night. Coming back from Cardiff."

"Last night when you were kidnapping me?"

"Well, yeah . . ."

"And why would I do that?" His face is wild. He grips the hair on both sides of his head so he's not holding on to the bridge at all now. "Why would I throw all my clothes over a bridge, huh?"

"You don't remember?"

"Of course I don't remember, that's why I'm asking you, you frickin' moron!"

I stutter. "I-I don't know why you did it, you just did it. You kept screaming that something was on you and you had to get it off."

He stops, turns back to the river. "Yeah . . . I do that sometimes."

"Why do you do that?" He twizzles the bottle. "You weren't . . . on something, were you?"

"I've forgotten what it's like *not* to be on something." He shoots me a look. "You think I put on shows like that 'cause I get such a natural kick out of it? I'm tired, OK? I'm tired of going to every corner of the globe and the only thing that changes is the wallpaper in my hotel room. Tour bus, hotel, venue, tour bus, hotel, venue, tour bus, hotel, venue. Round and round we go. If I wasn't tweaked every night, d'you think I'd put up with that shit? Go to this bridge place and get my stuff." He ushers me away like I'm a moth flapping around his halo.

"No," I say.

His face lurches toward me. "You will or I'll —"

"I can't get your clothes back. They're gone. Floating in the Bristol Channel by now. I know this must be really difficult for you to understand and I really am sorry."

He flings the bottle down into the water. I don't hear it splash below cos my heart's banging too much in my ears. "What do you care, you . . . kidnapper." He points at the water. His finger shakes. "That's what my life is now. That's all I'm good for." He sniffs. "Grohman won't let me get away — I'm his 'investment.'" He points his hard white finger at me. "He knows people. He knows people who'll find me and kill me. He's a complete nut ball."

"You're not exactly in a position to talk," I say quietly, but he doesn't hear.

"Bet the media are all over this. I'm one of their favorite targets." He throws me a look. "The paparazzi are after me. Always. There'll be pictures, photos."

"I'm sorry I've put you through this. I'd banged my head. I really wasn't thinking straight. I just wanted to spend some time with you. I thought it would be, I don't know, fun . . . or something."

"*FUN?* Do you know what you've done? Who the *HELL* do you think you *ARE?*"

"I'm just . . . a fan."

"Fan? Don't talk to me about fans! Stupid bitches. I see them outside the shows — fat, ugly lesbians, kidding themselves they're hot for me . . ."

"What? You don't know what you're saying."

". . . thinking if they put on enough eyeliner I'll see

them in the crowd and I'll be hot for them. 'Oh, Jackson, I'm a lost soul, too.' Bullshit. Talking to me like they know me from way back, just 'cause they once read a book I'd read. Whoop-de-fuckin'-do . . .'"

Tears drop down my cheeks. His voice rings around my head like a roulette ball. I'm still, like a sponge, sucking in every insult for every fan who's ever waited all day or all night in the cold. Who's saved up all their pocket money just to buy his album. Who's kissed his posters at night. Who's run away from home because of one of *his* concerts. He keeps on going, hammer blow by hammer blow, smashing down the perfect little house of love we've all built.

". . . just because they think that if they buy that key ring or that Regulators T-shirt, then they've got a little piece of Jackson to show off to all their friends. Just 'cause ya ain't got boyfriends, you buy into our crap thinking that somehow *we're* your boyfriends."

I bite my lip to stop the sob escaping but it doesn't help. I'm spluttering all over the place. "Y-you do care about the fans," I say, tasting salt water on my lip and licking it away. "You g-gave me my rock back. Last night. At the concert. You told off th-that security guy."

"What?"

"I lost my rock. You g-gave it back and you shouted at a security guy who stood on my —"

"I probably just wanted to shout at a security guy, that's all. I hate those guys. And before you say 'If it wasn't for us fans' and gimme all that shit, let me tell you something, Josie —"

"Jody," I squeak, but he doesn't hear.

"— there'll always be stupid fan girls, buying all the crap we put out, putting up our posters. Listening to our records, 'cause ya know what?" He glares at me. I don't even recognize him anymore. He is wild-eyed and sour. He is still the madman. He's just ditched his straitjacket.

"You're all the same. Sheep. Fat sheep, too." He looks at me, down to my feet, and up to my face and laughs evilly like a Bond villain. "And I've been over feeding you bitches for too fucking long."

My mouth hangs open. My sponge has just been squeezed out. I don't think. I don't even breathe. I take one step toward him and push him off the bridge.

NINE
WACKO JACKO

"I don't want any more chemo. Enough enough enough. It just makes me even more tired and even more old," Grandad once told me. He'd just tipped his tea tray onto the carpet and I was cleaning it up. *"I'm going out with a bang, Jody. I'm taking a different road out of here."*

My grandad hated being a burden on us as he got weaker. He wasn't meant to be weak. Inside, he was a fireball of energy and laughter — outside he was shrinking, drying up. Turning to dust. After his diagnosis, the color started running out of our house. When he'd gone, he'd pulled the plug right out. My grandad liked The Regulators. He liked the fact that their *The Punk, The Priest . . .* album was a concept album and told the story, in songs, of four men who escape Heaven in order to enter Hell. I used to show him my magazines, the pictures of Jackson taking his trash out or running away from hordes of screaming girls.

"They can't leave them alone for a bloody second, can they?" I remember him saying, as he went on this long tirade about the paparazzi and their treatment of celebrities. *"It's no bloody wonder they want to kill themselves, some of them.*

It's no bloody wonder that poor princess got hounded to her death. And poor Michael Jackson and all his problems. It's not right, it's not bloody right. Who's looking after these people for God's sake?"

"You were supposed to be talking him *out* of jumping, not pushing him in!" Mac shouts as he and Alfie thunder up the bridge to where I'm standing.

"I just . . . saw red. He called me fat. He said . . ." Mac runs to the side of the bridge and cranes his neck over. I can't go near, I can just hear the splashing about and shouting and ducks flapping below. I'm welded to the spot. "Is he dead?"

"Course he's not dead. But he's going to freeze to death in there. Well, go on."

I force my legs into action and run past him down the bridge and down again, sliding along the frozen mud on the bank and through the long reeds until I feel the coldest sensation on my legs and I'm in the water.

"I'm drowning, I'm d-d-drowning!" Jackson screams. He's in the middle, thrashing around, gasping and shouting and swearing and scared, though he must be able to feel the bottom with his feet. I wade out to him, not daring to slow down though every single nerve in my body is begging me to stop and get used to the icy water before I move forward. But I don't. I wade on out and throw both arms around him, making him lose his footing so I can pull him, awkwardly, as he thrashes around in my arms, toward the bank.

We both slump down onto the mud. "Bloody hell,"

I gasp as Jackson lies shivering and crying beside me. Within seconds I hear footsteps and Mac's there, coat off, wrapping it around Jackson from the front.

"It's OK, it's OK," he says, "come on, we'll get you inside and get you warm." He lifts Jackson to his feet, bundles him tightly in the coat, and guides him up the bank, leaving me lying there, like a rat in the shallows. Breaths pump out of me, and every one hurts. This just isn't Jackson. This just isn't what he's like. This isn't the man I fell in love with. My kindred thingy. This isn't the man who understands me. This is the celebrity my grandad was talking about. Driven up the wall by fame.

"No bloody wonder they want to kill themselves. Who's looking after them?"

That's why Jackson said all that horrible stuff about the fans. He's sick of being famous. He's sick of the celebrity. He's sick. And then, more abruptly than my head knows how to handle, the facts wash up and begin piecing themselves together.

I have to help him. I have to look after him. That's what Grandad meant. *That's* what *"Don't Dream It, Be It"* means. I couldn't help Grandad stay alive, but I *can* help Jackson!

I lie there, having my eureka moment for a bit, then slowly get to my feet and trudge up the bank, soaking and weighed down by my cold, soggy clothes. But on the inside, I'm warm with thoughts of my new project: Project Jackson. Project Celebrity Cold Turkey. And I know what I have to do. I have to get him back to my house, that's the first thing. Then I can look after him. I can bring him back to who he really is. But when I reach the top of the bank on the bridleway, Mac is alone. There's no sign of Jackson. There's a little movement in the hedge and Alfie returns from taking a wee.

"Where . . . is . . . he?" I pant. "Where's Jackson?" Mac nods toward the back of the library. Nobody is there, just some recycling bins and a red dumpster stuffed full of cardboard and shredded paper.

"Where?" I shiver, my eyes darting around the place. "Oh God, we've lost him again, haven't we? For God's sake."

Mac nods toward a recycling bin, a tall upright green one with a lid. He mouths, "In there."

I look at the bin. I crouch down beside it. "Jackson?" *Knock-knock.*

"Go away," comes an echoey, juddering sob. I can hear a clacking, too — his teeth.

"What's he doing?" I mouth to Mac. I'm juddering with cold, too.

"He saw Marge going into the back of the library. He thought she was the paparazzi."

"T-t-t-the w-w-w-what?" I shiver. "Why would he think that?"

"Because he's a paranoid wreck. He's convinced he's being watched."

"Marge uses a walker, doesn't she?" Mac just stands there, looking cold without his coat on. "Right," I say, flicking the brake up on the bin and going behind it to tip it onto its wheel. There's a heavy thud inside and I nearly tip the whole thing over but Mac joins me and takes some of the strain and we push it along together.

"The police station'll be open by now. The town's just coming to life," heaves Mac. "We'll drop him off on the doorstep and leg it."

"I'm not dropping him anywhere. I'm taking him home."

Mac stops. "No you're not," and pulls the bin away from me.

"I bloody am," I say, pulling it back.

"No way," he says, tugging it back again. "Alfie, come on, Alf . . ."

I tug again hard and this time I break away with the bin and Mac stands to the side, grabbing Alfie's leash up off the ground. "I'm going home and I'm going to call the police. You don't know what you're doing, Jody. This has gone way far enough. I'm going to tell the police."

I roll on with Jackson in the bin. "Do what you like."

"You can't keep him, Jody!" he shouts. A man walking a poodle stops along the bridleway on the other side of the bridge. Mac marches back up to me and whispers, "How are you going to get him past your mum and Halley? Dumbledore given you an invisibility cloak or something?"

An echoey sob comes from somewhere inside the bin. I keep rolling him on, taking the full strain of the sodden lump inside now. "I'll come around and get my stuff later," I call back.

"I don't want anything more to do with this!" he calls out.

"Fine!" I call back.

"And I'm still calling the police!" he says louder. "You can't look after yourself, Jody, let alone anyone else! Let alone someone like *him*!"

I don't stop moving until I've reached the end of Chesil Lane and see the blue door of number 25 shining in the distance. I roll the bin along the rickety pavement, the wet hems of my cargoes slapping against the concrete, until we get to the alley at the side of the house. Oh stunning. Gravel. I roll along regardless, going as quickly as I can, even though the bin is making such a racket on the stones and Jackson is inside, juddering around like a sodden wet lump and sobbing like a toddler.

Our garage is at the back of the house, at the end of the garden. It's the perfect place for Jackson. Grandad had a small lottery win a couple of years ago and had it converted into a drum room. He used to be a drummer in a band when he was younger, but had got out of the habit, so he said he was going to start drumming again. Then he got his diagnosis. Not only is it warm and secluded in the drum room, it's also carpeted and soundproofed. It's like my very own Room of Requirement for a rude, drugged-up rock star — carpeted, soundproofed, and a million miles away from his former habits — and momentarily I'm optimistic. It's also cluttered with boxes of Grandad's things that Mum put out for the Goodwill pickup the night before his funeral, things I rescued. I'd come down in the wee small hours to steal some of them back and hidden them in the drum room. I didn't want charity having all his stuff.

The front of the drum room is bricked up and a normal door has been put into the side wall. There's a cat flap at the bottom of it that Grandad had put in for Winston when he got the mange and couldn't come in the house anymore, but Winston ran off a few months after we moved in, which was, like, two years ago, and the cat-flap door's gone creaky and stiff.

"Phew, right. OK," I puff as I pull down the handle and push open the door, propping it open using the bin, while checking all around me for unwelcome faces. No one about, no one lurking in their backyards, four of which back right on to the gravel pathway that runs along the back of the house. I look for curtains moving in upstairs windows, body shapes behind glass, doors ajar, children playing, even cats roaming the wall tops. But no one and nothing is about. It's still too early for most people to have surfaced. I keep watching, lining up the bin with the opening of the door and lifting the lid for Jackson to get out. I expect a flurry of violence as the lid opens. But there is nothing. I peer slowly inside the bin and Jackson is cowering.

"It's all right," I whisper. "No one's around."

"I can't g-g-get out," he says, a meek look on his face as it tilts up toward me.

"You have to. I can't pull you out," I bark. "Come on, quick, before someone comes."

"I can't. I d-d-don't have . . . up-p-p-p-p-per body st-strength."

Without another word I snap the lid of the bin shut, wheel it around so it faces the other way, kick the brake down, and push it over so Jackson comes tumbling out of it and rolls straight into the drum room like a moldy potato rolling down a chute. I pull the bin away and step inside the room, clicking the door shut quietly and hunkering down beneath the two small double-glazed windows at the top in case someone appears to see what the rumpus is. Jackson lies shivering in a ball, plastered with sodden strands of shredded paper from the bin.

When I am sure the coast, or at least the garage, is clear, I straighten up and walk over to him. "It's all right," I say, without too much compassion. "You'll be safe in here. I need to take your clothes off," I say, starting to wrestle him out of Mac's T-shirt, but he's gripping on to it like his hands are claws, shivering and juddering.

"Need . . . m-m-m-my black-b-b-b-berriesssss." I can hear his teeth clattering again. He's gripping on tighter to himself so I can't get him out of the rest of the clothes.

"Jackson!" I shout and his shivering lessens and his grip releases a bit so I can start peeling the T-shirt off him, and then the freezing, soaking cold pajama pants, and, yet again, his soaking wet underpants. He grips on to me as I change him. I root around in a box labeled "Clothes" and find an old checkered shirt that I put straight on him. A spider crawls out of his sleeve and it isn't until I see it on his wrist that I realize Jackson's hands are clinging on to me.

"I'm sorry, I'm sorry," he keeps saying, and he's really sobbing.

"It's OK," I say, choking down tears myself. "I'm the one who needs to be sorry. Don't worry about that now. Let's get you better, OK?"

I can't find any pants but I remember seeing an old blue picnic blanket in one of the boxes so I start rooting through the one labeled "Holiday Gear." I find it, shake out the dust, and wrap it around his lower half. He looks so fragile with the blanket wrapped around him. I rub my hands up and down his arms to generate some warmth. He keeps shrinking away from me, probably imagining I'm going to hug him or something. He keeps apologizing for the names he called me on the bridge.

"It's OK, that wasn't you. That wasn't you. You're not feeling yourself."

"It wasn't me, it's not me. I don't know w-what I'm . . ."

"It's OK," I say, rubbing his arms on both sides. "I'm going to look after you, OK? I'll get you some dry pants from Grandad's room. He's got some he never wore, a couple of pairs that Mum got cheap — they've still got the tags on. And I'll get you something to eat, all right? Are you hungry?"

He nods, his teeth still chattering violently. Mine are chattering, too.

"OK. I'll get you something. It's nice and warm in here. I'll put the electric heater on as well," I say as I see it in the corner of the room beside the drum kit. I unravel the cord and plug it into the wall socket and within seconds a little whir starts up and waves of warm air ripple out. I sit the heater directly in front of Jackson on the carpet.

"OK?" I say to him. He's in a ball, shuddering under the shirt and blanket. He clutches the string around his neck and holds the key to his mouth. "I'll be back in a minute."

I creep through the door and lock it again behind me, turning the corner into the back garden. I part the leaves of the willow tree and see Mum in the kitchen window, washing dishes at the sink. She looks up and sees me and hurries to the back door. She comes out onto the patio and stops, drying her hands on a tea towel. She looks at my soaked and filthy clothes.

"Don't ask me any questions, Mum, OK?" I tell her, my jaw juddering with the cold. "I had an argument with Mac and I fell in the river. I'm OK, but please d-d-don't ask me anything else."

I know there's a million things she wants to ask, seeing as the last contact I had with her was a note saying I'd gone to Mac's. But she just nods. "OK. As long as you're all right," she says, letting it hang in the air like a question, but not a question.

"I'm fine. Hungry, but fine."

"I'll make you some breakfast," she says. "How was the . . . you're soaked . . . where's . . ." She stops herself.

"My stuff's at the pub. I'll get it later."

In the kitchen, my sister, Halley, is at the breakfast bar and looks up from her bowl of cereal. She takes one glance at my wet, muddy clothes and returns to her cereal without saying one word.

Mum comes back in and places a sheet of foil over a raw chicken sitting in a tray on the stovetop. She takes it to the fridge. "You OK with a veggie burger for dinner if we're having chicken?" she asks.

I nod slowly. Now that I know Jackson's not *actually* a vegetarian, I'm wavering. "Unless you want a bit of chicken with us?" I nod more certainly. Mum smiles. "Why don't you take a shower? I'll make you some bacon sandwiches.

How many rounds?"

"Five," I say, knowing I couldn't eat more than two, but thinking Jackson will probably want more. "I mean six," I say and disappear through the door on the image of Mum's face looking at me like she's just been smacked in the mouth.

TEN
PLEASE DON'T FEED THE DIVA

When Mum's gone to work and Halley to school, I make up a bed for Jackson behind the stack of boxes in the garage using the three huge duck-feather cushions off my bed and our picnic blanket. I'm so tired I could flop down myself and go to sleep right then and there, but instead I set about changing him into some of my grandad's unworn clothes — sweatpants, a long-sleeved black shirt, and a thick gray hoodie. I can't believe that the only things of Grandad's Mum didn't throw out were the things he never used.

I chuck all the wet river stuff, his and mine, in the wash, even the eBay shirt, which is supposed to be dry-clean only but I don't seem to care. I find the moon rock when I'm emptying my pockets. The moon rock that brought me closer to Jackson. That got me out of the mosh pit. That took me backstage . . .

In the kitchen, I balance Mac's sodden high-top Nikes on the radiator in the vain hope they might dry out and be good as new.

Mum's left the bacon sandwiches on the counter so I take them out to Jackson. He doesn't say a word, just scarfs down three, one by one, all the while rubbing the key around his neck. He crashes back onto my cushions and falls asleep. I feel his forehead. He feels hot, so I unplug the little heater and remove his hoodie. I go back into the house and put together a little box of entertainment for when he wakes up — some Stephen King books, a spiral-bound notepad and pencil case, a travel chess set, and three new tennis balls from Halley's gym bag.

Reality check — ugh. What . . . the . . . hell . . . have . . . I . . . done? What am I going to do when Mum gets home? When *Halley* gets home? I need to think up a plan quickly. I look at the clock — 9:20 A.M. I'm due in at work at ten. Hmmm, doubtful. But I've just had two days off, one for the concert that I'd booked ages ago, and one for the funeral.

I change into a clean work shirt and jeans and lace up my Etnies, and I go back down to the garage to check on Jackson, see if he needs anything before I go. The smell hits me the second I open the garage door. He's being sick. There's sick everywhere. And he's covered in it.

"Blaaaaaaaaaaaaggghhhhhh. Blaaaaaaaaaaaaaaaaaaaaaaaaaaaaaaaaaaaaaaaagh." *Cough, cough, cough.* "Awwww. Blaaaaaaaaaaaaaaaaaaaagh." This is how it goes. Several times. Followed by dry retching. I just stand in the door-way and watch.

And then it begins. . . .

"What the hell was in those sandwiches?" he shouts, still coughing. I stare at him, not knowing how the hell he's gone from peaceful, angelic sleeping man to violently puking maniac in twenty minutes. "What kinda," he shudders, "bacon?" *Cough, cough.* "Blaaaaaaaaaagh."

"I don't know, it was just bacon," I reply.

"Pig bacon?"

"No, yak bacon. Of course pig bacon."

His eyes are almost out on stalks with the effort of all the retching. "It was old."

"No it wasn't. My mum's really careful about expiration dates." And then I think, maybe Mum's cooked the vegetarian bacon instead. If you're not a vegetarian, you'd really hate that stuff.

"Look at me! You've poisoned me!" he spits, peeling my grandad's now sicky black long sleeve shirt off his body and stuffing it into a ball. He then throws it at me and my clean work shirt becomes spattered with flecks of semi-digested sandwich. He's been sick on the picnic blanket, too. He peels down the new sweatpants and once again he's standing before me, bollock-naked, and I don't know where to look. He exhales, spits on the carpet, then plonks himself back down on the cushions, covering his lap with an old Argos catalog. He points at me like his finger is a wand and he's about to turn me into a rat. "If you're trying to kill me, it won't work. I got an immunity to poison. A stalker tried it once."

"I'm not trying to poison you!" I cry. "Don't you think it might have something to do with all the vodka and pills and river water you've swallowed in the past twenty-four hours?"

He gives me this haughty look and I know he's run out of argument. He makes a face like he has a really bad taste in his mouth. "Get my blackberries and water. Bottled, not tap shit."

"I'll just go and drop my bucket in our alpine well,

shall I?" I snap. "I don't have any blackberries and we don't drink bottled water. Mum thinks it's a waste of money. And I haven't got time to clean all this up now. I have to go to work."

"Go to work, then." He starts flicking through the catalog, the garden hose section, pretending it really interests him.

"I'll get you some more of my grandad's clothes," I say warily, wondering what the hell he's going to come out with next.

"No, I want my own clothes."

"You can't have your own clothes. They're all on your tour bus."

"Go and get them, then."

"I can't."

"Yes you can. If you can hustle me out of a gig unnoticed, you can go and get my clothes."

"I told you, we're not in Cardiff anymore. We're nowhere near."

"Nothing in England is more than twenty minutes away, wherever you are."

"Where did you hear that?" I scoff. My eyes automatically flash toward his lap, and back to his face, trying to glue them there. "And Cardiff's in Wales, anyway. It's a whole other country."

"Well, you gotta get to an airport, then. Fly to Wales and get my stuff."

"No, you can't fly there from here. We could drive but . . ."

"So where's your car?"

"It wasn't my car. It was Mac's car."

"It was Mac's car," he whines, mocking my voice. "Go get Mac's car, then."

"I can't. We've had a row."

"Whatever," he says, finally admitting defeat. "Go and buy me some clothes, then. I don't want some old dude's threads." He leans back against the wall.

"Don't talk about my grandad like that. Anyway, Mum's only kept stuff he never wore." He looks at me and sighs. "There's a Kingsbury's in town. I'll go there and get something if you like."

"A what?" he says.

"Kingsbury's. It's a supermarket."

"No. *CLOTHES!*" he shouts. "I'm not wearing supermarket shit. If I've lost all my clothes, that's *your* fault, so you have to replace them. Gucci suits, D&G shirts, real leather pants . . ."

"Leather pants? Oh, trousers, right. I don't know. And I don't think you'll get Gucci around here. Mac's got Gucci sunglasses but he ordered them online. There's a man down at the covered market on Wednesdays that sells Moochi. He says it's a designer. . . ."

"What the hell's Moochi? That ain't no designer *I* ever heard of."

"I don't know. I don't know any designers."

"Jesus Christ," he sighs and his eyes roam across to a pile of puke. "You better clean that before it starts to stink up the place. And get some flowers in here or something 'cause it'll linger, I know what vomit's like. You do know where to get fresh flowers, don't you?"

"Yeah," I say in a meek voice. And then he starts counting off on his fingers all the other things he wants me to get.

"My blackberries. Cigarettes. Marlboros, not Lights. A skinny no-whip caramel macchiato with one Sweet'N Low and a dash of protein fiber powder. And get me a fresh fruit platter, will you? And God help you if there's bruises. I don't do mushy fruit." He flicks to the jewelry section of the Argos catalog.

I stand there transfixed on his mouth. "I don't have a clue what you just said."

"Coffee, goddamn it! If I'm gonna have to live in this armpit for the foreseeable then I'm gonna need a shit heap of coffee."

"There's a tea room on the High Street but I've got to go to work. I can brew you some instant?"

He looks like someone's just opened their rib cage in front of him. "Instant? I ain't drinking instant coffee. Why not just pour frigging anthrax down my throat?"

"Why are you being like this?" I say before I have time to think about why I ask it.

"What?" he says innocently, and then continues with his list of requirements. "Real coffee. Italian. I'll need access to wireless Internet, too. And a soft-headed toothbrush. I wanna brush my teeth."

He flaps his hand to shoo me out of the room.

I quickly change my top again for an old Slipknot T-shirt, shoving anything pukey in the basket for the second wash of the day, and all the while I'm trying to remember what he's told me to get. Cigarettes. I've forgotten everything else.

As I'm walking into town, yawning my head inside out, I'm racking my brain trying to remember what he's said. Fruit, no bananas? Caramel something-or-other with fruit and fiber? Blackberries. With every step I want to turn back and ask him, but I know he'll probably bite my head off. This isn't any Jackson I know. But he wants to stay with *me*. Of all the fans in the world, he's in *my* garage. I need to do whatever it takes to make him happy.

The shops are just opening when I reach the town center. I can't remember the caramel thing, so I get him a bunch of freesias and a selection of fruit (including blackberries) from the grocer's, a toothbrush from Boots, and I can't remember what cigarettes he wants but the newsagent won't sell me them anyway cos I'm underage. So I nip next door to the thrift shop and ask if they've got anything even remotely Gucci. The woman looks at me for a long time.

"No worries," I say, "I'll just have a look through the racks." And I'm checking all the labels but there's nothing Gucci or Dolce & Gabbana. There are a couple of fairly new T-shirts without labels in them, some jeans with a hole in the right knee, and a black hoodie, so I get them. I'm not sure about his shoe size but I'm guessing if he finds my DMs OK then he must be fine with a seven. Every pair the shop has looks like a lawn mower's gone over it so I decide I'll raid my wardrobe when I get home instead.

I'm pleased with my little haul when I get back. It feels good to look after someone else for a change. To be responsible for someone's welfare, even if that someone does talk to me like I'm a dog turd. I don't look after anyone, except when I'm at the day care, but that's my job. I'm paid to do that. But I'm not being paid for this and it turns out I'm quite good at it.

Jackson's obviously been rummaging through the boxes. He's thumbing through a cookbook when I get back, still half-naked except now he's wearing a pair of Grandad's Christmas tree boxer shorts so I no longer have to worry about my eyes darting to his crotch as he turns to Jamie Oliver's sausage hot pot recipe. He stands up and roots through the shopping bags in my hands. He pulls out the T-shirts one by one, flinging them over his shoulder.

"Wrong, wrong, wrong," he sings. He takes the toothbrush and studies the writing. "Medium head, wrong!" He takes out the fruit, piece by piece, and flings it hard at the wall. He upturns the basket of blackberries on the carpet in front of me and flings each of the apples against the wall behind me. "Bruised. Bruised. Bruised. And what do you call these?"

He rips the freesias apart. They lie at my feet. I stare at them until water clouds my eyes.

"Where's my coffee? My smokes?"

"I didn't get them," I whisper.

"What?" he says, leaning in with his hand behind his ear.

"I didn't get them. I forgot what you said." I start blubbing. "I'm underage. They wouldn't sell me any cigarettes." It's out of the blue, I didn't think I was going to, but I'm proper bawling it and I'm looking at him, but his face is just the same. Hard and sarcastic. I thought I was going to make him happy.

"Get me a coffee, right now. I don't care what kind. Black. Lukewarm."

I walk out of the garage like a robot, but one that's bawling its eyes out, make it to the back door, make it to the kettle, flick the kettle on, and put my hand in front of my face. I stand before the window and cry, sob, shriek. I'm so tired. But I can't sleep until I know he's happy, until he's cared for. That's my job now. It's like at work. I have to make sure the kids are OK before I can think about myself. I look at the clock. It's well gone ten so I'm completely late for work. There's no point going in now. I'll say I was ill or something. I take a red mug from the mug tree and search through the back of the cupboard for the French press coffee maker my mum got one Christmas but never uses. I find a packet of coffee, too. SELL BY JANUARY 2009. I scoop one spoonful into the press and wait for the kettle to boil. It clicks. I pour. I wait. I plunge. I pour it in the mug halfway, adding some cold tap water. I stick my little finger in. More cold water. Still too hot. More cold water. Just right. My finger throbbing red, I take it out to Jackson.

He's lying on the cushions with one hand reaching out for the mug, idly flicking through the Jamie Oliver book. I test the coffee to be triple sure it's the right temperature, then put the mug in his hand.

"Stir," he says, not even looking up at me. I take the spoon from the mug and stir it.

"NO!" he screams. "Counterclockwise, you idiot! I can't drink that now."

And that is it. That's all I can take. I rip the mug out of his hand, pin him back to the cushions with my knees on his chest, and pour it straight into his mouth. He struggles, gargles, gasps, coughs, splutters. The coffee splashes all over his chest and neck and the cookbook.

"There," I say, panting, dropping the mug onto the carpet. "Did the world end? No. Did you die? Just because something is *stirred* in a different direction does *not* mean you can't drink it!" I push him away from me and get to my feet, facing the door. My heart is punch-bagging it in my chest. I hate him. I hate him for being such a crushing disappointment. But what was I expecting? Perfection, I guess. And this is anything but. "Why are you like this?" I cry.

"Like what?" he spits.

"An arsehole. A complete . . . arsehole!" He's rolling around on the cushions, coughing. I'm shaking. "I dedicated my life to you."

He holds up a finger pointed to the ceiling. "That . . . is not my problem."

"No. It's my problem." I walk to the door and open it. "Go on, get out. If you're going to act like this, you can just go. This isn't what I thought it was going to be."

He wipes over his wet face with his forearm. "What did you think this was going to be? You thought you could keep me like your very own rock-star-in-a-box, someone to pet, someone to take for little walks and read stories to?" He rubs the key between his finger and thumb like it's a comforter.

"Just get out!" I shout.

He still doesn't move. So I march over to him, seize his arm, and pull him through the door. He struggles and rears back like a defiant cow scared of going in the slaughterhouse truck. His bare feet scrape the carpet.

"NO, NO, NO!" he protests, his free arm grasping at the door frame.

"YES, YES, YES!" I shout. I pull. I heave. And when I've pulled and heaved him out onto the grass, I push him away from me. He stumbles and lands facedown on the gravel path, but doesn't stay there long. Before I know it, he's scrambled back up the step into the garage.

He's hunched up against the back wall when I get back in there. I stand watching him, trying to catch my breath. He doesn't look at me.

"I don't know what I was thinking." I laugh like a maniac through my tears. "All I know is I'm tired and I don't want to be around you anymore. I thought you'd make every-thing . . . I don't know, better. I thought I could look after you, thought we could have talks about books and stuff but I know now how stupid I've been so . . . just go. Go back to your band. I'll give you some money for a train and clothes and stuff."

"I can't," he says. He doesn't get up. He doesn't go out. He slouches back against the wall. "I can't go back."

"Yes, you can. I shouldn't have taken you in the first place. The door's open. You can go and phone the police and tell them where you are and —"

"No, I'm not going back."

I sigh and fling the door shut. "Right. So . . . what, then?"

"Sorry," he blurts out, just like that.

I've no idea what to say. What would I do at work, with a

kid? I'd make them clean up their mess and I'd take myself out of the situation until they'd learned their lesson, that's what I'd do. "Right, well. I'm going upstairs and I'm going to take a nap. A long nap. You can clean all of this up. I'll get you sponges and stuff. And if you don't . . . I will call your manager."

"I'll . . . do that," he says. "I'll clean."

I'm nodding manically, like Mum does when she's angry with me. "Yes you will," I say as I leave and slam the door behind me. I go back minutes later with a bucket of soapy water, rubber gloves, and a sponge, and plonk it all down before him. I flounce out again on the sounds of him scrubbing frantically.

Upstairs, I'm lying on my bed but I can't lose myself. I'm thinking about Mum and Halley coming back later and Mum pegging out the washing and hearing him in the garage or Halley laying out her camping gear on the grass and seeing Jackson through the window. I'm thinking about Mac and why he hasn't come around to help me with Jackson yet. And most of all, I'm thinking about all those magazine articles about Jackson that I've bought because he was on the cover but never really read. I cut the pictures out but shoved the rest of the magazines in an empty box at the bottom of my wardrobe. I tried so hard not to read them because I didn't want to know what they said. Mac read them and delighted in telling me. About the models and actresses Jackson's been out with. The tantrums he's had. The photographers he's punched. The panic room he's had built on their tour bus when the rest of the band have to make do with their bunks. His paranoia about stalkers. Rehab. The hotel elevators his entourage are supposed to have emptied before he'd set foot inside them.

If all this and his performance in the garage is the real Jackson Gatlin then fame hasn't just gone to his head. It's blown his brains out.

I never believed a word of it. Even when Mac went on and on about it. *Did you see him hit that photographer? It's all over YouTube, I'll download it.* "Jackson's not like that," I'd said. "They're making it up to paint him in a bad light." *Did you get your Google alert about Jackass Gatlin today? Fancy him getting that air hostess pregnant.* "Jackson's not like that," I'd said. *Fancy him shagging that airhead actress. Thought you said he went for brainy women?* Other stars might act like this, but not Jackson. I never let the articles see the light of day, but now I'm fishing them out of the wardrobe and poring over each one.

And it's all there. The two million dollars he spent on a Vegas hotel suite before trashing it and using these priceless vases as bowling pins. The Grammy-night hotel orgy in Los Angeles. The high-stake, drug-fuelled poker game in Atlantic City. The maid he summoned to his room to turn his boiled egg up the right way. Without another thought, I swipe the zebra ornaments off my shelf with one *thwack*, and step up onto my bed to tear down the big poster from the wall. *Skritch.* Down comes another poster. *Skritch, skritch, skritch* go the individual months of my Regulators calendar. My band. My hero. My sanctuary. My mistake.

I step back down and grab hold of the magazines and the loose articles in one hand and I march back down the stairs. Out in the garage, Jackson's made an attempt to clean up one of the puke puddles, but is lying down on the cushions looking tired again. At least he's now wearing one of the T-shirts.

I brandish my proof. "If this is who you are then I don't want you here. I don't care that you don't want to go back." I throw the articles down in front of him. My head starts throbbing from where I fell down at the concert. That shiteous concert.

Jackson levers himself up on the cushions. He picks up the top two articles. "Gat's Just Not Good Enough" screams the first headline. It's about him throwing a wobbler at a restaurant because he was served a bruised peach. "Jack Attack" reviews the alleged meltdown he had after his requested humidifier and Pilates equipment weren't in his dressing room at South by Southwest.

He dips his head, like a child I've just bollocked for crayoning on the wall. I stop short of saying, "That makes me very sad," and plonking him in the time-out corner. He studies the articles before putting them back on the pile.

My tears drip constantly. "It's all true, isn't it?"

"Not all of it," he sniffs. "I don't do Pilates."

ELEVEN
HOT LEGS, COLD TURKEY

Woe is me. Woe to the max.

I don't know what to do. I've messed up, I know that. I need help. I need my grandad. He had a knack for always saying the perfect thing when I'd got myself in a hole and needed a rope. I need Mac like never before and, every time he crosses my mind, I get this horrible twinge of pain in my chest. He doesn't always say the perfect thing. He usually calls me a stupid cow and tells me what I've done is mentally ill. I call him on the landline and his mum says he's changing Cree's diaper and, when I call back about ten minutes later, his mum says he's taken Cree into town to get her new shoes. I keep thinking about him and Jackson on the Severn Bridge. He was so in control of him. He knew just what to do. I need him here. I can't do this on my own. I don't even know what it is I'm supposed to be doing, anyway. And even if he won't help me, I just want to hear his voice. Chat on the phone like we do, for hours. We don't even have to talk about the thing in my garage. We can talk about him and *Rocky Horror*. How rehearsals are going. When we're next going for a day out with Cree.

Mac was right. I can't look after Jackson. His mood is up and down all the miserable morning. He's irritable, he's shouty, when he's not demanding certain types of food he keeps yanking on his key necklace and rubbing it from side to side, making his neck all red. This gives me the extra worry that he's going to hang himself. I offer him the use of our shower, he chucks an apple at me. I post a cheese and cucumber sandwich through the cat flap, and within seconds the cucumber slices come flying back out at me like ninja death stars. As a last-ditch attempt to play the hostess, I post a note through saying if he wants to use the downstairs loo, I'll leave the back door open but it has to be before four o'clock as this is when Halley comes home. And I leave it at that.

I get the laundry out of the machine to hang it out to dry, and as my fleece comes out, I see the zebra zip pull Mac bought me hanging off it. I'm amazed it survived the wash. It reminds me of Mac and I get that horrible stab of worry again.

"He's a good boy, Mackenzie. He won't put you wrong, darling. You stick with him, girl."
"I will, Grandad."

But I haven't, have I? I haven't stuck with Mac. I've gone completely against him and now I'm in a mess. No, mess isn't enough to describe it. My *bedroom* is a mess. What I'm in is a landfill. I go upstairs to try sleeping cos my body is aching all over for it, but I don't expect I'll actually nod off. But after what I think has been half an hour, I open my eyes. Everything's different. It's dark outside my window. There are TV and metal noises downstairs and the clock by my bed says 7:32 A.M. I sit bolt upright, all sticky and hot, and it isn't until I get up that I realize I'm in pain all over. I turn on my light and lift up my T-shirt. In my mirror I see red marks and bruises beginning to form, I guess from the mosh pit. There's bruising around my ear where I bumped my head, too. I haven't felt a thing till now. My face is even more of a mess than usual — my hair is greasy and the white bits of my brown eyes are flecked with red. The second I set foot out of the door, Mum's there in her bathrobe, toweling her wet hair.

"You were sound asleep when I came in last night. Thought you needed the rest so I left you be."

Last night?! "Oh. Thanks," I say, my eyes barely wide enough yet. I've been asleep since two o'clock yesterday afternoon? Was it a dream? Was it all just some not-so-beautiful nightmare?

"Mackenzie called for you," she says, disappearing into her bedroom.

"Did he?"

"Yeah, a few times. Is your phone broken or something? He said he's left you texts."

"Oh. Yeah. My phone's . . . off." I look back in my room at my washing basket where I threw my soaking wet river-water clothes yesterday. Before I put them in the wash. My phone was in the pocket of my cargoes. My phone is dead. So it wasn't a dream, then.

Mum appears again. "I'm not prying, love . . ." she starts to say, which means she's going to pry. "But it must be bad for you to end up in a river. If he's hurt you . . ."

"No way, Mac had nothing to do with me falling in the

river. We had a row, I ran off, and I tripped and fell in. That's all."

She's so obviously waiting for further explanation but I'm not going to give her one. "Sometimes we choose the wrong one, love. I'm sorry if he didn't turn out to be what you think. I won't say any more but I always did wonder about him. You know, with his singing and dancing."

Oh how embarrassing. She thinks I made a pass at him and he told me he was gay. Well, that'll have to do, I suppose. I can't tell her the real reason.

"Anyway, he said he's at the Playhouse this morning and he wants to see you."

"Go along, to the Playhouse? To see him?"

"Yeah, I suppose," she says, frowning at me. "Don't you have work today?"

"Uh, I've got the day off." I don't have the day off. In fact, I don't expect I'll be allowed a day off ever again for failing to show up yesterday. I owe *them* a day if anything. But I need to see Mac — that's way more important than work. So I dredge up some courage and when I hear the hairdryer going in Mum's room, I call work.

"Hi, Hazel? It's Jody."

"Oh. Hello, Jody." Hazel reminds me a bit of Kathy Bates in *Misery*, to give you a mental image. She's short, brown-eyed, and smiley and she's got a backside like a sack of squashy yams.

"I'm not feeling very well today. . . ."

"What about yesterday?"

"Uh. I wasn't feeling very well yesterday, either."

"I called you several times, at home and on your mobile."

"Yeah, my mobile got stolen and . . . I couldn't get out of bed."

"Why, what's wrong with you?"

"I . . . think I might have caught something. From the river."

"What river?"

"The river by the library. I was . . . walking home the other night and I got mugged and . . . someone pushed me in the river." I'm going straight to hell.

"Oh, Jody, I'm so sorry. Are you all right?"

"Yeah, I'm OK now, but I'm still a bit shaky, you know. . . ." Jody Flook, you lying cow.

"Of course, of course. Well, you take next week off, then, recover properly. We've got some of those students in from the college on internships so we'll manage. Don't worry, don't worry at all. Bye, Jody, bye."

Oh. My. God. As lies go, that was a humdinger. Mac always says, *If you're going to lie, think about the trail of destruction it will leave. How it'll get back to your mum, who it might hurt.* Typical Mac. He's eighteen but thinks like an eighty-one-year-old. But I didn't think about anything when I told my boss I'd been mugged. The start of the call and I'm full on for a bollocking, possibly my second warning of three before I'm sacked, and now I have the boss eating out of my hand *and* a week off.

I shower and put on my clean Nirvana T-shirt and the black cardigan of Mum's twin set. I check on His Lordship through the cat flap. I can't believe he's still going to be there when I look in, thinking maybe he's done another bunk in the night, but all is as it should be — he's asleep and the room is a mini-bombsite. He doesn't stir at all, so I head up the street to the Playhouse.

The old guy at the box office, George Milne, doesn't want to let me in at first. I wonder if he remembers me from the other night in the parking lot. "Go round the back and put the code in if you're with NAOS," he barks, without looking up from his paper. He means Nuffing Amateur Operatic Society.

"I'm not with NAOS. I just need to speak to my friend. He's rehearsing *Rocky Horror* today. He's asked to see me. Please, it's really important. Just tell him Jody's here."

"Well, I can go and check, I suppose," he says, slowly putting his paper down.

"Yeah. Mackenzie Lawless. He's the lead. Frank-N-Furter. You can't miss him."

George disappears, mumble-moaning, and I mill about the foyer looking at all the old production posters and getting a near-uncontrollable urge for Junior Mints. George returns silently, looks briefly at me, and when he moves to go back inside the box office, Mac appears from behind him. He's wearing a faded Bath rugby shirt and black stockings and tottering along in the highest red patent heels I've ever seen. There's a folded newspaper under one arm and he's carrying my rucksack in his hand.

"What the hell are you wearing?" he says to me, eyeballing my cardi and Nirvana T-shirt combo and handing me my bag. "Marks & Spencer's grunge collection, is it?"

"Says the boy in the fishnets."

He smiles briefly, then something darkens his face. "What's that behind your ear?"

I touch the skin behind my ear. "Oh, just a bruise. From where I fell down at the concert."

"Let me see." He lifts up my hair and strokes it lightly with his finger and I get goose pimples down my neck. "Have you put anything on it?"

"No, look, it doesn't matter. I am in a serious shit-creek situation."

"I know," he says. "I called you loads of times yesterday. Where were you? I thought you'd been kidnapped 'n' all."

"Ssh," I say, eyeballing George's booth. He's returned to his paper and a crackly quiz show is blaring out of a little radio on his desk. Mac's standing there, hands on hips. I can't help but smile. "I didn't think you were speaking to me anymore. You went off in a mush."

"I wasn't in a mush," he sighs, all dramatic. "I just didn't want any more to do with that maniac. But I thought you should see this."

He folds out the newspaper and holds it up to my face until it's all I can see.

ROCK STAR MISSING.

I snatch the paper off him as we move into the foyer, then up the stairs to the first-floor bar area so we're completely out of George's earshot. I don't think I breathe out until we reach the room. A mirror ball twinkles high up in the center of the ceiling but all the shutters are down and the chairs are upended on tables. My voice drops to a whisper as I read on. "Shit. Shit, shit, shit!"

Mac sits down on a low-lying coffee table and crosses his stockinged legs. "Where is he?"

"Our garage. He doesn't want to go home. I told him to go and he just wouldn't."

He eyes me. "You actually *told* him to go?"

"Yeah. He's all over the place. And so's his puke."

Mac grimaces. "Not handling his scandal well, then?"

"He's a bloody nightmare, Mac. He's like Gollum. He swings from one mood to the next, calls me all the names under the sun. Remember that tantrum Cree had when we took her to the beach and she had about ten goes on that SpongeBob ride? He's like that. All the time. Sits there yanking on his necklace and spitting insults at me whenever I go near. And demanding . . . ugh. I bought him all this stuff and he threw it all back in my face, literally. But he won't leave for some reason. It's like he's scared of something."

Mac's eyebrows leap up into his forehead. "Well I won't say it."

"I know, I know, you did warn me," I sigh, turning to page six to read the rest of the article, my eyes pinging from one side to the other as I try and take it all in.

FEARS are growing for the lead singer of one of America's most popular rock bands, who has not been seen for two days.

Jackson James Gatlin, who fronts popular Chicago rock outfit The Regulators, was last seen backstage at the band's gig at Motorpoint Cardiff

Arena on 23 March. Since then his bandmates have been unable to contact him.

The 27-year-old, who has a history of depression, left no note and did not tell anyone who saw him that night where he was going.

The band's manager, Frank Grohman, said: "I remember seeing Jackson backstage just before the encore. His mood was level, he gave me no cause for concern. He was there one minute, and then he was gone. He's never done anything like this before. It's totally out of character."

Mr. Grohman added: "There's a lot of care and love for Jackson from friends and fans and we all hope we see him soon."

Gatlin has not answered any messages left on his voice mail since he disappeared, and his phone no longer functions. He is described as slim, 5 foot 8 inches tall, with dark brown shaggy hair. He has a tattoo of a flaming rose on his upper left arm, symbolic of the band's first album cover, and was last seen wearing a white straitjacket and jeans, part of his onstage costume persona, the Madman.

Anyone with information about Mr. Gatlin's whereabouts is being asked to call the missing-persons helpline: 0500 . . . .

"Whoa," I breathe out, folding up the paper.

Mac shuffles up and I sit down next to him. "You need to explain to Jackson that people are worried about him and hopefully we can just take him somewhere or . . ."

"Or what?"

"Or we can ring that helpline number and say he just turned up in your garage in a state and you don't know how he got there."

I shake my head. "I'm not just going to dump him. I brought him here. And he says he doesn't want to go back. There must be a good reason."

"He's probably just having a strop cos he's sick of touring. A couple of days away and he'll realize he has to go back. He can't live in your garage forever, can he?"

I bite my bottom lip hard. "He says he wants to stay there."

"Bit of cold turkey and he'll be back to some semblance of self. Then we can talk to him."

"Cold turkey?"

Mac uncrosses his fishnetted legs and recrosses them the other way. "Yeah. When junkies come off drugs. Let him detox for a few days. Keep him out of the limelight. Might do him a world of good. Maybe then he'll stop with the demands."

I'm doing that middle-distance staring thing. Mac pokes me in the side and I jolt out of it. "I don't know. I'm out of my depth, Mac. I need you." Mac says nothing, completely straight-faced, for which I'm quietly grateful. "Will you help me?"

There's a small but definite twinkle in Mac's eye, which could be the reflection from the mirror ball, but he nods faintly. "I'm involved now, aren't I? As usual, you've sucked me in."

I throw my arms around him and squeeze him so hard.

"Oh thank you, thank you. It's been hell without you there. I don't know what I'm doing."

"We haven't had a Jody drama for a while, have we, Presh?" Mac smiles so his cheeks dimple and something blooms in my chest. I've been dying to see that smile for days. "What was the last little Jody drama we had?"

"When I poured Sunny Delight over my head and got chased through the park by wasps?"

"No, there was one after that, wasn't there?"

"When I brought that injured rabbit home?"

"No, Christmas . . ."

"Oh yeah. Christmas." And that was all we needed to say. You only need to know three things — I was going through my die-hard vegetarian phase, Mum wanted to pick a fresh turkey from a local farm, and the police had to close the road in both directions.

"Do you want to come and see a bit of the rehearsal? We're only going through my songs today so they won't mind. You can sit in the stalls. Just don't laugh. Well, at the funny bits you can. But don't laugh at Mrs. Brooks on the piano, OK?" He gets up, tottering slightly on his heels.

"Why?"

"You'll see."

I'd forgotten how brilliant Mac is. I'm barely noticing Mrs. Brooks at the piano and her frantic arms. Mac owns that stage. Even without makeup, just a faded Bath rugby shirt, he *is* Frank-N-Furter. Unembarrassed, pouting, oozing confidence, strutting from one side of the stage to the other like a peacock, singing:

"Don't get strung out by the way I look,
Don't judge a book by its cover,
I'm not much of a man by the light of day,
But by night I'm one hell of a lover,
I'm just a sweet transvestite,
from transsexual Transylvania."

I swell with pride. That's my best friend — his voice as clear and as pitch-perfect as a professional's. His legs long and lean and graceful. His hands wide and expressive. I cannot wait to see the show. I'm going to be in the front and I'm going to clap the loudest. For a second I forget all about my own problems and just watch him. Then I remember. The punch of dread meets my stomach. I get up and signal to Mac just as they start running through "Don't Dream It, Be It." He gives me the ten-minute sign.

Once Mac's changed, we head back via the newsstand and Mac buys Jackson's cigarettes and a lighter.

"You owe me," he says as he hands me the shopping bag outside.

"I know, I know," I say. Then we head back to my house. I drag my feet the whole way. I know what's coming. As soon as Mac opens the garage door, a book flies past him, a hairsbreadth from his face.

I slam the door and lock it. "That's what I've had for the past two days."

Mac bends down to pry open the cat flap. "Jackson? It's Mac."

"*FUCK OFF!*" the beast shouts back. Something hits the wall inside.

"We're not going to hurt you, Jackson, OK? Can we come in?"

"No!" The kick drum flies against the door.

Mac turns to me. "Blimey."

"See what I mean? One minute he's OK, or at least he's not throwing things, he's just crying or something, and next he's like this. If I didn't know better I'd say he had PMS."

"Maybe he has," Mac suggests.

"What if he's always like this, Mac? What if this *is* Jackson?"

Mac shakes his head. "No. This is withdrawal." The two drumsticks pelt the door in turn.

"Withdrawal from what?"

"Whatever he's on. He's two days into full-on cold turkey. Has he been shaking and stuff?"

"Yeah, a bit. When I've dared to go that near." *Thud.* I can see Jackson through the window, throwing books about, bawling and swearing. But there's barely a sound to be heard outside, thanks to the soundproofing.

Mac kneels down and peers through the cat flap. "Yeah, he's well into it. This is the worst bit. We're going to have to see him through it. It's not like this is going to be a gradual thing, either. We've nothing to help lessen the effects. He's just going to have to deal with it."

"How do you know so much about drugs?" I ask him.

"NAOS. Half the cast are former drug addicts from the halfway house in town."

I'm not sure at all. This is so way beyond the beyondest of the beyond. "This could be dangerous, making him go cold turkey."

"I know. It's going to be a total shock to his system, so we'll have to keep a close eye on him. But he can't get any worse, that's the good news. Right, we need to Google it and find out exactly what to do. Must be a step-by-step guide on how to detox a junkie on there somewhere. It would help if we knew what he was on. Has he asked for anything drug-sounding? His stuff, his gear, Charlie, H, spliffs, meth, whiz?" *Thud.*

"No . . ."

". . . shit, blow, ganja, weed, dope, speed, rocks?"

"No, nothing. How can you get high off rocks? Do you lick them or something?"

"Not concrete rocks, Jode, rocks of cocaine. What about snow, smack, crack, crank, PCP, LSD? Has he asked for any of them? Anything that could sound like a type of drug?"

"No, I don't think so. I would have remembered. He's got this key around his neck that he's really presh about. Maybe it unlocks a box of drugs somewhere?"

Mac looks at me like I've just poked my tongue into his eye. He dips his head and I can tell he's smiling. Laughing at me.

"OK, maybe not. The only thing he keeps asking for are blackberries." *Thud.*

"Blackberries?" says Mac. "As in, more than one?"

"Yeah. I thought he meant fruit, but I bought him some and he knocked them all over the floor."

"Maybe he meant the phone, but who carries around two BlackBerrys?"

I shrug. "Jackson, I suppose."

"No, I mean, maybe they're not phones. Maybe the

blackberries are what he's taking. Maybe that's his name for them, the pills."

We go up to my computer and Mac makes himself comfortable on my chair. I stand behind him and drape my arms around his neck. Mac knows a little about a lot of things, which is just as well cos I know nothing about a lot more. And what he doesn't know he can find out in seconds with a fast broadband connection. His hand darts about on top of the mouse like an epileptic spider. He types "blackberry + drug" into Google.

The first result that comes up is an American medical website called Proclicyanide Sulphate — The Facts. And then there's all this science about what it is. I lean in, resting my chin on Mac's shoulder, as he reads aloud.

"'Proclicyanide sulphate tablets,'" he doesn't even stutter, "'or "red berries" as they are commonly known due to their red appearance, are recreational drugs. Their purpose is to promote energy and alertness, sometimes even temporary mania.' Right, so basically they're uppers. He's been taking them to give him an onstage high."

"But he asked for *black* berries, not *red* berries."

"I'm getting to that bit," he says, scrolling down the screen a bit further. "'Most users have to take effigysium sulphate tablets, or "black berries," to counteract the effects of the proclicyanide. These are used to bring one back to a version of calm, though in regular users this can be short-lived due to the craving for the former.' He must take the black berries to bring him down, only . . ."

". . . he doesn't have any black berries cos they went over the bridge with his clothes."

"Exactly. Look, 'side effects from red berries can range from violent childish mood swings, chronic inertia, agoraphobia, paranoia, heart palpitations, and even death in some extreme cases.'"

"Oh my God, Mac. What if he dies, what if he dies in my garage?"

"He's not going to die, is he? He's not taking them anymore. This is just the comedown. It's a bad comedown but it's still a comedown. He's shaking it all out of his system." He gives me a lingering frown. "*Where* exactly is he shaking it all out, by the way?"

"Everywhere."

"Grim. Well, as long as he's in that garage, he's safe, anyway."

"OK," I say. "What about his cigarettes?" I say, holding up the shopping bag.

"Yeah, that might take the edge off a bit," he says, taking the bag. I follow him back downstairs to the garage, where he pulls out one of the Marlboros and a lighter. He lights it, sucks in the smoke, and coughs it out. "Ugh." Then he bends down and tucks it through the cat-flap door, saying, "Jackson, want a smoke? Here, kitty, kitty." Then we stand well back.

Within seconds, the cigarette disappears and the flap snaps shut.

"Right. Keep an eye on him, keep his fluids up, and try and clean up after him. And if he behaves and he talks to you respectfully, he can have a smoke as a treat."

"OK," I say. I keep saying OK, like I know what he's talking about. Like I even know what's happening, what I'm doing, where this is going to lead. Nothing's OK, though. Nothing has ever been further from O and K in its entire life.

TWELVE

DIRTY LITTLE SECRET

Later, when the beast is asleep, we sneak into the drum room to attempt a cleanup. The drum kit lies in pieces, the skin torn on each drum, the sticks snapped. The beast himself lies legs akimbo on my nice duck-feather cushions, mouth wide open, dead to the world. Mac's aproned and gloved and wearing a face mask so he doesn't have to smell anything. He just about manages to scrape fruit slush from the walls before he has to run out and gag in the fresh air. He's such an actor.

"I'll stick the cushion covers in the wash, put fresh ones on," I whisper. Mac nods, peeling wet pages of an Argos catalog from the walls. But as I'm trying to pry the cushion out from under Jackson's head, I notice he doesn't look so good. I put my hand to his neck.

"Oh my God. I can't feel his pulse."

"What?" says Mac, running over to me. "No, he can't be . . . no, no, no . . ."

"I think he's dead. He doesn't have a pulse," I say, feeling frantically along his wrist.

Mac lifts Jackson's arm and releases his grip. The arm drops to the floor with a little thud. He is dead. He is heavy and pale and pulseless and dead.

And then he coughs.

"Jesus Christ." We both jump back as though zapped with a cattle prod. Jackson rolls onto his other side and goes back into his deep, corpselike sleep.

"I thought you said he didn't have a pulse?!" Mac screeches at me.

"I couldn't feel one!" I say defensively. "You check him if you don't believe me."

"No, it's OK," he pants theatrically. "I think. I'm just going to . . . lie here and . . . have heart failure." He slumps against one of the upturned boxes.

My hand is clutching a fistful of T-shirt. "So . . . that'll be the chronic inertia, I s'pose."

I get to my feet and tiptoe over to Jackson again, crouching down to inspect his neck. "He definitely doesn't have a pulse, Mac. Look, come and feel."

Mac eventually gets up and joins me by Jackson's head, somewhat nervous. "Oh for God's sake, you don't feel for a pulse there! I thought you were trained in first aid! You're touching his chin, the pulse is in his neck, like this." He puts two fingers against his Adam's apple. He fumbles around a bit. "Hang on."

"See, see what I mean? Maybe some people don't have them in their necks?"

Mac's bewildered. "It amazes me you found the right way out of the womb." He has a feel around Jackson's neck. "No, there it is," he says as his two fingers settle on a spot just under Jackson's jawline.

I feel for myself, still not convinced. This chronic inertia side effect should be relabeled the "looks dead" stage.

My fingers land on a little thumping spot deep inside his neck.

"Right, so he's not dead," sighs Mac, putting his mask back on. "God, he really stinks, Jode."

I can't deny it anymore, not that I've been trying to deny it, really. I've just been breathing through my mouth. He's been peeing in the corner, too, rather than using the downstairs loo as offered. His pants, my grandad's sweatpants, reek like a festering stable.

"Well . . . if he's not going to wake up," I tell Mac, "we could give him a bath."

"Can't you give him a squirt of Febreze or just keep changing his clothes?" Mac suggests.

"He'll still smell like a turd, just a turd wrapped in a clean T-shirt. Let's give him a bath." Jackson's mouth falls open and he starts snoring. I've heard lions roaring quieter, and OMG the breath! "I could clean his teeth, too."

Mac frowns, probably searching for a reason not to do this. "What if he wakes up when we're washing him? He'll go skitz."

I shrug. "At least his breath won't smell so badly when he's shouting."

"All right, *if* we can get him up the stairs, *you* can give him a bath. I'll help you get him up there but I ain't washing his crannies. I'm not going downtown."

I smile as I take Jackson under his arms, then Mac gets an attack of the guilts and tells me to take his legs cos they weigh less, while he takes Jackson under his arms. Jackson's not that heavy, but we both make a big deal of getting him out of the drum room, across the garden, and inside the kitchen. We're standing in the hallway, right next to the staircase, when a shadow darkens the glass in the front door. Someone's standing on our doorstep. I hear a jingle. A key in the lock. Mum. But it's only one o'clock, what the hell is she doing home in the middle of the day? And why am I worrying about why she's come home in the middle of the day? Point is, she *is* home in the middle of the day and we are carrying a very famous, unconscious, missing rock star who really shouldn't be in our hallway stinking of piss!

"In here!" I say quickly, nodding toward the coat closet under the stairs and I pull the door open with my elbow and Mac folds Jackson into me so he's doubled up, and we bundle him clumsily into the closet and shut the door.

"Mac, mask!" I whisper, and just as Mum steps through the door, he rips off both his plastic apron and mask and throws them both in the closet and shuts it.

Mum comes in, all of a bluster, loaded down with groceries. Mac stands against the closet door. I stand next to him, trying to look trustworthy. "Hi," I smile.

"Take these will you, Jode," she says. "Oh hi, Mackenzie. Here." She hands Mac a bag, too. He just stands there with it. She looks at him but he smiles sweetly. He reminds me of Jackson when he fake smiles. In most of the pictures I have of Jackson smiling he is doing that exact same smile. It doesn't look fake, but it is fake, and only an expert in fake smiles would know. Mum doesn't know. She trusts Mac, on the whole, as he's so much more mature than I am, but he's acting so sketchy at this moment I'm worried he's going to give the game away. Some bloody game.

"I've got it," I say, taking the bag, picking up another by Mum's feet, and taking them into the kitchen. Mum breezes in and dumps the bags on the breakfast bar.

"How come you're back so early?" I say, looking back out into the hallway where Mac attempts to move away from the coat closet. Jackson's hand flops through the crack. Mac folds it back in and stands against the closet door.

"I had to leave work early anyway so thought I'd do the food shopping. I went out to Lidl's for a change. Can't move for bloody baklava at Waitrose." This is Mum Code for "we can no longer afford to shop at Waitrose." "I've got to see the lawyer this afternoon. They're reading your grandad's will today."

"Oh," I say. Another plunge of dread. If Grandad's got debts, we could be out of a home. "Do you want . . . me to come?" *Please no, please no.*

"No, don't worry. It's a foregone conclusion, I think. I hope." She sighs wearily.

I have to ask. Sometimes I need more than a sigh or a bit lip. I need confirmation. "Are you worried? About, like, losing the house and stuff?"

She makes a little puff noise and starts unpacking the groceries onto the counter on top of a pile of mail. All bills. One from the funeral directors is on the top. "We'll find out today, won't we?"

"At least the divorce is through. You won't have to give anything to Dad." This is my attempt at a bright side, but the "D" word is enough to shove her deeper into her mood.

She grabs a carton of blood orange juice and some vegetarian sausages from one of the bags and makes for the fridge. I think about telling her not to bother buying veggie stuff anymore, as it's like an extra two pounds a pack and I'm not vegetarian anymore, not since I found out Jackson was the most arrogant piece of meat that ever walked the Earth, but I daren't. "What time have you got to be there?"

"The appointment's at half two. I wanted to take a shower and do my hair first, though."

"Well, I can put the shopping away if you want to go and shower. I don't mind."

She looks at me like I've just sneezed in her face but I'm hoping she'll soon come to the conclusion that I'm trying to build bridges. There I go with bridges again. But she takes the bait.

"Yeah, OK. Might put a color on it," she says, fluffing her hair at the back. "D'you think?"

"Yeah, yeah." I think about adding, *That nice auburn color really suited you when you put it on once before*, but I don't. For two reasons: (1) because Mum's radar always beeps when it comes to me overdoing it with the bullshit and (2) because her hair always looks bloody awful when she home-dyes it. So I just leave it at the two yeahs.

She touches me briefly on the shoulder and leaves the kitchen, passing Mac again in the hallway on the way up the stairs. I arrive to see him towering over her, smiling like a loon, and her looking up and giving him the dodgiest eye.

"What's that smell?" she says.

"Kitchen trash," I say, quick as a flash. "I've just put it out. They come today, don't they?"

"Oh thanks. I'd forgotten that. Can you do the others as well? I'm not going to have time."

I nod. Mac's making a halfhearted attempt to undo the laces on his Converse. "Takes me ages to get these off," he laughs nervously. "I'm all knotted up."

"You don't have to take your shoes off to go in the kitchen, Mackenzie." Mum smiles as she starts to go up the stairs. "It's a tiled floor."

"Oh, hahahahaha," he laughs again but stays put, still tugging at the laces. We both wait in the hallway and look at each other as we hear the noises that signal Mum's arrival up the stairs and creaks across the landing. We hear the bathroom door open. This is her getting clean towels from the wicker drawers. Then into her bedroom. Then the door to her en suite bathroom shutting. The water going on . . . and eventually, the shower door closing.

"Right, come on," I say, pulling the door handle on the coat closet. Jackson spills out onto the hallway carpet and with him comes the fug of unwashedness and it only makes me even more determined to get him upstairs as quickly as possible.

"Back outside, yeah?" says Mac as we pull him out.

"No, bathroom," I say.

"What?" he screeches. "We can't now your mum's here. She'll see him!"

"She won't," I say. "She's putting a color on her hair and then she's going to the lawyer's for Grandad's will reading."

"This is insane," says Mac as we roll Jackson onto his back and pick up where we left off, maneuvering him around the corner and up the stairs, Mac going first at the head. Each step is like a small mountain and we lump up so slowly I could scream. Halfway up, we get the giggles.

"Come on!" I try and say. "Keep going. Mac, stop laughing!"

Mac's in hysterics.

"Brilliant, just brilliant. Mac, come on, will you?!"

But once we finally regain our composure and begin moving up the stairs again, Mac trips on his trailing lace, loses his footing, and drops Jackson, so I take the full weight of him and we both fall *gadoink, gadoink, gadoink* down the few steps we've just climbed. Miraculously, Jackson doesn't wake up. I break his fall. Mac is poised like a waxwork on the fourth step up. We're both waiting for my mum to appear and wonder why I'm flat on my back at the bottom with a missing rock star on top of me.

"Are you OK?" Mac whispers down to me after a while.

"Yes. Just get him off me," I whisper back. He runs down and grabs Jackson under the shoulders.

Finally, once we're up, we take him into the bathroom, plonk him down on the floor, and close the door. I put the plug in the tub and start running the water. I pour in a shitload of ylang-ylang and crushed-diamond bath cream to get a foam started. I didn't know crushed diamonds even had a smell, but it's well nice. Mac starts to peel off Jackson's clothes, looking like he's pecking through a rancid trash can for a lost five pound note. I root about in the medicine cabinet for something to de-fuzz him. There's some Nair cream, but it smells like chemotherapy in a tube. I find one of my grandad's razors.

"I'll find him some towels," says Mac, rummaging through the wicker drawers before I can ask him to help me remove Jackson's pants. I hear Mum's shower whirring distantly.

"I can't lift him into the bath on my own, Mac," I whisper. "Just help me get him in."

Mac drops the two large white towels he's holding. I peel off Jackson's pants and fling them on the pile in the corner, draping a damp washcloth over Jackson's lap to spare his dignity.

Mac barges past me to take Jackson under his arms. "I'll get this end."

I step across Jackson and take his legs. On three, we hoist him up and into the bath. He slips down under the bubbles and I pull him back up. Mac watches as I soap up a sponge and begin swabbing Jackson all over his chest. I lift up his key necklace and swab under there, not daring to take it off as I know how presh he is about it. So here I am, sponging a female lust object, *my* ultimate hero, all over with soap suds. Water dripping out of the sponge onto his bare pink skin. My hands all over him, pulling him forward to wash his back. His back *side*. Wet. Skin to skin.

But it's not in the least bit erotic. It's like bathing a pig. A hundred-sixty-pound comatose pig, who might very well drown me if he wakes up. But he's showing no signs of waking up and I can't quite believe it because I'm giving him a fairly thorough scrub. And then he does wake up, sort of.

"Wha . . . s'whe . . . not . . . sez . . ."

And then his eyes close again and his face goes head-stone still and his mouth drops open. I breathe out and hoick him back up where he has slipped down under the water. His hair smells like an old man's toolshed — his breath like a drain. So it's all a bit too smelly and awkward to be erotic. I squeeze out some Wash & Go and start scrubbing his head.

"You could help. We'd get it done a lot quicker," I say to Mac, half turning my head in his direction.

He pokes his head out the bathroom door and pulls it closed again. "I can't hear your mum's shower going. I think she's finished."

"So? She's not going to disturb us in here, is she? Lock the door. I'll say I'm having a bath."

"Where am I supposed to be?" says Mac.

"I'll say you've gone home." I reach underneath Jackson to wipe him down below. Mac can barely watch. He stands there with his arms folded, studying the cobweb in the corner. "Go and get him some clean clothes, then. In my grandad's room, in the wardrobe."

Mac leaves the room like a cop in a shoot-out, his back sliding against the wall in case Mum pops out from somewhere. I prop Jackson up in the bath and take one of the razors out of its protective guard. I spray a blob of shaving foam on my hands and lather it all over his face. I nick him a couple of times but he still doesn't wake up. I then moisturize him using Halley's Nivea.

When I'm done with the razor, I rinse his hair with the plastic jug and attempt to brush his teeth.

Return of the Mac. He lies the two bath towels on the

floor and helps me heave Jackson out onto them so we can dry and dress him. He looks as good as new. Better. More like Shiny Smiley Magazine Jackson, not Post-Concert Sweaty Jackson, which is the only Jackson I've seen up until now.

"OK, here's what we've got. . . ." says Mac. He holds up a black-and-white tuxedo.

I didn't know Mum had kept that. I take the hanger and smile. A tiny piece of evidence that Grandad did once dress like a normal guy. "A little over-the-top maybe?"

"I thought it might bring back happy memories for Jackson of his Grammy-night paparazzi punch-up." I'm just about to argue when there's a knock on the door.

We freeze. Jackson's still spark out between us on the bath towels at our feet.

"Jode? I'm off to the lawyer's," Mum calls out.

"OK," I call back.

"What are you doing?"

"Uh, having a bath."

"Oh. Halley's staying at Nina's house tonight because they're catching the bus early in the morning, so are you OK to make your own dinner?"

Catching the bus? Oh yeah, she's going on an outward-bound thing. Mac flings me a hand towel and I quickly wrap it around my head so it looks like my hair's wet. I open the door a crack and poke my head out. "Yeah, OK."

Mum's at the top of the stairs with her power suit on. She starts to call out "bye" and then sees me. "Oh, there you are. See you later."

"Good luck."

She frowns. "You're all right, aren't you? I'm not asking any questions," she says defensively. "I just want to know." She comes to the bathroom door.

"I'm fine, Mum." She's looking at my nostrils. She always does this to check for white powder traces. She'll try to look behind me for bongs. Check to see if the toilet seat's down with traces of white powder on top of it. She saw it on *CSI: Miami*.

"Where's Mac?" she asks.

"Gone home," I say, closing the door slightly. "I need to wash my conditioner off now."

"Jode . . ."

"Sorry. See you later, bye."

I shut the door and flick the lock over. She's not convinced. I wouldn't be either. Mac looks at me and we both stop breathing until we hear footsteps down the stairs and the front door closing.

Once in a clean tuxedo, Jackson is carried back out to the drum room where we lie him down on the cushions and I move his limbs into the recovery position: on his side, chin up, arms laced to keep him in place, top knee bent at a right angle. Now he can continue his coma in comfort and I don't have to stress about him choking to death if he throws up again. It's one of the few things I actually remember from the first-aid course I had to complete for work. How to put someone in the recovery position and to always assess the situation before you act. Pity I couldn't remember where to look for a pulse, but still, I can only take in so much.

And the current situation is that Mac and I are both

knackered, but there's no time to waste. It's garbage pickup day. I can hear the clattering garbage truck a couple of streets away. With a bit of luck we can clean up the room and have the trash taken away without anyone knowing. So we get to work.

It's not the pukey smell that's bothering me as we bag up all the rubbish. It's not the torn boxes, the dirty walls, the dented skirting boards. It's the fact that I have to say good-bye to my grandad's things. Things I saved from the charity donation — clothes, reading glasses, books. The mannequin he nicked from Debenhams (now headless). Two multicolored glass bongs that used to sit on the windowsill in the lounge (now smashed). Ornaments he brought back from his travels — a plastic Taj Mahal (now snapped), a tiny snow globe of the Great Barrier Reef (now not so great), and a little Statue of Liberty on a brass base (now baseless).

"You OK?" Mac asks as each ruined item is thrown into the bin.

"Yeah," I say, and say no more. It hurts but there's nothing I can do. Everything's ruined. We clear the room completely, save for the coverless duck-feather cushions and the bucket. We then go through the house and empty the rest of the bins like Mum asked me to — anything to stop her from getting suspicious. Our trash bin is already full so we start to load up Jackson's hidey bin.

"Shall I do it, so we catch the trashmen?" offers Mac as I tie up the last bag.

"It's OK," I say. "It's not too bad. Silly hanging on to it all, really. It's not Grandad, is it?"

Mac shakes his head. "It's just stuff."

The trashmen are clattering nearer now. The truck beeps to signal their reversal into Chesil Lane. Two men in fluorescent orange jump out of the cab and start along the pavement, grabbing the handles of the green trash bins and flinging their contents up into the crusher. We leave the overflowing bins for the men and go back into the near-empty drum room.

"What now?" I say to Mac, expecting him to give me one of his treelike hugs, but he doesn't.

"Dunno," he says. "Fancy going shopping or something? I told Mum I'd be rehearsing nonstop so they had to put Cree in day care all day for once."

"What? No I meant what else can we do for Jackson?"

"Oh we're still on him, are we?" he sighs.

"What do you expect? I can't concentrate on anything else at the moment."

"How about getting a few DVDs out? Yeah, let's get some DVDs, popcorn, Ben & Jerry's, and make an afternoon of it. We can keep one eye on him and . . ."

"I can't," I say, "it wouldn't be right."

"OK, well, we'll turn it into research," he says decisively.

We find just enough energy to troop down the street to the pub and sneak up to the back bedroom to swipe every relevant DVD in Teddy's collection. Then we sneak back to my house, and all afternoon we watch them — *The Basketball Diaries, Dazed and Confused, Drugstore Cowboy, Totally Baked: A Pot-U-Mentary,* and, of course, *Trainspotting.* There isn't time to watch all of them properly so we skim, looking for scenes where a character goes through cold turkey. When *Trainspotting* comes to a halt, Mac gets up to take it out and place it back in its box. It's getting dark outside the living-room window. I reach up behind me and flick on the wall light.

"He just has to ride it out, doesn't he?" says Mac.

"And we just have to . . . keep an eye on him?"

"Yeah. A few days without his happy pills and his entourage might work wonders."

"What about the toilet?"

Mac shrugs. "He's got a bucket."

"Bit undignified, isn't it?"

"He could do with a bit of indignity. Remind him he's a human being."

"What if he tries to commit suicide?"

"How?" says Mac. "He's only got pillow feathers and a bucket."

The news is on. Channel Three.

Police are searching areas of South Wales and the West Country in the hope of finding American rock star Jackson Gatlin, lead singer of The Regulators, who has not been seen for two days since he came offstage at Cardiff Arena.

"Quick, turn it up," says Mac, fumbling for the remote.

Gatlin, aged 27, who has a history of depression, has not contacted his management or fellow

band members since his disappearance on 23 March. Bandmates say his passport and all of his possessions remain untouched.

Inquiries by detectives in London and Cardiff have drawn a blank, but revealed that he has not used his credit cards or contacted friends. The band have postponed a thirty-date concert tour of the US, due to start next Wednesday.

Last year the band, whose guitar-based rock is said to give a voice to alienated American youth, played at the Big Fish Festival in New Zealand as a threesome while Gatlin recovered from exhaustion in a clinic.

But a source close to the group said that since then the troubled musician, famed for his onstage antics, which include fire-breathing and backflips into the crowd, has steered clear of drink and drugs.

Anyone who may have seen anything unusual near Cardiff Arena on the night of 23 March is asked to contact the missing-persons helpline. . .

"Shit," says Mac, but we don't have a conversation about it, because just at that moment, his phone buzzes and it's his mum, asking him to look after Cree for the evening so she can go down to work in the bar. "Keep him locked in and don't feed him. It'll only give him more energy."

"I can't starve him. What about drink?"

Mac marches into the kitchen and returns minutes later with the carton of blood orange juice. I follow as he marches out to the garden, kneels down in front of the drum-room door, and hastily shoves the juice through the cat flap.

"OK, he's got drink. Now just leave him to it."

"Mac, I can't leave him. . . ."

"Yes, you can. Do not open that door, Jody, I mean it." He's got his serious voice on, like we've got a saber-toothed tiger in there or something.

When Mac's gone, I go inside and pretend to watch some wanky medical drama, trying not to think about Jackson. Pretty soon, the front door clicks. Mum's back from the lawyer's. She flops the free newspaper onto the armrest of the sofa and glances at me. Her auburn rinse looks rough as always.

"How did it go? Did we get the house?"

She sits down on the two-seater sofa opposite, on the edge. "Yeah. We got the house."

"Did he owe anything?"

She shakes her head. "No. He took care of it all. Can't quite believe it but, no, no debts. He even paid off the mortgage."

"So, is that the end of it, then? We get to stay here?"

"Yeah, we can stay here."

I'm expecting bad news. I always expect bad news, probably because I only ever hear bad news. Waiting for my exam results — rubbish news. Waiting to hear what Mum and Dad wanted to talk to me and Halley about — divorce news. Waiting to find out Grandad's test results — the worst news. But this, this is actually good news. No debts to worry about and we don't have to move again.

"That's not all, Jode," she says, leaning forward so that

Thompson-Nicola Regional District Library System

both her hands are touching her mouth, like she can't contain the words in there.

"What?" I say, preparing myself for the worst. *What? What? What? You're dying, too, now? You've got to have a leg amputated? What?!*

"Your grandad left us some money. You, me, and Hal. Quite a bit of money."

"Oh. Right." He said he was going to leave any money he had to the Rest Home for Elderly Break-dancers in Croyde. He'd been living off his pension for the last ten years so it can't be much.

Mum takes a deep breath. There are tears in her eyes. "You remember that lottery win he had a bit back?"

"Yeah. But he spent it on the drum room."

"No, he spent *some* of it on the drum room. Some of it he sent to elderly break-dancers. Adopted a couple of lemurs. But there was some left."

"Oh. How much?"

"Give or take . . . about a hundred thousand pounds."

THIRTEEN
LA DEVIAZIONE

As the week goes on, things take a turn for the better, as does Jackson's behavior. This is probably why I'm having this strange feeling of happiness. I've missed happiness, it's nice to feel it again. What makes the week that much more enjoyable is the fact that my sister, Halley, is still away on her school outward-bound training thing in the Quantocks with her Duke of Edinburgh herd, which means I've only got Mum to keep an eye on, but Mum seems to have a new focus in her life — shopping. She's never liked shopping before, probably because she's never had the money to like shopping before, but since the will-reading, it's like she's found a new hobby. Can't say I'm not worried, though. When Dad found a new hobby, casino investment, we ended up having to sell our house. But looking on the bright side, Mum's (1) much better with money than Dad and (2) out of the house a lot, which means less stress for me that she's going to find Jackson in the garage and go giraffe on me.

When he's not looking after Cree or rehearsing or working, Mac helps me watch over Jackson. We're like a couple of emo Florence Nightingales. Jackson doesn't really get up in the night, but during the day his behavior is changeable to say the least. One minute he'll be in one of his comas, the next he's a whole box of fireworks going off. During his hulk-outs, which last from anywhere between ten minutes to an hour, we lock the garage door and leave him to it.

The day after his bath, Jackson shreds my cushions. I bring him some lunch and can't help laughing. He's sitting in the middle of the floor, bollock-naked, surrounded by feathers, doing his extremely pissed chick impression.

"Aren't you angry with me?" he says, not looking up.

And quick as a flash, I return, "Nope. It was *your* bed. So you can lie in it," and I dump his sandwich and Doritos down beside his head. And that's that.

Most of the time, Jackson lies on the feathers shaking or just staring into space or reading the books that I post through the slot. Some books he shreds and posts back to me — some he actually reads and then shreds and posts back to me. I decide not to give him any more of my books to tear up and buy some in the thrift shop in town — *The Tenant of Wildfell Hall* by Anne Brontë, *An A Level Guide to Catch 22*, the fifth Harry Potter book, and two very dog-eared Stephen Kings, a book of short novellas called *Different Seasons* and one called *The Girl Who Loved Tom Gordon*.

"I don't want these ones," he yells through the cat flap.

"You've got nothing else to do, have you? Unless you want to leave?" I call back. He says nothing. I wait for a second and watch him through the cat flap when he thinks I've gone. He reaches for the Brontë book and opens it up. I'm feeling rather proud that I finally have him dancing around my little finger.

· The day after the cushion-shredding I decide I'll learn how to use the smoothie maker Mum gave me last

Christmas and spend the morning buying all the ingredients I need to make Jackson some power cleansing juices to build his strength back up — acai berries, soy milk, echinacea, wheatgrass. Costs me a fortune. The first attempt isn't exactly a success — I forget to put the lid on and get the full blast of blueberry and banana power pulp right in my face.

After two more days, when I'm sure it is safe to open the drum-room door, I take him in a chess set and set it up on the carpet. We attempt a game. Jackson loses and knocks over the board, of course. My grandad used to do the same thing during his final weeks, saying the chemo had sapped his brainpower. Jackson has no such excuse — he's just being a dick.

The day after that it's sunny so I leave the door of the drum room open and lie on the sun lounge chair in the garden with my MP3 player on. Jackson comes out as far as the doorstep, and sits down to do some writing in the notebook I'd given him. Noises of trash bins clattering about in the wind and kids kicking a ball around on the gravel path at the back of the house keep freaking him out so he scuttles back into the garage pretty soon. It's to be expected, I suppose.

Over the week, awful days turn into bad days, turn into OK days, turn into good days. On Thursday I put a yoga mat in the drum room and buy one of those exercise balls for him so he can get rid of his excess energy.

"What do you think I am, a fucking hamster?" he shouts and the ball comes bouncing back toward me but on the last bounce it gets wedged in the door frame. I kick it hard back at him and it pings off his head. He looks at me, struck by my lightning reflex. Ha.

"Sorry," he says. And he doesn't look at me, so I can tell he means it.

I'm learning and so is he — treat Jackson like a rock god, get a flying object in the face. Treat Jackson like a spoiled human being, get an apology. It's becoming easier.

He is getting better, or getting calmer at any rate. His hallucinations of spiders the size of cats and a sparrow hovering outside the window and calling him a moron are still happening but not nearly so much, and all his screeching and whining becomes like feedback in my ears — an annoying noise but ultimately just that. Noise.

Friday, and it's breakthrough day. I'm washing up the breakfast things when I see him come out of the drum room, close the door behind him, and walk across the lawn to the back door of the house. I wait. He knocks.

He stands there awkwardly as I open the door. His hair looks like a blackbird hitting a windshield, but at least he's wearing clothes. Grandad's tuxedo, now almost unrecognizably skanky and torn.

"I want to take a shower. Please."

"OK," I say, trying to hide my surprise, not least because he's said please for the first time. He hasn't said thank you yet, but I'm trying not to think about that. "The bathroom's at the top of the stairs. There's towels in the wicker drawers."

He nods and walks past me. I can't concentrate on anything while he's in the house. I hear the water running.

There's a really bad minute when I think about the Gillette razors in the medicine cabinet and when I hear a loud thump from above, I imagine he's up there, slumped on the tiles in a pool of wrist blood. Seconds later I hear the bathroom lock go and within a minute, he's back in front of me in the kitchen — wrists clean and wrapped in my grandad's navy bathrobe.

"OK?" I ask him.

He nods and gestures to the robe. "I found this in one of the drawers."

"It's OK," I say. Another item of Grandad's that missed Mum's cull. I'm amazed. I point toward the breakfast bar, where Mum's homemade carrot cake sits on a patterned plate. "Do you want some?"

"Does it have lumps in it? I don't do lumps."

"No, there's no lumps in it."

He slinks up on a stool. His shower hasn't done much to bring him back to life. His face is still china white and clammy and his lank, soggy hair still looks dirty. I can smell it. It still smells of cigarettes, just damp cigarettes now. He eats the carrot cake.

"It's good," he says, not looking at me. After a silence, where I can only hear the mushy chomping inside his mouth and his swallowing throat, he pulls out a small stack of papers from the bathrobe pocket. "I found all this stuff." I look at the papers. I know instantly what they are. I take them from him.

I sift through them. "Little games me and my grandad used to play. In the night, when neither of us could sleep. Sometimes we'd come in here and make hot chocolates and play games. Consequences. Hangman. Scattergories. He was pretty ill by then, though."

"I didn't ask what they were," he says, finishing his cake.

I shuffle the little notelets neatly and put them in my back pocket. He doesn't say anything else for a long time, just presses his finger down on his plate crumbs and then sucks it. I guess I have to make the next move, so I do. "We have to think about getting you back."

"Yeah. I'll just eat this. I'm real tired."

"No, not back to the garage. Back to your band. Back to The Regulators."

He shakes his head. "I'm not going back." He stares into the middle distance, like he's just seen a spider moving across the counter. His brilliant blue eyes don't seem to twinkle so much anymore and the whites of them are speckled red. "I'd rather die."

"You don't mean that." I smile but I know he's not joking. I just don't want to believe it.

"I mean it. If you kick me out, I'll . . . I'll, you don't know what I'm capable of, Josie. . . ."

I don't even correct him straightaway on the name thing as I notice his hand shaking on the tabletop, so much that his crumby plate is rattling. I put my hand out to place on his, but at the last moment, I reach for the plate instead and carry it to the sink.

"Must be all over the news," he mumbles.

"No," I lie. "It hasn't been mentioned." Immediately his hand stops shaking. "I won't kick you out. If you really want to stay. But . . . don't treat me like shit. I don't deserve it. And while I'm at it, my name's Jody, with a 'd.'"

He nods very faintly and goes back out to the garage, where he stays for the rest of the day.

Saturday, and it's just over a week since the concert. Jackson seems content with reading and sleeping, so I give myself the day off rock star–sitting and go and spend it with Mac at the Italian Market in town. I wait for him to join me outside in the pub beer garden, looking skyward. A wood pigeon is hooting away in the hazel tree above the swing, the one that's always there when Mac and I sit out. Ordinarily it would be annoying the arse off me, but today I don't even care.

Mac returns with two Cokes, Curly Wurlys for both of us, and a copy of the *West Country Chronicle* tucked under his arm. I don't ever want to see a Curly Wurly again but it's sweet of him to get one for me anyway. He's wearing a long-sleeved purple T-shirt and skinny blue jeans with DMs, his wallet chain swinging from his pocket. His black hair is two inches of straight-up fin on his head, held in place by extra-concrete styling wax, and his usual shock of blue. I'd kill to wear skinny jeans and DMs as well as he does but it's just not a good look for me. I know my limitations.

"You seen this?" He places the drinks and chocolate on the grass beside the swing and holds up the paper.

IS MISSING STAR IN SOUTH WEST?

A cloud comes over my day. "Oh my God," I gasp. "Oh my God. Why do they think that all of a sudden?"

He shrugs, opening up the paper. "They can't check every corner of the South West, can they? They're not talking about searching Nuffing and the surrounding Wolds yet, so until they are, he's fine where he is."

I chew my lip. "What about Mum? And Halley comes back in a day or so. One of them is bound to notice I'm spending so much time in the garage. One tells one, one tells another, someone snoops around. Someone'll find him, Mac. Mum's already suspicious with all the food that's going missing."

"She probably thinks you're going through a bulimia phase or something. She usually jumps to the most obvious conclusion."

I drag my feet on the ground so the swing comes to a halt and pick at the rust on the swing leg. "He told me he'll kill himself if he has to leave."

"He doesn't mean it," says Mac.

"He does, Mac." I start swinging again. "And it's not the drugs talking now. He's clean."

"All right, all right," he sighs. "Can we talk about something else now? This is supposed to be our day out. I don't want to talk about the thing in your garage."

"You brought it up. You brought the paper out."

"Only to show you . . ." The front leg of the swing keeps lifting up out of its bolt every time I swing backward. I stop and grab one of the Curly Wurlys on the grass, tearing it open and taking an almighty chomp out of it. I don't know why I do it — the taste of it makes me feel sick.

Mac sips his Coke. "You hear any more about Charlie's money? How much will you get?"

"Mum said she wants to spend a few grand getting the house sorted out. Pay off Dad's debts. And he's left ten grand for me and ten for Halley."

"Wow. That's great."

"Yeah. That's how Grandad wanted it, apparently. Mum's set up savings accounts for us. We can get the money out whenever we want, she just wants us to be a bit responsible with it until we decide. She's petrified I'm going to blow it all on Regulators DVDs and Coco Rocks."

"What are you going to spend it on?"

"Dunno. Liposuction maybe. Some new Converse. I'd quite like a malamute."

"What's that?"

"It's like a husky. Where's Cree?"

"Mum's changing her. Sorry she's tagging along. Yet again."

"I don't mind. I love Cree to bits, you know I do."

"Yeah, I know." Mac rests his head against the metal swing frame.

I touch the shark fin of hair sticking up on his head. Pretty solid. Work of art today. "You should tell your mum and dad if you don't want to keep babysitting her. It's not your fault your mum's gone back to working full-time now."

He shrugs. He doesn't want to talk about it, I can tell, cos he immediately returns to the subject of my grandad's money. "You could spend it on something Charlie would have wanted. You could . . . donate it to Bristol Museum or something, seeing as that's where he last went . . . you know, when we saw the Banksy stuff. He loved all that."

"What good would that do?"

"I dunno. Or you could put it toward community art projects or something. Charlie loved graffiti. Anarchy. Bedlam."

I laugh. "Yeah. Maybe . . ."

"But maybe he wasn't thinking straight that day," Mac adds.

My grandad didn't like thinking straight. Straight thinking was for boring people. Wobbly thinking was for trendsetters. Trailblazers. "He'd have wanted me to do something mad with it, like go to a rodeo or snorkel with great white sharks or something, probably while scattering his ashes."

"Yeah, probably," Mac laughs.

I study his hair again. "Perhaps I'll go somewhere amazing and scatter them, then. Put the money toward that." Mac nods. "Where's amazing? I always wanted to go to Italy. Or Vegas, we could do Vegas?"

"Italy sounds good," says Mac.

"He loved it when the Italian Market came to town. And he said he always wanted to see the Sistine Chapel."

"Bargain, well, that's it, then."

I squint up at him as the sun hits my eyes. "You coming? We could turn it into a holiday."

"Yeah?" he asks brightly, his smile all dimpled. "What do you keep looking at?" he says, suddenly getting all stressio about my constant frowns toward his hairline.

"Your hair. I think your roots are coming through a bit."

"What?!" he blurts out, instinctively doing his where's-the-nearest-mirror freak-out.

"Only a bit," I say. "But yeah, we could totally go away."

Then I remember. "Course, we might have to take Jackson with us."

"What?"

"Well, I can't leave him in our garage for a week, can I?"

Mac does his guppy mouth when he can't think of the right thing to say. "But . . . no, no, he'll be gone by then, surely. How long is he planning on staying here, for God's sake?"

"I don't know. I don't know what to do with him."

"Oh bloody hell."

The side door slams in the distance and Tish comes up the steps with Cree in her arms. Tish points toward us in the garden and Cree squirms to be put down. She toddles toward me faster than her legs can keep up, her little squeals filling the air. She's in a red-and-white sundress and white dolly bar sandals I haven't seen her wearing before.

"Hello, baby girl!" I call out and get up off the swing to greet her. She runs into my arms as she always does. "You got new soos!"

"Yeah, I got new soos," she says as I scoop her up. She points her foot out to show me. "They white."

"Yeah, they are white, good girl."

"My Kenzie bought them for me."

Mac and his mum are arguing. "You know we've got a bus of tourists booked in at one. . . ."

"And that's my problem, is it?"

"No, course not. We're letting you have the day off, aren't we?"

"Yeah, to babysit."

"Oh, stop acting so hard done by."

"We going to the tally inn?" Cree asks me.

Mac's getting the lecture from his mum about not letting go of Cree's hand and making sure he checks her diaper every hour. He's looking daggers at her but doesn't say anything more. I'm trying to hear what she's saying, but Cree's patting my cheek and trying to turn my face toward her. "Dody."

"Sorry, yeah, we're going to the Italian Market, that OK?"

"Kee coming to the tally inn?" she says, rubbing my earlobes, her blonde hair flyaway around her face like sunshine.

"Yep, you're coming, too."

Mac's face is stormy when his mum's gone back inside. I follow him across the parking lot with Cree in my arms.

"I don't mind if Cree comes with us," I tell him, trying to turn his frown upside down, but it's stuck solid.

"It's not about Cree, it's about them," he snaps. "They always just expect me to look after her. It's like they always just assume I'll do it. There's no choice or anything. Like, they cope when I've got a rehearsal or something, but Dad does *nothing* but work. And Cree *always* wants him."

"Cree's lucky to have you," I tell him, rubbing his arm. His arm stiffens. He's not just ranting — he's really pissed off.

"My Kenzie sad?" says Cree.

"A little bit," I whisper in her ear. She immediately shoots her arms out to him and he stops and takes her off me. She cuddles in and gives him the back pat. He sighs and closes his eyes.

"I'm sorry, Creepy Girl," he sighs, kissing her hair. "It's not your fault, is it?" She lifts her hand to his ear and twizzles his ear stud.

We walk up the side street and out onto the main drag for the market. The town center is closed off to traffic so people have parked their cars really stupidly two-deep in the road. I have to breathe in and sidestep past them through to the main market area.

"Solders," says Cree and Mac lifts her up onto his shoulders so she can see what's going on. Most of the town is out and about, along with a pulsing sunshine. There's an endless line of food stalls decked in Italian flags.

The first stall we come to is the wines stall. Stella Flaws, a pub regular, in a gold halter-neck top and jeggings, is stumbling about on these really high wedges, holding a wine glass. She wears this really thick fake tan that we're all supposed to think is natural. She always reminds me of a Cheeto I saw once on the floor of New Look.

Cree's holding the tops of Mac's ears and giddying him up like he's a pony.

"Giddy up, Mackenzie," I say to him, loud enough for Cree to hear.

"No, *my* Kenzie," she says defiantly, grabbing onto his forehead with both her hands.

Last summer Mac and I had been on a health kick and it had been Stella Flaws's keep-fit DVD we had borrowed to get into shape. We sprained our thigh muscles attempting two hundred stretches with one leg on the back of his sofa. Stella had advised us both to do the watermelon washout, too. We had to eat nothing but watermelon for three days to clean out all our toxins. Mac was so adamant we would stick to it he made his mum buy a week's supply of watermelon. We started one Saturday morning and by midday we were watching *Gorillas in the Mist*, practically inhaling ham, egg, and hash browns. I wonder if I should get some watermelons for Jackson and put him on a more intense detox for a few days.

Another woman, about three times Stella's size, is standing alongside her, grasping a wine glass with sausagey fingers. She wears all black leather and from a distance she looks like a stack of tires. This is Ann Rackham. She cut off her ear for a bet a few years ago.

Next to Ann stands a figure. A tall, wide figure in a hooded jacket. Duncan Buzzey, the town freak. I always thought he permanently wore his hood up because he had some hideous facial scarring or something, but no, it's just because he doesn't want to talk to people. He makes his way slowly along the stalls, sniffing things, tasting things. A lumbering giant with a fuzzy ginger face. Mac told me Duncan was in his final year at Nuffing Comp when Mac was just ten and in those days he was known as the BFD or "Big Fat Duncan." Nowadays, because of his expertise in selling weed to teenagers, he's known as the Big Fat Dealer. Buzzey's well sketchy. His eyes look like they've been poked right back into his skull and he's got so many pockmarks all over his face he's probably squeezed every zit that ever popped out of it.

"Look at Buzzey," says Mac. "Nice to see him out and about. Beats looking down his underpants and naming his crabs." Mac laughs at his own joke, trying to out-guffaw some lads cadging all the free chunks of pecorino from the cheese stall. I'm watching the BFD.

"I thought he was in prison," I whisper to Mac.

"No, but he's a bit of a hermit," he says, removing his Gucci sunglasses from his belt loop and delicately placing them on his face. "Never comes in the pub anymore. That was his dad who went to prison."

"What did he do?"

"Got caught bringing illegal immigrants over from Romania. He had like fifty of them working on his farm out in Carstowe. Got twelve years. Duncan said he had nothing to do with it."

At that moment, Duncan snaps his head around in our direction but doesn't look at us. He evidently heard his name, though. Time to move along.

"God, look at that lot," Mac says, gesturing toward the group of lads nicking all the free cheese. "All with the same knockoff Kappas with the tongues pulled out. All got the gold chains. All got the gold rings. All laughing the same. All got bad teeth."

"Yeah, and they're all about to stab us if you talk about them any louder," I say as Cree reaches her hand out to be got down, and we mosey over to the bread stall.

The sunshine beats down on us and I have to keep

squinting every time I look up. I'm not a summer person really so I resent it when it's this hot. I like it when I'm inside the house and I look out and see a blue sky, but being outside is a different story. I don't exactly dress for the weather. I daren't tell Mac I'm hot cos I know what he'll say. "Well, if you'd show a bit more flesh once in a while it'd cool you right off. Let's go shopping for summer tank tops!" Mac knows full well that for me to show more flesh, a nuclear fallout would have to blow my clothes off my back, so I just sweat in silence.

The lad lot is laughing like this, *hur, hur, hur,* and the guy behind the cheese stall is shooing them away. I tear off a piece of sundried focaccia and dip it in a complimentary bowl of olive oil.

"Kee have some," says Cree. I hand her some dipped bread. She chomps, makes a disgusted face, and duly spits it out all over herself. "My don't like," she says, scraping it off her tongue.

Mac leaves us briefly to grab two small plastic cups of something he announces as *Trebbiano d'Abruzzo* and hands one to me. I pick up Cree and give him an expectant look. "I'm not drinking, I told you."

"Go on. Just one. You're funny when you drink." He starts jigging about on the spot, singing, *"We gonna party like it's your birthday, we gonna sip Bacardi like it's your birthday . . ."* but I still don't want any.

"You know what I'm like when I drink. Anyway, knowing my luck I'll probably get arrested for underage drinking."

"They're more relaxed about drinking in Italy."

"We're not in Italy, are we?"

"Yeah but the guy at the booth is proper Italian. I heard him say, came over on the ferry with all his gear. So when in Rome." He swigs. "Oh, go on, just have a sip. You can do that poncey thing and spit it out again if you want. I'll never ever forget that time you . . ."

"Yeah, yeah, I know."

Mac likes to remind me of my antics while under the influence: the time I attempted to climb a lamppost after just two alcopops; or when I puked peppermint schnapps all over the neighbor's rose beds. But that's the thing about friends (and mums, and sisters, come to think of it) — they tend to prick you with those memories you'd rather forget. Like when you were fat, or when you pulled down your pants and peed on the dance floor at your cousin's wedding. Only being two at the time makes no difference, I still don't want to talk about it.

Mustachio and Ginger, the two policemen who came to the pub the morning after the concert, are at the market in their normal clothes and they've got their wives and kids with them, too. Mac gets cornered by Mustachio and wife, who tell him they're really looking forward to *Rocky Horror.* Ginger nods to me but doesn't speak, thank Cobain. Why do I always feel guilty when I'm around policemen? Probably because I always *am* guilty around policemen.

I'm watching the BFD. He is scratching his ball sack and yawning at the same time. He should be in a glass case, swinging on a tire.

People wander past us with plates heaped high with

cheeses, deep-fried oysters, triangles of pizza, and odd little alien vegetables on cocktail sticks. I make a mental note of all the sketchy things that I'm no wayski going to try — things at the cured meats and antipasti counter made from dried dolphin meat or pig's trotters.

Opposite Signor Salvo's outdoor pizza parlor a stall is selling every single shape of pasta. Mac buys a bag of *orecchiette*, which the man tells us (and we understand eventually) means "little ears." We look in the clear bag and the shells do look like little ears. This amuses Cree no end and she insists on holding the bag for the rest of the time.

The last stall is covered with fresh garlic and herbs. We sniff. The old Italian woman behind the counter is sitting beside her cash box, reading a newspaper. Her face is so long it looks like she's been hanging iron weights off her cheeks for centuries. Mac interrupts her reading to buy some mint for his mum. He tears off a leaf and hands it to Cree to sniff and she promptly eats it, then scrapes it off her tongue and onto his hand in disgust.

The old woman goes back to her newspaper. An Italian newspaper. I recognize the picture on the front page instantly. I see the headline. I tap Mac's stomach.

DOVE SI TROVA JACKSON?

Now, I'm no Italian, but I'm pretty sure that headline is asking where Jackson is. So the story's got as far as Italy, probably farther. Nobody in Europe knows where Jackson is. He could still be in England, in a garage, in the little market town of Nuffing-on-the-Wold. Or he could have got across the Channel. That would throw the local newspapers off the scent. If someone saw him in Italy. And then it hits me. If someone saw him *here* and took a picture and sent it to the papers saying they'd taken it in Italy, the media would *have* to admit he was nowhere near the South West. Wouldn't they?

Mac's singing to himself. I nudge him. "Have you got your camera on you?"

"Only on my phone. Why? Do you want to get a shot of you and the salami?" he laughs.

"No, I want to get one of Jackson reading that paper."

FOURTEEN
THE TALLY INN JOB

Cree toddles on ahead of me and Mac and rounds the gravel path into our back garden. When we get there, all we can see is her headless body sticking out of the cat flap. There comes one almighty scream from inside the garage.

Mac lunges toward Cree to pull her back, but her head is stuck fast.

"Shit, Jode! She's stuck."

"She can't be," I say, joining him to try and ease Cree's head back through the hole. At this point, Cree gets upset and starts panicking herself. Jackson is still screaming inside the garage.

"For God's sake, shut him up, will you? What's the matter with him?" Mac barks at me.

"I don't know, do I? Jackson," I call through the door, "it's OK, we're here, it's OK."

"Get it away, get it away from me!" he yells back.

I peer through the window. "He's trying to climb up the wall. I think she's scaring him."

Cree's screaming her head off, and Mac's talking to her really calmly, gently easing her head back through the little square hole. "There we go, easy, easy, easy . . . there you are."

And she's out. He lifts her up and cuddles her in,

looking at the thin red line around her hairline. She clings on and wails into his shoulder. "Kenzie's got you. Shit that was close, Jode," he says. "What if we had to call the fire brigade?"

"Oh God, it doesn't bear thinking about," I say. "Is she OK?"

He nods, kissing her forehead. "All gone, Creep. All gone now."

She sobs on his shoulder, looking at me as we enter the garage. "My hurt my ned," she says.

"I know. All gone now," I say.

Jackson's nervous to say the least when we approach him. He's huddled in a corner on his feathers like the last chick that won't leave the nest, eyeing Cree like she's got a forked tail.

"I just saw this head, c-c-coming through the door," he cries. "Scared the shit out of me. Thought I was seeing things. I wasn't, was I? I wasn't seeing shit again?"

"No, it's OK. It was Cree, Mac's little sister," I say, gesturing toward her. "Jackson, we've come to take you out of here for a little while. That would be nice, wouldn't it?" I start to tell him about my plan about the market, and he shuffles away from me.

"No, I don't want to. Someone will recognize me."

"No they won't. And it won't take very long," I explain. "You can put on a baseball cap and we'll just take a couple of photos of you reading an Italian newspaper under an Italian awning and then you can come back here again. It's just to throw the papers off the scent."

"But if the South West of England is hunting for him,

isn't he going to be spotted in a crowd full of people?" says Mac. Cree looks up from Mac's shoulder and stares at Jackson. Jackson is looking back at her and I'm waiting for him to make the sign of the cross.

"Don't think so," I say. "Who's really going to think he's here of all places? If you thought you saw Brad Pitt walking along the seafront at Weston, would you think it actually *was* him or just a look-alike?"

"Yes, if it's Brad Pitt, it's Brad Pitt. He might be doing a movie here. Or adopting someone."

"Well, I think it's worth the risk," I say, turning to Jackson again. "Come on, try it. If we get to the market and you freak out, we'll just come back."

"I'm not going," he mumbles. "Do it in here."

"We can't. A picture of you reading an Italian newspaper inside a feather-strewn garage is going to look like a hostage situation."

He shakes his head, scraping his fingers through his straggly brown hair. "No. Someone'll see me and it will get back to Grohman. He'll have his guys looking for me everywhere. He thinks he owns me . . . maybe he does. If he finds me, he'll make damn sure I never get to walk away from him again."

"Jeez, you're only in a band, you're not going back into some torture chamber," says Mac, but Jackson looks at him through dead eyes and I can tell that's exactly how he sees it all — the tour bus, the gigs, the hiding from the paparazzi, having every little thing you do photographed and put in the papers. *That's* his torture chamber.

Cree wriggles for Mac to put her down, still snuffling

from her cat-flap trauma. She toddles over to Jackson and crouches down with her hands on her knees. "Come on, Man," she huffs and garbles, "you hold my nand." This is what Mac always says to her when she's afraid of something.

Jackson looks at Cree, his eyes hardening. Mac steps forward, as though fearing at any moment Jackson will drop-kick his baby sister through the open door. But I hold him back. She knows what she's doing. For a two-year-old, Cree has perfect people skills. Comes from living in a pub, I suppose. She knows Jackson's afraid. She knows he needs someone to take his hand. Mac tries to teach her what to be afraid of and what not. Strangers — be afraid. Spiders — don't be afraid. Cree still hasn't quite got the hang of the stranger thing, though, and for some reason she's taken a deep interest in this one. Amazingly, Jackson lets her take his hand and stands up, dwarfing her, as she tugs him toward the door.

"Now put your soosies on," she says.

He looks blankly at her. "Susies? Who's Susie?"

She grabs one of my white DMs by the door and brings it over to him. She starts trying to force it on before his foot's left the floor.

Jackson's in a sort of catatonia as we wander through the town. He has on one of my old black hoodies and one of Mac's baseball caps forced so far down over his forehead his eyes are slits in his face. But I can tell he's watching every single person that passes. His head keeps darting from face to face, noise to noise, looking for signs of recognition, nudges in backs, pointing fingers. But no one's looking at him. They're all too busy trying to snatch the last free pieces of cheese or cups of wine. We make it to the far end, Cree pulling him all the way through the litter of market flyers and plastic cups on the ground. "Come on, Man," she keeps saying, dragging him all the while.

When we reach the herb stall, the ancient hangy-face woman is serving a customer. The Italian newspaper lies on the table behind her.

Mac does the honors. "Hello," he says, stretching his hand out to shake hers. She shakes it but her long face is wary. "Yeah, can you tell me how fresh your herbs are? I mean, what's the story? What's the process of them getting here?" He insists on talking about the carbon footprint and smelling her specimens. I lean as discreetly as possible into the canvas wall and sneak my hand underneath to grab the newspaper. I slide it along the table, off onto the floor, and out. The old woman hasn't noticed and Mac has bought some basil and a pot of sage, which he carries in a brown paper bag rolled up at the top.

"OK," I say as I rejoin him and Cree, looking over people's heads for signs of somewhere Jackson can sit. I see the perfect spot. "Over there."

Signor Salvo's has some wooden benches underneath large red umbrellas. People gather around the counter as the chefs toss dough and shovel pizzas from a small stone furnace. We watch the tables until a family leaves, and I shove Jackson until he sits down amid their scrunched up napkins and dirty plates.

I hand him the paper. "Put your hat up a smidge. We need to see your face a bit."

"My have picture and Man?" says Cree.

"No," says Mac, "not this one." Cree does her frustrated leg wiggle.

"We'll do another one in a minute," I tell her, and this seems to calm her down, though her leg still wiggles a bit. Mac steps back a couple of paces and lines his phone up on its side to take the picture of Jackson. He waits for the image to appear on the screen. "No, we can't see your face."

With some awkwardness, Jackson tips the baseball cap up slightly.

"Good," I say. "Look out toward the road. Go back a bit Mac, it's too close. It has to be natural, like he doesn't know we're taking it."

So Mac takes the shot of Jackson reading the paper, and a couple more of him pretending to sip from an empty coffee cup and scratching his chin, fully showing his face to the camera. I hope to God his shaking hand won't be blurry in the picture.

"Yeah, these are good," Mac says as he studies them on the screen. "Got the awning behind him, cover of the paper's in there and there's even an Italian pizza guy scratching his armpit with a spaghetti fork in the background, so that should be perfect."

"Bargs," I say. "When can you load them on the computer?"

"Whenever you want," says Mac.

"My have picture now?" Cree whines again and just for her, I sit her on Jackson's lap and take Mac's phone from him. She does her fakest little grin in preparation for the shot.

"Jackson, smile for this one, OK?"

"Say tees, Man," says Cree.

He makes a different kind of face than his usual painfully confused one, though I wouldn't call it a smile. "Cheese," he says, though for all the enthusiasm he puts into it, he might as well have said, "I have an inoperable lump."

"OK, all done," I say.

"I want to go back now," Jackson mumbles, his face glazed with sweat.

Cree walks up to him and takes his hand in hers again. "Come on, Man, let's go home. Can Man come see Roly?" she asks Mac.

"No," says Mac, "he needs to go back to Jody's garage now." Like we have to fold him up and pack him away.

"In a minute?" asks Cree, which is usually what people say to her when they don't want to do something.

"Yeah, in a minute," says Mac.

"What's a roly?" asks Jackson, still shaking, his skin as pale as raw pork rind.

"She's got this pet snail," Mac explains as we walk back through the market. "Mum won't let her have a rabbit. It's this tiny thing she keeps in a see-through tub at home. You can barely see it."

"Why does she want me to see it?"

Mac sighs. "Because she likes you, I suppose."

Jackson moves his baseball cap slightly and looks down at Cree. "Maybe tomorrow, huh, kid?" Cree nods. She takes his thumb in her hand and he looks confused but lets her and they walk in front of us.

We're walking back through the market and something spooks Jackson. Something spooks me, too, but I pretend not to have heard it. But I hear it again, and this time Mac hears it, too.

That's so him.

We're being followed. Toward the end of the market, where the numbers of people start to thin out, it becomes even more obvious.

Are you sure?

Yeah, it so is. Him what's been in all the papers.

You're having a laugh.

A different voice. *No it ain't, that ain't 'im. What would he be doing here?*

A gasp. *It might be. It looks like him. Get a picture, quick.*

And then we're running, following Jackson's lead, pushing past people, sidestepping strollers and wheel-chairs and bikes, and we're running hard. And the voices are running, too, following us. Mac grabs Cree and shouts, "We'll catch up with you later."

"OK!" I yell. "Shit!" We're at the car jam at the entrance to the market. Jackson takes a running jump onto a Honda and runs all the way over the hood and roof, and down and up onto the next one and down and up onto the next one, and I follow. I'm running on car roofs! *Thump thump bang bang thump thump bang* go our feet on the metallic floors beneath us, Citroëns, Chryslers, Renault Clios, Puntos, a Merc, and each one we climb is followed by a watery thud onto the wet road as our shoe soles land on the other side. Alarm after alarm goes *waa, waa, waa* in our wake, and Jackson's so wiry and fast I can barely keep up with him. I glance behind us. Our followers, the same teenage boys from the lad lot, are being told off by a tall bloke, probably for running on his car. Jackson slows so I can overtake him and guide us home. We sprint down Shepherd's Lane, then take a left, then a right, and finally turn onto Chesil Lane and up the gravel path at the side of our house. Jackson makes it into the garage first and crashes down into the feathers.

"Blimey, that was amazing," I pant, slamming the door behind us. "I've nearly been run over before, but I've never run over a car!"

"Neither have I," says Jackson, puffing and panting almost as much as I am. "God, that felt good. Good to get my legs moving, you know?" Once we get our breaths, we start LOL-ing really badly. "Your face," he says. "You looked so scared."

"Well, yeah," I say, bending over to relieve my stitch. "But you started running first."

"I know." He smiles. He tries to laugh again but it's labored, like he's trying not to be sick.

"I hate to darken the mood. . . ." I say. Feathers flutter down between us.

"I know," he says, smile ghosting from his face. "I've been seen."

I nod. "Probably took pictures on their phones, too."

"What if they were spying for Grohman or something?"

"No, they were just teenagers, local chavs."

"What's a chav? Is that code for something, like the CIA?"

"No, Jackson, they were just kids."

"Yeah, but they could be working for him!" he snaps, getting up and pacing over to the door. "It gets back to Grohman, he'll find me. He'll find me and he'll kill me. 'You try that again, Gatlin, you're gonna wish you'd never been born.' That's what he said to me. He knows people. He knows serious, serious people. . . ."

I go to laugh, because it sounds stupid and paranoid but Jackson's face stops me. "He's not going to kill you," I say. "You're his star."

He looks at me, points a shaking finger, and says, "You need to send those pictures. Now. Then you have to get me away from here."

FIFTEEN
I'M JUST A POOR BOY, NOBODY LOVES ME. . . .

Once a hot story takes, it takes like a flame to a sparkler. It threads its way steadily along until it either burns right out or explodes in someone's face. Usually, on the official Regulators website, pictures from a gig will appear within ten minutes of being taken. I rely on it for all the latest photos and downloads. It's the same with gossip websites, like Loose Lucy. She makes up all this stuff about whoever she wants and Photoshops pictures so people believe it. She'll write things like **JACKSON TO MARRY BRITNEY?** and **JACKSON SEX TAPE: ALL THE DEETS**. Another website, Chaos Theory, bills itself as the "World's Number One Celebrity Stalker Site," advertising that "if a celeb farts in the Arctic, I'll be tweeting it from Texas within ten minutes." They're two of the most fearsome gossip sites on the Net.

Anyway, Mac figures we didn't need to send off the pictures to every single website and newspaper in the world — just a couple of sources will do. So we choose the *National Sunday Press*, the one tabloid that my mum gets because she likes the word quiz, and Loose Lucy.

"We'll e-mail them the photos now. That way it'll be on Loose Lucy's site ASAP, and hopefully we can catch tomorrow's edition of the *Sunday Press*," says Mac.

"Are you sure we shouldn't send it to more places, though?" I ask him.

"No, it's big enough. Trust me. Only takes one match . . ."

"What?"

"Like that song." He then proceeds to sing it. *"Only takes one tree to make a thousand matches, takes one match to burn a thousand trees!"*

Mac keeps singing at full voice but I still don't get what he's on about. And I don't actually need to. By midnight, not only does the *National Sunday Press* website have our pictures, but Chaos Theory, and its whip-cracker Captain Chaos, is all over it. **MISSING ROCK STAR LIVING LA DOLCE VITA!**

By 2:16 A.M., it's on the news crawl on the BBC. **MISSING SINGER SEEN IN ITALY.** By 2:39 A.M., it's on CNN in America. **ROCK STAR JACKSON GATLIN SIGHTED. PHOTO EVIDENCE.** Everyone is going with the same story.

"I can't believe it!" screeches Mac as we scroll through each website in turn in his dressing room at the Playhouse later that morning. Jackson's in Italy. It's official. Probably.

10:14 A.M. — message board of the official Regulators site — **GATLIN IN AUSTRIA.**

10:29 A.M. — message board of Chaos Theory — **GATLIN GOES GREEK.**

10:31 A.M. — message board of The Regulators' Facebook fan page — **IS THIS JACKSON ON THE GREAT WALL OF CHINA?**

10:46 A.M. — a scratchy phone video of Jackson on YouTube, running away down a street with a brown-haired girl. The comments below the clip are all asking where it was taken and the video sneak is saying it's in the West Country but, much to my delight, no one believes it. They're all calling the video a fake. Bargain! "You can't possibly tell it's him," says Mac, swigging back a lukewarm mug of honey water. "At least on our photos there's no denying it *is* definitely him."

"But the more theories, the less people will believe he's still in England. He can lay low."

"No he can't, Jode," says Mac. "He can't stay in your garage forever now that he's clean."

I stare at him. His eyes are still and furiously blue like Jackson's. "He's only *just* clean, Mac. It's not safe yet. If he goes now, he'll be a sitting duck. Grohman sounds like a monster."

"What are you saying?"

"I don't know," I snap, getting up and pacing Mac's dressing room. I go to his clothes rail and run my hand along the sleeve of his black velvet costume.

"You want him to stay, don't you? You've got used to him being here and you're hoping for cozy little chats about art and all that," says Mac, actually reading my brain.

There's a knock on the door. A short, bald man in red trousers, yellow blazer, and bow tie pokes his head round. Geoffrey, director of NAOS.

"Mac, come on, son, we need another run-through while we've got Ann here. She's got to be back at her job by two for the afternoon shift." He disappears again, slamming the door.

"Why's he so antsy?" I ask Mac, who snaps down the

lid of his laptop and marches over to his costume rail to rummage for his Nikes, puffing flames. "Sorry. I'll get out of your way."

"No, it's not you. Got to do my bloody scene with Ann Rackham now."

"Don't you like her?"

"She's OK. But her mustache doesn't half itch."

At home, Mum's ironing in front of an omnibus episode of *Jeremy Kyle* entitled "He Dumped Me During Sex and Now I Want My Kidney Back." After a brief conversation where I reinforce the fact Mum doesn't need to scrape the meat out of the chicken and mushroom pie she's bought for dinner, I tell her I'm going out to the garage for a bit.

"You're spending a lot of time out there lately," she says as I'm going out the door.

I stop dead. Oh. She's noticed. Of course she has. I guess I was hoping that between working, shopping, and dealing with Grandad's will stuff she wouldn't have. She does still live here after all and I am always out there — even in the middle of the night. She must hear. It's not that big a house. I look at her.

She folds over Halley's school shirt on the ironing board and does the other side. "You don't have to talk about it if you don't want to. I'm not snooping."

"Painting," I say, without thinking at all about it. "I've . . . turned it into an art studio." Where did *that* come from? Sometimes the best excuses just pop right out, like really ripe zits.

"Oh," she says, settling the iron down. "Right."

"Grandad suggested it ages ago. Do you mind?" I feel I should ask.

She shakes her head and folds the shirt over again to do the collar. "No, I think that's a lovely idea. Glad you're making use of it."

"Thanks," I say, making to leave again, but again, she stops me with a statement.

"That'll be your space. I'll make sure Halley keeps out as well. We won't go in there."

And I know she means it. "OK. Thanks, Mum." I better do some art and get it out there soon, attempt to decorate my lie at least.

In the kitchen, I'm waylaid by the fridge, where I grab Jackson one of Mum's homemade pasties, some cooked sausages from the fridge, and an apple juice. He's asleep when I get in the garage. I shake his shoulder.

"Mmugh?" he mumbles.

"I've got some news," I say, kneeling down next to him.

"Oh yeah?" He wakes up a bit more and levers himself onto his elbows.

I place the pasty and the plate of sausages on the carpet beside his head. "The story took."

"The Italy thing?"

"Yep. Most of the gossip websites have got hold of it, and the news channels. They all say you're in Italy. They're all showing the photo. They *had* to believe it, didn't they?"

"Yeah." He seems shocked. He sits up fully, blinks his eyes wider, and leans against the wall. His eyes are droopy and shadowed. He looks in pain.

"This is good news, Jackson. It means the journalists will stop poking around England. For now, anyway."

"They won't stop," he says croakily and clears his throat. "This'll just invite more theories, more sightings." He closes his eyes and rubs them. "I'm just so sick of it all. I'll be like some ghost who people will keep saying they've seen. Like Elvis or Cobain. People will be trying to contact me on Ouija boards."

"Well you don't have to answer them, do you? Why worry about it? Besides, you're not exactly Elvis or Kurt Cobain. . . ." I stop myself. OMG, he's going to throw the sausages at me. "I mean, they're legends and you're . . ." He's going to stick them in my ears.

He looks at me. "I didn't mean I'm like them. Who is, for God's sake? I just meant, when people don't get a satisfactory answer to something, they make shit up. They'll still write fiction about me. Where I am, what I'm doing. And who even cares, right? Who the hell am I?"

"You're Jackson Gatlin," I say. And then I realize he was probably being rhetorical. Mac had to explain this to me once as I kept giving him answers to questions he didn't want answering and he got all annoyed and told me he was "being rhetorical."

"Yeah and who's Jackson Gatlin, huh? That wasted singer who can't go onstage unless he's had X amount of pills and X amount of compliments."

"No. That's not you. You've forgotten who you are, that's all."

"Oh, that's all? I know who I am, Jody. You reminded me when you called me an asshole and poured the coffee in my face. . . ." He rubs the back of his head. "Ah, shit."

"What's wrong?"

"I don't know. Did I bang my head?"

"Uh, yeah. We dropped you down the stairs. We were taking you for a bath last week."

"You gave me a *bath*?" He laughs. "Why don't I remember that? Jeez, I remember other stuff. The river and the coffee. And breaking the drums. You should have let me rot, Jody. You should have pushed me in that river and let it be."

I get up and walk to the door.

"Where are you . . . ?"

I'm already halfway up the yard, heading into the kitchen and up the stairs. In my room, I root through drawers for my finished sketch pad and then run back downstairs, as quietly as I can.

Jackson looks up as I reenter the drum room. "Jody, what happened then? Why did you . . . ?"

I sit down cross-legged and present him with the page of my sketchbook I was trying to find. "You've just forgotten who you are. Maybe this will jog your memory." The sketch is copied from an article about The Regs' debut album, *Needful Things*. The original picture was of Jackson and the band sitting beneath this beautiful pink tree, all wearing checkered shirts and boots with no laces. My sketch is just of Jackson, but closer up. He takes it from me and studies it.

"You did this?"

"Yeah. I never thought you'd be the first person I'd show it to."

"You trace it or something?"

"No, well, I copied it. It's from the —"

"The *Rolling Stone* picture? Yeah, I know. It's unbelievable."

I feel my cheeks burn. "I only copied it. I just really love that picture. You look happy."

"I *was* happy. The band was just starting out. It was all so new. That tree's a sakura."

"A saka-what-a?"

"Cherry blossom tree. We went to this signing in Sukagawa, Japan. *Rolling Stone* was there and they wanted to do this interview underneath it. The whole angle of the piece was this kind of 'we're a new band just starting out' thing. This tree was one of like a thousand that had been donated by a neighboring country they'd forged trade links with. It was its first flowering. Kind of a 'new band growing, new tree growing' kinda thing."

"Oh, right," I say, just about getting the link.

"I sat under that tree every night, wrote some lyrics under it. I had nothing but that tree for company at the end of every day, every single day. It felt like this strange, sheltering friend."

His words "strange, sheltering friend" circle around my head. I love the way he puts things. *Strange, sheltering friend*. Like me, I suppose. "Why didn't you hang out with the band?" I ask.

"I did, sometimes. I've lost a lot of weight since then."

"Yeah," I say. "Too much."

"You liked me when I was fat?" he says, incredulous.

"I just don't like seeing you unhappy. Even though it's kind of comforting cos it reminds me I'm not alone." My cheeks blaze. "Sorry."

He smiles, flicking through the other sketches in the book — other ones of him. His face. His eyes. His burning-rose tattoo. "I always wanted to be famous. But now, ugh. I can't turn it off. The other guys just seem to deal with it. Girls screaming in their faces until they throw up. Photographers climbing their fences. Breaking into their houses."

"That's awful. Why do they have to do things like that?"

"D'you buy the magazines with those pictures in them?"

"Yeah."

His eyebrows flick up. "That's why they do it. It comes with the job. I just don't know how to love it."

"You shouldn't *have* to love *that*," I say, all at sea for any other worthwhile comment.

"It's in my contract to love it. I see 'em lining up for *American Idol* auditions in Chicago. They'd give their right arm to have my life. My fame. Well, they can have my fame and keep their right arm. All you see is fake. It's Auto-Tuned, airbrushed acting. You don't see all the crap that goes on in between. I'm told what to wear, how to speak, how to sing, where to sleep, who to be seen with. I'm even told what to eat — 'Be a vegetarian today, Jackson. Be a vampire tonight, Jackson. The fan girls'll love it.' We don't ever stop touring. I hate it. But I'm stuck in it."

"Why don't you leave?" I say, thinking maybe he hasn't thought of it.

"Yeah, 'cause that'd be easy. Since Grohman took over, it's been all about the money. Gotta do these shows, gotta sing these songs in this order. Sometimes I sing something I wanna sing. No music, just me and the crowd. Usually 'Bohemian Rhapsody.'"

"My grandad loved that song. I wish I'd heard you sing it in Cardiff."

"I rock at it. It's my favorite part of the show, because it's my moment. No one tells me to do it. I just do it and the crowd loves it. Sometimes I do 'I Want to Break Free.' Royally pisses Grohman off. It's all about The Regulators brand to him — he doesn't care a dime about me, none of them do. In fact, it's fine by him if I'm doped to the gills. Then I can't answer back."

"So what was all that diva stuff before, with me, then?" I say, pulling my knees up to my chest. "You were ordering me about left, right, and center. You seemed to enjoy that."

He frowns and then breathes out, like the breath could fill a canyon between us. "I probably thought you were a runner. I'm used to ordering them around. Grohman employs them to hang off our coattails. Before you even say you're thirsty, there's a latte in front of you, that kind of thing."

"Bargain," I say. "I'd love that."

He scratches his chin. I hear whiskers grinding against his nail. "It's all over. Getting in the van, gigging, like we did when we first started, like we were doing when that article was written, *that's* music. *That* was fun. When we were kids starting out. It was exciting. Now it's all costumes and sales figures and security guards and what the record company wants. I'll probably end up Paso Dobling against Chachi from *Happy Days* on *Dancing with the Stars.* . . ."

I chuckle. "You've got money, success. Millions of women adore you."

He looks up at me. "Why? I mean, seriously, what is it about me you all love so much?"

I shrug, fumbling for words. I can't think of a single thing to say. It eventually comes to me. "You're our hero. We love how you're like us . . . an outcast. How you don't fit into the hole you've been put into. Like, a square peg."

"I'm like you?" He smiles. "You've met me. You still think I'm like you?"

"Yeah. You talk about it in your lyrics. About being in a world where nobody understands you. About being alone. And we both like art. And books. Stephen King and stuff . . ."

"I'm just a man. I'm not a hero, Jody. My image is engineered. You do know that? I don't mean to be patronizing or anything but you saw me on that DVD, right? Talking about my parents' divorce, Dad's death. Reading books on the bus? You probably went out and bought those books, too, right?"

"Yeah, and I liked them. Well, the Stephen King ones I liked. Mostly. Didn't really get a lot of the poetry. We've got a lot in common. My parents split up as well."

Jackson laughs. "Yeah? Your dad slept with prostitutes? Gave your mom syphilis? Your mom shoot your dad at point-blank range? That what ended it for your folks? What a coincidence."

I shake my head. "No. My dad had a gambling addiction. Mum kicked him out and moved us in with Grandad."

He leans in to me. "My mom kicked *me* out and adopted heroin. Your mom shoot up, too?"

I frown. "No, of course not."

"Don't put your life in the hands of a rock-and-roll band, Jody. We'll throw it all away," he says, looking pleased with himself, as though he's just bowed to an audience and gone offstage. *Fuck you, everybody, good night.*

I laugh, though I'm not sure why. I've heard that before. One of his lyrics perhaps? No, not one of his. It's Oasis. "You must like some people?"

"Not really. I don't get close if I can help it. It's their lack of trustworthiness, I guess."

The sky outside the top window is completely dark now. The only bedside light I could find him was Halley's old baby light display shoved in the coat closet, so I crank it up for him. It flashes out its beams of moons and stars all over the garage ceiling and a tinny little "Twinkle, Twinkle" jingle starts up.

He squints up at it, then back at me. "You look disappointed," he says.

"No, no I'm not," I say, thinking hard about what to say next, now that he's upset my apple cart and eaten every one of my apples. "I didn't really understand you, I suppose."

"Never meet your heroes, Jody. You'll always be disappointed." He looks up at the stars and moons on the ceiling. "They'll either turn out to be complete monsters or complete bores."

"My grandad used to say that. 'The reality will never be as good as the fantasy.'"

"It's true. A while ago I started getting real bad stage fright, just before we went on, like major throw-ups. Sometimes I'd have to go off in the middle of a set, puke, then come back on and sing. Grohman used to have to push me back on sometimes. It was torture."

"Didn't anyone help you?"

"Oh yeah, Grohman helped." He fumbles around on the floor for a pack of cigarettes, then for the lighter. He doesn't say another word until he's lit up and taken a long drag. Half the cigarette turns to ash. "He got me my own personal physician, who'd get me whatever I needed, whatever Grohman thought I needed. But I had to go onstage, I just had to. If I was sick, if I had broken bones, he'd have me full to the brim with painkillers. There was no choice. He had managed this band before that constantly let him down."

I had read about it in *Lungs* magazine. The band was called Eddie's Revenge. The lead singer took his own life on their tour bus during the Warped Tour 2006. Danny Ruffio. Twenty-three.

"Grohman wasn't going to make the same mistake again, I guess. He was the one who got me started on the pills."

"Grohman did?"

"Yeah. He could see me starting to slide on the whole thing, starting to hate it, so he said it was to give me back my confidence, arrogance. Energy. Excitement. Like when you chug an energy drink, you feel like you could bounce off a wall. One pill has the effect of two energy drinks. And then after a gig, I'll take a couple of black ones to bring me back down again, like a rock falling out of the sky. By the time we hit Cardiff, the night we met, I was doing five pills a night."

"Five?"

"Yeah. One wasn't kicking in at all. Two wasn't even cutting it. I got hasty."

"That's when you went offstage. After the first song, I remember you walking off. I thought you were addicted but you cleaned up, stopped drinking and everything?"

"Yeah, Grohman's PR guys put that out there to give people hope. He does this whole spin-doctor thing to make it look like I'm just so psyched to be in the band." He stubs the cigarette out on the wall behind him.

"So you don't enjoy anything about it?"

He looks at me for an endless time. His cheeks dimple and I think he's going to smile, but he doesn't. "I enjoy it when I've had my pills. I hate being addicted to those things, but those things are the only things that let me do what I do."

"But you haven't needed any for the last few days."

"No?" He actually smiles. I haven't seen him smile yet in the flesh, since the night of the concert when he handed me back the moon rock. I can see his proper dimples now and I remember why I wanted him so badly. Now he's smiling at me, without the drugs, without any pretense, and it feels like ten sunrises. He picks up my sketchbook, flicks past pictures of Mac, of my mum, of a bloke in the pub, a woman sitting outside the church smoking a cigarette. Mac in his Riff outfit when he was in the town production of *West Side Story*. "You go to art school?"

"No. I only draw people and stuff."

He flicks to a sketch I did of Mum falling asleep on the sofa. "You should go to art college."

My eyebrows rise involuntarily. "Oh yeah. Total Thrillsville. I hated school. If it wasn't for Mac, I'd never have gone in at all."

"You talk about Mac a lot," he says.

"Yeah. He's ... great. Mac saved you, do you remember?"

"What?"

"When we were coming back from Cardiff. When you had your hissy fit and threw all your clothes over the bridge. He pulled you back. Talked you down. He was amazing."

"I don't recall."

"I'm not surprised. I'd be pretty embarrassed if I remembered doing that."

"You're pretty into Mac, huh?" he says. "It's good that you're so close to him. Your boyfriend should be your best friend." His smile goes dimpled. "Recognize that? That's one of —"

I cut him off. "Yeah," I say. "It's one of your lyrics, from 'Tortuous.' 'Your boyfriend should be your best friend and the song that rocks you to sleep.' Very clever. But he's not my boyfriend, he's just my best friend. Mac's gay, anyway. He likes musicals and wears mascara and carries hand sanitizer around with him and stuff."

"I like musicals. I wear mascara, black nail polish. I'm not gay."

"I know, but —"

"Has he actually ever told you he's gay?"

I think hard for a minute, raking my hand through the feathers on the floor and wading desperately through my mind to find the moment he told me, the day that changed his life. I think back to the last year of school, all those snide remarks from Luke Mabley and those guffawing trolls who couldn't handle the fact that some boys didn't play rugby.

But however much Mabley would rip him, Mac never denied it. He would have denied it if he wasn't, wouldn't he? "He cries at the end of movies," I say, "and that ChildLine commercial."

"So?" says Jackson.

"And he only hangs out with me really because . . . I don't know why, really. I always think he could do better for a best friend than me, but for some reason he's stuck with me. And he used to take ballet when he was little. And he hates sports. And he likes shopping. . . ."

Jackson takes a bite of sausage and then a slug of juice. "Well, he seems to like spending his time with you. And" — he smirks — "look at the features you've picked out on these." He flips through the sketches. "His hands. His smile. His stomach when his shirt rides up . . . you've drawn that a few times. What does that say about you?"

I've gone furiously red in both cheeks and I pray he can't see it in the darkness. He turns past portraits of the bridge that I pushed him off, and my sister playing hockey, and the long shot I did of Grandad in his wheelchair, looking out over the top lake at Weston Park. He shows me the page. "That your gramps?"

I nod. "Me and Mac took him and Cree on all these

day-trips in his last few weeks. The day I drew him, we were at Weston Park. It's this stately home, not far from here. He'd fallen asleep beside the top pond. When we'd gone there months before, he was so full of life. He wasn't in the chair then. He'd gone skinny-dipping in the top pond. Threw his underpants into a tree. We got thrown out. They let us back in again the next time, though, cos they didn't recognize him. He'd changed. You know, he'd got really thin and stuff."

"Huh," he says, lying on the feathers, resting his head on his elbow. "He died recently?"

"Yeah. His funeral was two Tuesdays ago. Everything bad always happens on a Tuesday. My dad left. I got my GCSE results — that's like the main high school exams here, you can leave school younger than in the States. And Grandad got his test results. All on a Tuesday. The day he died, me and Mac took him out."

He frowns. "You . . . took him out? Like Tony Soprano? For real?"

"No, God no. We took him out for the day, on one of our day-trips, me, Mac, and Cree. He wanted to 'do young people things' to cheer himself up. His skin was all yellowy and he was so thin. There was a fair on just outside Bristol so we took him there. He wasn't allowed on the rides. I could see him way down below us in his chair. Cree was asleep on his lap. We tore through the sky on the roller coaster. He looked so sad. He had this toy monkey I'd won, Velcroed at the paws around his neck, and my bag of cotton candy on his head to make him look like he had hair."

Jackson frowns.

"Because of the chemo," I add.

"I know," he says, like that's not what he was frowning about. Jackson's just looking at me. I think he's going to say something else, but he doesn't.

"I remember we were walking past the fountains opposite the Hippodrome and Mac did this dance. He'd just been to a costume fitting for *Rocky Horror* and he was so buzzing. He did this routine to show Grandad and got absolutely soaked in the fountains. 'Don't Dream It, Be It' were the lyrics. He was doing all these thrusts and kicking the water and he took off this old woman's scarf and he was rubbing it between his legs and Cree was getting soaked as well and trying to copy him. It was so funny. People clapped at the end. I've never seen Grandad laugh so much. It looked like it was hurting him to laugh. He and Mac got on great." Jackson's eyebrows rise, then go down again, but he doesn't say anything, so I carry on.

"We went to see the Banksy exhibit at the museum. The queue outside was endless. Grandad pretended to have Tourette's and started flailing about in his chair and swearing so they'd let us in quicker. Grandad liked graffiti. 'Why would you rather see a boring gray wall when someone can put so many colors onto it?' he'd say."

"What an anarchist," says Jackson. "He sounds cool."

"He was. He wanted to go and get a Frappuccino, so me and Mac took him to Starbucks at the top of Park Street, this big steep hill with cool boutiques and cafés down both sides. I couldn't get the wheelchair up the step of the shop so I waited outside on the pavement and Mac took Cree in to change her and get the drinks. Grandad was just looking ahead. Mac came back with the tray and I reached to take my drink, and in that second, Grandad put his hand on mine and whispered, *'Don't Dream It, Be It.'*"

Jackson looks sheepish, blurring into nervous. "And then he . . . fell asleep?"

"No. He pulled the brake off and sped down the hill. I watched him do it. Zooming across side streets, weaving in and out of pedestrians. I heard him yelling all the way down, but it wasn't a frightened yell. It was happy. Like me and Mac on the roller coaster. When we finally got to the bottom of the hill, it was all over. He'd smashed straight through the window of this sex shop and he was covered in . . . frilly knickers and stuff. It was horrible. Local papers had a field day."

"Jeez," says Jackson.

I nod. "He'd tried it a couple of weeks before when we'd taken him to Longleat safari park. Tried to throw himself out of Mum's car as we were driving through the lions."

"Hope I die before I get old," says Jackson with a smile.

"Huh?"

Jackson starts laughing really badly.

"What's so funny?" I ask, really not seeing the joke. I look behind me, thinking maybe something's happened that I can't see. I touch my head, thinking maybe something's on it I don't know about. "My grandad dies and you think it's funny?" I feel the raging sting come into my eyes. This is absolutely the final straw. I'm about to get to my feet and sling his miserable body right out the door when he rolls back onto his side to look at me.

"Your gramps was a *legend*," he says. "Don't you see

what he did? He was dying, a terrible, undignified death, and there was nothing you or he or anyone could do to prevent that."

A tear drops from my eye. "Yeah, I know." I'm trying desperately to wipe my tears away before he sees but they keep dropping and dropping and I can't wipe them away fast enough. And then I'm hoping he *does* see so that he'll reach out and hug me and be all warm.

"You'd had a great day, a day doing all this fun, happy stuff that he could only watch from afar," he continues. "Your grandad knew his time was coming and he didn't just accept it, he beat death to it. He wanted *his* turn on the roller coaster. He'd probably been planning to do that all day. Got the trajectory of his chair just right, heading straight for a sex shop. Legend."

I hadn't thought about it like that before. I'd just thought how it was so like Grandad to do something like that. Something stupid, mindless, something so totally shocking and unexpected of an old man. Something people would talk about and laugh about.

"Better than dying at home, withering away in his bed like some old plant, don't you think?"

"I played 'Bedlam' at his wake," I tell him.

"You did?"

"Not me personally, but I put it on the stereo and . . . had a bit of a food fight. It was such a miserable day and they were playing such shit music. He liked that song. It just seemed right."

"That's so cool," says Jackson. "He sounds like a cool guy."

Suddenly, it is funny. After all this time, all the horrible stuff written about Grandad's accident in the local papers, all my stressing about it being my fault because I didn't notice he'd taken the brake off his wheelchair, it's really funny. We laugh together, like friends, not kidnapper and hostage. He sits up and returns to my sketchbook to finish looking at it. He turns to one of Mac with his full *Rocky Horror* makeup on. "I love that movie. When does Mac's version open?"

"Friday night. The audience dresses up and everything. I've ordered this well slaggy outfit from the costume shop. Maybe you could come and see it?"

"Maybe," he says, rubbing his key necklace.

I sleep with Jackson that night. Not *sleep* sleep, just sleep in the same room as him, on the feathers. We stay up for ages, talking about everything under the moon and stars. Childhood. Work. Parents and the lack of them. Politics, kind of. Climate change. It's so bargain. Such a nice time. And it's the first time I don't want to leave him. It's Jackson without the stink, without the drugs, without the fame, without the fear. I have fantasized about a night like this for so long. This is what I need. *He* is what I need.

SIXTEEN
SOMETHING COMES TO NUFFING

It's Monday. "Halley's back later," says Mum brightly when I go through the façade of walking into the kitchen yawning like I've just come from upstairs where I've supposedly been all night. I see something white out of the corner of my eye — a duck feather. I pluck it from my hair.

There's nothing to say. I know Halley's coming back from her Duke of Edinburgh training hike this afternoon. It's on the calendar. I know this. So I don't say anything.

"It'll be nice to have her back," Mum says. There's a definite spring in her walk, probably due to the fact that all those bills mounting up on the kitchen counter can now be shoved right up the funeral director's or the credit card company's or the gas man's arse. Maybe also due to the fact that she's got a whole new wardrobe. All thanks to Grandad. I'm glad. But I'm not glad that Halley's back. I'd been nursing the hope that her group might lose their compass and get lost on the Quantocks, just for a few more days. Maybe it'll be nice to have her back, it'll be nice for Mum, anyway, but it makes life a bit trickier for me. Hopefully Mum'll drum the whole personal space thing into her and I won't have to worry about her sniffing around the garage. I mean, my "art studio." That reminds me, I must get some art out there soon.

"Have we got any milk?" I say, pulling open the fridge door.

"No, I'm going to go grocery shopping on my lunch break. We seem to be getting through food like nobody's business at the moment." Mum says this a lot, usually as a hint that I must have the "munchies" from all the pot I must be smoking. "Don't stand there with the door open, Jode. You'll let all the cold out." I shut the fridge and start rearranging the magnets instead. "You back to work today?"

"Uh, yeah," I say. Oh, barnacles, it's Monday. Work hasn't even floated across my mind. I've had my "sympathy week" off (holiday, as far as Mum knows) and now I'm due back. I grab a piece of toast that Mum has done for herself and scuttle upstairs to find a work shirt.

I leave the house via the backyard so I can look in on Jackson in the garage. He's asleep, so I leave some orange juice by his head and close the door quietly behind me.

As usual I don't want to go to work, but today it's for the newest of reasons. I can't stop thinking about Mac. He's been on my mind all night, but I still can't unravel it all. What if Jackson's right? How *do* I feel? I don't know. Mac's my friend. He's been my friend for the past two years. What would he be like as a boyfriend? Why would he want *me*, anyway? It did cross my mind once, me and him being together. I've tried testing the gay theory, too. I left a magazine ad open on the breakfast bar, a perfume ad showing this half-naked man, just to look for a reaction. Mac was helping my mum fold laundry at the time. He put a pile of socks right down on it.

• • •

Work is awful. I'm late for a start, which isn't unusual, but it means I get a nice fat bollocking from my supervisor, Ashley, who chews me up and spits me out all over the linoleum in our classroom. We have a diarrhea outbreak, about our third so far this year, which means all morning I'm heaving small people onto changing mats and peeling off shitty Baby Gap jeans.

I'm on floor play over lunchtime, playing with those kids who don't sleep and haven't been sent home with the runs. The two kids who are awake are stabbing each other with wooden spoons from the holistic play tub. I do some crayoning on the craft table but neither of them is interested in joining me. I'm so frustrated I could scream. I don't want to be here. I decide I'll ask to leave early when the supervisors come back from lunch.

And then the sun comes out.

"Dody!" Cree has come in for an afternoon session. Cree's on flexi-time, which means when Mac can't look after her, she comes in to day care. He's obviously busy today, as Tish is looking stressed. I do love it when Cree's in, though, cos it at least means I've got someone to talk to. She has her black-and-white dungarees on and her new white sandals. She runs into my arms and I lift her up for a squidge.

"Where did you been?" she frowns, plucking on my earlobes.

"I've been here, waiting for you," I say to her.

"Why you not been to my house?"

"Uh, well, I've had a lot to do."

"Looking after the Man?"

"Uh y-yeah," I stutter.

"Can I come back to Dody's house and help with the Man?"

"Uh . . . hi, Tish."

"Hi, Jode," her mum smiles as she strokes Cree's ponytail and plonks down a little SpongeBob rucksack and the toy doctor case on a nearby chair. "She keeps on about this man at your house. She's drawn him pictures and keeps going on about showing him her snail. Your mum got a new fella?"

"God no," I laugh, more of a stalling tactic while I think what to say. "Unless she's got someone tied up in the garage I don't know about!"

We both laugh, though it's a little awkward, because of the whole not-a-million-miles-away-from-the-truth thing, and because I've just suggested my mum is a sex offender. "She must mean the man in the moon. We were talking to him the other night, weren't we, Cree?"

"Man in Dody's garage," Cree tells her mum. "Man's my fend."

Tish laughs. "He's your friend is he, sweetheart?" I laugh. It's too nonsensical for further questions and luckily Tish just puts it down as one of those kids-say-the-stupidest-things moments and says no more about it.

"I'll be back about five if that's all right. I've got to do a grocery store run and a few other bits and pieces, so can she have her dinner as well?"

"Tish, I could take Cree home with me and give her something to eat, if you want. I'm going to ask to leave about three o'clock, anyway. You won't have to pay for her, then."

"Oh, that's kind of you, Jody. Yeah, if you don't mind, thanks. I'll send Mac over when he's finished rehearsals at six," she says.

"My Kenzie pick me up," nods Cree.

"Sure that's all right?" asks Tish.

"Yeah, that's fine. We'll have fun, won't we?" I say to Cree and she nods with all her might.

"We go and see Man!" she smiles at her mum and leans out of my arms to kiss her good-bye and give her a brief "I love you but go away now" hug.

Cree clings to me like a barnacle all lunchtime. We play with the matching pairs of cards and do some coloring and she jabbers like she usually does, in her own little language, and for a while I just watch her, wishing my biggest challenge in life was getting the color inside the lines.

We lie down on the reading cushions and she bandages up my head and listens to my "bump bumps" with her stethoscope. The time flies, thank Cobain, cos I'm usually glazing ready for sleep by the time the others breeze back in from lunch at two o'clock. When they finally do come back, I take a deep breath and ask Ashley, or "Asslay" as Cree calls her, if I can leave early.

"No," she says, just like that, scraping her hair extensions off her face with a fake-nailed claw. "We haven't got enough staff to cover you. We're one child over."

Bitch. I flick her a V-sign when her back's turned, niftily turning it into a head scratch when she turns back.

She'd bloody well make sure there was enough staff if she had to go and arrange some more ushers or something for her wedding. So I slump down on the cushions in the book corner for the best part of an hour in a complete and utter sulk, reading to Cree. Ashley's always hated me, ever since I got stuck in one of the toy cars in the playground and had to be cut free. She thinks I'm stupid. I *am* stupid. But at least I'm clever enough to see that her fake hair extensions make her look like a horse. Anyway, I'm mulling this over when I get an idea. I take Cree into the diaper-changing room and sit her on the mat.

"Cree, we're going to play a game, OK?"

I can only do this with Cree because I know her so well and because she does pretty much anything I tell her to. She pulls her dungarees down and I take her diaper off. I take one of the diarrhea diapers out of the bin and get her to hold it right in the corner and go out to the classroom with it in her hand. I nip in the cot room next door to hide and watch through the window. She shuffles into the classroom doing her "I done a bad thing" face. She even delivers the line perfectly.

"My done a runny poo, Asslay."

Luckily, Oscar is awake in his cot so I pretend I have gone in there to get him up and return to the diaper room, completely innocent, to see Ashley cleaning Cree up on the diaper mat, flicking her horsey hair away from her face. Ashley's got her back to me as I walk in. Cree sees me and I put my finger to my lips and she smiles. I'm hoping Asslay is not going to twig that there's no actual poo on Cree, just the nappy, but then that does sometimes happen with very watery diarrhea, I've discovered, it shoots right out. I don't know much but I do know my shit.

"Oh no, not Cree as well," I sigh.

"Yep," says Ashley, huffing. "It's a bad one. It's just flown out of her. You'll have to call her mum. You know her, don't you?"

"She's out. She had to go straight to the grocery store. And her dad's running the pub."

"Oh for God's sake. If I'm ill for my bachelorette weekend . . ."

"I could take her. Then I could leave early and you won't be one child over. If you like?"

Ashley thinks for a second, then turns back to Cree, lifts her up, and pulls up her dungarees over her clean diaper. She strips off her gloves and drops them in the dirty diaper bin. "OK, fine. I'll sign her out for you. You'll take her back to the pub, yeah?"

"Yeah." I hand over a sleepy Oscar to her and she disappears into the classroom. I hold out my arms to Cree and she jumps off the mat into my embrace. We collect up her doctor's kit and rucksack and the pictures from her drawer and then we are out of there. Not so stupid now, Asslay.

"You little star," I whisper to Cree when we're out in the hallway and I give her a little kiss on her ear. Just as I'm about to press the buzzer to be let out . . .

"Are you all right now, Jody?"

"Uh, yeah, fine thanks, Hazel. How are you?" I set Cree down beside me on the doormat. She immediately bends down to investigate a wood louse that's crawled in.

"Did you get your wallet back yet?" Hazel asks me.

"What wallet?" And I'm busted. This little hesitation is enough to pull the plug on all my lies. I have completely forgotten why I told her I wouldn't be in. I'd been thinking I've just been away for the week, but no, I was on sympathy leave, wasn't I? For being mugged.

There's a really shiteous silence. I try and cover it up with a halfhearted joke about post-mugging amnesia, but Hazel's having none of it. "You weren't mugged, were you?"

My cheeks go volcanic. Cree hugs my leg. She can so tell when I'm tense.

I shake my head. "I . . . just don't want to work here anymore." It just comes out. I've been building up how to tell her for months, but I can never do it. And now I have. God knows why now, but I have. I've done it. I've told her.

I'm expecting the bollocking with extra bollocks thrown in for good measure, but it doesn't arrive. Hazel sighs and says, "I don't think your heart's been in it for a while, has it?" And she says it really softly, too. "Since your grandad . . ."

"No," I say. And I'm not lying this time. About the time Grandad got his results, that's when I started giving up on everything. Work was just the thing that got in the way before I was allowed to come home and talk to Grandad or Mac, or listen to The Regulators again. There's nothing else I want to do with my life, but I know I don't want to do this. "Do you need me to work out my month's notice?"

"No, it's OK," she says. "We've got loads of girls wanting part-time work. Just see out the week, OK? It's a shame, though, Jody. The children love you and you're very good with them. When you turn up for work, that is."

I attempt a laugh. "Sorry."

The conversation comes to an abrupt halt when Ashley comes out of the room, butting in to ask if she can have tomorrow morning off for her wedding dress fitting. Cree holds her arms up to be lifted. "We go and see Man, Dody?"

"Yeah, let's go and see the Man."

We get to the gravel path that leads along the side of my house and I immediately see the door to the garage is open. The back door of our house is wide open, too. I squeeze Cree tightly, wondering if Jackson's going to be in a state again. Suddenly I don't want her with me. I want her somewhere safe, but she's two and a half. There *is* nowhere safe. She's in my care. *I* have to keep her safe.

I put her down and we walk through the back door and there's no sign of Jackson.

"Hello?" I call out.

"Man?" Cree calls out. A tinkling in the distance. I hold her hand and we walk through the kitchen to the hallway and stop at the living-room door. I peer inside. And there it is, all over the floor. Millions of china pieces. My mum's bay window full of tacky ornaments is now my mum's *bare* window that *used* to be full of tacky ornaments. Smashed into billions of pieces on the carpet. My sister's hockey stick lies snapped in two on the sofa.

I reverse back out of the living room and shut the door before Cree can see what's happened. I can feel myself sweating as I maneuver her to the bottom of the stairs and grip her hand tightly.

"Hello?" I call out again. My heart thrums like a White Stripes bass line.

"Man?" calls Cree. She looks up at me and I put my finger to my lips. We creep up the staircase, hearing more and more noises as we go. In the bathroom. Something smashes in the sink. Something *boings* against the side of the bath.

Jackson stands before our empty medicine cabinet, glugging down an entire bottle of my mum's Night Nurse. Bottles and packets lie all over the floor and roll about inside the bathtub.

"What are you doing?" is all I can think to say. He's guzzling Night Nurse cough syrup is what he's doing, I can see that. Even Cree can see that. But he's still doing it. He turns to me, dark circles around his stormy eyes in the harsh white light of the bathroom. He drops the empty bottle.

"I needed something," he sniffs. "Something to knock me out. I can't sleep."

"But you're always asleep," I say.

"I woke up!" he cries. "I went in the house. Someone rang the doorbell. I heard it. A woman. She . . . she came around the back. She was calling my name. I need something, just to help me sleep, please . . ."

"No, this is what withdrawal is, Jackson. Mac says you're probably going to get these hallucinations for a while. I saw it in a film. You need to ride it out. Look at this place! What did you do?"

"Ride it out? I can't ride it out, I can't. She was here, goddamn it, I swear she was here!"

"Who?"

"She was blonde and she was wearing a yellow jacket and blue jeans and these ugly shoes. I swear to God she was here, Jody. She said she was from some newspaper. She knows I'm here. I need to sleep! I wanna sleep!"

"Dody," says Cree, behind my leg. That's when he notices her.

"OK, you need to calm down, you're freaking Cree out," I tell him as she hides behind me. "She doesn't understand it and to be honest, neither do I. You were fine last night. You didn't need anything to help you sleep then."

He slumps down beside the bath, as the curved side *boing-cracks* behind him. The little vanity mirror floats in the sink, water sloshing over the edge. "I didn't see her there," he says to me. He starts to cry.

"Why Man crying?" Cree whispers up to me.

"He's not very well," I tell her.

"Man poorly?" she whispers.

"Yeah, Man feels sick."

"Dody make him better," she nods.

I shake my head. I'm just watching him fall apart before my eyes. All over the sight of some journalist. If that wasn't just a hallucination or something.

"Poorly," says Cree, staring at Jackson. I'm amazed it's not bothering her more because he looks like a zombie. But without another word, she puts her dolly case down on the bathroom floor and gets out her Baby All Better Now instruments and sets them out on the floor — a pink thermometer, medicine spoon (with disappearing medicine), nasal aspirator, stethoscope, and bandages.

Jackson looks up at me. "What's she doing?"

"I think she's trying to make you better," I say, scratching my head at quite how he's going to take it. Cree goes over to him with the instruments. I'm on my guard as I always am when she goes up to strangers, especially if that stranger is a detoxing drug addict. He even *breathes* on her wrong and I'll do whatever it takes to keep her safe, I know I will. But it's OK. She puts her little hand on his greasy forehead and he just looks at her.

"Is he hot?" I ask her. She looks up at me and nods. "Does he need medicine?"

"Yeah. My got medicine," she says and bends down to take the toy medicine spoon and puts it up to Jackson's closed lips. He looks at me, then looks at Cree and opens his mouth. She presses a button on the end of the spoon and the medicine disappears.

"There you go," she says, picking up her plastic wipe-clean doctor pad and scribbling down what in her mind is a note for antibiotics.

A tear falls down from his right eye, and then from his left, and his head dips onto his knees.

"Cree," I say and she comes back to me and takes my hand. Jackson's sobbing, really sobbing fat wet tears onto Grandad's never-worn track pants. I bend down beside him. "You made a real mess downstairs." He nods again. "You smashed all my mum's china ornaments." He nods again. "My mum's ugly china ornaments." He looks at me. "Thank you."

He looks so tired. "You do believe me, about the woman who was here?"

"Yeah," I say, wavering. I don't really know that I believe him but I daren't tell him that.

"I was wide-awake. And I saw her. I went in to use the toilet and she was ringing the doorbell for a long time. I went back outside and locked myself in the garage but she came into the yard. I could hear her through the cat flap. She was calling out her name, saying she was from a newspaper." He rubs away a trail of water from his nose. "Please believe me."

"All right, OK. I believe you." I lean in toward him and envelop him in my arms as much as I can, like I'm trying to gather up a big pile of wood shavings, but he falls apart in my arms. He doesn't hug me back — Jackson still doesn't do hugs, whether he's terrified or not.

"Please, get me away from here. I don't care how you do it. I need to go somewhere where nobody knows me."

"Where's that?"

"I don't know!" he shouts.

"OK, OK. I'll figure it out, don't worry."

OK, let's assume for a second that Jackson's not lying, not hallucinating or dreaming. *Who* is this yellow-coated woman, *why* was she calling out his name, and *what* was she doing in my yard? What if he had been in the yard? She could have *spoken* to him. He could have run off again or, at worst, she could have blown this whole thing wide open and Jackson would have to be Jackson again, not plain old Man.

I'm in the kitchen making grilled cheese and Cree's drawing on the kitchen tiles with the chalk from Mum's shopping board. And I'm thinking things over. Thinking about Jackson and how hard he pleaded with me to get him away. *I don't care how you do it,* he said. He'll take anything. He's desperate. So that makes me desperate. And already the cogs are turning.

Bang. Clatter. The front door slams. I look at the clock. Oh shit. It's four already. Halley's home. I hear the tin mugs on her rucksack clanging against the wall in the hallway.

I turn off the grill and get the cheese sandwich out and leave it on the side. I bend down to Cree's height. "Shall we go and get my tin?" I ask her. She nods and reaches her arms up for me to pick her up. I have an old cookie tin filled with Hello Kitty trinkets and cutesy little knickknacks and novelty pencil tops and smelly erasers that I've collected over the years. Cree thinks it's the most magical thing in the world. It's guaranteed to keep her busy for a little while.

I hear a gasp in the living room as we reach the hall. I grab the cookie tin from under the stairs and hand it to Cree, who runs into the kitchen and sits down on the floor with it. In the living room, the bits of broken ornament lie untouched, Halley stands looking at it all in her tracksuit, her face as pale as the hideous china bell that lies smashed at her feet. She jumps as she sees me.

"Oh my God, Jody. We've been burgled!" she cries.

"No we haven't," I say, turning and going back into the kitchen to get the dustpan and brush from the cupboard under the sink.

She's still crying when I return to the living room. "Look at it," she sobs. "All Mum's ornaments. And . . . my hockey stick."

"I did it," I say, kneeling down carefully on the carpet and picking up the larger shards of china. I take yesterday's paper from the magazine rack and start wrapping it all up.

"What?"

"I did it. I broke them all. And your hockey stick. I was angry about Mum getting rid of Grandad's stuff and I was angry with you for just standing by and letting Mum do it and I just broke them all." I turn around and look at her. "So go on, call Mum. Tell her what I've done. Then you can get another gold medal for snitching, can't you?"

I go back to picking up the china bits, and a moment later, I hear her knees creak and she kneels down next to me and begins to help. "I won't tell her," she sniffs.

"You so will. You'll have to tell her something, you won't be able to resist."

"We'll make something up," she says. I catch her eye, offering her some newspaper to lay the broken pieces on. "I didn't want her to get rid of his stuff, either, but you know what she's like. I wanted to keep that little rock he used to have. The one he said fell from the moon. I went to get it out of the bags the night before the collection but I couldn't find it. Every time I asked Mum about it, she just snapped at me. She can't even go in his bedroom. It's like she just wants him gone from everywhere, even though this was his house."

I say nothing. She'll be hunting the moon rock down if she knows I've got it.

"I mean, most of his stuff was pretty rank, wasn't it . . . but . . ."

"It wasn't rank," I snap.

"I didn't mean rank, I just meant, like, well, stuff you wouldn't want to hang on to. Like his bongs and his smelly old books and his weird clothes."

I huff. "Whatever."

"You must be so angry with Mum, Jody, to do all this. I didn't realize."

"Yeah. Well, now you do."

"You've always been the favorite, for Mum and Grandad. Even Dad. You're the Golden Child."

"What? How am I the Golden Child?" I cry. "You were there when I opened my crap GCSE results. I've just walked out of a dead-end job. I've got a criminal record for disorderly conduct. And as for Dad, don't you think he'd have been in touch in the last year if I was his favorite?"

She swallows. I think in some sadistic way, this has made her feel better. Her face relaxes, though the tears still rain from her eyes.

"It's not because I'm some kind of favorite, Halley. It's because I'm a walking disaster. I'm always something to be concerned about. Mum doesn't have to worry about you with all your Duke of Edinburgh achievements and trophies. You're the Golden Child for her."

"What about Liam-slash-Sid, the truck driver?" she says.

"Oh, yeah. I forgot about Sid." We both sort of smile.

Halley frowns, her head dipping. She shuffles up the carpet on her knees and takes the dustpan. She starts brushing away at the smashed china. "She made you a veggie burger both nights when you went to the pub, just in case you came back. And she cried in her sleep."

We catch each other's eye. Halley and I couldn't reach an understanding if it was an inch away, that's how I thought it would always be. But this little moment is good. I have a feeling a little fire has been put out.

"I'll buy you a new hockey stick," I say. "That Nike one you've had your eye on."

She smiles. "You don't have to. Get me a ticket for the next Regulators concert or something. We could go together."

"Oh, yeah. Don't know when that's likely to be, though."

"No, I suppose they'll have to find him first, won't they?" she chuckles, wiping her cheek.

I pause for a second, the weirdness of what she's just said ringing in my head. She helps me finish clearing up the broken bits and even insists on devising a plan to get me off the hook with Mum. She takes the sample pots of peach paint off the mantelpiece and hands one to me. She then proceeds to paint over the bare wall. I follow her lead, filling in the gaps until we've painted the whole section. She goes to the window and opens it on both sides.

"And then a gust of wind came and . . . whoops! Sorry Mum," she shrugs.

I laugh. "If I tell her that, there's no *way* she'll believe me."

"She'll believe me. I've got a clean record . . ."

". . . apart from Sid."

"Yeah, apart from Sid. But she won't have a go at me nearly as much as she would you."

Who'd have thought it? My own little cow bag of a

sister, bailing me out. I have spent years thinking one of us was adopted because we don't look or behave alike, and suddenly we're like the two talking peas in the pod on that frozen vegetable commercial.

At 6:31 P.M. precisely, while we're enjoying our roast beef dinner for Halley's homecoming, the doorbell *bing-bong*s. Mac has already come to get Cree, I think nervously, so it can't be him. And there's that plunge of dread again.

SEVENTEEN

99 PROBLEMS BUT THE SNITCH AIN'T ONE

I pray that the kitchen TV is on loud enough so that Halley and Mum haven't heard it. But they have. Halley has.

"I'll get it," she says, still in baby-girl-hasn't-seen-Mummy-for-a-week mode.

"No, I will," I say. "It'll be Mac. He said he was coming over later." Halley stops in her tracks and sulkily gets back up on her stool. Mum has a mouthful of cabbage.

I see the shadow through the glass in the door the second I step into the hall. She's on our welcome mat. I can see the yellow of her coat. I close the kitchen door behind me and make my way slowly down the hall to face the object of Jackson's terror. I open the front door.

"Hello," she smiles, showing a mouthful of pure white teeth like a piano lid opening. "Could I speak to Jody please? I've got the right house, haven't I?"

She seems nice enough and very pretty. She's got all the hallmarks of every guy's dream woman — perfect curves in her casual yellow-jacket-and-blue-jean combo. Her face is pieced together as perfectly as a new peach. Full red lips, petite nose, long eyelashes, blue eyes, and the whitest blonde hair. Behind her is a bright pink Volkswagen Beetle, like a giant bubble-gum balloon.

"Uh, who are you?" I say as politely as possible, smiling as best I can.

"Oh, I'm Sally Dinkley," she giggles, her voice squeaky and children's TV host–ish. I don't know why she's giggling. "Did you get my card? I put it through the mail slot this morning." She laughs again, flashing her glittering teeth. Am I supposed to laugh? I look around behind me on the floor. A little white card is poking out underneath the doormat. I bend to pick it up.

SALOME JANE DINKLEY
WEST COUNTRY CHRONICLE
REPORTER

Her contact details are on the back. Mobile phone. E-mail. Skype address. She continues. "I am talking to Jody, aren't I? You e-mailed some pictures of Jackson Gatlin to the *National Sunday Press* from your Hotmail account? Well, the paper I work for, the *Chronicle*, has picked them up. I called by this morning but no one was in."

The security light decides to come on above my head. Bit late, seeing as the squeaky-voiced intruder and I are already mid-conversation. "Yeah, yeah, I was at work. Sorry."

She laughs, again. It's not even funny. I guess it's a nervous thing. "Silly me, silly Sally. *Doink!*" She shoves the heel of her hand against her forehead in a "stupid me" gesture. "Well, I thought it might be a good time to call around and have a word with you. Is now OK?"

Her face stays smiling like a waxwork dummy, even

when she's stopped talking. It's terrifying. It unnerves me so much I'm stuttering. "Uh, we-we're in the middle of dinner. It's not really convenient."

"Oh. Right. Well, I'm staying in Nuffing, so perhaps I could stop by tomorrow morning?"

"I've got to work. Why do you want to talk to me about it?" This is a whole different story now, it isn't an e-mail to a faceless, nameless journalist miles away in London. This is a real-assed journalist on my doorstep and I'm hiding a celebrity about fifty feet away.

"Well, basically," she says, eyes alive like she's telling a story about a magical elf in an enchanted wood, "we were very excited at the *Chronicle* when we saw those pictures and I wanted to have a chat with you about them. I grew up near here, actually."

"Oh, really?" I say weakly, though I don't intend it to sound quite so sarcastic.

"Yeah," she says merrily, like we're old friends or something, "in Randle-on-the-Wold. Anyway, I saw your pictures in our pressroom when I was hanging around our news editor's desk. Everyone was going crazy of course, but, well, I was a bit confused."

"Oh, why's that?" I say, praying she can't hear my heart tub-thumping its way up my throat.

"Well," she giggles, "it's very odd, I know, but the pictures don't seem quite right to me. And I wondered if you could shed any more light on that." Her face freezes, and it becomes clear that she's not going to say anything else until I have.

I frown. "In what way? I mean, I saw him myself.

He was just sitting there, at this table, eating, reading a paper. . . ."

"In Italy?"

"Yeah." I remember Halley's bags are still lined up in the hallway behind me, so I open the door a bit wider for Dinkley to see. "I've just come back."

"Oh. Right. Well, it's so bizarre, I mean, I can't even believe I'm saying it, but . . . are you sure you took the pictures in Italy?" She laughs and it's echoey, like a cave laugh. I'm not laughing.

"Yeah. I think I would remember where it was taken."

"Of course, of course. How was the weather?"

"Oh, OK."

"Didn't go outside much?"

"Yeah, why?"

"Well, you're not very tanned." She smiles and chuckles.

"I don't tan easily," I say. "It's my freckles."

"Right, right. Well, in that case I must ask have the pictures been Photoshopped in any way?" She says it as a throwaway comment, thinking she shouldn't really be asking but is obviously desperate to. "Was this all a joke is what I want to know." Her smile drops like wet rags.

"No. I don't even know *how* to Photoshop stuff. Look, me and my friend were walking through this market one day in Venice and Jackson was just sitting there, reading this paper. My friend got his phone out, took some pictures, and then he went off. Jackson, I mean."

"Just walked off? Just like that?"

"Yeah."

"Who is this friend that went with you?"

"Mac . . . I don't want to drag him into it, OK?"

"Oh sure, sure. Look I'm not trying to pry, I'm just trying to get to the truth. You must want to know the truth about what's happened to Jackson Gatlin, don't you? Everybody else in the world does. This is a very big deal, Jody."

"It's not that big a deal, is it?"

She gawps at me. "Uh, yeah it is. Jackson Gatlin's disappearance is big news. He's a big star, ever since he slept with that what's-her-name from that film with whatsit DiCaprio."

"That was a lie."

"How do you know?"

"I d-don't," I stammer. "I just don't believe everything I read in the papers." I gulp. What have I said? I'm itching to step back inside. The breeze along our path is whipping up now that the sun's gone down and I'm hungry. I think about the half-eaten roast going cold on my plate.

"Everyone's very worried about his well-being, too. His fans, his friends, his bandmates, his manager. I mean, he just vanished. No explanation. Gone. *Poof.* No note. Nothing."

Or rather *Nuffing,* I think to myself. "Yeah," I say. "It's been on the news."

"How did he seem to you when you saw him? You said he was eating something?"

"Uh yeah, a pizza."

"Flavor?"

"Pepperoni, I think."

"Are you sure it was pepperoni? Jackson is a vegetarian, you know. Maybe the sausage was vegetarian sausage, do you think?"

I do some speedio thinking. "There were little pieces of pepperoni on his plate. He'd taken them off the pizza. It must have been a pepperoni pizza." Dinkley nods. Phew. But . . .

"Why would he order a pepperoni pizza if he then took the pepperoni off?"

My teeth clamp down. "I don't know. Maybe he doesn't speak Italian very well."

"So why would he be reading an Italian paper?"

"Look, I was just there. We just happened to be walking through. We saw him, we took some pictures, and we left. That's it."

"OK." She pulls her jacket in around her as the breeze whips up a little more. "Any chance I could just come in for a sec —"

"No," I say, more harshly than I mean to. "Sorry, I've really got to go."

"Fine, fine," she says, taking out a small black pebble thing that looks like Mac's iPod and rubbing the screen like she's dusting off flies. She taps it. Lines appear on the screen. She's writing notes. "I'm not saying you know any more than me," she smiles, "it would just be good to get your slant on it, being such a big fan and everything. Don't you think?"

"Why do you want my slant on it?"

She does that *doink* thing again. "So sorry, Jody, did I not say? I'm doing a follow-up article about where *I* think

Jackson is. See, I don't think he's gone to Italy at all. I think he's somewhere round these parts. Somewhere in the West Country. I mean, just for argument's sake, let's say you got your pictures muddled up when you got back from Italy. You went to the Italian Market on Saturday in Nuffing town center and saw Jackson Gatlin there. You uploaded your photos on the computer and, for some reason, you thought you'd seen him in Italy, but in fact you'd seen him in the Italian Market *here* instead. Quite likely, isn't it?"

She's like a retriever who's got the whiff of a dog biscuit in my pocket. She knows something. I have to front this out. I have to throw her off the scent. I have to pretend to throw it far away so the bitch'll run after it. I wish Mac was here. He'd know exactly what to say to shut her down. Nothing fazes him.

"I think I know the difference between Venice and Nuffing High Street," I say. "Why would you even think that?"

"Well, two reasons really," she says. "For one thing, at the front of your picture there's a flyer on the ground for the Italian Market in Nuffing."

"Uh . . ." She must have held that photo under a pigging microscope.

"And two, the Italian guy standing behind him in the photo? He runs the pizzeria in Nuffing High Street. I grew up in Randle and I went to school for a time in Nuffing. Me and my friends always used to go down to Salvo's at lunchtime, you know, how girls do, go in just to sip Cokes at the bar and ogle the waiters? Well, that man in the photo is Salvo. He's well known in these parts." She giggles so shrilly it's sending electric shocks up and down my back. "So, do you think you could help me figure this one out?"

"I'm sorry, I don't think I can," I say, reaching behind me for the door.

"Jody, wait, please. I just want to know which parts of the photo are true and which are falsified, that's all." She's talking to me so soothingly, it's like she's telling me I've got a tumor or something. "We just need to know the truth. His fans deserve to know where he is, don't they?"

"If you want to know the truth, no, I don't think they do," I snap. "Why can't you leave him alone?"

"Because he is a major celebrity and that makes him public property. And because the public is worried about him and it's my job to find out if he's OK. He has a history of depression. Drugs." She says it quietly, as though saying it will offend our neighbors.

"So?"

"I have insider information that when he supposedly went into rehab a couple of years ago, he actually tried to commit suicide. Threw himself off a bridge. He was fine but . . . well, there was brief talk that he'd tried it again but with the arrival of your photo it's given everyone hope that he's OK, happy even. That he's just taking a break from it all. Do you know what I mean?"

I nod, praying that neither Mum nor Halley comes out of the kitchen to see what's keeping me. I hear the *clink-clink* of plates being scraped.

"I mean, wouldn't it be great to finally find him?" she says. "To be the one to tell all his fans he's all right, *happy* even." She's looking at me like I'm an abused puppy on one of those anti–animal cruelty commercials. "Just have one final think, Jody. I'll give you another chance, OK? Where is he?"

Where is he? Not where *was* he, or what do you think happen*ed*. Where *is* he, she asked me. She knows!

"It's OK," she says, "no one's going to be angry. If you're protecting his privacy, that's very honorable. But why are you protecting him? What does he want with you? Do you owe him something? Are you related to him in some way? Did he threaten you just after the photos were taken? Did he get violent? Where's the phone the pictures were taken with? Did he break it?"

"No . . ."

"Look, I'd probably do the same if Michael Bublé decided he wanted to leave showbiz and join some circus or something. If I found out where he was and he asked me to keep his location private, I would."

"Michael Bublé?"

"My mum listens to him in the car." She laughs. "Probably a bit old for you. But listen, if you've seen Jackson Gatlin in Nuffing, though God knows why he's in Nuffing, then you can talk to me. I will tell everyone exactly how it is. And who knows, maybe I can get hold of some tickets for their American tour? Maybe plane tickets? Bit of swag? Yeah?"

She's onto something, she knows she is. She's pulling every trick she can think of. Strumming on my heart-strings. Interrogation. Bribery. She's like a kid reaching for a bite of a cookie. She's going to keep coming back until she's got a bite and, when she's got a bite, she'll want the whole cookie. She'll want to speak to Jackson, she'll want to break the story. She'll want to bring him back to the world so he can go back to where he was before I took him away from it. But he won't want that. He'd rather die. I can't think what to say. I have to speak to Mac.

And at that moment, I love my mum more than anything else in the world.

"Jode, d'you want custard or cream on your crumble?" she calls. For once, her voice sounds like a thousand beautiful notes rising into the air, not one dirty black cannonball falling on my feet.

"OK, look, I've really got to go, that's my mum."

"I'll come by tomorrow, then. Perhaps we can grab a coffee in town? Or maybe a pizza?" She winks.

"Yeah, all right," I force out. I don't know what else to say.

"OK, I'll meet you at the Whistling Kettle in the High Street. About one o'clock."

"Yeah. OK."

"Great, oh, that's so great, Jody. You won't regret it. And it's on me, OK? Least I can do," she says, with another patronizing wink.

No, it's on me, I think. It's all on me now.

"Who was that?" says Mum when I reenter the kitchen. "You've been gone ages. I put the rest of your dinner under the grill."

"Jehovah's Witnesses," I blurt. "One of them was cross-eyed. I felt bad." It usually *was* Jehovahs whenever I answered the door, so this was a nice neat excuse to throw out on this occasion. I never had the heart to tell them to leave or to slam the door in their faces. Except when one of them tried telling me Grandad was wanted for an angel and I had a right go at them. "I don't believe in angels," I told them, "I just believe in Jackson." And then I shut the door in their faces.

Now look where my religion has got me.

My last potato and few carrots have gone all shrivelly under the grill, so I gollop down my strawberry-rhubarb crumble and race straight upstairs to call Mac, only his phone goes to bloody voice mail. Rehearsals tonight, I forgot. It's the performance on Friday.

"Shit," I say, my frantic heartbeat the only sound in my ears. She bloody knows!

I can't go out and check on Jackson until after ten o'clock cos Mum is fannying about at the dishwasher and Halley's doing the laundry from her camping trip in the utility room. He's OK, though. I take him out some leftover dinner and crumble with custard and a couple of games to play — Connect Four and Operation. I've been trying to rotate his toys like we do with the children at work, to keep him entertained. When I go in, he's drawing on a sketchbook I've given him.

"Oh hey," he says. He accepts the food and scarfs all of it down, apart from the pieces of soggy rhubarb in the crumble, which he leaves lined up around the edge of the bowl. I just watch him and listen to his guzzling sounds. There *is* no good way to tell him about Dinkley so

I don't think I'll mention it. He'll have another sick-fit. I don't want to see that crumble again.

He has a little bit of color in his cheeks when he's done eating. "Any news?"

I shake my head and smile. "No, no news."

EIGHTEEN

JODY POTHEAD AND THE HALF-ASSED SNAIL

I have to wait until the next morning on my walk to work before I can talk about the Dinkley Bombshell to Mac. After the ninth attempt, he answers his phone.

"Mac, thank God, where have you been?"

"I'm at the Playhouse," he says. "We're so busy. We were doing this scene last night and there was this almighty crash and half the scenery came down. We've spent half the night fixing it. We all had to pitch in and —"

"A reporter came to the house yesterday. Jackson saw her through the window. She came back last night and asked me about a billion questions. Mac, she knows, she knows he wasn't in Italy."

"Whoa, how?"

"One of the photos. There was a bloody flyer for Nuffing Market on the ground and she recognized the Italian bloke at the counter. What the hell am I going to do? She's staying at the Torrance. She's determined to sniff him out." There's a long silence. I can hear Mac's breathing. "Hello?"

"Yeah, I'm still here, I'm thinking. What did she look like? She might have been in the pub."

"Bleached blonde hair, a yellow Primark jacket like Halley's got, five-inch heels, skinny . . ."

"Tell me everything she asked."

"I can't, I'm already late for work. She wants to meet me for lunch at the Whistling Kettle. Can you come to the day care center before one?"

"Yeah. I'm at the Playhouse 'til then, anyway. Then I've got Cree so she'll have to tag along as well. I'll try and nip out to check on Jackson in a bit. Nobody'll be home, will they?"

"No. Mum's in Cardiff of all places at some work seminar and Halley's at school until seven for netball."

"Right, I'll be at the day care about twelve, then. 'Kay?"

"'Kay," I say and off he goes.

All morning at work, Dinkley's in my brain like a head-banger's headache. Her words *Where is he? Why are you protecting him?* are on a constant loop. As bad days go, it's another world-record-beater. Snotty noses and shitty arses a-go-go and Ashley barely speaks to me, except to bark orders. Even the part-timer is looking at me like she's on the ghost train and I've just sprung out of some crevice. I think they're all secretly glad I'm leaving. At least then they might get some enthusiastic college student filling my shoes who actually turns up on time. The children I'm responsible for today are Kezzy, Mitch, and Jaden. Lovely. All bases covered — one to cough in my face, one with chronic thrush, and one who screeches in my arms until his mum comes back for him at lunchtime. Superb.

In fact I'm holding Jaden (plus taggy blanket, teddy, blankie blanket, bottle, and sticky pacifier) when the door buzzer goes at 11:30 A.M. That'll be Mac. I hand Jaden over to the part-timer, whom he promptly has a nice kicky tantrum on, and catch sight of Ashley glaring at me through her false eyelashes.

"I'm just saying hello to Cree," I explain. She seems to accept this but, quite honestly, I wouldn't care if she didn't. What's she going to do? I have like three days left so I'm zero bothered.

"Dody!" says Cree and her whole face lights up as she sees me. I can always count on her to make me feel good. I lift her up and she snuggles in, then pulls back and grabs my earlobes as usual when she wants to talk to me, woman to woman. "Dody, my brought my snell today."

"Did you? Where is he?" I say, looking at Mac, who is carrying Roly's see-through plastic animal carrier. All I can see is grass and a few twigs inside. "Is he asleep?"

Cree shakes her head.

"She thinks he's d-e-a-d," Mac spells out with a wry smile. "But she's not sure. She wants to ask 'the Man' for his opinion." He rolls his eyes.

"Man wants to see my snell," Cree explains. "He won't come out of his shail." She sighs. "He just won't come out."

"Maybe the magic Man can talk him out, yeah?" I say to her and she snuggles in again. "Did you see him?" I ask Mac.

"Yeah," he says, adjusting his beat-up black fedora on the back of his head and checking his hair in the porch mirror. "I looked in on him on my break. He wanted the loo but your back door was locked."

My heart hurts. "Oh no. I forgot to leave it open for him."

"He's fine. He took a piss in the flower bed."

"Stunning. On my mum's polyanthus I suppose."

Mac smiles. "Give me your key. I'll go back and unlock the door for him."

"No, I'm coming, it's fine. Wait here a minute. . . ."

I go back into the classroom with Cree in my arms and stride across to the coat hooks to get my bag. "Is it OK if I take my lunch now, Ashley?"

"It's not twelve o'clock yet," she says, looking up from her Play-Doh birds' nest, which Mitch proceeds to bash with his fist the moment her face is turned.

"It's an emergency," I say, which it kind of is. I mean, if Jackson's got to go, he's got to go, and there are limits when it comes to my mum's flower bed. I hear no further argument, which doesn't mean there isn't any, since once the door is shut I would put money on the fact that they all start bitching about me.

We walk back to my house and look in on Jackson. Cree immediately runs in with Roly's animal case and shows him. "My brought Roly."

"Hi. Sorry, I forgot to leave the door open," I tell him.

Jackson puts the book he was reading down by his side and takes the animal carrier from Cree. "Where is he? I can't see him."

She shakes her head. "He won't come out. Fink he's died-ed."

Jackson peers into Roly's carry case, squinting like he's conducting an experiment. "Nah, he's probably just asleep." He looks up at me. "Is it OK if I take a shower?"

"Sure, yeah, of course, absolutely," I say. "I'll go and get everything ready for you."

·"Come on, Creature," says Mac, holding his hand out

for his sister, but she sidles up to Jackson. "No, my want Man to make Roly come out."

Jackson gets to his feet and shakes off the feathers. "He probably just needs some new leaves or something, Cree. We'll go and find some, okay?"

She nods, staring up at him like he's Santa Claus, and they both walk past us out into the yard, where they start foraging around in the flower bed for bits and pieces for the snail, Cree hanging on to Jackson's hand all the while. I can tell Mac's not happy about it at all as he follows me into the kitchen. "So who's this reporter, then, and when are you going to tell him you've talked to her?" He jerks his head toward the yard when he says "him."

"Her name's Sally Dinkley. And I'm not going to tell him. Yet. One mention of the word 'reporter' will tip him over the edge, and I've only just yanked him back from it."

"Sally Dinkley?" says Mac as we begin up the stairs. "That's definitely her name?"

"Yeah. Why?"

"I went to school with someone called Sally Dinkley."

"She said she went to Nuffing for a bit."

"Yeah. She was a few years above me, though. Left before you came."

"She's just starting out as a journalist, apparently," I tell him. "I've seen her gossip column in the *Chronicle* — she just talks about the different lipsticks she's tried and who she thinks the mayor might be shagging." I search for fresh towels.

"I think he ought to know, Jode. So he can prepare if she comes around again."

I walk into Mum's bathroom and get some shower gel. Mac follows me in. He's standing right behind me when I turn around. "You just want him gone."

He shrugs. "Yeah. I can't lie, I do want him gone. The longer he's here, the worse this is going to be. For you, in the long run. But you should tell him about Dinkley. Just so he's aware."

"No, there's no point. Anyway, he's seen her. He's already on high alert. If she comes around here again he'll be able to avoid her."

"Jody!" a voice calls.

I look at Mac. Mac looks at me. We both turn to stone. It's not Jackson's voice. It's not Cree's voice. It's not even Mum's voice. It's Sally Dinkley's voice. And it's coming from outside.

I turn and peer through the bathroom window. You know that saying "speak of the devil and he appears"? That's exactly how it feels. Like we have the devil herself standing in the middle of my backyard, calling up at the window. Except this devil wears Primark.

"Oh my God," I say with the small amount of breath I can muster.

"Where's Jackson?" asks Mac, peering slowly out the window.

"Where's Cree?" asks Me.

We both leg it downstairs, through the kitchen and out the back door. It's starting to rain. Dinkley's standing underneath a pink umbrella in the center of the yard like a large scary garden gnome, still in her yellow jacket, her designer heels sinking slowly into the damp grass.

"Oh, Sally, hi," I pant. There's no sign of Jackson or Cree anywhere. "Sorry, I thought we were meeting —"

"At one o'clock, yeah I know, sorry, I thought I'd see if you were here first and walk down with you if that's all right? Not quite sure where it is. I think it's relocated."

"No, it's still where it's always been," I pant.

"Oh." She does the *doink* thing with her hand on her forehead. "Should have known. Well, anyway, I'm here now. What a lovely house you've got."

"Thanks."

"And who's this nice young man?" she smiles, shielding her hand over her eyes to look at Mac, who is just as out of breath as I am.

"Mackenzie," he says, offering his hand like he always does when he meets someone new. "You used to go to Nuffing Comp, didn't you?"

"Uh, yes. I thought I knew your face," she says, batting her eyes.

Mac blinks. Droplets of rain hang on his eyelashes. "You were on the school magazine committee."

And then she snaps her fingers like she's plucking a thought out of the air. "Got it. On a poster I just walked past."

"Oh yeah, *Rocky Horror.* We're putting it on at the Playhouse on Friday night."

I bring the conversation back to its point. "I'm sorry but I can't talk to you now, I'm afraid," I say to her, not in the least bit afraid or sorry. "Something's come up, so . . ."

"Oh, Jody, you are quite a noodle, aren't you?" She laughs but her eyes don't. I can tell she's getting pissed off with me.

Mac points at her. "You left Nuffing Comp a year early, didn't you?"

"Good memory! My family moved."

"Why was that?"

"Well, I think that's probably a story for another time," she chuckles. "Jody, I'm afraid we really must speak because I've got to get my article in by seven o'clock tonight at the very latest or else it won't make tomorrow's edition. Just five minutes?" she says, looking around the yard, her eyes settling on the drum room. The door is open. She must have seen him in there with Cree — there's no way she couldn't have. She gets out her electronic pebble and starts dusting it again.

"No, I tell you what," I say, thinking of a bone I can throw her. "Mac's dad owns the Pack Horse, it's a pub just up the street. It's open all day. Why don't you meet us there about six? Then we can get everything out in the open and —"

"Marvelous," she says, "yep, that would be perfect for me. I'll bring my laptop and we'll do the interview and I can e-mail it straight off. And maybe we could do some photos, somewhere picturesque?"

"The restaurant's got a garden with some pampas grass?" suggests Mac.

"Lovely," she says, putting her pebble thing in her satchel. "Well, I'll drop by around six-ish, then, OK?"

"Fine," I say.

"Great," says Mac. "And we can talk about school days. Happiest days of your life and all that." Her smile wipes from her mouth.

She wanders slowly toward the far end of the yard and

just as she gets to the drum room, she glances inside. To my amazement, she keeps on walking around the corner and out of sight.

"Where the hell's Cree?" says Mac, forehead stretching back in alarm.

Once my heart restarts and my legs remember how to bend, I run to the open door of the drum room. No Jackson. No Cree. It's just the feathers. And books. And the bucket. With any luck she'll have thought we keep ducks in there or something.

"It's empty."

We run inside the house, into the empty kitchen, empty dining room.

"If he's touched her, if he's touched one hair . . ." Mac's threatening as we go into the living room, and we both let out a sigh of utter relief as we see Jackson cross-legged on the carpet and Cree, next to him, cross-legged on the carpet, and on the carpet before them sits a leaf. And on that leaf sits a tiny snail shell.

"Oh thank God," says Mac, bending down beside Cree and putting his hand on her head.

I'm still panting. "Did you see her?" I say to Jackson.

"Who?"

"The woman, the reporter. Sally Dinkley."

Jackson gets to his feet, his face draining of all color. "No. She was here again?"

"Yeah, in the yard. She was in the yard. You were outside. You must have seen her."

"It started to rain. Your sister wanted to come inside and show me the snail."

Mac lifts Cree up. "You saved the day, you little super-star," he says, tickling her. She wriggles about in his arms. He turns to Jackson. "That was way too close. If it wasn't for Cree, you'd have been seen. It'd be all over."

I dash out to the kitchen to lock and bolt the back door, and on my way back into the hallway I pull the blind down on the front door so no one can look through the glass.

The phone rings out in the hallway. God, what if it's her? What if it's that bloody woman again, asking about bringing a photographer or something with her to the pub? When the answering machine doesn't kick in, I go to answer it. But it's not the bloody woman. It's Mum.

"Jody," she sighs as I answer. "I'm glad I caught you, I've been trying your mobile. I'm sorry, love, but I'm stuck in the worst traffic jam ever, so I'm going to be late back. Halley's staying at Nina's after netball. Can you get your own dinner? There's some money in the coffee jar under the sink. Go and get yourself a fish supper or something. It's chaos here."

"Where are you?"

"Trying to get out of bloody Wales but something's happened on the bridge. They've just closed it and they're trying to turn us all around. They said on the radio some clothes have washed up so they think it's a suicide. Either that or that singer's been found, the one who's been in the papers. The one from that group you like."

"What?" I cry.

"Yeah, there's flashing lights and all sorts going on. Girls with flowers and banners have passed me, so God knows, it's bloody chaos. Like some protest march out of the seventies that your grandad used to go to. I'm going to have to find another way back, so I'll see you when I see you."

"OK. Mac's here with Cree. Don't worry."

"Oh good, you won't be on your own, then. All right, love, see you later, bye."

I slam down the phone and dash back into the living room. They're all gathered around the snail on Cree's hand. Jackson's trying to poke inside it with a toothpick. I grab the remote and slide down onto the carpet before the TV, jabbing the POWER button, willing the blackness to go to a news broadcast.

"Jode?" says Mac.

"What is it, what happened? Who was on the phone?" says Jackson.

Flick, flick, flick, flick. I flick through every channel until I get to the news. And the scrolling headline is there.

MISSING SINGER'S CLOTHES FOUND IN BRISTOL CHANNEL. JACKSON GATLIN FEARED DEAD.

"Oh shit!" says Jackson, a worry line appearing in the middle of his forehead.

A picture of his face flashes up. "Man!" says Cree, pointing at it.

"Yeah," I say, almost laughing.

"I'm dead!" Jackson laughs.

"You're dead!" Mac laughs.

Then I see Cree's face. She's looking up at Jackson, the leaf with her snail on it balancing on her open hand. "Is my snell dead, Man?"

He rouses himself from his own situation for a split second and bends down to her level. Her little nose starts flaring and her bottom lip disappears like she's about to cry, but Jackson says the perfect thing to stop her in her tracks.

"No, he's not dead. He's just hiding. He just wants to hide away for a little while. Be by himself, that's all." And he looks up at me, and for the smallest second, the slightest shadow of a smile crosses his face, then disappears.

NINETEEN
DEAD AND GONE

To the whole world, Jackson Gatlin is gone, never to be seen again. There's no corpse yet, though the divers are still looking. But all his clothes have turned up, even his shoes. There's no way he's still alive and well and living in a domestic garage in the West Country, no way. No sane person would ever believe that.

So who is the man in my living room, swinging a little girl around by her arms as she squeals happily? Just a man, I suppose.

Mac and I sit on the sofa watching the news unfold. Watching the same images again and again and again because there's nothing else to report — some clothes have washed up, fans are there on the bridge, crying, being moved along by police, throwing roses over the side. Some are lighting the roses with cigarette lighters before throwing them off the bridge, in homage to Jackson's burning-rose tattoo. Some have "JG" written on their cheeks in black marker. Some are showing their tattoos of Jackson's face and lyrics all up their arms. Jackson himself isn't paying any attention. He's playing with Cree on the floor. Well, Cree's playing with him. He's just sitting there, not quite understanding what she's doing or why she's combing his wet hair using the plastic knife and fork she ate her mini meat pie with. She giggles as she combs his hair down over his face and he blows out so it messes up. She combs it back and he blows it and she giggles again.

Jackson looks up after a while. "I'm, like . . . dead. I'm totally the deadest, ain't I?"

Mac scowls at him, like he's just interrupted a really interesting comment the windswept reporter's making, even though we've probably heard it six or seven times before. "They haven't found a corpse yet, I'd hold your horses if I were you."

"It all points to them finding a corpse, though, doesn't it? It's awesome."

I don't think his deadness is awesome at all. I'm watching those fans on that bridge, a thousand broken hearts all cracking in unison. It's about as un-awesome as you can get.

The clock on the mantelpiece chimes three o'clock. Mac turns to me. "Shouldn't you have been back at work at one?"

I bite my lip but that's the most I do. "I completely forgot." I don't actually make any further effort to go back to work, though. They know what I'm like, and I'm leaving on Friday anyway so it hardly matters. No point going back at all.

Sally Dinkley comes to my house *again* that afternoon. Knocks on the front door and waits. Rings the front doorbell and waits. Knocks again. Calls out to me. Waits again. We sit on the sofa, all four of us (well, five if you count Roly inside his leafy carry case). We've got our fingers on our lips so Cree knows we really mustn't make a peep. Eventually

Dinkley gets the hint. Me and Mac are on PAUSE, watching each other, the TV on MUTE, a jumbo bag of Doritos on the sofa between us, rooted to the endless news bulletins but unable to move for fear that she's suddenly going to ram-raid the front door with her bubble-gum Beetle.

"What are you going to say to this Dinkley woman when you meet her at the Pack Horse?" Jackson asks me without looking around.

"No idea," I say. "Don't think I'll bother to go now that this has happened. I'll just stay here."

"You have to. She's still convinced he's here some-where," says Mac, flicking channels to another news station. "She'll think finding the clothes is a red herring. It'll just make her more determined. She's studied that photo. There's no way she's going to believe he jumped off the Severn Bridge two weeks ago, is she? No, you'll have to meet with her and tell her the photo was a hoax. I'll come with you and say I Photoshopped it or something. Go all grief-stricken, make it look like you're really sorry you lied now that he's dead and everything."

"I can't just act grief-stricken."

"Yeah you can. I'll sneak you a couple of glasses of wine first. That should do the trick."

"Then what happens to him?" I say, nodding toward Jackson, whom Cree has deemed fit to wear two of her pink teddy barrettes in his hair. "If I convince her that he's dead, what's going to happen to Jackson, then?"

Jackson turns around and looks at both of us in turn. "You gotta go and shake her off for good. And then you gotta get me out of the country."

"Oh yeah," Mac says, snapping his fingers. "Just like that. We do it all the time, Jode, don't we, help get missing rock stars out of the country? I've got a fleet of planes in *my* garage."

"Mac," I scold but Mac's not listening to me, he's just looking at Jackson.

"Well, how do you expect us to do it? Have you any idea how hard it is to get in and out of this country? Any country, for that matter? Even if we get you a boat, you have to face some form of customs somewhere. And unless you know someone who can knock up a false passport . . ."

"Well, what, then?" says Jackson.

"Well," I blurt out. It's what I've been mulling over for some time. They both look at me. "We do know someone who can get people in and out of the country, don't we?"

Mac's blank. "Do we?"

"Yeah. The BFD."

"Who's the BFD?" says Jackson.

"He's this sketchy guy who lives in Nuffing and he got caught bringing illegal immigrants over from Romania a few years ago."

"No, no, no," says Mac. "I told you Duncan had nothing to do with that, it was all his dad. I never said Duncan was involved with that."

"No, but he must have known something about it, mustn't he? You said he's a well shady character. I bet he'd find a way if someone paid the right price."

Cree takes her barrettes out of Jackson's hair and clips them on his ears instead.

Mac shakes his head. "No way, Jody, we are not getting involved with the BFD and you are definitely not giving him a penny of your money, no way."

"But if that's the only way —"

"*NO!*" Mac shouts. "We can disguise you, Jackson. We can give you a bit of cash for the road and I'll even drive you to the nearest ferry port, but from then on, you're on your own."

He gets up off the sofa. "I've got to go."

"Mac, don't be mushy," I say. "Please, can't we talk about this?"

He turns to me. "I'm not mushy. I've got a rehearsal. Cream Puff, come on, we've got to go."

"No," Cree whines, with wobbling leg. She puts Jackson in a choke hold. "My stay with Man and Dody, Kenzie, no!"

"It's fine, she can stay here," I tell him. "Will you come back here afterward?"

"Do you want me to?" he says, looking at Jackson, then back at me.

I'm confused. "Well, yeah, to pick up Cree."

"Yeah, yeah, I'll be back about five-ish. Bye, Creepy."

His sister gently removes one hand from its clutch around Jackson's neck to wave him good-bye, wary that he might scoop her up and take her with him. But he doesn't. He leaves, and she gets Man to herself, so she's happy.

A convincing disguise is the essence of all covert operations. In most of the Shakespeare I failed at school, someone was either dressing up in drag or pretending to be dead or in hiding, and it usually turned out all right.

Apart from *Romeo and Juliet*, I suppose, when Juliet disguised herself as dead and Romeo topped himself, but I try not to think about that.

So me and Cree set about trying one of my mum's blond hair colors on Jackson, but it doesn't take. It's just dark brown with the slightest of gold tinges. He looks like I've just sneezed glitter all over him. Cree insists on helping to wash it off but she gets bored midway through and starts soaping her hands and rubbing them all over the toilet seat.

"We'll cut it," I suggest.

"You ever cut someone's hair before?" he asks me.

"No. But men's hair is easy to cut, isn't it? I used to watch my mum cutting Dad's."

"All right." He seems up for anything, so we go down to the kitchen and I find Mum's bag of hairstyling equipment under the sink. I drape the plastic gown around Jackson and find the scissors. Cree decides to give Doctor Dolly an impromptu haircut, too, putting her up on the stool beside Jackson and draping her in a tea towel. She has to hack a bit as her blunt craft scissors don't work very well on hair.

I start snipping away at his ends. *Snip, snip, snip, snip.* He stops my hand. "You got any clippers? Electric razor, anything."

"Uh, yeah, I think so," I say and make toward the cabinet to get it out. "Dad had a grade two for a while."

"I think we should go all the way."

"Huh?" I say. Then I realize he's talking about the clippers. "You want to shave it off?"

"Yeah. I'm known for my hair, so if I get rid of it, I'll be less known."

"Are you sure you want to?" I put the scissors on the breakfast bar and stoop to search for the clippers in the cabinet. They're all the way in the back under a pile of dusters.

"Yeah," he says. "Put it on the shortest setting."

Cree has two hands to the scissors and is trying to hack through Doctor Dolly's neck with great concentration on her face, tongue out and everything.

"Jackson . . ."

"Yeah."

I come around to face him. "What are you going to do once you're disguised?"

"Disappear."

"Where to?"

"I don't know yet."

"What if . . ." It seems like the right thing to say. Maybe it's too much, though. I mean, I've only been thinking about it for about five seconds but . . . "What if I gave you some money to . . . get out of the country properly."

"Still wouldn't be enough for a jet pack."

"It would. Five thousand pounds would be more than enough to get you somewhere."

"Five thousand pounds?" he shrieks. "Where the hell did you get that kind of money?"

"My grandad left it to me in his will. I can go to the BFD and say I have five thousand pounds if he can get you out of the country."

"Uh, no way. No. Way. I'm not taking any money from

you. You're a kid. And taking your grandfather's inheritance, Jesus, that's just way outta line. I may be an asshole but I ain't a bastard."

I click the clippers on. *Buzzzzzzzz.* "I want you to have it," I say. "The money. Grandad told me to do something. 'Don't Dream It, Be It.' That's the last thing he said to me. . . ."

"That doesn't mean giving your money away to the first loser who comes along," says Jackson. Cree's moved on to a thinner area of Doctor Dolly's body to snip and has almost made it through one of her ankles. *Buzzzzzzzzz . . .* "Why is she doing that?" he asks.

"She's a child. That's what children do. It's how they learn," I tell him. "Jackson, please, it would make me feel better." *Buzzz . . .* I turn the clippers off. "If you want, think of it as a loan. You can send the money back when you get settled. If you say no, you'll be offending me. And you'll be offending my grandad, too."

Jackson looks to the kitchen tiles and the clumps of his hair at his feet. "Whoa, you've cut off a bunch!"

"You told me to do it," I say. "And stop changing the subject." I walk around to face him. "I want you to have my money."

Without another word he takes the clippers out of my hand and glides them right down the center of his head. *Buzzzzzzzzzzzzzzzzzzzzzzz.*

"Looks like I don't have a choice, then."

I feed Cree some spaghetti on toast and settle her in front of *SpongeBob* in the living room, which wild horses couldn't tear her away from, while I go upstairs to the bathroom where the light's better to finish off Jackson's scalping. And we're in the bathroom, looking at his hair, or rather head, in the mirror when the front doorbell rings. Oh. My. Effing. God. Mum. Halley.

But no. They have keys of course. I nip downstairs to answer it and turns out it's Mac.

"How's Tiny Temper?"

"She's fine. She's got *SpongeBob*. Come and look at this."

I lead him upstairs to the bathroom where Jackson's looking at his head in the mirror. "There's someone I'd like you to meet."

"Oh," says Mac, holding out his hand. Then he stops. He withdraws. He really looks at him. "Oh my God. I thought you were . . . shit, it's not the same guy."

"I know, ain't it great?" Jackson grins. His eyes are watery. He keeps blinking the longer he looks in the mirror. His hands feel over his newly shaved head, again and again. He looks brutal. Hard. Not like my sweet-smiling Jackson of before, with the floppy brown hair and the electric blue eyes. Now his head is bare, his eyes sad. He's a totally new man.

"Oh," says Mac, as though something's pricked him in the buttock. He removes something from his back pocket. "I nicked these from the makeup room at the Playhouse, for the disguise. Thought that would be a good start. But I guess you're quite a bit ahead of me on that front." He hands Jackson two little plastic packets.

"Contacts?"

"Yeah. They're dark, so people won't recognize your eyes. I wear some like it in the show. *Rocky Horror*'s being sponsored by the optician's in town so we get them for free. Try them."

Jackson peels off the foil on one of the packets. He's worn lenses before. I've seen a few interviews where he's had them in for effect — once with the stars and stripes across them, and one when the band dressed up as cats for an article in *Lungs* that was all about how much "pussy" they got on the road. Charming, I know. Another story I only scan-read at the time. He sticks his index finger in the packet and pulls it out again with the lens suckered on the tip. He moves it gently around until it lies cupped on the end of his finger. Before too long, his sea-blue eyes are black as night.

"Oh my God! You look incredible!" I tell him.

"Not quite," says Mac. "Why do you insist on dressing him in this never-ending succession of dodgy jogging pants?"

I frown at him. "Excuse me, these were my grandad's clothes."

"And he hated them, too, that's why he never wore them. Your mum only bought them for him cos they were drawstring and he kept losing weight. I'll dig out some of my last-season stuff from home. No point having a brand-new look if you're still going to wear saggy castoffs."

"Cool," says Jackson. Mac almost smiles, and we're then so busy deciding what clothes Jackson will need for his new image, we don't even notice Cree bum-shuffling one at a time up the stairs to see what all the fuss is about. She stands in the bathroom doorway and looks at Jackson. Her nose flares, bottom lip disappears, and before we know it, she's tipped her head back and started wailing.

Mac goes to pick her up. "What's wrong?" She clings on to him like a crab, huffing and whimpering in his arms. She's still looking at Jackson.

"Cree, it's OK," I tell her. "It's Man." Cree shakes her head, nose still flaring in and out.

I step forward and put my hand on her back. "She's shaking. Cree, it's Man. He just hasn't got any hair. Take the lenses out, Jackson. They do make you look pretty evil."

Jackson turns to the sink and takes his contact lenses out, putting them back in the packet. He turns to Cree. "That better?"

She sucks in another huff, then eventually lessens her grip on Mac and puts her arms out to Jackson.

"What does she want?" he asks me.

"Uh, duh? She wants you," says Mac. Jackson's clearly shocked at this but he reaches out and takes her from Mac anyway. She immediately snuggles into his chest, still huffing, and holds on tightly. She really didn't recognize him.

"She loves you so much," I say, more to myself than anyone else.

"Can't think why," he replies, looking at her like she's a little leech and he's watching her suck his blood for medicinal purposes.

"She probably thinks you're Dad," says Mac, going back through the door and downstairs.

Jackson holds Cree closely but he looks wrong with a child. She's cuddling him but he's not really cuddling her back, he's just letting her. Letting her because she's small. Unformed. Has potential to be a person he can trust, perhaps. Not like me. A fully formed, untrustworthy fan who just loves him for his manufactured image. Cree doesn't know any better, like he didn't when he was young and innocent and just starting out.

"How 'bout we go and play with Roly? In the yard?" he says to her in his best child-friendly voice. "Want to go and find him a girlfriend?" She nods against his shoulder, then lifts up her head to stare at him. She pats his skull.

He pats his head, too. "Do you like it?" He smiles at her.

She frowns. "What you done to your ned?"

TWENTY
MUST HANG SALLY

I have good days and bad days and these can be best described by the kind of music I like to listen to. Black Keys days are good days. Nirvana days are doubtful days when I need to check my head. Queen days used to be the days I spent with Grandad when me and him and Mac and Cree would go out in the car, to Weston Park or Glastonbury, singing along, headbanging, and laughing — happy-beyond-belief days. And every day, The Regulators appear at least twice, including once to wake me up, and again to lull me to sleep. It occurs to me that I haven't listened to any music for days. This is probably why my brain feels like a scrunched-up ball of paper — I need a drumbeat or a steady bass line to help iron it out sometimes.

Today started off so obviously as a Nirvana kind of day but now it's changing into a Hole or Distillers day or some such other angry tampon rock. I'm frustrated and I'm petrified all in one bad-tempered bundle as we head off to the pub to see the Wicked Witch of the West Country. Cree's falling asleep on Mac's shoulder but she wakes up the minute we get into the main bar of the Pack Horse and puts her arms out for Teddy. He's too busy serving pints behind the counter to take her, so Tish does instead, and heads upstairs to give Cree a bath.

Mac snags us a bottle of wine from the cellar and we go and sit in the restaurant's garden to eat Curly Wurlys — although I don't eat mine — and wait for Sally Dinkley. We can see the street snaking up the hill at the far end of the pub parking lot, so we'll be able to see her car as she leaves the Torrance Lodge. No way a woman like her walks anywhere. I'm nervous. I guzzle a couple of gobfuls of wine to get going on the grief. We're still talking about ways to throw her off the scent.

"We could get a human arm, tattoo it with a burning rose, go to Cardiff, and chuck it in the River Severn," I say, grabbing at any straw that floats across my brain. *Glug, glug.* "Maybe we could take Alfie and pretend we found it when we were walking him. She'd have to believe he was dead then."

Mac bats his eyes. "I don't think she'd believe it if she saw his whole corpse washed up, let alone some random arm. And where are we going to get an arm from, anyway?"

I shrug, sitting astride the bench seat, one leg on either side. "I dunno. The hospital or something? They sawed a guy's feet off in *Shallow Grave* and took them to the hospital to be put in an incinerator. Maybe they have spares?"

Mac doesn't respond this time, he just stares out across the parking lot. I swig at the wine. My glass is soon empty. "Tub her up," I tell him.

"Slow down for God's sake, Jody," he says, topping my glass up regardless.

"You said I had to be grief-stricken." I shrug. "I can only do that when someone dies or I've had too much wine."

"Dinkley's not stupid, despite appearances. She's clever

enough to have spotted the flaws in our Italian fiasco. You're going to have to be convincingly grief-stricken if we're to throw her off the scent, not just hammered."

I'm not really taking in what he's saying here. I'm thinking back to all of Teddy's DVDs Mac and I have watched, where a journalist or just some well nosy person is trying to prove something exists when everyone else won't believe it, like the scientists in *E.T.* And the creepy guy in that one where Tom Hanks finds a mermaid. And the bounty hunter in that one where the family befriends a Bigfoot. How did they all throw the nosey parkers off the scent?

But the pink bubble gum on wheels is a-coming, we can see it now, pulling out of the Torrance Lodge parking lot and along the street, blinker blinking when it gets to the pub. The car turns in, disappears for a little while, and appears moments later. Now we can see the blonde head and yellow jacket and the mincing walk of Sally Dinkley.

"Shit," I say, my brain fogging as I try desperately to remember the ending of *Splash*.

"Shit," says Mac. Dinkley presses her keys and the parked bubble-gum balloon blinks.

The wine's beginning to kick in. I'm hazier now, but not quite grief-stricken yet. "I don't know what to say, Mac, I don't know what to say. My mind's gone blank. It's useless!"

He just looks at me. "Just deny everything. And if you can, cry."

Harry and the Hendersons, I keep thinking. What happened to Bigfoot? How did the kids get E.T. away from the government? How did the mermaid escape from the scientists? I just can't remember.

Sally Dinkley runs down the length of the parking lot, as much as you *can* run in five-inch Louboutin heels. Fake Louboutin heels, Mac informs me. "No way a newbie hack on some local rag is going to afford kosher Louboutins."

I'm too drunk to fathom what he's talking about, or care about her footwear for that matter, as she *clip-clop*s toward us. I can already hear her making apologies.

"Sorry, sorry, sorry! I know I'm late, *doink*." She does that stupid hand-against-forehead thing again, which is starting to annoy me as much as anything's ever annoyed me in my life. "Have you been waiting long?"

"No," I say. We've been here about twenty-five minutes but I'm starting the whole "deny everything" order as instructed by Mac as I have absolutely zilch other options. I can't summon any tears, so all I can do is look mournful. Elliot ran away with E.T. That's what the whole bike scene was about. Maybe Jackson and I could run away? On bikes?

"So," she says, sitting down next to Mac on his side of the bench, directly opposite me. "Ooh, sorry, can I get you both drinks?" She gets up again and pulls her handbag up her shoulder.

"We can't stay long," says Mac, getting up and moving around to my side of the bench. So now we're both facing her as she sits back down and starts rooting around in her oversized red leather bag for a small laptop. She starts it up and roots around in the bag again, pulling out some stick, which she shoves in the side of it. I'm getting more

and more panic-stricken by the second, desperately foraging around in my mind to remember what happened at the
end of *Splash*.

"Oh, OK, we better crack on, then. My story's going to
print tonight so . . ."

"Did you not hear the news? About Jackson Gatlin?"
I mumble. "They found his body. In the River Severn."

"No, they found his clothes," she corrects me, flapping
her hand. "Red herring. Now . . ."

Mac interrupts by shoving his hand underneath her
nose. "Mackenzie Lawless." She shakes it warily. "I don't
think you fully recognized me earlier. I think you were
only at my school a year before you left. Just before your
A level exams, wasn't it?"

"Yes." That's all she says. "Jody, if we could make a
start?" She checks her watch.

But Mac's not done. "Nuffing's a really small town.
Everybody knows everybody, like you knew Salvo the pizza
man from our pictures. Small minds. Long memories."

"Oh, so you're the friend in Italy? Right, well, if we
could begin . . ."

"Yeah, I think I might know a little about you," says
Mac. "Didn't one of the substitute teachers get you pregnant or something?"

"That was *not* me!" she snaps. Her whole face changes
color. It's no longer pale with the slightest hint of rose to
her cheeks. It's red. Angry red.

"Oh, why did you leave so suddenly, then? Was it
something to do with the lesbian PE teacher and her daily
knicker checks?"

"Oh my goodness, look, I haven't come here to —"

"— what, sell Viagra to seventeen-year-olds? Come on, *one* of them must be you."

"I don't have time for this. Jody, can we go somewhere more private, please?"

But I let Mac carry on. I don't know what he's doing or where all these allegations are coming from, but they're working. Dinkley's getting well twitchy. "See, I've done a bit of digging of my own," he says, "and I know for a fact you used to edit our school magazine. And it was *you* who made up all those stories. People hung for it, though. Four students were expelled for that Viagra story. Miss Chambers the PE teacher got the sack. But did you own up and say you'd made it all up to fill pages? Noooo. Just as long as you made the headlines, that's all you cared about, wasn't it?"

"You can't prove any of this."

"And you can't prove Jackson Gatlin isn't floating down the River Severn, can you? Now I suggest you take what little evidence you've already got, hop on your glittery pink broomstick, and bugger off back to Bristol, all right?"

"You can't stop me from running whatever story I like. I have my own column."

"No, I can't. I can't stop you writing yet another false story in a whole sea of false stories. And when Jackson Gatlin's body *does* wash up, which it will, you're going to be very embarrassed indeed. I've got a blog. Two thousand followers so far. And I'll be blogging about this until the cows come home."

They stare each other down for a little while. Dinkley gets up. "His body won't wash up. He's alive, I know he is.

But for how long, who knows? Believe me, if you *are* covering for him, I'm going to be the very least of your worries."

"What are you talking about?" I slur. I'm actually slurring now. Crying, no. But slurring? Check.

"I'm talking about a roadie who was found beaten to a pulp after the same concert in Cardiff where Gatlin went missing. I'm talking about a St. John Ambulance member having her face rearranged in the sick bay of said concert where Gatlin went missing. I'm talking about the bass player, Pash Fredericks, having his nose and three fingers on his left hand broken on the night of the same concert in Cardiff where Gatlin went missing. Spotting a pattern yet?"

I hold my breath. That's what Jackson's been trying to say; no wonder he doesn't want to be found.

But Mac just looks at her, as cool as an iceberg. He shrugs. "Rock concerts are dangerous places. People get hurt all the time."

Dinkley's equally as cool. "I've been researching into Frank Grohman, the manager of The Regulators. Very shady. He has ways of getting information. If Jackson Gatlin *has* gone AWOL, I'm sure Frank Grohman would give anything to know where his star performer is right now, probably more than I would." She turns around and begins to walk away. She turns back. "You're both hiding something. I know you are. And by the time my story's made the rounds tomorrow, everyone else will know, too. Including Frank Grohman."

"But you just can't prove it, can you?" sighs Mac. "It's sad, really. You'll run that story, nothing will come of it, and that will be that. Just more bullshit. You're so hungry for attention it's quite depressing." He smiles. "I mean come on, Sally, a world-famous rock star, hiding away in the tiny West Country town of Nuffing-on-the-Wold? Who the hell is going to believe that?"

"Mac, don't," I mutter.

"It's all right, it's fine," says Sally. "You're obviously threatened because you know I'm close to something. Give it another day. Something will come out of the woodwork. Or someone. I will find out, you just mark my words."

Dinkley marches back up the parking lot to her little pink bubble and heads back to the Torrance and Mac doesn't say one more word until she's on the road.

"That was a close one. Didn't think we'd turn that around."

I turn to him. "We didn't. She's still going to run her story."

"Yeah but it won't mean a thing. It'll just be talk."

I tip my empty wine glass upside down and rest my chin on it. "You don't have a blog, you liar, let alone two thousand followers."

He grins. "And she doesn't have a shred of actual proof that Jackson's in Nuffing, does she? So it looks as though we're both running false stories."

And all of a sudden I remember the endings of all those films. *Harry and the Hendersons. Splash. E.T.* I remember what happened to the alien, the Bigfoot, the mermaid at the end.

They were set free.

And that's what I *have* to do for Jackson, or else he's

going to be all over the papers. Hounded. Hunted. A freak show. He won't be able to handle it. He won't be able to escape from Grohman. He'll hurt him. It's up to me to help him. It's the only way he's going to be able to get on with whatever life he wants to have. My nose starts to flare like Cree's does when she's about to cry and, before I know it, there are tears in my eyes.

"Wine kicking in, is it?" says Mac. His arm encircles me. "Come on, it's OK, it's OK."

It's going to be hard to let him go, as much as I wanted to be rid of him in the beginning. Because he's Jackson. He's my hero. And he's become this weird kind of garage-dwelling, pee-stinking, constantly hungover friend. But it's what I have to do, I know that now.

"She won't leave. She'll find him. I've got to set him free, Mac."

Maybe *that's* what *"Don't Dream It, Be It"* meant. Maybe Grandad wasn't talking about me at all. Maybe he meant that for Jackson. Getting him a new life abroad. Getting him away from his torture chamber. But how am I going to do that? I can't get him out of my *garage* without being seen, let alone the *country*. I know I can't do it. And I know Mac can't help me.

But I know a man who can.

TWENTY-ONE
THE BFD

Halley makes me breakfast — toast and jam and cornflakes in the bowl we always fight over, the free one we got with the Rice Krispies. She did this the morning after Grandad's death, too. Today she's done it because she's read Dinkley's article and knows how I feel about The Regulators. It's in the morning paper. Front page. Dinkley has written everything she said she'd write about — Pash getting beaten up, Frank Grohman's unsavory past, the St. John Ambulance woman's plastic surgery, everything. It's time for drastics. I eat the breakfast, just to please Halley, and shove the paper through the garage cat flap on my way into town.

As I've mentioned before, I have a tendency to do stupid things. In my short sixteen years, I have inadvertently caused two fires, been cut free from a toy car, been arrested for damaging public property, and caused a semi-serious road accident while in the process of liberating fifty farm turkeys. But this is probably the stupidest thing I've ever done.

I'm first in the queue when the bank opens. I take out the full amount I'm going to offer the BFD, but I only take half of it around to his place that morning. I stuff the other half under my mattress. My dad always used to tell me that in poker games he would always start low with his stake until he knew "the lay of the land" or, rather, knew how good the other players were. So that's what I'm doing. Though in my case, I'm lowering my stake until I know exactly how dodgy the BFD is.

The outside of Duncan Buzzey's flat is about as skeezy as skeezy gets. It's right at the end of Albert Lane, which looks like Knockturn Alley on a bad day, and the door looks like it's been kicked in. Mac would go ballistic if he knew what I was doing, if he knew I'd been within ten feet of this place. But here I stand, pressing the intercom, admiring the "F" and "C" words scored into the brickwork. There's Coke cans and condoms jammed up the gutter, it's cold and pissing with rain, and somewhere in one of the flats opposite I can hear a baby screaming at the top of its lungs — it's that kind of vibe. I'm sick with nerves. Buzzey's a lout. He's done time for theft and drug dealing. He's everything I hate about the human race kneaded into one fat, flatulent lump.

"Murgh?" comes the scratchy response from the intercom.

"I need to speak to Duncan Buzzey," I say, very slowly.

"What *scratchy* want?" His voice sounds like he's eating something crunchy.

"I need to speak to Duncan. It's urgent."

"Nah, fumph off."

The receiver clicks down. I look back up the lane to check no one's around. I grab hold of the moon rock in my jacket pocket with one hand and press the button hard again until it stops buzzing. *Come on, Buzzey, I'm buzzing you. I'm not going to stop buzzing you, Buzzey. . . . buzzzzzzzzzzzzzzzzzzz . . .*

"Whaaat?!"

I exhale. "I've got money."

A scratchy silence follows. The receiver goes down. *Buzzzzzzzzz*. The door clicks open.

I push through the door, and pick my way through a stack of unopened boxes and packets. The stair carpet is greeny-gray and thick with clumps of mud and tiny bits of gravel. A cluster of mismatched sneakers lies in the corner of the first-floor stairwell, worn down at the heels and holey at the toes. I start slowly up. The walls on either side of the stairs are orange. There is no banister.

At the top of the stairs, the walls turn the same color as the stair carpet, gray-green, and I can see a TV flickering in a room to the right. I'm stupid to have come here on my own, I know I am. I know, I know, I know. But it's the only plan I've got.

"Who are you?" says the garbled phone voice, clearer now. The TV is loud but I can just about hear him. He's sitting in a moldy brown armchair facing *Car Booty*. I move across into his line of vision, seeing as he makes no effort to look around at me. He's a huge, hulking boy-man in a stained green T-shirt. He has a tray on his lap with three foil containers on it — one for rice, one for curry, one for a cracked-up popadam.

"Hello, Duncan."

Duncan looks at me again, for a longer time, up and then down. I only went to Nuffing Comp for my last year of school, so I didn't know that much about him. All I knew was what Mac had told me. Despite this, he still recognizes me. "You used to go to Nuffing Comp, din't ya?"

"Yeah. Someone told me you could help me out with something."

He looks me right up, then right down again. "Oh yeah?"

"Your dad," I say, my mouth dry.

"I ain't nothing to do with my dad. If you've come here from the *Chronicle* or summing, I ain't saying nuffin'."

"No, I'm not from the paper. It's not about your dad . . . as such. But it's about what he did."

"I don't know anything about it, darlin'."

"You must."

"Nah, them immigrants, that was all me dad, all me dad, that was." He sniffs and moves the tray onto the coffee table in front of him. There's a bald patch amid his otherwise thick, greasy ginger hair and for a second I think I see something scuttle across it. I hope to God it's my mind playing tricks. "What's it to you, anyway? You want a pet Romanian or summing?"

His arm moves to the back of his chair and he crosses his legs in a proper bloke-crossing-legs pose.

"No, I don't want to bring someone into the country, I want to get someone *out*."

"Who?"

"A friend."

"What's he done?"

"Nothing. He's not a criminal or anything, he just needs to leave. I can't tell you any more."

"Bad, is it? Done someone in?" He leans over to the right for the lager by his chair, his fat fingers like baby legs. He knocks back the dregs of the can, then half-crushes it and throws it toward a trash bin by the TV, already over-flowing with half-crushed lager cans. There's newspapers all over the floor, too. I double-check for signs of Jackson, but they're old newspapers by the looks of them.

The massive wodge of money in my jeans pocket may as well be a hot coal, I'm so aware of it. "I can't tell you," I reply, getting irritated. "Can you arrange it or not?"

"How do I know you ain't bugged or summing?" he says, rearranging himself in his underpants and getting fairly out of breath in the process.

"I'm not, I swear! Believe me I don't want to be here! I just need to get someone right out of the country as soon as possible and I'm willing to pay. So will you help or not?"

"I gotta check you ain't bugged first. Take your top off."

"Good-bye," I snap and march straight back through the living-room door. I can hear him laughing. I want to run back in there and shove what's left in that curry container right over his melon head. I want to tip up the coffee table and throw it against the wall. But I don't. Because I need his help. And for some reason, I still think, even as I get to the top of the stairs, that he will help me. I'm two steps down and I hear his voice again.

"All right, all right, I was only having a laugh wiv ya, weren't I?" *Hur, hur, hur.* "How much you got, then?"

I troop back in slowly. "Five thousand." He barely raises an eyebrow. At this point, I take out the money. "I can give you two thousand five hundred for any customs documents he'll need and the same again for travel costs and stuff."

"Ain't possible," says Buzzey.

"I know for a fact your dad brought two women over from Romania for half that!" I shout. I'd looked it up on the Internet that morning.

"Yeah, well, that was a few years ago. We been through a little credit crunch since then, or hadn't you noticed?"

"Yeah, I *had* noticed," I say, still clutching the money, scanning the dank brown room heaving with junk, clutter, and dust. There's a definite dark brown shadow in the far corner that could or could not be a cat turd.

"I been signed off sick," he says, leaning back, yanking his trousers up over his spilled belly.

"Off skiving, more like," I mumble.

"Uh?" he says. He's helped himself to another mouthful of popadam dipped in cold, greasy curry. He itches the second of his three chins with a yellow-stained finger and reaches for the remote to change channels.

"Can you help me or not? Can you get him out quickly and quietly and never tell a soul about it or not? I haven't got time to play games."

I've never seen anyone flick through TV channels quite so fast, but he eventually settles on *60 Minute Makeover* and goes back to his popadam. He knows full well I'm on tenterhooks. He alternates between staring at me and the envelope. *Crunch, crunch, crunch.* "Where've you got five grand from, then?" he eventually says through a spray of crispy bits.

"My grandad. Charlie McGee. He died a couple of weeks ago. He left an inheritance." I gesture to the envelope. "This is it."

"Yeah, I heard about that. Took a bit of a tumble, din't

he?" I start out the door again. I don't want to hear it if he starts on about Grandad. "That all he left ya?"

I turn back. "Yes," I lie. I wasn't about to tell him exactly how much he'd left me. He'd want all of it.

He leans forward in his chair. "You give me five, and I'll see what I can do. And that's a discount. I usually ask for ten. You caught me in a good mood." He holds out his baby-leg fingers to take the envelope.

"No, half now, half later. Please." I'm saying please so as to appeal to his better nature. He must have one, some-where, beneath all the fat.

He holds up his filthy yellow hands. "That's the deal. No half-arsed two thousand now, two thousand later crap. You give me five grand, I'll get him into Europe without the pigs sniffing around him. I'll do the whole lot."

"What's the lot?"

"Everything. I'll get 'im out, get everything ready . . ."

"What, like a passport?"

He wipes the back of his hand across his nose. "Depends what I can sort out, dunnit? It'll be professional and all that. International driver's licenses, dummy credit cards, passports. Stamps for the passport so it'll look used."

"It will?" I say. "And you'll get him as far away as pos-sible, you won't dump him in the middle of the North Sea or . . ."

"I'll get him as far into Europe as he wants to go. Well, my associates will."

"Your associates?"

"Well, yeah. I'm just the organ grinder, I got monkeys for things like that."

"What if I don't . . . really trust you?"

He shrugs. "Ain't my problem." He shovels another scoop of curry on a crisp of popadam into his gob. "You can't have that many options if you've come to me. So are we in business for five grand, then, or what?"

I rub the moon rock in my hoodie pocket, waiting for the voice in my head to tell me what to do. I try to listen to my heart; that's what people say in movies, don't they, when they're not sure about something. But my heart's just doing its usual beat thing and I don't understand what that means. However, my head is telling me not to trust this guy with a Monopoly note, let alone five thousand of my grandad's money. I have to be sensible about this. I have to be Mackenzie about this. So I say no.

"No. I can't give you five thousand pounds just like that. Two thousand five hundred now, for the documents, same again when I hear from him when he gets to Europe."

"I ain't buggering about with all that."

"Fine, let's forget it, then," I say finally, stuffing the money back in my pocket and turning to leave again, this time for good. My head is a whole mosh pit of new worries. I am completely out of ideas as to how to get Jackson out of the country. I wasn't too pleased with my idea of approaching the BFD, anyway, but now even this option is out, due to his total unwillingness to strike a deal. I guess I'm not one of his usual teenage boys who'd sell their own feet for a tenth of weed.

I reach the fourth step down this time and I hear his voice call out.

"Oi!"

I don't move. He wants this, he's got to waddle and get it. I keep walking, slowly down the staircase. I am standing on the bottom step when the voice comes again, at the top.

"I can have the papers by tomorrow." I turn. I look up at him. "I'll need three passport pictures of him by tonight. And a name." I nod. "I can have it all in place by Friday."

"The quicker, the better."

He picks at his teeth. "It'll take as long as it takes, darlin'. These new biometric passport chips make it well 'ard to clone. And you can't just shove a new photo in 'em, you gotta have it digitally imaged. It ain't a walk in the park."

"I don't care. Just get it done, OK?"

"It'll be done, don't fret your little head. Just get me three pictures of your mate, the one who's 'not a criminal,' all his details and his new name. I'll set everything up first. You breathe a word to anyone that I'm helping ya, no more Big Friendly Duncan."

I pull the money bundle out my jeans for the last time and hold it at arm's length to him. "Half now, half when I get the papers?"

He nods and his pudgy, yellow-nailed hand reaches out and takes it.

And then I'm down the stairs and out the door and I don't look back. I keep walking until I turn the corner of the street into an alleyway, which leads into the High Street, and it's here that I break down. I clamp my hand to my mouth and sob. The cry is in place of the fear I had to suck up walking into Buzzey's flat. It's losing my grandad's money on the longest long shot in history. It's five thousand pounds going toward a drug industry that's put Jackson in this hideous situation in the first place. And it's for Jackson himself. Because I know, if only Duncan can pull this off, I'll never ever see Jackson again.

Jackson's sitting on his feathers reading when I get back. *The Girl Who Loved Tom Gordon*, which I haven't read yet but it's apparently about this girl who gets lost in the woods and starts to believe her hero, this baseball star called Tom Gordon, is watching over her, kind of protecting her.

My own hero is more angry than happy when I tell him about my visit to the BFD to get him out of the country.

"You didn't go on your own, did you? Mac went with you or something?"

"No," I say. "He thought the whole BFD thing was a very bad idea. He doesn't know and he's not going to know, OK?" Jackson scrapes his palm over his shaven head, just like Mac does when he's annoyed with me. Except Mac's got hair and gel and stuff on his head so it takes a bit longer. "I knew you wouldn't let me do it, anyway."

"Damn right. What the hell were you thinking?"

"You said you wanted to get out of the country. The BFD is one of those guys who know how to get you things. He's going to get you a passport and a car to get you across. . . ."

"Hmm," he says.

"You do still want to go, don't you?"

"Yeah," he says, but there's a little note in it that indicates otherwise.

"I've just paid Buzzey to get you across to Europe on Friday, Jackson. You better not be chickening out on me."

"You paid him already?"

"Yeah."

"How much?"

"Two and a half thousand."

"Jesus H . . ."

"It's halvsies. Halvsies now and halvsies when he's got your documents and everything."

". . . Christ . . . and everything? You don't even know what he's gonna do to get me out of here! He'll stiff you with some forged crap and you won't be able to do a damn thing about it."

"No he won't."

"How do you know? Look, I'll get your two and a half grand back somehow. Just forget about giving him any more."

"I can't forget it, can I? There's no other way. We either take a chance on Buzzey or we stay here and you get found by Sally Dinkley or, even worse, Grohman, and shoved back on that tour bus . . . or shoved out of it in the middle of a desert or something."

He shakes his head. "You're gonna lose your money. You'll lose your money and I'll still be here and she'll find me."

"We're desperate, OK? You read her article that I posted through your door this morning, didn't you? Pash has a broken nose and three broken fingers. That roadie's on life support. That St. John Ambulance woman needs plastic surgery. You said yourself Grohman's never going to let up until he's cemented you into a pillar on the motorway or something. I'm not letting anything happen to you. Not when I could stop it, no way."

He dips his head.

"They'll never leave you alone, Jackson."

He thinks about this. He nods.

I get to my feet. "I'm going to find Mum's camera. I think Halley borrowed it on her outward-bound trip. We need to take some photos of you. OK? Against that wall will be perfect."

He picks up *The Girl Who Loved Tom Gordon* again. "I musta read this story a dozen times. I'm glad you got me this one. It's my favorite of his."

TWENTY-TWO

THERE GOES MY HERO

Another day, another bullshit headline.

I SAW SUICIDAL ROCK STAR ON BRIDGE

Some bloke is claiming he saw a man matching Jackson's description, in a hooded sweatshirt and jeans, on the Severn Bridge, where he was "staring out to sea and thinking things over." Usually I would be infuriated by such a lie, but it's actually OK. It's helping us. We need the distraction. We need people to believe he is dead. Yeah, he went to the Severn Bridge. Yeah, he was suicidal. Yeah, yeah, yeah.

But there are slightly more pressing issues at hand today. It's Thursday. I dropped the photos through the BFD's letter box last night, pretending I was visiting Mac at rehearsal. I also gave him Jackson's new name. I'm wondering if Buzzey will have found them or whether they're hidden under all the packages and pizza leaflets in his stairwell. I wonder if he recognized Jackson from the photos.

Halley's hanging around me as I separate my and Jackson's laundry. She's trying to get a conversation going, swinging the microwave door backward and forward.

"Aren't you going to be late for school?" I ask her.

"I s'pose." The microwave door bangs shut. "What are you doing in the drum room?"

"What?"

"You go out there a lot."

"Yeah, I just . . . like it out there. Reminds me of Grandad."

"Oh," she says and we leave it at that.

Jackson has worked up the nerve to give his disguise a test drive, so we arrange to go to Weston Park in the afternoon with Mackenzie and Cree as soon as Mac gets off from work. And as soon as I have collected Jackson's new passport and stuff and given the rest of the money to the BFD.

So it's back I go to Knockturn Alley, where I heave myself once again up the filthy staircase, the second wodge of cash safely tucked in a sealed white envelope in the zipped pocket of my messenger bag. The BFD's sitting there like before in his armchair, watching a rerun of *Supermarket Sweep* on cable, eating a bowl of what looks like rabbit poo in water.

I fumble about in my bag to find the envelope and stand there with it in both hands, waiting for a sign of recognition. Eventually, the audience bursts into applause, signaling a commercial break, and Duncan settles the bowl down on the coffee table and looks at me. He holds out his hand and for a split second I think he's going to shake it, but he's looking at the envelope. I hand it to him. He opens it and starts counting the money. He looks up at me when he's done. "Cool. Cheers for that."

I stand expectantly, watching a large drooping cobweb

swaying in the corner of the room, waiting for him to pluck out a crisp new red passport from behind his chair, or a large envelope carrying details of Jackson's new persona. But he remains sitting there, just looking at me.

"The passport, then? His papers?" I eventually splutter out. "You did get the photos? And his new name and . . ."

"Yeah, yeah, Tom Gordon . . ."

"Thomas Gordon."

Buzzey pulls his gray elastic-waisted sweatpants up from where they have slipped down. "Everything's in hand. Have 'Mr. Gordon' waitin' at the cab stand outside the library at ten thirty tomorrow night. There'll be an unmarked white Rover waiting."

I stammer. "Wh-what do you mean? You said you'd have his papers ready today. You've got five thousand quid of my money. . . ."

"Nah, I said it depends what I can sort out, din't I?"

"You liar, we agreed!"

"Ah, ah, ah," he says, pointing a finger up to the ceiling. "We never signed nuffin', did we, darlin'? Now I've sorted out the transport side of things, so you've paid for that. You get 'im there, to the taxi stand for dead on half ten tomorrow night and Mr. Gordon'll get his papers from the driver. Right? That'll get him out of Blighty. Then it's up to 'im."

I breathe in, getting the full force of the musty, tangy room smell in my nostrils. "But —"

"Don't mess me about, sweetheart. You really don't wanna mess me about." He leans forward in his chair and spoons in a mouthful of chocolatey water from the bowl. There's a long wet mark all down the front of his Republic of Ireland shirt. "I'm many things, sweetheart, but I ain't a liar."

I'm so frustrated I could chew the arm of his armchair clean off, but I just stand there and do something I haven't done for years — I stamp my foot. All that money and *NOTHING* to show for it. I remember my dad saying the same thing once or twice before.

The morning at the BFD's flat is a long, dark train tunnel, but the afternoon feels like the breakout. It's definitely a Queen day. In the car going to Weston Park, we blare out "Bohemian Rhapsody" and we all join in singing, with Cree doing the "Scaramouche" bits in her own little way. The day is so much better now it's almost as though it's a totally different one, like we're in a different universe. The sun has painted the sky gold and we sit with our shoes off on the vast green lawn in front of a yellow stone building called the Orangery, rolling a ball for Cree to toddle off and fetch. Every single time one of us rolls it, she squeals and trips and stumbles after it and brings it back, first to Jackson, then to me, then to Mac. But mostly Jackson.

"You all right?" says Mac to me, out of nowhere.

"Yeah," I say, in that quivery way people do when they're so not all right.

"You've been really quiet."

"Just thinking about Jackson and stuff. What's going to happen and stuff. Just stuff."

"It'll be all right. We'll work something out. I'll learn to sail if I have to and we'll sail him to some island somewhere." He laughs.

"You can't bloody wait to get rid of him, can you?"

His smile drops. "I didn't mean it like that. . . ."

Cree flops down onto Jackson's chest as he lies back on the grass, and when he *oomphs* in pretend pain, she giggles and does it again. Today she's insisted on wearing her pink flower-fairy tutu, her Halloween pajama bottoms, and white sandals. She wouldn't win any beautiful baby competitions in it, but I wouldn't want her to, anyway. Jackson, meanwhile, is spending his first day in his black contact lenses, which Cree has just about got used to. He's wearing all Mac's last season castoffs — Levi's, long-sleeve Calvin Klein T-shirt, and a black biker jacket Mac found at the back of his dad's closet. Styled by Mac, he looks like he's about to mince down a runway.

Cree is sprawled on Jackson's chest like a beached jellyfish. He goes to say something to her but she interrupts. "I'm a mickle baby, I am."

"A what?" he asks, turning his head toward Mac.

"That's what Mum and Dad call her," he says. "They didn't think they could have any more kids. Then one day Mum was serving in the bar, had a pain, and about half an hour later, out popped Creedence."

Jackson laughs. "Don't tell me. Creedence Clearwater Revival was playing on the jukebox?"

"Yeah," says Mac, leaning on his elbows so his white T-shirt is taut across his chest. "'Green River.' My dad plays it all the time. And they tell her she's this miracle baby."

"Oh, a *miracle* baby. That actually sounds as though it might be true," says Jackson, looking into Cree's eyes as she fiddles with a button on his shirt.

She rests her head on his chest. "My can hear the bump-bumps, Dody," she tells me.

"Good girl." Jackson frowns and looks over to me. "She can hear your heart," I tell him.

"Oh," he laughs. "So I *am* still alive, then."

We follow rickety flagstone paths into terraced gardens scattered with flowerbeds that are so symmetrical there isn't a blade of grass out of place. There are ten different gardens at Weston Park, like different rooms in a house. Different gardens to suit different whims or times of day, gardens to picnic in, sit in, read in, look at the hills in. It's too quiet for me, really. I like noise and a bit more *wah wah* going on. So did Grandad, although the top pond at Weston Park was his favorite place to skinny dip.

"Cree, get down," Mac calls. She's trying to climb onto the fountain at the center of the terrace. She kicks off when Mac pulls her back. I wish I could still climb stuff sometimes — you know, trees and walls — like I did as a kid. But you can't climb when you get to my age. It's frowned upon. They put spikes on top of everything, anyway. I know this from experience.

We've all got things on our minds that afternoon as we sit around a table in the park's courtyard tearoom. I'm thinking about the five thousand quid I've just chucked down the swanney, trying to fathom any possible way that it has gone to a good cause. Mac's probably thinking about opening night at the Playhouse tomorrow and biting his black fingernails in between bites of scone. Jackson Gatlin, former lead singer of American rock outfit The Regulators, who nearly topped the Billboard chart one year ago with their second album *Strapped for Cash*, is sitting opposite me, delicately spreading clotted cream onto one half of a scone and feeding it to a two-year-old girl sitting on his lap. The last time I was here, sitting in these chairs in this same area of the courtyard, I was looking directly at Grandad and wondering exactly how long he had left with us. I look at Jackson and the same thought crosses my mind.

"It's nice here," says Jackson, removing a mushy strawberry from the top of his scone. "Ya know, in America, these are called biscuits. Not sweet ones with strawberries; plain ones. We have them with, like, chicken and gravy."

"Urgh," says Mac, swallowing down a large chunk of scone and looking pained.

"Nah, it's good." Cree leans forward and takes the spoon out of the jam and tries spreading some more onto her half of the scone. Most of the jam ends up on the tabletop. Jackson still looks awkward with her, but she's sitting quite happily on his knee like it's the safest place in the world. He looks at her eating the scone and frowns. "How come you keep missing your mouth, Cree?" he asks her. "She, like, totally keeps missing her mouth."

"She's two," says Mac, scrunching up his napkin and reaching for her. "Come on, Creep, we need to change your diaper." A full-on head-back tantrum because she wants Jackson to do it is narrowly avoided because Mac's learned my tactic of immediate distraction. "Look, look, birdies!" he says, pointing up into the sky as they go off toward the toilets. Cree's squinting skyward and wondering what the hell he's talking about.

Jackson's looking at Cree as Mac takes her. I'm

looking at Mac's jeans, wondering how he finds ones that fit his arse so well.

"Cree's really taken to you," I say.

"She's a sweet kid," he says. "Always thought I'd have a kid someday."

"You did?"

He nods. "Well, doesn't everybody when they're young? You think that's the way it's gonna go. Marriage. Kids. It wasn't meant to be. Never met anyone I really fell for and I can't seem to give back what they give me."

"You're still young. Anyway, what about that model you went out with? That Cassandra ....."

"God, no. That was a publicity stunt. I just went to the VMAs with her. Grohman *paid* her. The fans don't actually want me to have a girlfriend, of course, but Frank sets me up with these models every now and again to save face. So I at least appear normal. Engineers a few pregnancy scare stories, just so the album sales don't drop. Can't disappoint the fan girls now, can we?"

"What do you mean, you can't give back what they give you?"

"Love, I guess," he sniffs. The sight of the mushy strawberry he's put on the side of his plate is obviously offending him as he drapes his napkin over it, like it's some dead body at the side of the road. "I don't really feel love. My therapists all tell me it's a childhood thing, I don't know."

So he hasn't got attached to me at all. He hasn't even thanked me for everything I've done for him. Not that I'm surprised, I suppose. I don't think he was actually expecting to be kidnapped, or expecting to thank anyone for kidnapping him, never mind how many hot washes of his clothes I've done since he's lived with me, or how many sandwiches I've made him. Or how many coffees I've brewed him. Nights I've stayed up talking to him. That hasn't mattered at all.

He smiles and dips his head. "Cree will forget me soon, anyway."

"She's not a goldfish. You must care a little bit. About her . . . about me?"

"I don't miss stuff. I just don't. I don't have that thing inside me."

"What, humanity?" I scoff.

Jackson's human enough to get the hint that the subject should be changed. "Have you and Mac talked about your little attachment yet?"

I snap myself out of my daydream. He's still going on about me and Mac and how we should be in a relationship. "Don't mention it. He'll be back any minute. You'll embarrass him."

Jackson looks around. "I don't see any sign of him. Haven't you at least thought about him that way before?"

"Of course I've thought about it."

"Interesting," he says, sipping his coffee and leaning back in his chair.

"What's interesting?"

"I just think it's kinda interesting. You say you don't get along with your family. You've quit your job. No boyfriend. What's to stay here for? So you could, if you wanted to, come with me. When I go away. Whenever that will be."

I'm stuck for words. "Where did that come from?"

He shrugs. "You told me in the garage that night that you think of yourself as a lost soul. Like me. You couldn't give me one thing in your life, now that your grandad's gone, that makes it worth sticking around here for. You said yourself there's no future with Mac because he's gay. And neither he nor Cree is in your family."

"Don't rub it in, will you?

"So you want them to be? You love them both?"

"Of course I do . . ."

"You said the last few years have been all about The Regulators. About me, your dream guy. And now I'm giving you the chance to get away from here for good, start a whole new life with me, a whole new persona."

"I—"

A waitress drops a stack of plates and cutlery, which smashes and crashes to the cobbles below. I jump. Jackson doesn't even turn around. "Were you just full of it?"

"Full of what?" I reply, annoyed by the loud, over-apologetic clearing up of dropped cutlery and plate fragments.

"Full of shit." He shrugs, all matter-of-factly, like he knows me better than I know myself. "You say I'm your guy and you've built your life around me. You say that concert was the best night of your life."

"It wasn't the best night of my life. It was probably one of the worst, actually."

"Why?"

"Because it was horrible. I queued up all day, got puked on, spat at, crapped on, crushed, to see about three songs, and then my bloody moon rock went missing and you gave it back to me and . . . that was good . . . but then I got dragged off and stamped on and I fainted and hit my head . . . ugh, the whole day was hideous." My voice gets louder and louder.

An old lady who's sitting by a table next to us, all hunched over and grumpy like Winston Churchill, turns her wobbly head in our direction and tuts.

Jackson drops his voice to a whisper. "So why did you put yourself through it all?"

"Because I wanted to be at the front. To be close to you. I thought it would . . . I don't know. Maybe you'd wink at me or something and I'd be more than just a face in the crowd. I did it because I loved you."

"Loved me? As in past tense loved?"

"Yeah."

"So when you look at me now, do you love me? Would you go through all that again for me? Would you kidnap me again?"

I'm stuck again, no words will come out, no words will even show up ready to be sent out of my mouth. There's nothing waiting in the wings.

"No," I eventually say. "I was hoping for the 'Grandad and Jimi Hendrix experience.'" He frowns. "I just wanted to meet you. I thought you were going to make everything better."

The truth was no, he hadn't made everything better. But he had made things clearer. I know now that I don't love him anymore. He's just Jackson to me now. He's important, but he's just a guy. What's that line in that Hugh Grant film where he's a poor bookseller and she's this famous actress? She's just a girl, standing in front of a guy, asking him to love her? Well, I'm just a girl, sitting in front of a rock star, wondering why I bothered.

"It'll be amazing. We'll do so much, see so much of the world. It'll be awesome."

"I don't want to come with you," I say.

"Say again?" he says, leaning forward.

"No offense. But, I don't want to come with you, when you go. I don't know why, I just . . . I don't belong with you."

"That's the difference between us. I don't belong with anyone."

But where *do* I belong? I wonder.

We buy some seeds in the shop where we meet up with Mac and Cree.

"You OK?" Mac asks me.

"Why do you keep asking me that?" I snap and then try and laugh it off. "Yes, I'm fine." My chest squeezes.

"Sorry I asked," he says and I blush. I want to tell him about the BFD. He'll kill me but before he kills me he'll at least try and sort it out. Make me feel better about it. If I cry, Mac might not shout at me. He'll hug me. He always hugs me when I cry.

I wish I knew what love felt like.

Watching Jackson on the DVD for the first time felt like love. My chest felt thundery and I kept rewinding. And I just wanted to kiss him. I just wanted to do nothing else but kiss him for the rest of my life. But when I look at Jackson now I don't feel like that at all. He just feels like a very annoying elder brother and the last thing in the world I'd want to kiss. When I look at Mac, I think I want to rewind. I actually want to touch him in some way. God. Weird or what? But I do. I keep rewinding.

Jackson promises Cree we can go up to the top pond and feed the swans. He wants to see where Grandad used to swim. Grandad's become a bit of a hero in Jackson's eyes and I know, I just know, he's going to jump in, too, if there's no one around. It's all part of this newfound freedom thing. He's going to jump off the stage and crowd surf for a bit. He's going to suck out all the marrow from life, do all the carpe diem stuff my grandad did. He's been asking about my grandad a lot the last few days and he says he's going to live life like he did.

Nobody's going to stop him doing anything from now on. The garage won't contain him for much longer. Even though I haven't told him he's leaving tomorrow, he still seems ready to go.

At the back of the formal gardens there's a wooded valley and along it runs a stream that connects the lower and top ponds by landscaped waterfalls. As we walk through the valley along a stony track, going against the flow of the river, Jackson's running after Cree, who's squealing and getting all excited, and her laugh is like falling pennies. The sun glows down. It's the perfect day. She toddles after the rolling ball on the path ahead of us and, for the first time in days, Mac and I are alone. We have time to talk. But it's weird. I can't look at him without imagining things.

How it would be if we were together. Like, *couple* together. Kissing and stuff. Kissing him all the time. All this saliva comes into my mouth when I think of it. I check my chest. It's a bit thundery.

"It feels like we haven't been anywhere, just us, for ages," I laugh. I'm nervous. I'm never nervous around Mac. My cheeks explode and I put my hand up to scratch the side of my face nearest him so he doesn't see.

Mac flaps a fly away from his face. "I know. *He's* kind of taken over."

"*He's* asked me to go away with him, when he leaves."

Mac says nothing. Eventually he laughs. "How's that going to work, then?"

I shrug. "I don't know. He just asked me."

"So you're going to leave with him? You've known the guy two weeks."

"I haven't said I'll go. It's a pretty amazing offer, though. Isn't it?"

"Yeah. Sure. What have you got to stick around for, after all?" he says, with more than a hint of sarcasm threaded through his voice. "Regulators is your life, that's what you say, right?" We come across a large clod of dried mud on the path. He kicks it out of the way.

"It's not like that. He just asked me. It's just an option."

"You'll go, I know you will. He's everything to you."

"No he's not."

"He is, you love him to bits. That's why he's here, isn't it? To be your dream man and ruin my life."

"What do you mean, ruin your life?"

"Forget it."

"No, what does that mean, Mac? Tell me you want me to stay here with you."

I stop walking. Mac carries on for a bit and then stops and turns around, his arms flap once against his sides. "You waited all day to see his concert. You kidnapped him. You were willing to sell your soul to the BFD. I can't compete, can I?" He turns and keeps walking.

"Why would you want to compete?" I say, gaining on him, but he doesn't hear, or if he does, he doesn't show it. "Say I do go with him. Wouldn't that be better?"

"No, it wouldn't be better."

I want him to say something, *anything* to make me believe what Jackson says is true. I want him to say he loves me so much he couldn't bear it if I left. So I push the button. "I think I'm going to do it. I think I'm going to leave."

"Fine. Do what you want," he says, walking faster.

I don't know what to say. But I don't have to say anything, because at the next moment the most frightening noise I've ever heard is suddenly in my ears.

And I realize I've heard it before. From Jackson. It *is* Jackson.

Before I know what's happening, Mac and I are running, sprinting along the track toward the sound. It comes again, and again, and we pick up speed. I'm trying to understand what he's yelling, yelling all the time. *Scream. Scream. Scream. Scream.*

And then I realize what he's yelling.

Cree.

TWENTY-THREE

CREE'S POND
WATER REVIVAL

We sprint toward the top pond and, when we get there, Jackson's just standing on the edge, combing the water frantically with his eyes.

"Where is she?" Mac shouts, pelting to the edge of the pond and plunging straight in, a great crash of water behind him. My hand automatically grips the moon rock in my jacket pocket. Cree's nowhere. I scan the pond. It seems endless and still and dark with green weed. Cree's pink ball bobs alone on the surface.

"She ran after the ball!" Jackson shouts at me. "She fell. I couldn't get there in time — I didn't see where she went in."

At one end, the pond feeds into a small cascade, which sucks the water down into another smaller pool and from then on into the trench that runs right the way along the entire valley.

What if she's caught in the weeds? What if she's caught in the sucking pull of the cascade? It's a ten-foot drop down into the next pool. That's if she doesn't drown before she gets there.

"She just disappeared. One moment she was in front of me, next she was gone."

My heart is a huge hand thrumming its fingers on a tabletop. Mac's not going to find her. I just know he's not going to find her. I wait. What was it I learned in first aid? *In an emergency, assess the situation.* He bobs up and takes a huge breath.

"Where the hell is she?!" he screams out.

"She was right here!" Jackson yells back. "Oh God, no."

"Why didn't you jump in, you fucking coward!" He disappears back under the water before Jackson can answer. Not that he was going to answer. He's scared. He hates water. I know that from when I pushed him off the bridge. I leave my body. I urge myself to wake up. Nothing happens. I wait. And I wait. I grind my fingers against the moon rock and pray for Grandad to guide me, tell me what to do. Mac bobs up and frantically down again but there's nothing. I kick off my sneakers and lower myself down into the water. I bob up. I wait. I can just about feel the bottom with my feet. It's gritty and scummy. My soles roll over rough rocks as my open fingers comb the water, desperately looking for clues. I breathe in and just wait. My heart bangs in my throat. The pond's so murky I can't even see my own hand. It feels like she's been gone for an age, but it can't be more than seconds. *There's still time. There's still time.*

I could cry and never stop. But I keep looking, just standing there, stupid and helpless, looking, my hands swishing through the water, back and forth, back and forth. I just wait, I don't know what for. I just know I should stay here, not dive under. Just wait. *Wait. Wait. You'll see her, just wait. Don't go under. You'll see her. Just. Wait.*

And then I see it. Fifteen feet away from me in a clump of weeds. A white sandal.

I dive straight under and swim blindly to where I saw

the sandal and I reach out and I grab it — a sandal, a sock, a leg, a body, and then something tears. Pondweed. She's stuck. I push her body up and feel the weed tear away from it, up, up, up toward the surface of the water. The weed covers my face, it's over my mouth, it's in my mouth. I swallow dirt. But she's out. And I'm out with her. And I hear the beautiful noise of her crying so hard.

I stride through the weed and water toward the bank. I reach for dry land and claw my way up the mud with one arm wrapped around Cree. I drag us up out of the water, my heart beating so fast, my lungs pumping so hard, and I slump down onto the bank. I put my hands on Cree's back and feel her ribs, her lungs working hard underneath. Her strong coughs ripping through her body. I sit up, I rock her, counting down the seconds. She coughs harder and throws up a bit. I sit her upright and rub her back. She cries my name. She says it perfectly, in between sobs and coughs.

"Dody."

I scrape the weed away from her face as I hold her to me like the baby I always forget she is. I hold her close — I could hold twenty of her, she is so tiny. She coughs so hard her little white face bursts into purple.

"It's OK, it's OK, you're all right," I say to her, wiping her face and cuddling her tightly. "Cree, you're OK. Jody's here."

"My . . . want . . . my . . . daddy." She cuddles into me and she's shaking so hard her hand keeps slipping on my rubbery arm. I look out to the pond. There's no sign of Mac. He'll kill himself trying to find her, I know he will. He's always getting the third degree from his parents whenever

Cree comes out with us. Make sure he changes her diaper every hour. Keep hold of her hand. Don't let her wander off with any strange men.

Twenty seconds. Thirty. Forty. He's not coming up. He's not coming up. *Come up. Oh God, come up, come up, come up. Please.*

Jackson calls something and runs over to where I'm sitting with Cree on the bank. I'm still looking for Mac.

"Oh my God, where is he?" I start to cry. Cree's still howling and coughing in my arms, gripping on to me.

"Where is he?!" I shout at Jackson. He just stares at me.

And then Mac bobs up near the swan island and, as I close my eyes, my tears fall like never before. He searches around and sees us on the bank. I thank the sky above me. He front-crawls to where we are. Jackson sits down on the grass a few feet or so away. Mac wades out and runs immediately to me. He snatches up Cree and she clings on to him. I've never ever seen Mac cry before.

"Oh my God, oh my God," he keeps saying, and his hand clings on to her wet blonde ponytail at the back. "It's OK, Kenzie's here, Kenzie's got you." Cree's coughing and sobbing on his shoulder. The three of us are crying. And then I feel it. I feel the pain more than I've ever felt anything before. Another minute and Cree could have died. We could be pumping her lifeless little body on the bank right now. I thought I'd felt terror before. I thought I'd felt the worst I could possibly feel, but that wasn't this. This is real. It burns like a nightmare.

Mac looks down at me. I'm shaking so hard and can barely see him through tears.

"You got her out?" he gasps.

I nod. I sniff. "I saw her sandal in the middle —"

He bends down and with Cree in between us he hugs me, grabbing my head with one of his hands. "Jody . . ."

I don't think anymore. I lean forward and kiss him hard on the lips. It's violent and wet-pond watery and at that moment all it means is sheer relief. "She's OK," I whisper as our foreheads rest on each other's. "She's OK."

The four of us slop back along the path toward the parking lot. Jackson doesn't say one word. But Mac says plenty.

"Stupid, selfish, idiot! Why weren't you watching her? Why weren't you holding her hand? Why didn't you jump in before we got there?"

Cree starts whimpering on Mac's shoulder. She's looking at Jackson. Jackson's got his head down, his hands wedged into the pockets of his Levi's. Mac's Levi's.

"You don't think about anyone but yourself," he goes on at Jackson. "Why didn't you go in after her straightaway? Because you care more about your own safety than anyone else's, that's why."

Jackson yanks on his key string, the first time I've seen him do it in days. The sun is going out for the day and the grass in the shadows is cold to the touch. After a while, Cree's little huffs are the only sounds on the air. Even the birds high up in the treetops seem to have stopped their incessant warbling.

We make it back to the car in silence. Mac hands Cree to me as he opens the trunk and we stand her up to get her out of her wet things, wrapping her up in the picnic blanket to keep her warm while we get her spare clothes out of her SpongeBob bag. She holds on to me as Mac changes her. She's all shivery and so small, like a little pink shrimp. She keeps asking for her daddy, sometimes Mummy, but mostly Daddy, and she's clinging to me hard. I ask her once if she wants a cuddle with Jackson while I go to the toilet before we set off, but she shakes her head defiantly. I don't want to leave her, anyway.

We don't report what's happened to the staff at Weston Park, but there's no getting away from telling Tish and Teddy about it. Cree doesn't want to sit in her car seat so I cradle her in the back. Mac has the heating on full blast to keep her warm all the way down the motorway.

"You're going to see Daddy now. We're going back to your house and you can give him big cuddles." I kiss her on her head and all at once there are tears on my cheeks.

"My daddy cuggles," she repeats.

"Yeah. Yeah, he will give you cuddles," I say. I'm holding on to her really tight. Jackson remains absolutely silent, riding shotgun. Mac won't even look at him.

We get back to my house and drop Jackson off at our back gate. He holds the door open and leans in. "Mac, I'm sorry," he says. Mac says nothing. "I screwed up."

Mac nods, his jaw clenching, still staring resolutely at the street beyond the windshield as the Saxo's engine ticks over. "The sooner you leave, the better."

Jackson doesn't even argue, he just nods, closes the car door, and walks back over to the drum room, opens the door, and goes inside.

I don't say anything, either. I don't even look at Mac. He's waiting for me to get out of the car. "I've got to take Cree home and tell Mum and Dad," he says.

"You're not taking the rap for this on your own. I'm coming with you."

"Jody, get out," he snaps.

"No. I'm not leaving her on her own in the back." Cree starts whimpering again in my arms and before I know it Mac's put his foot down on the pedal and we're speeding up Chesil Lane, on our way to the Pack Horse. The second we park the Saxo, Mac leaps out, leans in the back, and snatches Cree off me, so he's holding her as we enter through the back of the pub. Teddy's behind the counter, counting up the lunchtime take. The second Cree spots him she starts full-on crying out for him.

"What's happened? Why . . . why's she . . ." Teddy's all confused as to why Cree's hair is damp and why she's in utter despair for a cuddle and clinging to him with strength he never knew she had. Why Mac and I are wet and muddy and my hair is straggly and dirtier than usual. Teddy's face grows whiter with shock as we tell him, leaving out all the bits about Jackson. Mac takes the full blame.

"Me and Jody were talking and . . . throwing the ball to her and she ran after it. We weren't looking. She fell in the pond."

"Bloody hell, Kenz, what were you bloody playing at, not watching her?! God, I think I'm going to be sick," he says, sitting down on an upturned bottle crate and rubbing Cree's back. She's completely calmed down now, her face against his shoulder and sucking her thumb. Now that she's got her dad, she's relaxed. All her angst and crying has transferred to him. His face is sheet-white. "I should have been there," he keeps saying. "Why wasn't I there?"

"She's OK, Dad," says Mac.

Teddy's shaking. He gives Mac a brief glance. "Jesus, she could've drowned! My poor little girl. Look at your hair, all dirty." His whole hand shakes as he strokes over her damp ponytail. He's deffo on the verge of blubbing.

Teddy's right. If he'd been there, it wouldn't have happened. She wouldn't have got near that pond, let alone gone in. I bite my nails again, only there's nothing there to bite anymore. All my nails are in fragments on the backseat of Mac's car.

There's footsteps along the corridor and Tish appears through the beaded curtain at the back of the bar. "I thought I heard voices, d'you have a nice . . ." she starts to say and then sees us, sees Cree, sees Teddy's ashen face, and immediately the panic sets in and she takes Cree's dazed face in her hands. "Oh my God, what's happened?"

Mac and I tell her, almost word for word, what we've just told Teddy, again leaving out the missing-rock-star-that-came-with-us bits. It's even harder telling her because she does cry. They both start shouting at us then, at which point Cree starts crying as well. It's a total nightmare of crying and accusing and shouting, and most of the shouting and accusing is directed straight at Mac.

"Don't take it out on him," I interrupt. "I was there, too. It's my fault as well."

"Leave it, Jody," says Mac.

"I tell you time and time again you've got to watch her cos she wanders, but do you listen?" Teddy cries. "She could have died because of you!"

At this point, Mac marches straight through the bar and upstairs. I hear a door slam in the distance. Moments later there are thumping footsteps down the stairs and the kitchen door opens and slams. He's gone to his dress rehearsal about an hour early. I'm not aware of my heart beating a path out of my throat anymore, or my lungs ballooning in and out. I'm completely numb. I just feel dirty, like I want an endless hot shower. I think it must be shock, if not from what happened at Weston Park, then because of what they've just said to Mac.

I have to say something. "It's not fair, telling him she could have died. She's OK. It was an accident."

"Go home, Jody," says Tish, all quivery voice. "It's all right, we're not angry with you."

"We bloody are!" says Teddy. "The pair of 'em should've been watching her better." Tish rubs her temples. Her hands are shaking.

I turn to go, but I turn back. I don't know what I'm going to say until I hear it coming out of my mouth. "When was the last time you took Cree out anywhere? For the day? We take her out all the time, me and Mac. All she wants is you two, but you're always busy. You palm her off on Mac all the time. . . ."

"I beg your pardon," says Teddy. "Don't talk to my wife like that."

"Your wife? Not your barmaid, then? Just cos Cree's not

old enough to stock bottles or clear glasses she's probably not on your radar really, is she?" I can't help myself. I can't stop it coming.

"How dare you!" says Teddy. "Running a pub is a 24/7 job."

"So is having kids! You can't just have them and then let them get on with it. It's the same at the day care. Kids cry all day for their parents, but they're too worried about paying for the mortgage or remodeling the kitchen to be that bothered. You don't realize how much she needs you. All she ever wants is her daddy and you're never ever there!"

"How dare you!" Tish shouts. "You don't know what you're talking about."

"Yes, I do," I say. There's no stopping me now. "Mac told me you were the same with him as a kid, too. Always making excuses. Can't go and see him in his Nativity play, got to be back for opening up. Can't go and see him sing at the school concert, who'll run the pub? You missed out on Mac's whole childhood. And you're missing out on Cree's, too!"

"Get out, Jody. Go on, go home, you've crossed the line," cries Tish. Teddy's rocking Cree and just looks shell-shocked. And then Tish and Teddy start riffing between themselves.

"This is just like last time," Tish says, sobbing. "We weren't there then, either."

Cree escaped from Bumblebees one day (one of the few days when I had genuinely been out sick). She had just learned to walk and she managed to undo the lock on the gate in the yard and wandered out into the street, which is right by the main road through Nuffing. It was sheer luck that one of the ladies from the sandwich shop was walking past.

Teddy just nods and strokes the head of his now-sleeping little girl.

Silence. "So what are you going to do about it?" I ask them. They both look at me. "Take her to the Easter egg hunt in the woods next weekend? Go and see Mac's opening night tomorrow? I bet neither of you have ever been to one, have you?"

Silence again. Tish sniffs. Teddy sighs. "We always think about going," Teddy mumbles.

"I think you should go home, Jody," says Tish.

And without one more word, I do.

TWENTY-FOUR

BETWEEN A ROCK GOD AND A HARD PLACE

I take the long way back to my house, through the churchyard, and sit on one of the benches for a bit, looking at the graves. There's a slug moving its way down one of them, the nearest one. I wish I was it. Comes to something when your life sucks so bad you want to trade places with a slug. I stare at the pub across the road. I shouted at Mac's parents. They're going to hate me now. They'll never want me at the pub again. If we hadn't gone to Weston Park, Cree wouldn't have nearly drowned. If I hadn't kidnapped Jackson in the first place, we wouldn't have taken him there like he wanted to. It's all because of me. I use the phone booth to try and call Mac but his phone just rings and rings. I call again and it goes straight to voice mail. I don't know how long I'm sitting there, headstone-watching and churning over the day's events in my head, but it's getting dark by the time I leave. I go into the house via the backyard, hoping to look in on Jackson before dinner, but the kitchen light's on and Mum's in the window, running the tap into a saucepan. She sees me and smiles. I smile back. I look across to the garage and when Mum's back is turned, I open the door and look inside. Jackson's gone.

Oh my God.

The back door opens. Mum appears. Yet again, she

greets me when I'm fresh from a dunking in dirty water, except this time the pondweed and dirt are pretty dried into my clothes.

And yet again, she doesn't even ask.

"All right? How was Weston Park?"

"Mmm, yeah," I tell her. And I explain, "Cree fell in the pond. I fished her out."

She looks at me as I walk into the utility room and start stripping off my jeans and socks. *Where the hell has he gone? Has he left? Is he hiding? Has Mum caught him and forced him to shell broad beans for dinner? Where. The Hell. Is. He?*

"Blimey," she says. "Is Cree OK?"

"Yeah, she's fine. I'm going to take a shower, all right?"

"All right, dinner'll be about forty minutes. Beef Wellington."

"Lush."

So I'm in the bathroom, showering away, but I'm thinking the whole time about my incredible vanishing hostage. I'm thinking about all the places I need to go and look for him. Back down by the river. The train station. I wonder if I could borrow Alfie again without Tish and Teddy noticing. I wonder if they'll let me after I bawled them out. I wonder what excuses I'll give Mum when I suddenly have to dash out after dinner. I step out of the bath, wrap a towel around me, and out of nowhere, there's a *chink* on the window. And another *chink*. And another.

"What the —" I lift up the catch on the window above the sink and shove it open.

And my moon rock comes flying toward my face.

"Hey, it's me," comes a voice. An American voice. I climb up onto the sink, holding my towel in place to look down into the yard. There's no one there, but it's Jackson's voice. The moon rock appears again, and I realize it's suspended on a long string. A shoe lace. It's dangling down. I pull on the string.

"Jackson?" I whisper.

"Come on up, the moon is fine," he says.

I throw on a clean T-shirt and jeans and slip on my Converse and sprint back downstairs. Halley's safely watching *Hollyoaks* in the living room and Mum's emptying the dishwasher.

"Where are you off to now?" she asks as I leg it past her, my hair dripping all over the tiles.

"Just . . . to the pub. I have to give something to Mac. His iPod. I forgot to give it back to him. I won't be long."

"You've got twenty minutes."

I shut the back door and walk directly to the center of the grass. I look up. Jackson is sitting on the lowest part of the highest roof peak, just above the flat bit where Grandad used to moon-bathe, and dangling his feet just above our bathroom window.

"What are you doing up there?" I whisper up at him.

"Just wanted to be up high," he calls back.

"Ssh!" I say. "Someone'll hear you."

"No they won't. There's no one around. You can see everything from up here, it's great. Come on up."

"How?"

Jackson guides me up the garden wall, along the top of it, and I have to do a bit of shimmying up the rose trellis and onto the flat part of the roof. I tiptoe over to him and he dangles the moon rock down to me again. I take it. He's tied it to both of his shoelaces. "How did you get this?" I say, taking it from him.

"It fell out of your pocket at Weston Park. I picked it up."

"Oh. Why are you up here?"

"Everyone looks down," he says. "No one can see me up here. Your sister came out to hang out the laundry. And later your mom came out to take it in again cos it started to rain. Neither of them looked up and saw me. It's nice being up high. I can really breathe up here."

"That's nice, why don't you come down off there now? It's dark," I say.

"Is Mac still angry with me?" he says, looking far out into the night.

"I don't know. I tried calling him but he's not answering." Anxiety sits piano-heavy on my chest. I'm worrying about the helicopter I can hear somewhere in the sky that could be sweeping the county looking for him. I'm worrying that the kitchen roof is going to cave in under my weight. I'm worrying that Jackson's going to fall. I'm worrying about the slates he's spent God-knows-how-long dislodging and piling up around him like a throne. "Mac didn't mean it," I say. "What he said about never wanting to see you again. He's just scared about what could have happened. He didn't mean it."

Jackson looks at me sideways. "Yeah he did. He's got every right to hate me."

"That's not true. You're great with Cree."

"No, Cree's great with *me*," he says. "And I could've let her die today."

"Listen to me!" I tell him. "We were all there. We should all have been looking after her. I'm a trained nursery nurse. Well, I work in a day care. And Mac's her brother. Cree isn't your responsibility, she's *ours*. The only reason you're here at all is because of me, so if it's anyone's fault, it's mine. Oh God, look can you come down now and go back in the garage, please? You're giving me a heart attack being up here."

He laughs.

"What's so funny?"

"Nothing. I just can't believe I screwed things up again. I finally meet people I can get along with and then it ends in disaster. Grohman's right. Everything I do turns to shit. I can't make good of anyone's lives, especially my own." He launches a lump of moss high into the night.

"That's not true. You made my life better."

His laugh is sour. "Did I? How bad was your life before you met the wonder that is me? What single aspect of my miserable wasted shit of a life made *yours* better?"

"Well, you've certainly made it more interesting for a while."

I bite down on an already throbbing nail that I've been chewing since the car ride home from Weston Park. "Maybe I *should* come away with you, Jackson. Maybe *that's* what *'Don't Dream It, Be It'* means. Me being out of the way. And Mac doesn't seem to care one way or the other." Before I can speak again Jackson pipes up. He's smiling.

"I was clowning, Jody. I don't want you coming with me. Why would you want to? You belong here."

"No I don't. Not anymore. I was so rude to Mac's parents. They started laying into him and I just went mad. I've never seen Mac so upset. He probably hates me, too, after what happened with Cree."

"Poor, poor you. Poor tough-luck you." He jumps down onto the flat roof to stand before me. I wait, holding my breath, waiting for the sound of the back door opening. Waiting for Mum to appear below and ask me what I'm doing up here. He struts to one end of the roof. My blood runs like mountain water in my veins. "These GCDC tests you didn't pass, were any of them in getting the hint?"

"I don't —"

"Mac's a guy. I'm sure the only way he can talk you out of coming with me is if he tells you how he feels about you, and he can't do that. He'd rather face an entire audience, his hometown, wearing stilettos and fishnet stockings, than do *that*." He's smirking at me as if he's so clever.

I try and win back a point. "So he's just going to let me leave, is he? That's how much he loves me?"

"What am I, a therapist? But I saw the way he kissed you in the park."

"That was just . . ." I stammer, glad he can't see me blushing in the dark. "That was just because of Cree."

He doesn't say anything more, just shimmies back down the rose trellis and along the wall at the edge of the yard and jumps down onto all fours at the end of the flower bed. I follow him down and we creep back into the garage and close the door. "Where do you think you'll end up?"

He shrugs. "Who knows? It's exciting. Not knowing every single tiny detail of where I'm going, where I'm gonna eat my next meal, how I'm gonna get there. I don't care."

There's a hideous silence, during which I have a hideous thought. "You're not going to kill yourself, are you? Is that what you were going to do on the roof? Were you just waiting for me to watch or something?"

He shakes his head. He reaches across and picks up one of the dog-eared Stephen King books I got him from the thrift shop. *Different Seasons.* He opens it at the last page of "Rita Hayworth and the Shawshank Redemption." "You ever read this?"

"Yeah, of course. Well, I've seen the film. I didn't know it was a book, too."

"It's a novella. OK, you remember Andy, the main character in *Shawshank*? How he had everything set up in a different-name bank account just waiting for him when he got out of prison so he could disappear into a whole new life?" I remembered the end of the movie where he's digging his escape hole in his cell wall, behind this huge poster. "Well," says Jackson. "I kinda been digging a hole behind my poster, too."

"Huh?"

He finds the key string around his neck and holds it out to show me. I've seen it a thousand times but it doesn't mean anything until that moment — the moment he tells me where the lock is.

"About a year ago, we did a European tour to promote the *Strapped for Cash* album. Around the same time, I got depressed and I knew I wanted out. We did a couple of gigs in Zurich and I opened up my very own clichéd Swiss bank account."

"Why?"

He points at me. "You're the only person in the world I've told this to. I opened the account in the name of Tom Gordon. That's what I wanted to be known as if I ever got out of the band. My new identity. I think it's about time I went and unlocked that box, don't you?"

Realization slams into me like a punch. He had it all planned. He had a whole new persona already laid out for him that nobody in the world had a clue about. That was the name he'd wanted on the passport. Thomas Gordon. The name of the man who opened the offshore account. Thomas Gordon. The name of the man in the photos I'd given the BFD. Thomas Gordon.

I smile. "You bastard."

"What?"

"You've had this planned all along, haven't you? You were never going to kill yourself."

"I don't know about that, I came pretty goddamn close a couple of times there. But call it my rainy-day escape plan. I always dreamed it's what I'd do. I never got the chance to, until now. Thanks to you. That time before, when they said I was in rehab in New Zealand?"

"Yeah?"

He shakes his head. "I'd tried to do a disappearing act then. Had it all planned. Access to money no one knew I had. Got the documents through an ex-roadie Grohman fired years ago. Ran into Pash at the damn airport. So I was whisked safely back into the limelight. Balls-deep in limelight. Grohman did some damage control with the press and all was well, though he certainly kept me on a tight leash after that. Son of a bitch. That night in Cardiff, though I didn't know it at the time, another door was opened for me. Another way out."

"You'll never be in The Regulators anymore, will you?"

"As far as everyone but you is concerned, Jackson Gatlin will never walk this Earth again."

I reach out and wrinkle up the sleeve of the black Calvin Klein T-shirt — *Mac's* Calvin Klein T-shirt — to reveal his burning-rose tattoo. "What about that?"

He looks down at it and sneers. "That's the least of my worries."

"But won't you miss any of it? Singing? Performing?" He shakes his head. "I used to pretend you were my boyfriend," I tell him. "At night, whenever I couldn't sleep, I'd listen to Regs on my MP3 and close my eyes and imagine you right there with me. Singing just for me."

"You won't do that anymore?" he says.

"No way," I say. "Well, I'll still listen to rock. I don't know if I'll listen to The Regulators again. It would be too strange. You're like some weird brother to me now."

He smiles his dimpled smile and pats the feathers next to him. "Come here." I crawl across the feathers and sit next to him. "You're making my dream come true. So, I'll do the same for you. I'll give you an exclusive, backstage, all-access pass to Jackson Gatlin's final performance."

He lies down on the feathers.

"What?" I say, not quite sure what he means.

"Lie down here."

I shake my head. "No."

"I'm not going to do anything, Jody. Come on, humor me." He pats the feathers next to him. I lie down, staring into his eyes. "I'll sing for you. What would you like me to sing?"

"Ooh, this is way cringey!"

"Come on, pick a song. One of our slow ones? 'Tortuous'? Everyone always wants 'Tortuous.'"

"No," I tell him, looking dead into his eyes. "Do you know any Fang Morrison songs?"

"Van Morrison? What one? 'Crazy Love'? 'Brown Eyed —'"

"'Brown Eyed Girl,' yeah, that's it."

"OK," he says and starts to sing. And for the first time ever, I feel his breath on my cheeks. The breath I've been imagining for so long. Hot and perfect. And I close my eyes. But he doesn't stroke my hair as I've always imagined. And in my mind it's not him singing anymore. It's Mac.

TWENTY-FIVE

LAST FAMOUS WORDS

Friday arrives with gray skies and drizzly windows. Mac's phone is off all morning. I'm guessing he's still not talking to me so I leave it, and once Mum and Halley are out of the way, Jackson comes in the house and I finally tell him he's leaving tonight. I push all thoughts of never seeing him again out of my mind as I help him pack my black rucksack with a few items of spare clothing and a new toothbrush. I gulp down a rush of tears as I'm raiding the cupboards for long-lasting foodstuffs to take with him — beans, crackers, cheese. All morning I daren't look at his face for too long, because it keeps catching me — that thought. That unbearable thought that after ten thirty tonight, he'll be gone forever. Before the concert, I'd look at the posters and the magazine articles and the TV interviews and I'd know that I'd see him onstage again some day and I'd know he really existed. But after ten thirty tonight, that'll be it. He'll get in that car as Jackson James Gatlin, but when he gets out again, he'll be plain old Thomas Gordon. Nobody.

Jackson can't wait. He keeps talking about all the things he's going to do. These cliffs in Indonesia he's going to jump off. This art gallery in Australia he's going to visit. That blossom tree in Japan he's going to sit beneath again. The day goes so fast, like galloping horses I just can't hold back, no matter how hard I dig my heels in the dirt.

At four o'clock, I walk into town and buy Mac a large good-luck card. I write it in the shop. Then I walk around to the posh flower shop. They've got into the *Rocky Horror* spirit, and I buy Mac the nicest bunch of black roses. I take both around to the Playhouse. I want to see Mac, even if he doesn't want to see me. I open the stage door. I'm confronted by a group of people in white makeup, corsets, and garter belts. They're holding plastic cups and chocolate-chip cookies and are coming up from the room under the staircase, the actors' canteen. They meander past me like a long multicolored river, all giving me funny looks, like I'm the freak. I stop a short fat bloke, who turns out to be Ann Rackham in a wig.

"Have you seen Mackenzie Lawless?"

"Yeah, he's in his dressing room," she says, and then rejoins the group of players as they disappear up the stairs to the first and second floors.

I walk along the corridor that runs parallel to the back of the stage to find Dressing Room One, all on its own at the very end. The door is shut. I can hear music. I lean in closer. It's that song again — "Brown Eyed Girl." I knock. After a little while and a lot of clunking around, the music disappears and the door snaps open. Mac stands before me. And for the first time ever, I know what I feel when I'm looking at him. I feel the thunder.

"Oh," he says. "I thought you were Geoffrey. Just done my opening song about six bloody times. I'm sick of it." He returns to what he was doing before my interruption: changing. He flicks off his sneakers. I walk in, still clutching the oversized card and bunch of black roses. He turns back to me and twizzles a finger in the air to make me turn around so he can take off his pants.

"Why?" I say. "I've seen you naked before." And then I wish I hadn't said it cos suddenly I remember I was sneaking a look at him when he took a shower at our house once. I know it's a bit pervy but he was coming out of the bathroom, I was coming out of my room, his towel slipped, he grabbed it, I saw his ass. That was all I saw. Honestly.

"I've never been *that* drunk in front of you," he says. "Go on, turn."

I turn. "Why have you done your opening song six times? You know it backward."

"I did," he says quietly. "Nerves are kicking in today, just when I least need them."

"You don't get nervous. *I* get nervous."

"Are you coming tonight?" he asks.

I turn back around. He's in a long-sleeved black mesh top that's threaded through with silver and there's a bath towel around his waist. "Course I am. Front row. And I'm picking up my costume from Fancy That on the way home and Jackson's going to do my makeup for me." I present him with the card and flowers. He smiles at them, not me, setting the card down on the neatest dressing table I've ever seen and the flowers in the sink along with another bouquet he's got. I walk over to them and fumble with the other card. "Who are these from?"

"Sorry bouquet from Mum," he says, sitting down in the towel in front of his mirror. The flash in his hair is red. "She's only coming to the first half tonight."

"She's actually coming?" I'm amazed.

He picks up his hair straightener and starts running it through his hair. "Yeah, I don't know what's come over them. She's going home at the intermission and Dad's coming to the second half. They don't want to leave Cree." He pokes about in his makeup bag, pulling out his hand sanitizer, foundation, and tube of mascara. He unscrews the mascara and starts fluffing it about his lashes. "He's never *ever* seen one of my shows."

Wow. What I said actually made a difference. I can't believe it. I can't believe they worked something out for both of their kids. I want to hug him but he's busy applying the mascara. His hand is shaking.

"Do you want me to do it?"

"No, it's fine," he says. I suck in a big deep breath and let it out. He turns and looks at me. "I daren't ask if you're OK, after the last time I asked."

"Jackson's leaving. Tonight. Hopefully."

"About time." It's just mumbled but I hear it all the same. But then he stops mascara-ing and turns around again. "He really is going? Where? How?"

I swallow. "The BFD. I know what you're going to say, but he's fixed everything." Mac just stares at me. "He can do it, I know he can."

"You . . . what?"

"I gave the money to the BFD."

"You . . . stupid . . . your grandad gave you that money!" he shrieks.

"Yes, I know where it came from, thanks. And he told me I could do what I wanted with it."

"He wanted *you* to do something with it! The BFD will piss it away, Jody! It would have been more productive to burn it. God, you idiot! You could have done so much with that money."

"No I couldn't," I say. "I didn't know what the hell to do with it. I didn't want it, I told you that. I don't give a shit about money. If it meant having Grandad back, I would have given the BFD every single penny."

"How much *did* you give him?"

I don't want to tell him but he's looking at me so bug-eyed, I feel I have to before his eyes pop right out of his head. "Five."

"FIVE GRAND?!"

"Yes, five grand. No one else was going to help me, were they?"

"NEITHER'S HE!"

"He will. I know he will."

Mac shakes his head. His voice is calmer now but there's a thread of hate running all the way through it. "I just don't believe what you've put yourself through for that waste of space."

"My money. My risk. My decision. So save your lecture, OK? I'm not interested."

"What about our holiday?" says Mac, looking up.

"I've still got five grand left."

He shakes his head. "No, you need to put that in a secure vault somewhere and leave it alone. You'll have no savings left at all at this rate."

"Stop talking to me like you're my dad or something!" I shout at him, not that my dad ever encouraged me to save, quite the opposite in fact, but a normal dad would. "I'm fed up with your bloody preaching to me. I *KNOW* I've done the right thing. Jackson *HAS* to get out of here and I found the one way he could do that, so leave me alone."

"Well, I suppose there is one glimmer of light at the end of the never-ending tunnel of doom. If the BFD *does* perform the miracle of the disappearing rock star, then at least *I* won't have to deal with him anymore."

"What's he actually done to you?" I ask. "Apart from what happened yesterday, what's he done that's so wrong?"

He doesn't answer. I'm so frustrated I could scream in his face.

"So are you going with him, then? I assume you are." He smudges a fingertip of mascara into both his eyebrows.

For some reason, I let him think that I'm still going with Jackson. I want to know if he cares enough to stop me. "We have to meet the car at ten thirty."

He nods, clicking the mascara back in the tube and picking up a small eye-shadow stick with electric blue powder at one end and smoky black at the other. He dabs some more over both his lids, all clumsy, and he has to keep dabbing away at the corners where he's messed up.

"Let me do it," I snap, stepping forward.

"No, it's fine," he says. I step back. He runs the straightening iron up his spiky layers again and quickly hairsprays over it to keep it in place. He picks up his silver glitter spray and starts squirting it all over his head. "I won't see you off tonight. Show doesn't finish 'til quarter to. I'd miss my encore."

He's not going to beg me to stay. Ask me to stay, even. I knew it — he hates me.

"No, I . . . I know. I'm still coming tonight. Jackson wants to come as well. We'll see most of it. We'll just have to skip out a bit early."

He stops spraying and slams the can down on the side. "You're making the biggest mistake ever, Jody. I thought you were stupid before, but this . . ."

"Yeah, well, you know me." I laugh, thinking he'll laugh, too, but he doesn't. He gets up, looks at me, sparkling all over, like my moon rock when it catches the light. His mouth is as thin as a pavement crack. "Good luck for tonight," I say and move back toward the door. He sighs.

"And what happens after tonight?" he says finally, turning to apply some black lipstick. "You're not going to be here." He strides over to his clothes rack and flicks down a pair of black fishnet stockings that have been hanging over the rail. He starts fumbling with one of them, stumbling about on one leg trying to put it on. "You don't give a shit about me, do you?"

"Of course I do."

"So wrapped up in yourself and your stupid bloody deadbeat rock star."

"Don't talk about him like that."

"Why shouldn't I?" he says, one leg finally netted. "He's driven a wedge right between us, Jody. If you can't even open your strobe-light dazzled eyes for one minute and see that, then I feel sorry for you."

"I know I've been preoccupied with him lately and I've—"

"Preoccupied? You're infatuated with him!"

"No I'm not, Mac, I'm not infat—"

"Oh yes you are. Everything you do, it's all about him."

I feel in my pocket for the moon rock and clutch it hard. "You were there, too. You helped me. You helped me look after him."

"Because that's the only way I could see you. But he's always bloody there, like a bad smell. If he's not singing in the background, he's staring down at me from your wall, and now he's in your bloody garage. I can't talk to you without him being there. Can't say what I want . . ."

I step forward. "What do you want to say? He's not here now, say it to me now."

For a second he looks me straight in the eye and I hold his blue-black gaze until I feel my cheeks starting to burn. But then he blinks and starts groping around with the other stocking. "What's the point? You wouldn't listen, anyway."

My heart's like fists on a door. "I'm listening now. Tell me. Tell me what's wrong."

He stands up straight. "How about the fact that I waited for you all day outside that concert. All day."

"No, you didn't. You went into town. You met your cousin —"

"Ally's digging for fossils in Arizona, has been for six months. I just used him as an excuse in case you felt sorry for me being on my own all day. For sitting in my car for five hours after the shops closed. I needn't have worried, though. Not like you were going to leave that queue for anything or anyone, was it? Not like you were going to think about me for five seconds."

"Why didn't you tell me your cousin wasn't there? I'd have —"

"What? What would you have done? If you'd known would you have come out of your precious queue and kept me company? No, you wouldn't. You don't give a shit about me just like Jackson doesn't give a shit about you and *I'm* the only one who can see that. You know what? I don't give a shit about you anymore, either. Why would I? It doesn't get me anywhere. He's obviously the one for you."

His words skin me like a hot blade. "You . . ." A dozen words flash up in my mind as to what I should say. Bastard. Prick. Wanker. Arsehole. But all he's done is ignite the truth. He's not a bastard. He's not a prick. He's just been bottling his resentment for too long and now it's all vomiting violently back at me.

"Why did you wait for me all day, then? Why did you do that? Tell me, Mac."

"Just go. Have a nice life. Just go." He finishes attaching his stockings. There's a dirty great run all up his right leg. "Oh shit!"

"If you tell me not to go, I won't."

"Oh, what's the point? There's no contest, is there? You worship the ground he walks on."

My chest is pounding so painfully. I don't even want to look at him anymore. He hates me and now I hate him, too. That's how it's supposed to be.

"I'll go, then."

"Yeah. Go," he says, turning back to his mirror and rooting through every compartment of his makeup bag again. "Tell Ozzy Osbourne I said bon voyage."

I'm crying as I walk back toward his door. Through his door. Along the corridor toward the stage door. By the time I'm on the street, I'm crying so much I walk straight into someone.

"Sorry," I sniff. Then I realize who it is. Yellow jacket. Waxwork smile. Sally Dinkley.

"No problem," she winks. "Oh, you're not looking well, Jody. Something you want to get off your chest, love?"

"Wh . . . you're still here?"

"Yeah. I've got a ticket to *Rocky Horror*. I'm not quite done with Nuffing yet, Jody. There's definitely something about this place. I'll see you later, yeah?"

She says it like we're meeting up at the mall to go shoe shopping, and carries on walking past me.

"What are you still doing here?" I call after her. "What are you doing?!"

But she doesn't look back, just disappears through the stage door.

A million images of Sally Dinkley's evil face hurricane around my head as I walk into town to collect my outfit from Fancy That. I can't even remember paying for it, picking out the red feather boa, speaking to the man behind the counter, even. I'm still thinking, thinking, thinking about it when I get home. I don't want to be thinking about Mac but he's all I can think about.

"How's that?" says Jackson, stepping back from me and holding my little makeup mirror in front of my face to show me his handiwork.

I look like one of Jack the Ripper's prostitutes. Black eye shadow. Rosy red cheeks. Lips like Salvador Dalí's sofa. Hair with more crimp in it than the eighties and a small costume tiara in the middle. "Bargain. Thanks."

"Too much?" he says.

I shake my head, wrapping the feather boa around my neck. "Just right, actually." I fidget about in my black-and-red tutu. I have black fishnet stockings on and my black DMs and a little red bolero cardigan of Mum's to go over my shoulders. I look well rough but I'll fit in if nothing else. "Mum'll be back in a minute. You better get back in the garage."

"OK," he says, putting the mirror down and grabbing the heavy rucksack from the stool. He disappears out to the yard and I stand at the window, watching him. Watching the garage door shut behind him. I stand there until I hear the front door slam. Mum. And Halley.

"All right?" says Mum, lumbering in with bags of groceries. Waitrose bags. "Ooh, wow. Look at you."

Yeah, look at me. Just look at me.

I stand by the crossing, across the road from the Playhouse, watching them through the glass. It's well weird to see people like old Marge from the library in a black corset with a pink feather boa around her neck, but she doesn't look out of place. That's how people dress when they go to see this show. There are men in black corsets and garter belts, too. A couple of women are in short bridal gowns with frilly white garters and there's a man walking around in a doctor's coat and see-through heels. There are women in white underwear with long beads around their necks, giggly on wine. Groups of girls in black silk suits with Day-Glo pink and green shirts underneath, black masks across their eyes, and feather crowns on their heads.

I don't feel right. I wasn't going to come at all, after our argument, but I still want to see him, even if he doesn't want to see me. The crowd inside the theater is slowly disappearing into the auditorium. I think it's time.

I run back home through the gravel alley and creep across to the drum room, keeping one eye on the kitchen. Mum is making her and Halley hot chocolates to settle down for three hours of soaps, like she always does.

"Jackson?" I say. He's waiting for me on his pile of feathers with my black rucksack alongside of him. He's not dressed up for the show. He's wearing Mac's old clothes, the black leather jacket Mac pinched from his dad's closet, gray hoodie underneath, a black-and-white checked scarf, jeans, and a gray knit hat.

"Teddy's going to kill Mac if he finds out you've got that," I say, nodding at the jacket.

Jackson smiles. He puts his gray hood up. "I didn't know what you wanted to do with the feathers."

I shrug. "I'll sweep them up later. Shall we go, then?"

The show has started by the time we sneak in through the back of the auditorium but Mac hasn't come on yet. Jackson looks out of place in his normal clothes. *Everyone* else is dressed up. But that's how he wants it. He doesn't want to play dress up anymore. He's done enough of that as the Madman. Tonight is the first night he's just himself. He hasn't even got his contacts in.

People are up in the aisles, singing and dancing along to "Time Warp," and there's some drastic dance moves going on all over the place so we can't get through to our seats at the front. So we stay at the back, behind the barrier, behind the sound-mixing desk. It's still a pretty good view. I'll still be able to see Mac.

He struts on about three minutes later from the trap door underneath the stage. He looks phenomenal. A black corset over his diamanté see-through top. Bright red heels. His hair the usual black spikes with the new shock of red, but it glitters in the stage lights. And he is amazing, better than amazing. He is the only one to watch. I don't see anyone else onstage, just him. Song after song, all I see is Mac.

Jackson says something but I don't hear it. He nudges me again.

"Intermission."

"What?" I say, sneezing as one of my red boa feathers tickles my nose. He lifts up my wrist to show me the time. Suddenly it's half past nine. We've been watching the show for over an hour.

We hide in one of the stalls in the ladies' toilets for fifteen minutes, to allow people to come and go and get drinks and warble on about how good the first half was. In between all the bathroom noises — the creaky door opening and banging shut, the hand dryers blasting on and off, water splashing, toilet seats clattering — I hear so many good things.

Who's that boy playing Frank-N-Furter?

He's wonderful, isn't he? He ought to go to London, the West End.

That Frank-N-Furter, what a body! Is that Teddy Lawless's son?

Yeah, I think I saw Tish, too. Must say hello.

He's fantastic. And he's only eighteen.

I've never fancied a bloke in high heels before. D'you think he's gay in real life? He's got to be, doesn't he? To play a character like that.

He might not be gay, just a really good actor.

Yeah, that kid's going to be famous, mark my words.

Jackson looks at me over his rucksack and whispers, "Yeah, he is. Poor bastard."

The woman in the next stall drops her program as she leaves to wash her hands and doesn't come back for it. I reach down and pick it up. I flick to Mac's headshot and look at him. He's top of the bill. His write-up says about his school acting, his experience playing Riff in *West Side Story*, and his hopes of starring on Broadway. "I'll get there some day," says his quote. "'Don't Dream It, Be It,' as the song says." And he will make it some day. And I feel so sad all of a sudden.

The banging doors and splashy taps and chatter and whirr of the hand dryers gets less and less and eventually stops altogether. I slowly venture out of the stall to check everything's clear. And Sally Dinkley is standing by a hand dryer, smiling at me.

I pull the door of the stall shut behind me. "Sally."

"Jody," she says. "Thought I saw you come in here a while ago. You're not having trouble, are you?"

I shake my head. "No. I'm fine. I'm just going back for the second half." I stride to a sink and press the soap dispenser, lathering my hands up. Sally walks to the stall I've just come out of. She touches the door ever so slightly. It doesn't budge. He's locked it.

She nods to it. "Someone in there with you?"

I shake my head, rinsing the soap off my hands. "No. It must have locked itself." I go to the hand dryer and shove my hands underneath it. The horrible loud blast of air covers us until my hands are dry and I've thought of something to say.

"Who's in there, Jody?" I shake my head. She smiles, *clip-clopping* slowly toward me in her death-defying heels. "It's him, isn't it? He's in there, isn't he?" She looks as though she's going to burst out laughing, such excitement in her eyes.

"No one's in there."

"He is, isn't he?" She knocks on the door. "It's OK, you're amongst friends."

"Sally, please . . . no one's in there, OK?"

"Jackson, come on, what are you so afraid of? I'm on your side."

My throat constricts, but I still find enough air to shout, "It's not who you think. Get away from the door!"

Dinkley looks at me. "Jody, I'm not going to hurt him. I just want to see him. Look, I'm not the Big Bad Wolf here. . . ."

"No, you're just a pig!" I shout, and with all my strength I push her backward and she totters *clip, clip, clip, clip, bam*, slamming hard against the hand dryer and sending it into a drying frenzy. I can barely hear my own breath wheezing in and out of me as she slumps to the floor. She lies beneath the furious dryer, her blonde hair dancing all around her head on the hot air, and yet she's out cold.

"Oh shit. What have I done?" I crouch down to feel the place on her neck where Mac showed me. There's an awful wait. And then I feel the bump bumps.

The dryer stops. A door creaks behind me. Jackson comes out of the stall, his hood up over his hat. He stares at Sally's unconscious face. He opens his mouth to speak but I speak first.

"She's not dead, it's OK. I wasn't thinking. I didn't know how to stop her opening the door. I'm sorry, I'm sorry. She was going to find you. . . ."

He places his hand on my shoulder. "I wasn't going to lecture you. I was going to say, we need to tie her up. She's obviously here to cause problems. You gotta do something with her, just until I'm gone. OK?"

I fumble for the right words to say, my hand angry with pain, my fingers aching as I stretch them out. "Yeah, I suppose. What am I going to tie her up with, though?"

It takes ages to bind up and gag Sally with my feather boa and the gaffer tape I've used to hold up my stockings. We eventually get her into the end toilet stall. I keep checking her breathing, like a good first aider, and try to leave her on the floor in the recovery position as best I can, which isn't easy when her legs are halfway up the stall wall. We can't risk sticking around in case she wakes up, which means I'm not going to see the second half of the show. We've missed most of it trying to tie her up, anyway. "Don't Dream It, Be It" is playing quietly on the speakers in the lobby as we leave, and the words run round and round my head as we make our way down to the library to meet the white car.

It's colder outside, or maybe it's just the same as it was before, only I'm noticing it more now because my neck is bare. Or perhaps it's because as Jackson and I are walking in step along the pavement, I'm realizing this is the last time I'll walk beside him. The last time I'll see him in the flesh again. I just can't think about it, so I'm concentrating on how cold I am. The icy night air slaps against my throat. I check my watch: 10:16 P.M.

"Are you really going to go through with this?" I ask him as we scurry along the pavement.

"Yeah," he says. "You think I'm chicken?"

"No. It's just such a . . . change. You're stripping all your life away."

"Yeah, I am. I'm shedding my skin. For the first time in a long time, I'm clean. It's a good thing, Jody. This is a good thing."

The town is pretty much deserted. A few take-out places glow with life and at the pub on the corner opposite Mac's pub, a cluster of smokers stands beneath a lamppost with their cigarettes. I want to reach out and hold Jackson's hand as we walk, but I resist. He's walking too quickly, so much so I have to skip every so often to keep up. Finally, we reach the post office and the walkway across the river, opposite the bridge where I pushed him off two weeks ago. I gesture toward it as we cross the walkway, but he doesn't seem to understand the joke.

There is no white car at the taxi stand. We sit on the bench outside the library, watching and waiting. We both sit right on the edge, as the bench is wet from where it's been raining earlier. I feel so stupid in my *Rocky Horror* outfit. I want to wipe off all my makeup right there, so I look plain and inconspicuous like Jackson. So I look like I'm waiting for a taxi with Jackson. I want to get in the taxi with Jackson. We still have a few minutes before the car's due.

"I could come with you," I say suddenly, to the paving stones beneath my feet more than to him. "I don't think I belong here anymore. Mac hates me. Grandad's gone and he's the only one who ever understood me apart from Mac. There's no point in me being here. Let me come with you."

"You're just stressing because of that reporter. It's all right. She won't be able to prove —"

"I'm not worrying about her," I tell him, remembering the pain in my right hand. "I don't care about her at all. Once you're gone, I'll just bullshit her, it doesn't matter. Let me go and get my stuff, and I'll come with you."

"No. There isn't time."

"There is. I'll just get some clothes and my bankbooks and we can be off. Five minutes, just give me five minutes."

I can't hold my tears in anymore. "Please don't leave me. You don't have to talk to me if you don't want to. I could just be, like, your sister?"

He pats me a couple of times on my knee, hard. "It's all right. Just, stop crying."

I look at his hand smacking my knee. "What are you doing?"

He looks at me. "I don't know. You know I don't go in for all that huggy shit." A white car pulls up and joins the end of the line of taxis. Right on time. He stands up. "Car's here," he says, swinging the rucksack onto his shoulder. My rucksack.

I claw at him, begging him. "No, please don't. . . ."

His hand is on my shoulder. "Let's do this quickly, OK? Come on."

"Don't do that," I say, shrugging him off. "Don't hold my shoulder. That's how my dad left me. That's how my grandad left me."

"I'm sorry. I don't know what else . . . Look after yourself, OK? You knew how this was going to end." The car engine revs at the back of the line. I can't see the driver's face.

"Please," I beg. I grab hold of his hand. "If you go, I'll have nothing, no one. You and the band, Grandad, Mac — you were the only things that made it better."

Jackson shakes his head, then moves my hand up to his mouth and kisses it. "I'll send your money back, once I know where I am."

"No, I don't want it back. I don't want any of it back, you keep it. It's yours."

He smiles. "Thank you, Jody. For everything."

He walks away from me and over to the white car. It's turned around. Brake lights on, exhaust pipe chugging.

Dignity already hanging by its ankles, I sob like I've never sobbed before. I watch as he hitches up his gray hood over his head and opens the back door of the car, throws my rucksack inside, and steps in without another look back. The brake lights go off. The car moves away.

"It's not fair," I whisper to the starless sky. I shake my head. I rip my tiara out of my crimped mess of hair and sink to the ground. I crouch to my knees and cry like I'll never stop. The next sound I hear is footsteps. Running footsteps. I look up. Jackson's running back to me. The white car has stopped at the edge of the parking lot, brake lights on, back door wide open.

He's running back to me. He's coming back to me.

I stand up. He slams into my arms and squeezes me so tightly. He feels so strong, not like he was two weeks ago when he was limp and could barely stand up straight. He feels tight and full of pent-up energy just waiting to explode. I never ever want to let go. If I let go, that will be it. He'll just be Thomas and I'll just be Jody. And I'll never see him again. I'm hugging him like I should have hugged Grandad before he left me forever.

"I don't want to let you go," I *huff-huff* in his ear. "Please don't make me let go." I squeeze harder onto him, breathing him in, trying to memorize every sense so I can draw it over and over and over again, but images of Grandad flash through my mind and confuse me. I feel him crumble away from me, like a rock of sand in my fist. He came to me as Jackson James Gatlin, singer, born 3 September, beautiful, big blue eyes, messy brown hair, teetotaler, vegetarian, Stephen King–fanatic, broken-homed, bookish, bliss on legs. He's leaving me as Thomas Gordon. And I don't know anything else about him now.

He's Mr. Nobody now. Just how he wants it.

He looks at me. He walks backward, turns, and runs to the white car and gets in.

I don't know if the driver of the white car will get him across the English Channel. I don't know if he'll make it to Switzerland to get his money. To get where he needs to go. I don't know. I know how those fans felt as they stood on that bridge and threw flowers into the muddy water. Those fans who are calling suicide helplines. Those fans who have rushed out and got tattoos so they don't have to feel the inside pain anymore, so that they can feel some other kind of pain from the unbearable sense of loss I'm feeling now as I watch that white car drive away. I am just one of those fans, but I've been given so much more than they have. I'm the only one who knows he's not dead. Kidnapping him did make the world of difference, but now it's torturing me with a world of pain. My brain is an even tighter paper scrunch of sadness, and Grandad wheels fast into my mind. I stand sobbing — my mouth wide open, waiting to say something to a world that's so empty and dark and awful to me now, I can't see straight. Everything hurts so much. Grandad. Jackson. Mac. They all keep my world on its axis. Two of them have gone forever and one of them hates me. There's nothing left. My world is rolling fast down the hill and there's no one to hold it back.

I turn to face the bridge. To face the river. The river I pushed Jackson into when he first arrived. Where he was so horrible to me. I wish he'd been horrible to me just now. I wish he hadn't hugged me. It made it worse. It wasn't as warm as one of Mac's hugs, but it still reminded me of him. He's the only other person who hugs me like that, wrapping me up completely in such a hard, safe lock like that. I wish I wasn't alive. I want to jump off the bridge. I want to feel the pain of that cold water again. I don't care how shallow it is. I want to drown.

But I can't see the bridge. There's too many tears in my eyes. It's too dark. And there's a transvestite in my way. Just standing there.

I stare at Mac's face for the longest time. He stares back.

"Wh-what are you . . . you should be onstage. You'll miss your encore."

"I've already missed it," he says. He's got tears in his eyes, but he's trying not to release them. He's dabbing his eye at the corner with one of his black fingernails. "My makeup's running."

"You'll miss your enc-core," I say again, overwhelmed by another surge of tears.

He steps toward me. He's even taller than usual in his high heels. He hitches one leg up and undoes the strap, then the other one, and he throws his shoes behind him onto the ground. "I thought I'd missed you. I thought you'd gone, Jode."

I shake my head. "I just said all that to make you

jealous." I'm huffing on every word. "You were jealous, weren't you?" He nods. "Why? I'm a disaster area, Mac. You'd be better off without me."

He shakes his head. Water drips down from both his eyes. "No I wouldn't."

And though I don't see it coming, he moves closer toward me and we face-smash into the longest kiss ever — the saddest, wettest, messiest kiss I've ever had. And we're both soaked and we're both sobbing. And our makeup smears together so it's all over our faces.

I pull back, but he holds my face in his hands. "I would have gone, if it wasn't for you," I say. "When we argued, I thought you hated me. I thought I *should* go, then."

"But you didn't," he says, all serious voice, and kisses me again and it's like a thousand strobe lights and the loudest, dirtiest guitar chord smacking me in the face.

And it's better than all of that. Because he's real. Rock steady before me.

And it's because it's Mac. "I love you, Jody," he whispers.

And because it's really mine.

THE GIRL WHO LOVED

Three Months Later

"Jody, can you nip down to Waitrose and get some more hot dogs?"

"Yeah, in a minute," I call back. Me and Mac are sitting on the sofa, holding hands and watching TV. The latest boy band, FOS, are on *MTV Newbies* talking about their latest single and there's like a million girls outside the TV studio screaming for them and holding up placards.

"We're just so blessed to have such great fans," says one of them and waves through the glass window behind at all the fans lined up outside the building screaming and tearing their faces off, but they can't hear him. The others turn around and make stupid faces at them every so often and lift up their shirts to show their washboard stomachs. The girls are in meltdown but can get no closer.

"It's such a big joke to them," I say. "And before you say 'don't take it so personally,' I can say that because I *have* been there. I *do* know what I'm talking about, as you well know. Can I look at the picture again, just once more, then you can delete it."

He shifts over and removes his phone from his back pocket and rubs the screen to find the picture. Then he hands it to me. I stare at it, the picture of He-Who-Must-Not-Be-Named — that's what we call him now — with Cree on his lap at the Italian Market. Cree's beaming, as cute as a little apricot, but I can barely see his face under his baseball cap. I still like looking at it.

"You can delete it now."

"Sure?"

"No. But you probably should."

"I'll keep it, it's fine. It's a nice one of Cree."

Mac lies himself down with his head on my lap, his feet dangling over the edge of the sofa. "You're my groupie now, aren't you?"

I lean over and kiss him on the mouth. He's so warm to kiss, warm and soft. I could spend whole days kissing him. The only thing I used to kiss before him was the cold moon rock, for luck, or a wall poster. Both were always freezing cold. I ended up giving the moon rock to Halley. I had to. I kept losing it. It brought me nothing but trouble, but it made her so happy. She keeps it on a little stand on her windowsill. Every time I walk past her bedroom and see it, I remember Grandad as I should, and I remember how much he loved both of us, me and Halley. And how much we both still miss him. Halley bailed me out over Dinkley in the end, too, when Dinkley came to our house the day after *Rocky Horror*. She brought the police with her.

She beat me! She beat me and tied me up with her feather boa and she locked me in the toilet. And she had him with her, Jackson Gatlin. I'm telling you, she did! Why does no one believe me?! She kidnapped him. She must have!

Halley said I was with her the night of the show. She

thought Dinkley was an old school enemy bearing a grudge and that I was nursing an injured duck in the garage. Turns out, she went in the garage on the night of *Rocky Horror* to take the duck some bread, but it had gone. She thought a fox had killed it so she tidied up the feathers to spare my feelings. The moment Dinkley presented the empty drum room to the policemen was priceless. It'll stay with me forever, if I can fit it in. There are so many priceless memories in my head, I'm not sure there'll be enough room.

I trace my fingers up and down the sides of Mac's nose. He loves it when I do that.

"You look nice today," he mumbles. "Lemon suits you."

"Don't you start. You're worse than Mum. 'Nice to see you in something other than black for a change,'" I say in my best whiney Mum voice.

Mac chuckles. "You always look gorgeous to me, Presh. Lemon, lime, candy-striped."

I smile. "You've changed your tune. A few months ago you'd have done anything to *Project Runway* me into something fashionable."

"Yeah, well, tunes change," he says, leaning his face up toward mine for another kiss. "You all right today?"

"Yeah," I shrug, trying desperately to smile so he doesn't think I'm having another depressive moment about He-Who-Must-Not-Be-Named. I had a bad day yesterday, angsting endlessly over why he hasn't been in touch. It really gets to me, the not knowing. Three months solid I've felt like this, on and off. More on than off. It hits me out of nowhere. Sometimes I get this chilling feeling, like I know he's definitely dead. Like I've had a premonition and the

next time I switch on the news there'll be an announcement that they've found his body somewhere between
here and God-knows-where. Or worse. That Frank
Grohman's tracked him down and got his minders to beat
him to death. I even went back to the BFD and begged him
to get in touch with his contact and let me know where
he dropped him off, just to have some information. But he
wouldn't say a word. More than his life's worth, blah, blah,
blah. I can't sleep for thinking about it. Wake up early,
racing heart thinking about it. On the plus side, though,
I've never done so much art in my life. Endless paintings.
Capturing landscapes in my memory. Capturing moods.
Capturing him.

I don't want to know everything, even what continent
he's on. Just that he's still around, that something hasn't
hurt him between here and there. I did get this strange
certificate through the mail some weeks back from the
Prostate Cancer Charity, thanking me for my very gener-
ous donation, telling me about all the screening equipment
it will buy. And my mind ran wild, thinking that could have
been him, donating on my behalf. I told him I didn't want
my five grand back, so what if he'd gone ahead and given it
to them instead? I just didn't know. I didn't know a single
thing for certain. And it hurt like death.

The boy band debut their latest single. It's the usual
soft, warbly crap. I long to hear some skin-stripping
rock to clean my ears out, and direct the remote control
through all the music channels to find some. They had a
Regulators day on MTV recently but I couldn't watch it.

It kind of hurt. I've been dying to know what's happened to the other members of the band since Jackson's "death." They aren't even mentioned anywhere anymore, except in articles about Jackson. I know they broke up soon after. Lenny's side project band pops up on MTV every now and again but The Regulators, as I knew them, are gone forever. There was a memorial service for Jackson on the Severn Bridge last month, when the band thanked all the fans who'd created a shrine to him there. The shrine's still there. Tealights in saucers and rain-spattered flowers and damp, torn posters and lipstick-stained CD cases mark the spot where everyone thinks he jumped in. I've never been to see it, though, and I never will.

"Jody, hot dogs, please!" calls Mum again.

I sigh. Mac and I have been trying to evade the party celebrations for most of the afternoon, having done a few rounds of "Ooh haven't you grown" and "You two dating?" and "My boyfriend Mac and me are both going to college together in the fall — he's studying drama, I'm studying art." We just want a break.

"Can't you send Hal?" I call back.

"Not on her birthday, no," Mum shouts. I fling Mac upright and he follows me out to the kitchen. The breakfast bar is covered in bowls of chips, crudités, dips, mini sausages, and cakes, and in the very center is Halley's cake with a massive "15" candle in the middle of it. I take a couple of macaroons, shoving one in my mouth and sneaking one behind my back for Mac. Mum comes back in the kitchen from outside.

"Jody, hot dogs, now, please? Teddy's doing seven sorts out there because he thinks we're going to run out." She hands me a tenner.

The barbecue is on the patio outside. Mac's dad is doing it (his first barbecue in ten years, hence the smoke) and has even shut the pub for the afternoon, the first time since, well, forever. The yard is filled with all sorts of different chairs and kitchen stools and Halley's friends and Mum's friends from the bank. Tish is there, too, with Cree, looking in the flower bed for snails. (Roly mysteriously disappeared from her animal carrier, so we told her he and Man had gone to live on a happy farm in Australia. It was the nicest thing we could think to say that wasn't close enough that she'd want to go and visit.) Some pub regulars stand around the barbecue with pints, laughing and trying to sort out the smoke problem. A couple of them are the builders who are going to start on Mum's addition next month. She's using some of her money to have the kitchen extended and my bedroom's going to be bigger, too. It'll have its own bathroom and, get this, its own *staircase* that will lead straight down into the garage, which has now officially become my art studio. How cool is that?! Halley's getting all new bedroom furniture and a puppy and private tennis lessons, so she's happy, too.

"I want to go to the Trose!" says a little voice as Cree runs in from the garden in her new summer dress with the little dragonflies on the shoulders.

Mac scoops her up. "Oh you heard that, did you? No, you won't like it at the Trose. It's run by the nasty witch."

"The nasty witch is at the Trose?" she asks, twizzling

his ear stud. Mac nods. "Will the witch eat me up?"

Mac nods again and winks at me. We've lost our last bastion of privacy today what with Mum turning the garage — my art studio — into a walk-in gallery for people to view my canvases. She's insisted I put them all out on the easels she bought me so people can go in and look at them. So embarrassing.

"I want to come to the Trose, Dody." She puts her arms out to me.

I take her from Mac. "You can come to Waitrose, Cree. I'll make sure the nasty witch doesn't come anywhere near you."

"OK, Dody." She smiles at Mac who tickles her until she's writhing like a little fish in my arms.

We go out to the hallway. There's a stack of mail on the hall table. A menu advertising "Gluten Free Night" at the local fish bar, a Carnival Cruises holiday leaflet for Grandad, a phone offer for Halley, and, amazingly, two envelopes for me. I haven't had *any* mail in weeks. I've given up on the whole rushing-downstairs-when-I-hear-the-letter-box thing. I put Cree down and hand one of my envelopes to Mac. "Could this be our tickets at last?" I ask him.

He smiles, tearing it open. "Yep, two tickets, two weeks." He kisses my head. "Our first holiday. Just us and Italy for two whole weeks. It's going to be amazing."

He's right, it will be amazing. I can't wait. We've got tickets to see Van Morrison, live in Venice, while we're there, too. Mac says I need to "exorcise" the concert demon. I'm happy about it, I am. But going away just reminds me about him. He-Who-Must-Not-Be-Named. How he went away. How I don't know how far he got or if he's OK. If he's happy now.

I hope the gondola ride is as romantic as Mac says, not all open sewers like I've heard.

I hope I don't fall in. I hope I don't make some scene in the Sistine Chapel when I'm attempting to scatter Grandad's ashes.

I hope not. I really hope not.

I note the postmark on my other envelope. Weird symbols and a mountain. Definitely foreign. I stand looking at it for a long time. I almost can't bear to open it.

"What's that one?" Mac asks.

"I don't know," I lie. But I do know. I know exactly what it is and it's what I've been waiting for. Praying for. I'm shaking as I rip open the envelope.

And a single pink cherry blossom falls out onto my hand.

PERMISSIONS

Many thanks to Richard O'Brien for his permission to quote "Sweet Transvestite" and "Don't Dream It" from *The Rocky Horror Show* (© Richard O'Brien/Rocky Horror Company, 1973).

"Don't Look Back in Anger" by Noel Gallagher, from the album *(What's the Story) Morning Glory?* (© Noel Gallagher/Oasis, 1995), quoted with kind permission of Oasis.

"Black" by Eddie Vedder and Stone Gossard, from the album *Ten* (© Pearl Jam, 1991), quoted with kind permission.

"Bohemian Rhapsody" by Freddie Mercury, from the album *A Night at the Opera* (© Freddie Mercury/Queen, 1975), quoted with kind permission.

Every effort has been made to trace or contact all copyright holders. The publishers would be pleased to rectify any errors or omissions brought to their notice, at the earliest opportunity.

ACKNOWLEDGMENTS

Barry Cunningham, Imogen, Rachel, Esther, Laura, Elinor, Chrissie, and the wonderful Chicken House. Kirsten Stransfield and Nicki Marshall for their amazing editorial skills.

My lovely mum, Auntie Maggie, and Uncle Roy for all the grist that keeps the mill going. Jamie, Angie, Alex, and Joshua for the loan of their house to home my wayward rock star. And to Josie, who named my baby Cree. My cousin Emily Snead (sorry, Em, I just had to use the puke experience). Owain Gillard for his all-seeing eye.

Matthew Snead, who wanted a line of his own in this one.

The usual suspects plus some new ones — Manic Street Preachers, Allie Moss, The Prodigy, The Killers, Paramore, Kings of Leon, Green Day, Foo Fighters, Antony and the Johnsons, 30 Seconds to Mars, Oasis, Nirvana, Pearl Jam, Avril Lavigne, Metallica, Queen, Van Morrison, and the endlessly inspirational My Chemical Romance for being the constant soundtrack to my thoughts.

Holly Grainger, Adam Lambert, Seth Gabel, Lorraine Ashbourne, Dakota Fanning, Monica Potter, and Billy Connolly. Although you didn't know it, these characters wouldn't be who they are without you.